The yellowbacks... classics of popular fiction

The yellowjackets or yellowbacks were a great series of bestselling adventure and crime thrillers that had its origins in the mid to late 19th century following on from the 'penny dreadfuls'. They virtually began the mass market revolution of the early 20th century with a clear standard format and imprint/series livery (what would today be called branding). Hodder & Stoughton published the yellowjackets in two main series with series run dates of: 1923-1939 and later 1949-1957.

As the tagline ('where thrillers really began') on the back cover implies, the imprint and series focused on thrillers that were the bestsellers of their time. This current reissue or retro revival if you will, brings back many of these masterpieces, now classics in their own way and extends it further by including key titles from that period that were either great crime or thriller or even general commercial fiction (including sub-genres of noir, horror, gothic, romance, westerns, etc.) influences of their time. There are some perennial favourites and many rarities either lost or not easily available being revived in the current series. Writers and characters ranged from adventure heroes like Bulldog Drummond, Allan Quatermain, Richard Hannay or the Saint through thriller grandmasters Edgar Wallace and E. Phillips Oppenheim, crime and mystery maestros like Patricia Wentworth, G.K. Chesterton, Agatha Christie and the Detection club, to western and swashbucklers like Zane Grey, Max Brand, Captain Blood and even romance or general fiction classics like Hermina Black, Denise Robins, Marie Corelli or Stella Morton. These were books that had storytelling at their heart and always entertained.

The yellowbacks had both hardback (with varying design elements) and paperback (which built the series look) versions with the latter still carrying the imprint 'yellowjacket'. The current reissues pay tribute to both and use an amalgam of elements from both editions while retaining the complete yellow (or 'mustard-plaster') livery with the author's name in blue beveled type with a 'simulated emboss' effect and a white outer 'outline', and the book title in black. These reissues retain the distinctive size of the original mass market paperback and follow the three main category variations—the thrillers (crime, westerns, mystery, adventure) had blue lettering for the author's name, while romance and softer general fiction had red; and other categories like humour had green.

For more detail and a full list of titles visit https://www.hachetteindia.com/home/yellowbacks

THE SEAMARK OMNIBUS OF THRILLS

VOLUME 2

THE SEAMARK OMNIBUS OF THRILLS

Seamark was the pen name of Austin James Small (25 July 1894–15 January 1929) – an English writer of thriller, detective, science fiction, adventure, romance, and western novels and short stories. Most of Small's titles appeared in Britain under the pen name Seamark, while his American publisher preferred using the name Austin J. Small. Several film plots were based on his stories. Small was born Austin Major Small in Luton, Bedfordshire, on 25 July 1894. He later changed his name to Arthur James Small. He ran away to sea as a boy and travelled the world, serving in the Royal Navy during the First World War, where he was a champion heavyweight boxer. He met and was inspired to write by Jack London and adopted the pen name "Seamark" to comply with Admiralty regulations. He began his literary career in the early 1920s publishing new westerns and detective stories in British pulp magazines.

In 1924 he produced a western novel, *The Frozen Trail*, and three romantic novels in 1925, before publishing *Master Vorst* a.k.a. *The Death Maker* (1926), a science fiction novel in which a secret society based in London develops a means of destroying the human species with the help of a bacteriological weapon. He went on to write half a dozen detective novels, another science fiction novel, and many short stories.

He was found dead in Kensington, London, on 15 January 1929, from suicide by gas inhalation.

THE SEAMARK OMNIBUS OF THRILLS

Austin J. Small

VOLUME 2

THE MASTER MYSTERY
—the grim case of the theft of the Gairlie Rubies
THE SILENT SIX
—the terrible vengeance of a master criminal

HODDER AND STOUGHTON
YELLOW JACKET
hachette

The Seamark Omnibus of Thrills
First published by Hodder & Stoughton, UK in 1937

This Hodder Yellowback edition © Hachette India 2025
(Registered Name: Hachette Book Publishing India Pvt. Ltd.)
An Hachette UK Company www.hachetteindia.com

1

The texts in these editions in most cases have been reprinted as is, with minimal editorial changes and by and large no bowdlerizing for political correctness; though in some editions, a few words and phrases considered archaic, or those considered offensive now, along with archaic punctuation may have been modified in places to make the text more accessible to today's readers. The narratives, language, beliefs, social mores and/or cultural depictions, in these volumes are a reflection of their times and must be viewed as such. They may also contain certain cultural, racial and gender prejudices and stereotypes that may be outdated or clearly wrong then and wrong today; but their removal would be tantamount to claiming these prejudices never existed. The Publisher does not endorse or support those depictions or stereotypes; and these books have been made available for a discerning audience that will read it for entertainment value and a chronicle/record of popular fiction of past times.

Cover design by Priya Singh adapted from the original classic yellowjacket by Hodder & Stoughton.

Cover illustration by Ishan Trivedi.

Series note: Some of the books in the series (unless otherwise credited) may have cover or inside illustrations from the original yellowbacks or early editions, and while full restoration has been attempted, some images may be grainy or faded due to the condition of the original material. The end notes or bonus material or blurb details may have been sourced from the public domain or free use publications such as Wikipedia and attribution is hereby made also allowing similar free use reproduction from here. Sources requiring further specific attribution may write in and further detailing and/or corrections shall be made in subsequent printings/editions.

Reprint specifications may be subject to change including but not limited to finishes, paper, colour sections.

ISBN: 978-93-5731-493-0

Hachette Book Publishing India Pvt. Ltd.
4th & 5th Floors, Corporate Centre,
Plot No. 94, Sector 44, Gurugram - 122 003, India

Typeset in Electra LT STD 10/12.5 pt by Manipal Technologies Limited, Manipal

Printed and bound in India by Manipal Technologies Limited, Manipal

FSC www.fsc.org MIX Paper | Supporting responsible forestry FSC™ C043100

CONTENTS

THE MASTER MYSTERY

The grim story of the theft of the Gairlie Rubies, praised by *Public Opinion* as "A first-rate detective story."

I

Of all the extraordinary features that served to make the theft of the Gairlie Rubies the master mystery of the generation, not the least amazing was the method of the robbery itself.

True, in the days that followed, mystery piled on mystery until the initial robbery became a mere puzzling complication in the welter of insoluble enigmas that arose around it, and when the Silent Death began to stalk through the wide halls of Gairlie Castle the shadow of a terrible fear hung like a black cloud over the great household.

Kennedy, of the Yard, admitted that it betrayed all the symptoms of a latter-day miracle. The man who lifted the Gairlie Rubies succeeded in performing the utterly and patently impossible. For over a month Scotland Yard was flat on its back, out to the wide.

The Gairlie Rubies are known all over the world and have a *cachet* all their own. Collectors speak of them reverently, not without awe. At least three impeccably-organised gangs of big-scale crooks raise their hats to a sigh at the mere thought of them.

There was the tiara, a coiling circle of shimmering fire—three hundred and seventy stones caught in a spider-web of platinum, a glittering sheen picked out in flashpoints of silver and old wine. There was the collar, six rows of scintillant blood-red marbles blazing with all the fiery lustre of dragon's eyes. There were the eardrops, deep and slumbrously carmine as pigeon's blood. The corsage, a breast piece of crimson iridescence, the shoulder clasp, the armlets, and the great pendant.

Eight hundred and eleven perfect stones. That is the muster of the Gairlie collection. Lord Gairlie spent twenty years of his life and £150,000 cold cash in their accumulation. There was nothing like them in the universe. Eight hundred and eleven eyes of red-glowing fire, flashing and burning and blazing like red-hot cores torn from the very heart of the Fires Eternal. Matchless. Incomparable. A masterpiece of the patience, art, and ingenuity of the jewel collector.

They were worn, on an average, twice a year. The insurance companies balked at more. So they graced the two most brilliant functions in the whole magnificent run of the London season. The Grosvenor Reception was one; the Court Ball the other.

They reposed elegantly on the noble person of Lady Gairlie. She walked abroad, a soft murmur of envious sighs following her progress, like the gentle rustle of a breeze whispering through ripe corn. A gracious lady, with the poise and presence of a Regency Duchess—and exquisitely aware of that whispering in the corn. There was regal beauty in her carriage, she, the wonderful "Lady of Flame" of the society writers, her head and shoulders a living torch of crimson brilliance.

Gairlie had raked the world for his rubies, from Burma to Peru, from the Cape to Samarkand. He had bought them carefully, and with shrewd discretion. The gathering of them into one huge collection had placed their value beyond computation. There was no comparative on which to strike a value. They were like the Cullinan Diamond, unique, and for that reason as safe from robbery as the Crown Regalia. The biggest, the great pendant stone, known popularly as the Burning Star, was as large as a walnut. The smallest was bigger than a marrowfat pea. From the criminal point of view they were not negotiable, for there was not a dealer in the land who would not have recognised any of them on sight.

Yet vanish they did. As smoothly and as silently as dawn comes to distant waters. There was no sound, no suspicion, not a fingerprint left behind, no shadow of a clue—no nothing—except the thunderous fact that they were no longer there.

The jewels were kept in two great strongboxes, which operated on an entirely new locking principle. Each box required seven different keys to open it; and the system of unlocking was ingeniously intricate. The keys had to be inserted in the locks in a certain order and then turned according to a schedule known only to Lord Gairlie himself. Not until that was done correctly could the box be opened.

The boxes were of polished armour-steel, fire-, drill-, and acid-proof. When not in use they were housed in the vaults below the castle. Only once previously had an attempt been made to steal them. And that was when, some years before the war, a lone adventurer along the highways of daredevilry cut a tunnel from the spinney to the castle wall—and was engulfed in the black flood that leapt to meet him out of the darkness. For the Gairlie vaults were protected by a wall of water—the bricked-up remains of the great moat which, in feudal days, circled the castle.

But the thief, or thieves, who finally got away with the gems were far too clever to pit their brains against subterranean water-locks. They waited a more subtle opportunity, and, in doing so, accomplished the seemingly impossible.

It began with great and magnificent doings that day in Gairlie Castle. The occasion was one of such happy omen that the famous rubies were to be brought out and worn, for the third time that year. It was the coming of age of Lonora, Lord Gairlie's only child and heir to the splendid heritage of the great Gairlie estates. She was a beautiful girl, blessed with the twin gifts of her mother's good looks and her father's brains.

And none denied her father's strength of intellect. Almost alone among the great landed families, Gairlie had brought his estates through the cataclysms and financial upheavals following the world war immune. All around him the oldest families of the Empire tottered, hung for a few desperate years in the balance and fell. Heads of vast estates, unable to compete with ever falling revenues and ever rising taxes, broke up their lands and sold them to the speculators, leased their castles to the new rich or sold them outright to the war profiteer. Nobles, whose titles went back to the parchment sheets of Domesday Book, bowed their heads to the storm, closed down and reduced their households to gardenless villas in London or flats on the fringe of Mayfair.

But Gairlie came through, not merely immune, but with added lustre to the family name. And Lonora came of age with a liberal share of her father's abilities, and all her mother's grace of charm and feminine sweetness.

The castle was full and there was an atmosphere of gay expectancy in the air, for a particularly happy announcement was expected during dinners that night.

All the world loves a lover, and certainly all the world smiled its cheerful encouragement on Tommy Delayn. Tommy was known everywhere a decent, clean-living young fellow aspires to be known. One international athletic accomplishment is enough for most men, but Tommy seemed to have made a habit of doing most things well. Wimbledon knew him. He had given—and taken—wholehearted clouts in squared ring at the National Sporting Club. He wore Corinthian colours and the Test Eleven was one short without him. Not a bad record for a boy still on the threshold of twenty-eight.

The one point against him was that, unlike Gairlie, the elder Delayn had not weathered the post-war storm. Crisis after crisis had hit him. Rumours had begun to circulate. The old stability of the House of Delayn had suffered, its foundations were crumbling. Rumour became club gossip when Delayn senior relinquished his great estates in the north and retired to a small manor on the Wolds.

Tommy knew things were bad. How bad he did not dream—until midway through that ghastly interview with the family lawyer, three months after his father's death.

Fate stage-managed the stroke with masterly judgment. The timing of it was devilish—a malicious jest that had no spark of humour in it. It was reserved for that great day at the castle.

The engagement had been kept secret for a long time; the announcement was not to be made until Lonora's birthday. That was the perfectly happy arrangement they had come to on that wonderful August night when Tommy, with a ring in his fingers and a wobble in his voice, had proposed and been accepted.

And that great day had dawned. Tommy, almost one of the family even then, had arrived overnight. Both Lord and Lady Gairlie knew him thoroughly well and liked him, though Gairlie was apt to smile tolerantly on his assumption of business responsibilities. For Delayn professed to be an experimental chemist. He had a tumble down little laboratory somewhere up at the smelly end of Tottenham Court Road, and on occasion he spent a good deal of time there.

But nobody dreamed of taking Tommy's activities seriously. "Delayn," said his friends, "was cut out for an athlete, but as a business proposition he was off the earth. Tommy a chemist? Ha, ha! Good joke, chaps. Tommy couldn't mix a seidlitz powder."

And yet the President of Haloran's, Ltd., one of the greatest industrial concerns in the north, thought so well of one or two of his propositions that he had had long business conversations with him, and, now and then, came south specially to see him. But Tommy's friends were not to know that. And Tommy was not the man to tell.

He woke early, with a delicious sense of elation. The cold bright sunlight of a cloudless February day was streaming in at the wide windows, and there was the crisp tang of the salty Channel in the breeze.

Halfway through his dressing he stopped and looked round with a puzzled frown on his face. Something was missing from the little heap of things on the top of a chest of drawers.

"Dashed funny," he muttered. "I'll swear I put it on that ledge last night—sure I did—with my watch and cash and stuff. Now where the devil—" He broke off and went over to his bedside table, groping about among the odds and ends there. Suddenly he stood upright again and scratched the back of his head.

"Well if that doesn't beat the band," he said. "I'm hanged if my book hasn't gone too!"

For some seconds he stared down at his things, trying to focus his mind back to his last waking moment the previous night. Yes, he remembered perfectly. He was reading that book last night when the clock struck eleven. A dry, unexciting volume, but one that had a peculiar interest for him, *The Uses of Vegetables in Industries.* He was surprised to find it so late; verifying the time by his own watch he marked the page, put the book on his bedside table and switched out the light. It was the very last thing he did before sleep claimed him. And now the book was gone. And so was his diary, that rather valuable little notebook in which he made rough references from day to day. He could swear he put that diary along with the other things. He hunted round for a bit and then rang the bell. One of the male staff, the plateman, answered it.

"Oh, Barson," said Delayn, "you unpacked my things last night, didn't you?"

"Yes, sir."

"Notice anything of a little leather-covered diary knocking about among my stuff?"

"No, sir."

"Or a big book, about twice as thick as the average novel?"

"Yes. sir; I put that among the other books by your bed. At least, there were two or three big books, and I put them all there together."

"H'm! You didn't come in here again last night after I'd gone to sleep?"

"No, sir. I did everything I had to do while you were having dinner. Why—have you lost anything, sir?"

"Well, I won't say 'lost' anything—it would be perfectly ridiculous to think they're lost when there's plenty of things here much more worth taking. But I simply can't find them, that's all. And I am absolutely certain they were both here last night. There's my cheque-book, loose cash, watch, wallet with a couple of hundred pounds in it, a valuable ring in an open case—all these are here, untouched. So it's infantile to imagine anyone taking such stupid things as an entirely worthless diary and a book that can be bought for a guinea at any library. But what I *do* want to know is where are they?"

"Excuse me, sir, but you sleep with your window wide open." The plateman was looking serious.

"Yes, always. What about it?"

"And I'd like to bet long odds your diary was a red one."

"Quite right. Red leather. Three-and-six in the Strand. What are you driving at?"

"And your book was red, too?"

"I know it was. What of it?"

"You've lost them, sir. Lost them both. You'll never see either of them again." Barson spoke with his eyes fixed steadily on Delayn, and there was a half-frightened solemnity in his voice.

"Barson, what the dickens are you talking about?" Delayn looked at the man as though he had suddenly gone queer in the head.

"It's true enough what I say, sir," said the plateman. "Common talk among the servants, sir. Take a look round this room, sir. You won't find another red object in it. If there had been it would have gone too. For all I know there may be something else gone. Yes, the little red stud-box that was over there against the mirror."

"By Jove, yes; I think I remember that," said Delayn with a sudden rush of uncomfortable interest. "A little red lacquer box with queer little Japanesy figures cut into it."

"That's it, sir. Red! And it's gone. If your eiderdown had been red you'd have lost that too. I believe you'd lose the very carpets if we were fools enough to have 'em red."

"But—but—what?" Delayn gaped at the man in blank astonishment.

"Been going on now, sir, for some months," declared Barson stolidly. "Red things; only red things. You could leave a million pounds in banknotes in a room with all the doors and windows wide open and they wouldn't be touched. But if you put a red box of matches alongside of 'em, them matches would go. If you put a red pencil on top of 'em you'd lose it. Last week one of the maids lost a ha'penny slab of raspberry toffee and a lipstick out of her handbag—and eight golden sovereigns what she'd saved up wasn't touched."

"Barson, you're dotty!"

"Not me, sir! I've seen too much of it. This is the thirty-fourth time things have been missing. God alone knows how it happens. I've known him get into locked rooms and never show a trace how he done it. Christmastime we lost a big red vase out of the library—not a finger-mark anywhere—just the vase—gone! Sometimes we almost feel it's a haunt. Red satin slippers, red table-centres, ornaments, flowers, anything so long as it's red. And once we lost a pot of strawberry jam. If it had been marmalade it wouldn't have gone."

"But, man alive—there must be some explanation. Who is it? Who does it?—"

"That's where you've got me, sir. If we knew, it wouldn't be so bad. At first her ladyship thought it was one of the servants gone a bit queer in the head. Got a kink for red things, sir, or something like that. We've set guards here night after night—weeks on end. And for weeks nothing happens. Then, right in the very room where we haven't set a guard, in he pops, takes what he fancies in the red line, and nobody's a penny the wiser."

"Then you think it's a man?"

"Can't say, sir. But we always calls it 'him.' Don't know why. Just came natural like. He comes and goes like a shadow, gets through locked doors as though they wasn't there. A fair knockout—and gettin' on some of the maids' nerves, too. You can take it from me, sir, you'll never see your red book again—nor your diary."

Delayn paced up and down the room with his hands thrust deep in his trouser pockets, furrows of concentration drawn heavily across his forehead. "Holy Hades," he muttered. "This is weird! Why the deuce—all right, Barson," he jerked, "that will be all. I'll have another talk to you about this later on"

He finished his dressing in a hurry, intending to get down and have a yarn with Lord Gairlie about it before breakfast. Gairlie would know all the ins and outs of the matter, and would surely have a great deal to tell him that must be beyond the servants' knowledge.

But downstairs he found that Gairlie had done the gracious thing. He had turned out an hour earlier, breakfasted alone, and gone out on a hack for an hour's run. It was a broad wink to Tommy that, as Lady Gairlie always breakfasted in bed, Lonora and he could have their first meal on that delightful day *têle à tête*.

So, instead of a discussion with his host on the possibilities of invisible marauders with red complexes and kleptomaniac reactions, he had a charming half-hour with Lonora. And the moment he saw her all thoughts of sordid things fled his head. She was standing by the great old leaded window looking radiant. A shaft of brittle white sunlight burnished her hair to a golden sheen and glossed the skin on the soft curves of her neck till it gleamed like polished marble. Lonora would have been counted a beautiful girl, even among a bevy of beauties. She was not exactly pretty in the modern sense, but she had carriage, grace, and a wonderful dignity. The skin-deep type of beauty was not Lonora's—hers was feature-deep, a beauty that belonged to Greece before ever it migrated across the continent and blossomed again in the lines of an English girl. Her hair, out of the hard morning sunshine, was brown; not quite so dark as her mother's, but full of a rich, lustrous warmth. And her eyes were of such a vivid, arresting blue that Delayn swore she had recourse to the blue-bag every morning.

"Good morning, Tommy," she said softly, as he pushed in through the door.

"And to you, Lonora," he said, hurrying over. "You're looking perfectly delicious today. Feeling nervous?"

"Not a bit. I'm going to enjoy every minute of it. Covers are going on for two hundred and fifty! Almost like old times again—hunt balls before the war, with all the County in the Big Hall. Dad's ordered all the special old plate to be brought out of the grisly old dungeons—and mother is going to wear the Rubies."

"Great. I've never seen her yet as the Lady of Flame."

"Well, you don't look as though you were worrying over nerves either,"

"Nerves? No, I'm not nervous. Shall be tonight, though, I'll bet. I'll make a perfectly marvellous meal—swallowing the lumps in my throat. Where's dad?"

"Boundary riding, like the darling he is." She rang the bell for breakfast.

Halfway through Delayn's first cup of coffee the butler entered with a telegram for him. He slipped it open and his face, according to Lonora, fell six yards in four seconds.

"Oh, but this is the absolute limit," he declared, glaring at the flimsy.

"Anything wrong, Tommy?"

He handed the telegram across, and she read it: "Must see you at once. Urgent. Serious news. Signed Gilbraith and Gilbraith."

"And who are Gilbraith and Gilbraith?" she asked. "They sound like a music-hall turn."

"Nothing so entertaining, my dear," replied Delayn with a worried frown. "Gilbraith and Gilbraith happen to be the family solicitors. They've been holding an inquest on my father's affairs; I've been badgering them for weeks to get down to it and let me know exactly where I stand. I've been hoping they'd get some sort of an estimate out a fortnight ago, but apparently the whole estate was in such an appalling mess that they've only just got through."

"But, Tommy, surely you're not going to town today?"

He shrugged. "Read what it says there," he said gloomily. "My last words to them before I came down were: 'Don't you dare send for me unless it's something absolutely imperative. If you do I'll brain you.' I'm afraid it must be something pretty bad, dear—they know why I'm down here."

Lonora glanced at her watch. "You'll have to go up by car," she said. "The trains are no earthly use to you. There isn't another till eleven-thirty."

Delayn nodded. "I can be in town before then," he said. "I'll take my own car and risk the road traps. I can finish my business, whatever it is, and be back here just after lunch. That's about the best thing to do, I think."

"All right, Tommy. A smooth journey and a quick return. And—"

"Yes—and? "

"Good luck when you get there."

He kissed her and hurried out, calling for his car.

II

The offices of Messrs. Gilbraith are in Lincoln's Inn, quiet austere rooms set off with old mahogany furniture. There is a stale smell of old books about them, and a still staler but less definable aroma that seems to be compounded of last month's tobacco smoke, last year's furniture polish, and last century's dust.

Both the partners were present, two courtly, troubled-looking old gentlemen, who had survived somehow from an older, more courteous generation. Delayn was sitting in an uncomfortable-looking chair, facing them, trying to get his thoughts down to bedrock. A glance at either of their faces was enough to show that something portentous was in the air. They both looked as though they wished with all their souls that someone other than they had been appointed solicitors to the House of Delayn.

"Yes, but I don't quite get the hang of your meaning," said Tommy awkwardly. "I know dad had a stormy passage round about nineteen twenty-one, but he had assets all over the country. Why send for me to tell me I'm not a millionaire? I know it."

The elder Gilbraith coughed and fingered a huge sheet of blue paper in his hand. "They—ah—those assets disappeared, Mr. Delayn. I'm afraid this will be something of a shock to you, and I am asking you to steel yourself to hearing the worst."

"The worst. Good God, man, what do you mean?"

"I mean that your father died utterly bankrupt. It was that knowledge that killed him."

Delayn swayed slowly to his feet. "You mean—I'm a pauper," he managed to get out at last.

Gilbraith nodded and looked hard at his rows of damnable figures.

"You haven't a farthing," he said. "Indeed, you are not only penniless—you owe several thousands of pounds."

Delayn shuffled vaguely on his feet, his hat and gloves dropping with a gentle plop on the table-top. He opened his mouth and shut it again, bleakly, out to the wide, wide world. Through a painful mist that clotted his eyes he saw dim visions flitting, broken and shattered. The tall, high towers of Gairlie; a banqueting hall ablaze with lights; at the head of the great tables, Gairlie with his lady, a shimmering fire of flashing red; on her left Lonora, girl of a thousand dreams, and opposite her—what? An empty chair? A cowed Harlequin, braving it out, feverishly waiting the fall of the mocking curtain to crawl away into the ultimate darkness? His bemused brain failed to compass it. As though from the very dawn of time, across numberless ages, he heard the stifled, helpless voice of the elder Gilbraith—the voice of an old man who loathed the things he had to say, but had had to say them.

"Simply could not help ourselves... sure you will appreciate our motives... affairs only very partially straightened out... but already so obvious that we had to send for you... dreadful if you compromised yourself any further at Gairlie Castle... crash complete... creditors already clamouring... too sorry for words to tell you..."

So it came and went. Odd little scraps of information, a death stab in every line of them. Delayn never knew how the rest of the interview went, could never quite remember how it ended. He groped his way from them and stumbled out of the office with the weight of all the world spinning round in his head.

That it should come on that day of all days. That was the wickedest cut of all. Delayn did not know it, but that was the first link in the long chain of events that was to lead him on and on to the very shadow of the gallows.

Like a man in a dream, he drove back to Gairlie—another link in the chain. Looking back, he realised afterwards, with a surge of horror, by what perfectly innocuous sequences of events an utterly damning case can build itself up round a perfectly innocent man, throttling him, smothering him, condemning him even to that loop of coiled rope in the grey of a dawning.

He drove slowly. He was physically unable to make that car travel fast. He just had to go slow in order to keep time with his bemused faculties. From the castle to the lawyers' office took him two and a quarter hours. From the lawyers' office to the castle took him six. And at that point the third link slipped in.

He went quietly in through the lodge gates and stopped his car as the great walls of the castle closed around him. The desperation of his plight hit him then, like a blow between the eyes. Somewhere in that great building a glorious creature was waiting for him, a girl who, gladly and unquestioning, was preparing to pay him the greatest compliment any woman can pay to any man—the free and sweet surrender of all she has and is. There was something miraculous in the glowing thought of it.

And—and somehow—he had got to go in and tell her that for him the dream was ended—that all his world had come crashing about his ears, choking him in its own dust. Somehow—how in God's name he was going to do it he didn't know—he had got to face her four-square and to tell her that there would be no happy announcement during dinner that night, or any other night.

And also in that building there was the grim old figure of Lord Gairlie to be met and—and well, explained to, he supposed.

That was going to be a horrible business, too. Gairlie could be as frigid as a chunk of Polar ice when he chose.

And without doubt this would be one of the occasions when he *would* choose. But Delayn was fair to him even in that disastrous moment. What else could he do, he argued. Gairlie would be thinking solely of his daughter. Poor, tragic Lonora. It would be awful for her. Delayn could picture the whole harassing situation. The dinner drawing near its end—and no announcement, no sign of an explanation from the courtly figure at the head of the table; the air of strain in the great dining hall; Lonora playing up to her mother like a little hero and trying not to give herself away; the quick glances from eye to eye along the glittering tables; the end of the dinner and still no announcement, the whole thing developing into a fearful unbearable anti-climax—with Lady Gairlie sitting at the top there, her head and shoulders a blazing mass of red-gold fire, to burn him all the deeper with its savage splendour.

"God!" he muttered. "What on earth can I *do?*"

He stared at himself in the glass reflector.

"Tommy Delayn," he said unsteadily, "this is where you get off and walk. What can you do? You can shoot, you can play tennis; you can kick a football up and down a field. You can knock a chap's chin off. You can score boundaries like falling off a fence, and you can ride. All of which is fine—if you've got a fortune behind you. And that's the hell of it. The moment your banking account takes a front seat in an overdraft all that stuff becomes just—silly. And the rest is made up of mortgages, debts, bills, and demand notes. And, by God! A Paradise kicked to smithereens."

He fingered his chin hopelessly. "And on the other side—what? What in the name of fortune can I line up against all that? A half-baked chemical laboratory; a brace of ideas that may, or may not, keep me out of the Bankruptcy Court for a month or two, a racing auto (the ghouls will grab that in the morning). An engaging manner (yes, I s'pose I've got that), a perfectly marvellous desire to get up out of the mess, and—and"—he stared critically into the mirror—"m'yes, *not* too good looking. Loa the good-looking men. That dint in my nose that Battling Brodzky gave me spoils me for the beauty prize. Otherwise not too bad. And, having agreed with all of which, where on earth do I get off *at?*"

An ostler approached, startling him out of his reverie.

"Can I get you anything, sir?" he asked.

"*Yes,*" said Delayn savagely. "All the Gairlie Rubies, neatly, on a big gold tray."

Poor idiot! The fourth link snapped on there, almost as loud as the clang of a closing cell door.

The ostler looked at him oddly as he climbed out. He noted the tense face and the white lips, the slight trembling of the hand when it rested on the door, the queer little laugh he gave as he walked away.

Turning, he called back over his shoulder. "Stick the car up somewhere handy, so that I can get out in a hurry if I want to. I may not be staying on to dinner, after all, and the stables are choked with cars."

And that was a parcel of news that staggered the ostler, for the servants were as alive to the occasion as the guests themselves.

Gairlie Castle stands in wide-sweeping grounds where the green hills of Hampshire kneel down to the Channel's glitter. The walls are of solid masonry two feet thick and absolutely unscalable. Here and there a great patch of age-old ivy clings to the walls, and there are flat green lawns right up to the stonework. Two great square towers stand sentinel at the ends of the long wings; in olden days beacons burned on them at night as landmarks to ships at sea. There were rumours of secret passages and chambers, but if they existed, none had ever been discovered. Tommy knew every stone of the grand old place, and loved it all.

He went moodily in through the great entrance hall and up to his room by a side staircase. He didn't feel like meeting any of the other guests just then and he didn't want to face Gairlie until he had got rid of the dust of the road. He stripped and tumbled into a cold tub, gasping and spluttering at the chill of it—Hampshire water is devilish chilly at the best of times—then he had a steaming hot one, with a yard of mustard in it. By the time he had changed, shaved, and dressed again, an hour had passed.

A footman entered just as he was finishing, a gorgeous apparition in full plush and powder.

"His lordship's compliments, sir, and at your convenience will you please go to him in the library?" said the flunkey.

"Be there in four minutes," answered Delayn, pushing the hairbrushes through his thick mop of hair. And that was the fifth point registered against him in as many hours.

Tommy found Lord Gairlie waiting for him, his back turned to the steady warmth of a glowing peat fire. Gairlie was a handsome man, in a cold, autocratic sort of way. His hair, grey-white as his moustache, was still plentiful; there was still life in it, despite its colour. His face was tanned to a virile brown, and his lines were well cut, reliant. His cast of features seemed to typify an army general or a judge of the High Court far more credibly than a successful director of great industrial concerns—Gairlie's interests ranged from wood paving blocks to artificial silk.

"Good afternoon, sir," said Delayn, closing the door. "Sorry I left you so incontinently this morning, but I had an urgent call to London. I was just coming to see you when your message arrived."

Gairlie looked at him keenly. "Take a cigar, my boy. I want to talk to you," he said. Already there was a suspicion of tension in the air that communicated itself to both men.

"I want to see you about an extremely personal matter," said Gairlie. "It is a matter which I had hoped you would have had the fairness to broach yourself. I am referring to your financial position." It was the Gairlie way, the way that had taken him to the top of the tree.

Delayn felt the skin at the back of his neck begin to tingle. Why the devil hadn't he gone straight in to Gairlie when he got back? He had a genuine grievance against the way Fate had built up that drastic situation for him, and he was feeling fierce and sore about it.

"It was about that that I wished to see you, sir," he said awkwardly. "You see—"

"Why leave it until tonight?" The question was like a wind off the Pole. "The matter should have been finished and forgotten months ago."

The palms of Delayn's hands were going cold and sticky. He slid a finger nervously round the inside of his collar. If he could have come face to face with Destiny just then he would have belted the living hide off it.

"Lord Gairlie, I had no intention of evading my responsibilities," he said doggedly, "I've only just got back from town. The lawyers wired me this morning. I—I feel ten thousand sorts of a cad about the whole wretched business, but I couldn't come to you before because I didn't know the position myself. The auditors have only just got to the bottom of dad's affairs."

"Very unfair of you, then, to come to such a definite understanding with Lonora. Don't you think so?" Gairlie did not give him an inch. "Surely you know that your father's position could be intelligently assessed by others outside your immediate family circle? Delayn was heavily committed in every big collapse of the past five years."

"I know, sir, I know. But I was out of contact with things at that time. I was in Australia, trying to score runs off the toughest bowling on earth. Lonora and I had decided to become engaged even then. Ours was not the affair of a moment, we have been meeting at every possible opportunity for over three years now. For heaven's sake believe me when I tell you that I honestly thought that I was in a fair position to offer Lonora marriage. Had I not, I would have drowned myself rather than have compromised her for a single moment. And," he finished bitterly, "drowning for me would be something of a pleasure right now."

Gairlie shot a swift, searching glance at him. There were drawn lines round the young mouth, and on his face a look of sullen harshness, throttle back. Gairlie saw it and understood.

"After I have finished this interview with you I am going up to see Lonora," Delayn said.

"Well?"

"I am going to insist on the engagement being immediately broken. And I must ask you not to refer to it tonight."

Gairlie was silent for a moment. Then he said quietly, "Like that, eh?"

Delayn turned his head away. "Yes—like that," he said.

"You've left it late in the day."

"I didn't know myself until ten o'clock this morning."

"Are things as—bad as that?" For the first time the hint of steel slipped out of Gairlie's voice.

Delayn eyed him squarely. "I'm afraid they are, sir," he said quietly. "I'm worse than a pauper—paupers don't usually owe thousands. And I do. You'll give me an hour with Lonora, won't you, sir?" The last request held something of a plea in it. It was wistful, but tight-lipped still.

Gairlie shrugged. "Of course," he said. "It will not be easy for either of you. I am deeply sorry about this, my boy. I will see Lady Gairlie myself. There is much to be considered."

Delayn assured him on the point. "I shall go back to town tonight," he said. "That is the squarest way out. If I am not present at the dinner you can scarcely be expected to make an announcement."

Gairlie held out his hand. Delayn took it, joylessly, and crawled out of the room with a sudden blur swimming across his eyes.

Lord Gairlie, who knew more about the affairs of the House of Delayn than did Tommy himself, accepted the situation with stoic philosophy. He had been more than half expecting it. In a few quiet, unemotional sentences he explained the whole thing to his wife. Just for one shattering moment it seemed as though the pluperfect calm that stamped her caste was going to desert her. But with an heroic effort she mastered the storm that was pent in her ample bosom, and gazed stonily at her husband.

"Richard," she said, "this must not become public tonight. Tommy is leaving before dinner you say?"

"As soon as he has seen Lonora, my dear. The only thing for us to do is to carry on as though nothing had happened."

"Do you wish me to wear the Rubies, Richard?"

"Most decidedly, my dear. The original intention was to wear them in honour of Lonora's coming of age—not her engagement."

"Then if you will get them for me, I will arrange for their cleaning. There is little time."

Gairlie rang for the butler. Together they fetched the boxes from the vaults, and took them straight to Lady Gairlie's boudoir. She was waiting for them; she rang for the plateman, whose duty it was to clean them before they were worn. He was an old and trusted servant of the family; over half his life had been spent in the faithful service of the lords of Gairlie Castle. Lord Gairlie opened the boxes and laid the jewels out on the green baize cleaning-table. The whole magnificent collection lay there, winking and blinking in the glare of the light.

Gairlie went down to dress, and Lady Gairlie was left alone with the marvellous collection, waiting the arrival of the plateman.

The boudoir was up on the third floor, at the end of a great square landing that was really an upper hall. There were two windows, with a sheer fifty-foot drop outside. Between the windows and the lawn beneath was just a bare wall. There was no handhold whatever, except another window ledge right away on the ground floor, and a broken lightning-conductor that trailed away down the wall. That was all. At that point there was no ivy, no anything that could have borne the weight of so much as a baby. A fly might have climbed to those windows—but flies can't carry off heavy jewellery.

Moreover the windows were double-locked on the inside; had been for years. And those windows were used purely for the admission of light. Ventilation was supplied through a circular opening in the wall higher up. It was a vent, like the porthole of a ship, ten inches in diameter; a suction-fan, drawing fresh air into the room, stood on a bracket inside it.

The room was plainly furnished. There was a dressing-table with wide side mirrors, two chairs, a divan and a gate-legged cleaning-table. Round the wall were high mirrors, on all four sides, giving a remarkable illusion of immense space all round the room. Lady Gairlie could stand in the centre of that room and inspect a thousand reflections of herself at once.

Every detail of her toilet could be scrutinised from every angle. As a "final touch" dressing-room it was perfect, but as a possible hiding-place for a thief it was ruled out. A cat could not have found cover there, much less a man.

Lady Gairlie glanced at her wristwatch. The plateman seemed an unconscionable time in coming. She went to the door and looked up the wide sweep of the landing. The plateman was not to be seen, but coming rather diffidently towards her was Tommy Delayn, nervous, irresolute, unhappy. Tommy Delayn, looking as though he wanted to find some quiet place where he could bury himself.

"I—I'm trying to find Lonora," he said awkwardly. "Could you please tell me where she is? The butler thought she was with you."

Lady Gairlie put her hand on his arm. "I want to see you myself, Tommy," she said gently. "Poor boy; perhaps it's not quite so bad as it seems. You can wait for Lonora in my room. Keep your eye on the rubies, won't you? They're all laid out for cleaning on the table. I'm just going along to see what has happened to my plateman."

She smiled and hurried across the landing to the stairs. Delayn did not even go into the boudoir. The door was wide open and he saw the magnificent array of rubies set out on the green baize table. He just walked across to the great oak balustrade that ran round the whole of the landing, and leaned against it, watching Lady Gairlie, on the far side, going down the stairs.

He drew idly at a cigarette, the boudoir and the jewels forgotten. There were other things then that filled and overfilled his brain. And anyone, to get into that boudoir, *would have to go past him.*

Lady Gairlie was gone a bare five minutes. He saw her returning on the lower landing, with Lonora, white and trembling, hanging on her arm. Just behind the two ladies was Barson, the plateman, carrying a tray of powders and velvets.

Lady Gairlie paused at a door a little way down the landing and beckoned him. Lonora went in, a pathetic figure, not even looking at him. Delayn went along, Lady Gairlie held the door open, and pushed him in with a little womanly pat on the shoulder. "I hope it won't be too hard for you, Tommy," she said.

Delayn went in and she closed the door very gently.

The plateman had reached the boudoir as she turned. He stopped dead in the doorway and switched his white, scared face round. The tray of polishing things fell with a crash.

"My God—my lady—the rubies!" he gasped. "They're gone!" Lady Gairlie gazed at the plateman as though he had suddenly gone raving mad.

"*What* did you say?" she demanded with an imperious little shiver.

"The rubies, my lady. They're not here!" the man stammered agitatedly.

Lady Gairlie sailed in—and stopped as though she had collided with a wall. The baize table was empty. Not a single stone was left on it—or under it—or anywhere around it.

"W—w—what shall I do, my lady?" quavered the thoroughly frightened plateman.

Lady Gairlie gazed blankly round the room. "Do?" she muttered vaguely. "Do? What *can* you do? They're not here. Barson, don't you realise?—They're gone! What can have happened?" Her thoughts broke off short. She was scarcely aware of the stupidity of her own expressions.

"Mr. Delayn!" she gasped at last. "Mr. Delayn was the last one near here. Run and get him—hurry! No—no! Not that. Mr. Delayn mustn't be disturbed yet. Go straight down and tell his lordship to come up here." Then again she halted between doubt and urgency. "No—that won't do. Don't go yet, Barson. Oh, in the name of mercy, what shall I *do*?"

At the very outside she had not left the boudoir for more than five minutes. And Delayn had been standing there the whole time. It was obvious to assume that he had not moved. Equally obvious was it that if anyone had got into that room Delayn would have seen him. Certainly no stranger could have passed him, for Delayn knew every servant in the castle. No; the Gairlie Rubies were gone and nobody but a thief—a bewilderingly elusive thief—could have taken them.

"Barson, you must not leave my sight," she said decisively. "That is for your own good, you understand. There must be no possible link between this room and any other part of the house until a thorough investigation has been made. And until you receive permission from Lord Gairlie himself, not a single word of this to a living soul."

A maid was passing on the landing below. Lady Gairlie leaned over the balustrade.

"Marietta," she called softly. "Go to your master and tell him I wish to see him immediately in my room."

She returned to the dressing-room and spent the next five minutes, in company with Barson, feverishly turning the whole place upside down. They searched everywhere where a ruby might have found a possible hiding-place, ransacked the whole boudoir in a hunt which they both realised was abortive before they began.

Lord Gairlie arrived to find her on her hands and knees dismantling the cushions from the built-up divan. He stopped in mute surprise on the threshold.

"My dear," he said in astonishment, "what on earth are you doing?"

"Barson, close the door," commanded Lady Gairlie. She waited, firm-lipped, while her order was obeyed. And then, without any show of hysterics, informed her husband of exactly what had happened. She recounted the whole episode, loudly and clearly, from the time she left Delayn on guard till the time Barson swung round in the doorway and let the tray fall.

Gairlie went white to the lips. It was some time before he could comprehend the magnitude of his loss. The rubies, his precious, wonderful rubies, gone? He couldn't believe it. It was all a ghastly, silly mistake. And yet there was the evidence of his own wife—coupled with the mountainous fact that the rubies were missing. He groped blindly for a chair and sat down heavily.

He heard his wife's voice quietly in his ear.

"Pull yourself together, Richard. The rubies can't be far away. Perhaps Tommy can throw some light on the matter. He was here the whole time. At least he will know whether anyone entered or left this room while I was out of it."

"But, Myra, this is awful," he muttered. "No engagement, no rubies—what on earth will the guests think?"

Lady Gairlie turned and dismissed the plateman, giving him a last warning to silence. "Go straight to your room," she said. "And stay there till I send for you again."

"Myra, this is more serious than you think," said Gairlie.

Lady Gairlie did not answer. She was looking at him queerly.

"Where—where do you say Delayn is?" he asked after a painful silence.

"In the second room along the landing."

Lord Gairlie went out of the room without another word. The key was sticking in the lock of the door behind which Tommy was crushing the life out of his own romance. Gairlie turned it quietly, locking Delayn in. He turned. His wife was standing by his shoulder, a look of dumb wonderment in her eyes.

"Myra, my dear, go and phone for the police," he said grimly.

"Oh, Richard," Lady Gairlie gasped. "Not the police—not—not yet. Surely you will wait and hear what Tommy has to say? He may be able to—"

Lord Gairlie held up an authoritative hand. "My dear, this is no time for minor considerations," he said quietly. "The rubies are gone. There is only one course open to me. The jewels can't have been taken out of the castle yet. The police must be called in before it is too late."

It was Yardley, the local inspector, who answered the call. He listened in silence while Gairlie recounted the events of the past hour.

"I'd like to see the actual room where it happened," he said at last. "And I'd like Lady Gairlie to come with us."

The three of them went along to the boudoir.

"This is the room," said Lady Gairlie. "The rubies were all laid out on this table. I went downstairs for Barson, and when I got back they were gone."

"Tell me, my lady, did Barson actually go into this room?"

"No. I saw him. He was never out of my sight. He only got as far as the doorway."

"H'm. That puts Barson out of reckoning. Who else was on the landing, my lady?"

"Only Mr. Delayn—so far as I know."

"And he was standing here, you say?"

"No, a little farther along than that." Lady Gairlie positioned herself exactly where she had found Delayn when she returned. "He was leaning over the balustrade," she said.

Yardley stood in the same place and screwed his head round. From that spot he could see into the room and the gate-legged table was right in the centre of his vision.

"Mr. Delayn is above suspicion, I suppose, my lord?" he asked after a thoughtful silence.

"Oh, absolutely!" said Lady Gairlie emphatically. The inspector looked from her to her husband—and his gaze stayed there, for there was something in Gairlie's eyes that made him check up suddenly.

"Oh!" he said softly, and went back into the boudoir.

He examined the windows critically. "Haven't been opened for months," he said with decision. "Look at that dust. And the two frames are still stuck together with the last coating of paint they received. When was this room last repainted, sir?"

Gairlie thought for a while and then said: "Some time last year—about June, I should think. As a matter of fact, those windows are never opened."

Yardley glanced up at the ventilation hole. "Well, he couldn't have got in *there*," he said. "Unless he was a monkey. That hole is barely a foot across."

"Ten inches exactly," said Gairlie.

"What is there outside there, sir?"

"A sheer drop to the lawn below. Fifty or sixty feet at the very least."

"I'd like one of those windows opened so that I can see for myself," said the inspector.

With some difficulty they got the window open and Yardley leaned out. It was exactly as Lord Gairlie had said. The wall fell sheer and unbroken to the bottom. And it was as flat as a sheet of paper. It was the same above.

Yardley got back into the room. "Whoever stole your rubies, sir, stole them from *inside*" he said flatly.

"Exactly," said Gairlie. And again Yardley caught that queer look in his eyes.

Yardley toured the room. "About these mirrors," he said. "Are they fixtures?"

Gairlie nodded. "Yes; I had them built in two or three years ago."

"There are no secret panels behind them? None of them that swings out if you press a button and reveal a cavity behind?"

Gairlie laughed. "Oh, no," he said. "You can take it from me, the walls of the room are solid. The mirrors are built into the walls; they are immovable."

"Very well, then; point number two," said Yardley. "Whoever lifted your rubies came in through that door and went out through that door."

"Quite," said Gairlie.

Yardley looked at him hard.

"My lord," he said, "you must give me all the facts."

Gairlie cleared his throat.

"Whom do you suspect—up to now?" he asked defensively.

"I can't suspect anyone yet, I've only got half the evidence. For all I know, there may have been a dozen people along this landing between the times Lady Gairlie left this boudoir and returned to it. In that case the field is widened by exactly so many people."

Gairlie was silent for a long time. Then, very quietly, he said: "I have told you all I'm entitled to tell you."

Yardley mopped his forehead with a big silk handkerchief.

"Lord Gairlie, you're not helpful," he grunted. "The last time you needed my services was in connection with an extraordinary outbreak of petty larceny in this building. All sorts of silly little thefts—and always the missing article was red. Well, now the rubies are gone. *And you couldn't get anything much redder than that.* Come, my lord, out with it—this is no time to shelter friends—where do you make the connection?"

"So far as I can see there is absolutely no connection whatever," declared Gairlie. "I agree that the persistent pilfering of red-coloured things from Gairlie Castle is a mystery entirely beyond my comprehension. Over and above which, those thefts have never ceased. According to Barson there was another one this morning—or rather last night."

"Indeed? '

"Yes. Mr. Delayn reported the loss of a red scientific volume and a little red diary."

"Mr. Delayn did?"

"Yes, early this morning."

Yardley tried a new line. "Tell me, sir, has Mr. Delayn been here before when red things have disappeared?"

"No. Not once to my knowledge."

"H'm. Wrong again. Mr. Delayn is marrying your daughter, isn't he, sir?"

"No. Not now."

Yardley looked his surprise. "Since when, sir?" he queried.

"Since this evening."

The inspector dropped his voice so that Lady Gairlie did not hear his next question.

"Will you please tell me why?" he asked.

Gairlie seemed to grudge his answer. "Mr. Delayn was informed by his solicitors this morning that he is hopelessly insolvent—bankrupt," he said.

Yardley drew a deep breath.

"I see," he said. "Thank you. Now you have circumstance, opportunity—and *motive.* I'd like to see Mr. Delayn now."

Lady Gairlie went down to Tommy's room without a word. She knocked on the door, and after a little while repeated the knock, ever so gently. Then, under cover of turning the handle, she softly turned the key. Delayn stood there, cowed and miserable, but he looked at her firm-lipped and steady. Lonora was lying on her face on a couch in the corner, her shoulders quivering with deep, silent sobs.

"Come outside, Tommy," Lady Gairlie whispered. "Dad wants you in the boudoir. It's—it's rather important, dear. I'll stay with Lonora for a while."

Delayn went out, dumb, too unsure of himself to speak.

He pushed in moodily through the boudoir door and stared in puzzled surprise at the uniformed man inside.

"Tommy, this is Inspector Yardley, of the local force," said Gairlie. "He has called in connection with—ah—with certain things that are missing from Gairlie Castle. Barson tells me you lost a book and a diary this morning. You also probably know that a good many other things have been stolen from time to time. Tonight something else has gone and Yardley wants you to tell him what you know."

"With pleasure, sir," said Tommy mechanically.

"Mr. Delayn," said the inspector, without any beating about the bush, "there have been some serious developments in this business of red things being stolen from the castle, and I want you to do your best to concentrate on what you were doing and what you saw on this landing about an hour ago."

"All right, inspector, fire ahead."

"You remember, when you came up to see Miss Lonora, you came as far as this room?"

"Yes. Lady Gairlie was in here, waiting for the plateman."

"I want you to tell me exactly what transpired from that moment."

"Nothing much. Lady Gairlie asked me to stay here for a minute or two while she went downstairs to find Barson. I stayed. And after two or three minutes she came back with him. That's all."

"Why did she want you to stay?"

"She didn't like leaving the rubies unattended, I suppose. It's one the insurance people's rules, I believe, that the jewels shall never be left once they are out of the vaults."

"And you stayed in this room?"

"No. I was smoking a cigarette at the time, so I stayed just out there by the balustrade."

"I see. And did anything happen while you were there?"

"Happen? In what way?"

"Well, did anyone pass you on the landing?"

"No. Not a soul."

"You could see both sides of the balustrade?"

"All round it."

"Then nobody went into the boudoir during Lady Gairlie's absence?"

Delayn clicked his tongue impatiently. "How could anyone possibly go in if there was nobody there?" he exclaimed testily.

"I mean, did *you go* in?"

"No. I didn't move from the balustrade."

Yardley began to look a bit worried. Delayn's answers were coming so frankly that his half-formed suspicions were beginning to totter. Either Delayn was the most consummate actor he had ever seen in his life, or he was the biggest fool on the face of the earth. With an innocence that was pathetic he was slowly and remorselessly condemning himself out of his own mouth. He had repeatedly committed himself to an assertion that could never be hedged—that no other soul in Gairlie Castle *could* have taken those rubies.

Yardley took him up again.

"Let me try this way, sir. Did you *hear* anything while you were there smoking?" he asked.

"Nothing. The landing was deserted."

"Think again, Mr. Delayn. Think as hard as you can—the tiniest scratch of sound that might have emanated from somewhere *here in this boudoir?*"

"No, inspector; absolutely nothing. I'm sorry; I don't seem to be helping you in your task, but it is useless for me to pretend a knowledge which I do not possess."

"How long was Lady Gairlie away?" demanded the officer.

Delayn was non-committal. "Only a few minutes," he said.

"You can't get it any nearer than that?"

"I'm sorry, no," said Tommy acidly. "I had something else to think about just then."

Yardley ran his fingers through his hair. The net was surely closing round Delayn, and it was Delayn himself who was pulling it tight.

And then through the haze of trouble that clouded his brain Delayn began to sense the air of aggression that tinged the voice of the inspector. This cumulative questionnaire seemed to be directed at him—against him. There was the sinister craft of the Inquisition in that long lead-up of interrogatives.

"I say," he blurted suddenly. "You seem to be getting mighty near the bone, Mr. Inspector. You don't think *I've* been developing a passion for other people's belongings, do you? I'll assure you on that point. Blue is my favourite colour."

Yardley looked at him with a dangerous flicker in his eyes.

"You'd prefer the turquoise to the ruby, eh?" he said.

Light began to dawn on Delayn. The hard tan of his face drained away to a dull parchmenty hue, and his jaws opened slowly in sheer unbelief. His gaze travelled with painful slowness from the policeman, calm, businesslike, and competent, to Gairlie, worried, anxious, and all at sea with himself—and from Gairlie to the green baize table, horribly empty. With an effort that was as much mental as physical he forced his eyes back to the inspector.

"Good God!" he gasped.

Yardley rose and quietly shut the door. "That's it, Mr. Delayn," he said shortly. "They're gone! Have you anything to add to your previous replies?"

Tommy shook his head helplessly.

Yardley turned to Gairlie. "My lord," he said, "I am calling in Scotland Yard on this. Too big for me altogether—and too risky! If you allow me to use your telephone I'll get right through now. Mr. Delayn, I must ask you not to leave this building until I give you permission."

Gairlie looked across at Tommy with a gaze that was not quite steady. He seemed as though he wanted to look away, but could not. He was in a quagmire of doubt and difficulty, but somehow it wasn't merely that that was responsible for that queer harassed look.

Delayn eyed him back coldly. Yardley had pronounced his ultimatum and all the squealing in the world wouldn't stay the slow revolutions of the wheels of the law. Objections would only strengthen the inspector's suspicions. Any requests for Scotland Yard to be kept out of it would have to come from Gairlie. And Gairlie remained silent. There was nothing for Delayn to do but to accept the situation. He thrust his hands into his pockets and eyed the millionaire.

"I'm sorry about this, sir," he said quietly. "But I can't help thinking you haven't been quite fair to me—all things considered."

"I don't think I understand you," replied Gairlie stiffly.

"I'm not referring to my own troubles just now. But considering the inexplicable circumstances that rose around me on that balustrade, I think the very least you could have done was to have acquainted me of the facts before calling the police."

Gairlie's eyes lowered and he looked for help from the inspector.

"Would the result have been any different?" asked Yardley sharply.

"Probably not. But somehow it doesn't seem cricket to question a guest like this when he is in entire ignorance of the reason for it."

"I had to take this course in fairness to everybody within these walls," said Gairlie stubbornly.

"Bilge," snapped Delayn. "All right, Mr. Policeman, you go and do your 'phoning. I'll go to my room and stay there to your convenience. You have my parole. Lord Gairlie—I shall not embarrass you with my presence at dinner tonight." He turned and with a curt nod to the inspector went out of the room.

Yardley made a few brief notes on a pad, and then looked up quizzically.

"Didn't seem much like a guilty man to me," he said.

Gairlie fidgeted with his watch-chain. "I didn't infer that he was guilty," he jerked. "Delayn is probably Britain's most famous amateur sportsman—no one but a lunatic would couple his name with a suspected robbery."

"Suspected!" snorted Yardley. "The rubies have gone, haven't they?"

"Come to my library," said Gairlie, opening the door.

When they reached the library Yardley 'phoned through to his own headquarters in the town, talking rapidly to his chief. The inspector was quickly down to the bones of the matter in hand.

"I think so, Chief," he said. "Yes. An absolute mystery. Can't get a line on it anywhere. Only one suspect so far. A guest, yes. But even so it's a mystery how he got rid of the stuff. What? Yes—the whole collection; not a stone left. They need a box a foot square to hold them all. Delayn couldn't possibly have hidden them on his person. There isn't a clue of any sort. Lord Gairlie swears to the integrity of the servants. If Delayn did it he must have had accomplices, and I can't see who they are or how they worked. They couldn't have got upstairs without being seen. And he couldn't have dropped them out of the window because the windows are locked. Took me five minutes to get *one* open. To me, it's Yard job, pure and simple. You agree? I'm glad of that, sir. Eh? Yes, I'll get right through now. Ring off, will you, please. I'll come and see you as soon as I've put the Yard men square."

Gairlie maintained a stolid silence, listening intently while Yardley spoke, striving to complete a dialogue from a monologue. Yardley was pounding the instrument impatiently, trying to get his call. At last he got through to the Superintendent and got a priority call through to the Yard. "Rush that call, miss," he barked. "I'll wait."

In a few minutes Yardley was through to the Commissioner himself explaining the whole case in a long string of succinct details. The Commissioner's only comment when Yardley had finished was "Dam extraordinary."

"I can't see daylight anywhere," agreed Yardley. "My chief advised me to get through to you before any of the guests leave."

"Right," came the answer. "You'll want a good pair on this I'm sending Kennedy and Stanforth. They're a good team, know all about the London cracks—you've probably got a couple down there unbeknown to Lord Gairlie—and they've worked in double harness on most of their jobs. They will come down by fast car. You'd better meet them at Winchester. You can give them all the facts on the way down. They can start straight in on the job."

Yardley turned from the 'phone.

"I want a car, sir," he said shortly.

"A car will be ready for you in two minutes," said Lord Gairlie.

Yardley hurriedly packed up his notes and stowed them away.

"I'll get back as fast as that car can travel," he said. "Scotland Yard asks that you keep your guests here—all of them—until their men arrive. And while I'm waiting for that motor I'd like to have a look round outside."

He took a strong flash-lamp and went out on the dewy lawn. A thin sickle of moon was pulling slowly up, just above the tree-tops. Its light was hardly strong enough to be of much assistance, it made the surrounding shadows too black. But right under the boudoir windows where the great wall went ponderously up into the night, a long white patch of clear moonlight lay, some twenty feet square. It illuminated the exact spot where anyone would have to stand when establishing communications with the windows above.

Yardley switched on his lamp and quartered the ground inch by inch. To right and left of the window line he went, on his hands and knees, with his torch full on. He travelled slowly, a black, crouching figure behind a circle of glaring light. For fifty feet along the wall, and over an area of thirty feet away from it, he crawled, scanning every tiny patch, scrutinising every blade of grass. And the result was just a marvellous and profound blank. There was not a footmark, nor a dent, nor even the faintest impression on the short-cropped turf that might have yielded a clue as to how the Gairlie Rubies had vanished from the room above. He thrust his lamp into his pocket and went down to the waiting car.

III

Nearing eleven o'clock that night an overheated car approached the gates of Gairlie Castle. The driver sounded the horn for the lodgekeeper to open the gates, but Kennedy touched his arm.

"Don't go through," he said grimly. "We get out here."

He clambered out, stamping about in the road to get the stiffness out of his legs. Stanforth came out after him with Yardley behind.

Kennedy was of stocky build, rather on the short side, stumpy and somewhat solid in his movements; but his face carried the assurance that though his actions might be inclined to hang fire a trifle, there was nothing but a high-speed brain under his hair. His eyes were quick and restless—and unfriendly.

Stanforth was his able second. He was taller, looser—nearly lanky. He was one of those "unexpected" men—who look older than they are—and so very unlike a detective that one was rather incredulous to know that he was even remotely connected with the police.

Kennedy approached the gates and stared up the dark drive.

"A lodge, eh?" he said. "Bright lights. Dozens of guests arriving right through the afternoon. Lodgekeeper on the alert. A dog couldn't get in or out of these gates without him seeing it. The man who got the Gairlie Rubies got in somewhere else. Only a fool would come down here. And he was no fool."

"Any other entrances to this estate?" asked Stanforth, turning to Yardley.

The inspector shook his head. "The boundary walls and fences run right round," he said, "and so far as I know, they're unbroken."

"Any hedges?"

"Only here and there. But they're very thick and kept in first-class repair."

Kennedy nodded. "Stanforth, you go round to the right; I'll take the line to the left," he said "First job is to find a breach in the hedge or a weak section where a man could climb—with a load."

He turned and swung away by the high wall, the beam of his lamp playing ahead of him.

There was one thing Kennedy did not know when he started off on that search. And that was that the Gairlie boundary was fourteen miles round. Roads run through it, villages dot it, rivers cross it, but the boundary walls and fences continue. The only breaks are at the public highways, and there the junction of wall and road-hedge is even more securely built. But it was just as well for Kennedy, and for the prestige of the police in general, that he made that tour.

For towards the end of half an hour he found what he was looking for, a distinct break in the hedge that converged on a lonely lane, a hole in the stout hawthorn bushes that could be crawled through with a certain amount of ease. And what gave him infinitely more satisfaction, there was a clearly defined track leading from it. Only the very regular passage of a human being could have worn the grass like that. Someone had made that breach wilfully, and not too recently either. The lower stems of the hedge had been cut through with a knife and the wounds were already healing over with a soft powdering of pollen-like green.

Kennedy switched his light down and tried to distinguish the boot-marks. But the grass grew right up to the hedge and no isolated footprint was discernible. He swung the light from side to side to see if, by some lucky chance, a bare patch of earth might show the print of a boot. But nothing showed there, and he decided to leave that part of his investigations to daylight.

And then he stopped like a rabbit scenting a stoat. Something was shining back from the grass in the very centre of his beam of light, a bright red eye that leapt to the light from the darkness around in a single blob of shimmering fire. Kennedy knew it instinctively. It was one of the Gairlie Rubies.

That wonderful collection was not unknown to him. Its description was one little item among the thousands that comprised the stock in trade of his calling.

Kennedy stooped and picked it up. A great blood-red ruby on a chain of gold. His pulse gave a jump. It was the biggest and most wonderful of all, the pendant stone, the famous Burning Star itself.

The fact that he had performed almost a miracle, that within half an hour of sighting the gates of Gairlie Castle he had found a very remarkable clue, at night, lying in a tiny tuft of grass in the immensity of a fourteen-mile circle, and that he had found that clue as a direct result of his own logical reasoning, passed him by. The only thing that concerned him was that he had got it; and round that fact his bulldoggish sentiments played.

His line of argument continued mentally along the same jerky avenue as his speech. "Early thefts of red things from Gairlie only preliminary to the big haul. Same man responsible. Night worker. Afraid of the daylight. Came in through this entrance every night. Clue at other end of this trail. Some new method. No good hanging round here. He's finished. Made the big haul. Won't come again. And there'll be no more red things stolen from Gairlie Castle."

He coiled the chain round the Burning Star and slipped it into his pocket. Then on hands and knees he began crawling through the hedge, scrutinising every tiny tuft and patch of weed with his torch. But there was nothing more. He emerged at the other side of the hedge and stood up, casting about with his light to pick up the trail again. He found it easily enough. The trampled line of grass led away from the hedge on a slant into the muddy cart-track. The trail pointed up the lane, but was lost in the maze of wheel-tracks and hoof-marks the moment it left the grass.

Kennedy paused for a moment, thumbing his chin. "Trail points *up* the lane," he mused. "That means he goes down the lane. Too darn wise to leave an open book behind him. Lane leads to the main road, I suppose. Reduces the area of search to somewhere south of here."

He went out and stood in the lane, looking keenly up and down. It was nothing more than a wagon-track between two high hedges, a mere communication way between two sections of the Gairlie farming operations. Wisps of hay and wool along the out-jutting bits of hedge confirmed that surmise.

"Are you looking for anything?"

A deep, almost sepulchral voice from the opposite hedge startled him so much that he dropped his torch. Coming as it did with such shattering unexpectedness, Kennedy was nearly knocked off his balance. He made a hurried grab at his torch and strode across.

Kennedy pressed the button of his torch and flashed the light full.

The man neither moved nor spoke. In spite of the eye-aching brilliance of the light he did not flick an eyelid. It was an extraordinary face, set on an extraordinary figure. Grim, dour and immensely strong, with deep lines and big-built features. It was the face of an ex-prizefighter, a heavyweight, too, with a beard on. A face with which only a fool or an armed man would engage in heated argument. The eyes were big, but as relentless and hard as a mountain in a storm. Big eyes sometimes express generosity and timidity. But there was nothing of those qualities in the motionless pupils that looked up unwaveringly at Kennedy. The lips, too, were pressed close together under the black moustache, and there was an unforgiving line about them. The chin line was obliterated by the beard, but the whole aspect of the face was one of silent, morose strength. His chest was titanic, a huge depth of strength and virility, and there was not a pound of superfluous flesh on him. Standing up he would touch six foot four, and not look over-tall for his immense gorilla-like proportions. But he did not stand up. He just sat there, immobile, staring steadily past the beam of light, at Kennedy's astonished face.

"Good God! *You?* What in hell's name are *you* doing here?" gasped the man from the Yard.

"If you switched off that cursed light I could see who you are," came the level answer. There was no surprise in that voice, no fear, no emotion of any kind, just a quiet, restrained announcement of an obvious fact.

"I'm Kennedy, down on a job. The castle. Sent for. Got on to the tail end of a line already. What in thunder—"

The heavyweight Sphinx blinked.

"I live here," he said. "Just down in the village. My name is John Argle. And I'll trouble you to keep on calling me John Argle. If you don't it means that I'll have to shift my damned pegs again. And I've had enough shifts to last me a lifetime. Put that blasted light away."

Kennedy stuffed the torch into his pocket and sat down beside him.

"John Argle," he said softly. "I wouldn't spill your beans for all the nickel in the Mint. How long have you been here?"

"Three years."

"Great stuff. You're the man I want. Got a big job on. Bit of trouble at the reception. You—"

"Guest lost a tiepin?"

"No. Someone has done a fade-away with the Gairlie sparklers. All the heap. I've found one. Got it here in my pocket. Here, take a look at it. That's the Burning Star. Worth fifty thousand in the open market. Who do you know round here? Anyone likely to be cute enough to get away with the swag inside five minutes?"

"No. They don't grow 'em that way in Hampshire villages."

"Anybody badly in debt? Younger sons of local squires; undergrads likely to pull out a 'varsity rag?"

"No. The only ones I know anywhere near your street are the local drunks."

"Forget them. This was done by a considerable piece of brain, walking about on two acrobatic legs."

"Well, start a new line, Kennedy. I'm in the mud."

Kennedy was quiet for a moment. Then he jerked, "Come here often?"

"Every night," said the steady voice.

Kennedy jumped. "Gosh!" he muttered. "Since when?"

"Ten months ago."

"Every night—at this time?"

"Yes. I never miss. Unless—I—you know what I mean."

"Unless you're away? Right, I've got you. Listen, John, you know who comes through that hole every night?"

"Yes. I know."

"Who?"

"Betty Ralston."

"Who?"

"Betty. A maid at the castle. I'm engaged to her. We have an hour together every night. She will be coming soon. I cut that gap for her. She slips out for an hour every night and comes to the lane here so that she won't be seen."

For a long time the detective was irritably silent. Instead of an explanation to a brain-twisting criminal plot he had stumbled on a village romance. Then his deductive faculties began to pick up their beat again. The Burning Star—how did that get there? What was the connection between Betty Ralston, the great ruby, and John Argle's trail?

"Has Betty been out today?" he suddenly demanded.

"No, she's been too busy. She's late now."

Kennedy nodded his satisfaction. "That means that the thief who got the rubies was slick enough to find out about your secret meetings here and to use your trail. I'll get back to the other end of that track. Ought to be something waiting for me there. And don't mention this to your Betty. Quite enough leakages without having a woman chattering."

John Argle grunted, and Kennedy crawled back through the hedge, following the trail up to the castle with his light. There were no more rubies on the way, and at the end he found nothing but a disappointment. The trail petered out in the smooth gravel walk that circled the great flowerbeds. He hunted around patiently, trying to find where it crossed to the lawns, but the thief had been too clever even for Kennedy's trained eyes.

He went round to the stables—and found an ostler.

"Somewhere over there," he said, pointing to the left, "you'll find two men following the boundary line of the estate. Tell them to come back here; Kennedy wants them. You'll find them all right. They'll be using strong torches."

The ostler did not question the matter. "Yes, sir," he said," I'll go and shift a couple of cars out of the fairway first—they're in the way."

"Oh, so you're in charge of the cars, are you?" said Kennedy, motioning him to stay. "What time did Mr. Delayn get back this evening?"

"About six o'clock, sir."

"Notice anything unusual about him?"

"No, sir—er—yes, sir, now you come to mention it. He seemed very worried—upset like."

"Did he say anything?"

The ostler paused uncomfortably. This was betraying a hero of his, a sportsman whose feats he had followed with avidity in the newspapers.

"Come on—out with it!"

"He asked me to park his car near the gates, sir, so that he could get away in a hurry if he wanted to." The ostler was doing his best to say a little and leave a lot unsaid.

"Go on. That's not all."

"Said he might not be staying to dinner after all."

Kennedy pulled the man up close to him.

"Look here," he growled. "You're the fifteen-hundredth man I've questioned who's had to have it dragged out of him by the roots. Don't try to face me out. Loyalty is all right in its place, but when it's holding up the recovery of half a million pounds worth of rubies, we call it 'being an accessory after the fact.' You're holding something back. Come on—what was it?"

There was no getting away from that autocratic tone, and the man wilted under its dominance.

"I—I asked him if I could get him anything," he said awkwardly, "and—Mr. Delayn said 'yes.' He said: 'Bring me all the Gairlie Rubies on a big gold tray,' he said."

"Oh! He said that, did he? All right. That will do. But another time don't be quite so slow. Off you go and take my message."

Kennedy, thinking hard, made his way to the great main entrance and pealed the bell. He was shown straight into the library, where Lord Gairlie, reduced to a bag of frayed nerves, was waiting for him. Gairlie had just passed through the most ferocious three hours of his life, and he carried evidences of it. The dinner was held according to programme—Gairlie had to go through with that—but neither Delayn nor Lonora was present.

And in the midst of it Gairlie had had to stand up and hint at explanations, a speech that would have brought perspiration to the forehead of the most skilful politician in the House. And Gairlie laid no claim to mastery of oratory. In the end he gave up trying to skate over ice already broken, and came out with the flat announcement that not only were the Gairlie Rubies gone, but that Scotland Yard had been called in. It was the only way he could tell them that no one could leave Gairlie Castle without police permission.

He told them haltingly, that owing to sudden circumstances beyond the control of any living person, the engagement of his daughter Lonora to Mr. Tommy Delayn could not possibly be made public that night, but he hoped that time would deal gently with the matter and explain a great deal that he himself was not privileged to discuss.

It was a relief to get it over, a still greater relief to receive that call to the peaceful seclusion of the library. Away from felicitous guests and too often repeated expressions of sympathy.

Kennedy entered, unhurried, competent, taking a mental photograph of Gairlie as he came towards him.

"Good evening, my lord," he said. "I've got most of the details. You don't mind getting right down to business, do you?"

"I'm glad to, Mr. Kennedy. The butler tells me you have already opened your investigations."

"Tell me, sir, what department of the house is Betty Halston in?"

"She is the still-room maid. That is the butler's department."

"Ring for him. Do you trust that girl?"

"Oh, implicitly. She's quite a pretty little thing. I doubt if there's an ounce of evil in her."

Kennedy waited in stony silence till the butler appeared, a tall, portly man, cast in the ideal butler's mould, with a profound dignity of presence.

"Harris, this is Detective Kennedy, of Scotland Yard—he wishes to speak to you," said Lord Gairlie.

"About a girl named Betty Halston," cut in Kennedy. "Has she been out of the castle since, say, six o'clock?"

Harris thought for a few seconds and then said quietly: "Not for a moment, sir."

"Right. Thank you. Think no more about it."

Kennedy turned to Lord Gairlie as the door closed,

"Would you recognise your property if you saw it, sir?" he asked.

"Why—yes—of course," said Gairlie, losing a shade of colour.

Kennedy dropped the Burning Star into his hands. "Take a look at that," he said. "That's yours, I think."

Gairlie's face drained bone-white. He stared at the jewel like a man in a trance.

And then the colour came mounting back to his face again, a rush of hectic red that brought back with it a chuckling smile—almost of relief. With an easy gesture he tossed the ruby back.

"No go, Kennedy," he said, still smiling. "You can have that. It's no earthly use to me."

The amazed detective caught it and remained staring at Gairlie, his mouth open and a look of pained astonishment on his face.

Gairlie chuckled again. "Glass," he said smoothly. "Red glass. A wonderful copy. Somebody has pulled your leg."

Kennedy fingered the jewel bemusedly. This was a complication that knocked his world sky-high. All his shrewdly constructed theories about the Gairlie robbery smashed into smithereens as he gazed at the fake. For the first time he began to discredit his own idea of a straight robbery. There was more in it—a great deal more. And for the life of him he couldn't figure out what. The new orientation of his case showed a mystery within a mystery, a plot behind a plot, and he found himself up against a deadlock in deciding which was his principal target. Plot and counterplot were as baffling as each other.

"Are you sure this is glass, sir?" he asked at last, hoping against hope that Gairlie had made a mistake.

"Crystal, extremely good crystal," replied Gairlie. "There is a tiny vapour cloud in the bottom point of the Burning Star, minute, but visible to an expert. That piece of glass is clear. Again, there is a difference between white gold and platinum. My stone had a platinum link connecting with the chain. That one in your hand is white gold."

Kennedy sat down, muttering thunderous things under his breath.

For half an hour he hammered at the facts with Gairlie, going over the points with dogged persistence, taking the case right down from the point where Gairlie had gone down into the vaults for the two strong-boxes.

But Gairlie ruled him out. "You're playing with the substitution idea," he said. "And you're on bad hunting. No one but myself ever goes to those vaults. No one has access to the keys. Those keys are kept in a separate safe here in my library—built into the wall there. The key of it is here on my wristwatch, an ingenious part of the chain. I bring the boxes up one under each arm, right into the boudoir. I opened them myself and laid the rubies out. And they were *my* rubies. No, you can dismiss any substitution theory. Utterly impossible."

He sent for Lady Gairlie and they went over it all again. Even though Gairlie himself was the losing party, Kennedy's bulldog tenacity began to exasperate him; and he made his irritation known.

"I want the facts," declared Kennedy stubbornly. "I want to know just what happened, and—just what didn't happen. I'd like to go up examine the boudoir."

All three of them went up, and Lady Gairlie reconstructed the whole episode, using Kennedy as a deputy for Tommy Delayn. Four times re-acted it, and at the end of it Kennedy expressed the sum-total of thoughts with a dissatisfied growl.

"Couldn't be done," he grunted, "not if Delayn's straight. Nobody could have got into this room without his seeing them."

He stumped over to the windows and prospected round from there.

"Boils down to this," he jerked. "*Somebody* stole 'em. Somebody with hands and feet and a body and head. And there's only two ways into this room Through the door; and through the window. That's it—in a swimming bath."

"There's the ventilator," hazarded Lady Gairlie helpfully.

Kennedy squinted up at the hole again. He had given it a quick scrutiny the moment he entered, but the ventilator was automatically a discarded factor.

He shook his head. "Even a Living Skeleton couldn't crawl through that hole, my lady," he said. "And before he could reach it he'd have to climb the wall outside. The man doesn't breathe who could do it."

He threw up the window and stared out. Ten seconds were enough. He pulled his head in and snorted. "Bah, a trained monkey couldn't do it. The man who stole your rubies, my lord, came in through that door. Fetch in Mr. Delayn, please."

Stanforth arrived while they waited, and Kennedy sent him off to make a tour of the rooms. "See if you can recognise any of the guests," he said. "The Chief has an idea a couple of West End crooks may have helped themselves to an invitation. Lord Gairlie says he knows personally every guest who sat down to dinner. But those rubies went before dinner. Take your time, I'll send for you if I want you in a hurry."

He turned to Lady Gairlie as Stanforth left. Delayn was just entering.

"I'd like you to stay here, if you will, my lady," he said. He shot a shrewd look at Delayn as he came in. He was a firm believer in first impressions, and with an uneasy feeling under his coat, he found himself admitting that his first impressions of Delayn were wholly favourable. There was nothing "smart" or smooth about him, nothing impudent or over-obsequious, not a single hallmark of the modern swell cracksman was noticeable. He was just a young, fairly good-looking boy who was obviously worried out of his life.

"Mr. Delayn, I'm Kennedy of Scotland Yard," said the detective brusquely, "and I must ask you to give me fair answers to a few questions."

Tommy nodded. "Inspector Yardley has already questioned me a good deal," he muttered. "But if—"

"My questions will be a little more personal," grunted Kennedy. "To begin with, what time did you leave Gairlie Castle this morning?"

"Soon after eight."

"Arriving in London at—?"

"Half-past ten or thereabouts."

"About two and a half hours for the journey, eh? You went to see your solicitors, I believe. What for?"

"Candidly, to be told I was something worse than a pauper."

Kennedy made a note of the exact answer. "At that time you believed you were a millionaire," he suggested.

Delayn smiled feebly. "Well, a fairly rich man," he agreed.

"Rich enough to offer marriage to Lord Gairlie's daughter."

"Quite," said Delayn, flushing.

"What time did you start back from London?"

Delayn passed a troubled hand over his forehead. "I haven't the vaguest idea," he said. "I—I think it was some time about midday."

"And you didn't get back here till—what time?"

"Very late, I know."

"Very odd, wasn't it? Taking all that time on a return journey? You were long enough in between London and here to make all sorts of—arrangements?"

Delayn went white. "I did not leave my driving wheel," he said.

"At the gate you spoke to the ostler. He asked if he could get you anything. Do you remember your reply?"

The clock ticked along slowly. For long seconds Delayn sat trying to recall what he had said, a deep frown of puzzlement across his brow.

"No, I'm blessed if I can remember," he said.

"You said you'd like him to bring you all the Gairlie Rubies on a gold tray."

"Did I? What a damfool thing to say."

"It was," snapped Kennedy. "Then when you got in you shut yourself up in your room."

"I was tubbing," remonstrated Tommy in surprise.

"Nevertheless, with all that mass of happenings to account for to Lord Gairlie, you did not go to him."

"But I did," protested Delayn, his face the colour of a tomato.

"Lord Gairlie had to *send* for you—an hour before dinner. Can you account for it?" Kennedy almost threw the words at him.

"N—no. But I was going down anyhow. I was brushing my hair when his lordship sent for me."

"Just so, Mr. Delayn. I'm arresting you. Now. On the charge of being implicated in the theft of the Gairlie Rubies from this room, shortly before seven o'clock today. You must come with me to the local station. You will spend the night in cells. Sorry, but duty is duty. Will you give me your parole?"

Delayn winced. "Of course I will," he said quietly. "I won't try to escape."

Kennedy turned to Gairlie. "I'll take him along in my own car," he said. "Get your hat and coat, Delayn."

Lord Gairlie, looking fearfully unhappy, stepped forward.

"Kennedy, this isn't really necessary, is it?" he said with an effort, "I will stand sponsor for Mr. Delayn's parole. The evidence, I admit, is bewilderingly against him, almost overwhelming—I think Mr. Delayn himself realises that—but at the same time the whole thing is preposterous."

"Can't help it, sir," said Kennedy obstinately. "If this were a civil case it would be different. But it's criminal. And whether the suspects person is a duke or a dustman the law goes through."

"But I protest. I am bringing no charge against Mr. Delayn. All I want is the rubies back."

"The matter is out of your hands the moment you call in the police!" Kennedy was inexorable. "Delayn's my man, and I want him."

"I'm sorry, Delayn," Gairlie turned impulsively to the hot-faced boy, Lady Gairlie was standing near the door, embarrassed misery on every line of her face. She looked too ill and too hopelessly dazed to speak to him "But—but what can I *do*?" asked Gairlie helplessly.

"Nothing, my lord. He comes up before the magistrate in the morning."

In a painful silence Lady Gairlie opened the door and they passed out. She just managed to squeeze his arm as he went blindly past her, a motherly touch of sympathy that brought a great lump into his throat. Gairlie himself stepped up quickly behind him. "Can I do anything, boy?" he asked in a husky whisper.

Delayn shook his head. "No," he said quietly. "And I don't want you to try. I can't help thinking that you haven't played the game in this affair. Good night, sir." Lord Gairlie fell back, staring at his retreating figure.

Lady Gairlie went down into the hall with them. She thrust a great box of cigarettes into his pocket as he went out. A minute later the purring hum of a high-powered car droned away into the night.

IV

Kennedy rubbed the sleep from his eyes and sat up in bed. Stanforth had been asleep when he got back from the police station overnight. He read Stanforth's note.

Nothing wrong with the guest lists. All satisfactorily accounted for. Have seen them all and recognise no one known to us. Have heard about Delayn. Lord Gairlie told me. I agree. Very obvious.—Stanforth.

He climbed out of bed and groped to the window. Stanforth was still sleeping. A pitiless pall of rain blotted out the view, and a bleak wind swept round the casement.

"Brrh," he rasped, and pulled the window shut.

Stanforth stirred and opened his eyes.

"What's doing, ol' man?" he asked, heaving up among the bedclothes.

"Rain, hail, sleet, mud, cyclones, typhoons and hurricanes," came the disgruntled reply. "Over and above which it's darn cold. Hallo, what's this?" He pushed the window open again and looked out. Lying on the coping, so water-soddened that it toned with the brown woodwork, was a piece of imitation leather. It had been torn off on a nail, a thin triangular piece of stuff that somehow seemed vaguely familiar. He laid it carefully on his dressing-table.

"Everything O.K. last night?" growled Stanforth.

"Yes. Local police agree with us. But—" He rubbed his chin reflectively. "Somehow young Delayn doesn't seem to fill the bill," he said.

"I felt that way about it after what I heard last night from the servants. *They're* with him to a man—and woman. We are the two most unpopular men in Hampshire. They seem to blame us for it."

Kennedy rang for shaving water. "Good, square, clean-looking young chap. Can't seem to reconcile myself to it either," he muttered. "Still, you never know what a high-spirited youngster will do when there's a lady concerned. Make fools of themselves all day and all night. Say, Stanforth, how does Gairlie strike you?"

Stanforth looked over his knees and screwed up his eyes.

"Bull's eye," he said softly. "I only saw him for about a minute. And he didn't impress me half as well as did the youngster. If you ask me, he's got something on his mind he hasn't told us, or I'm very much mistaken."

Kennedy grunted. "Old aristocracy. Upset a bit. Don't like this sort of thing happening in their houses. Mighty touchy about it. Delayn wouldn't have much to do with him last night when I was taking him away. Gairlie tried to come over with the olive branch. But the boy wouldn't have it. Very much on his dignity. The old lady was great."

"Think there's more than Delayn in it?"

"Must be. He's only a tool. They've played him up and let him stand the racket. The old game. The boy can't squeal. Gosh! I'd like to make him talk. We'd rake in the cleverest gang in London."

Kennedy was groping about on his dressing-table.

"Where's my damation razors?" he growled. "Hey, Stanforth, did you shift my razor-case when you came to bed?"

"Haven't seen 'em. Where'd you put 'em?"

"Here, on the table. Along with my sponge bag."

Kennedy suddenly stopped in his search and wheeled round.

"Hell, Stanforth! They're at it again," he barked. "That case was red."

"Eh? Good lord! So it was." Stanforth was crawling out of bed and reaching for his dressing-gown.

Kennedy picked up the bit of imitation leather from the dressing-table.

"This was a bit of it," he snapped. "Off the cover. Outside the window stuck on a nail. Torn off by somebody getting out of the window, Say, where do we go from here?"

He looked round the room irritably.

"Who opened those windows?" he demanded.

"Not me. I prefer mine warm. They were shut when I turned in."

"So they were at two o'clock this morning when I got back." He went to the window and inspected it. "Plain slip catch," he muttered. "Open easy with a knife from outside. Nothing to go on there." He gazed down the walls, a flat, bare expanse of masonry that would have defied the most wonderful cragsman on earth.

"Well, if this doesn't beat the band," he exploded wrathfully. A footman tapped with the hot water.

"Is Lord Gairlie up yet?" asked Kennedy.

"Yes, sir, his lordship is dressing."

"Tell him I'd like to see him urgently, as soon as he is at liberty."

Kennedy finished dressing in a preoccupied silence. This case was getting right beyond his powers of anticipation. He would have staked life that the mysterious thefts of red things would have ceased as soon as the big haul was made. And yet here, on the very next morning, within twelve hours of lifting the great prize, his own stupid, worthless razor-case—

A hurried pattering of feet sounded along the landing, heavy feet that were not used to running, and were making a great labour of it. There an abrupt knocking at the door, and Harris, the butler, thrust his head in.

"Gentlemen, awful news, please come to the servants' hall at once. Lord Gairlie will join you there." Harris was almost too agitated to get his words out coherently.

"What's wrong?" said Kennedy quickly.

"One of the maids, sir, dead—murdered, sir."

"What? Who?"

"Betty Halston, sir."

Harris was shivering. His fat, good-natured face protruded round the door like a full moon which in some odd way had become able to register emotion. And the emotion printed there was sheer unthinking fright—a fear that went right down into the very roots of terror. Having delivered his news he lost his grip. His teeth began to chatter as he stuttered out the rest of it.

"They—they f-found her in the li-library, sir," he stammered, "f-found her dead and cold—all lying in a heap. We—we—we took her to her room, sir—and—"

"Murdered? How do you know?" cut in Kennedy. "What happened? Are there any wounds on her?"

Harris shook his head violently and swallowed hard.

"No, sir," he said with a rush. "That's the awful part, sir. She isn't marked. Can't find anything wrong with her at all, sir. Except she's dead. And her dress, sir—her dress—it's"

"Yes? What?"

"It's all turning red, sir! Red! *Red!* My God, we're all bewitched in this house!"

Harris swayed into the room, made a weak effort to get to a chair missed it by a yard, and slithered to the floor.

Kennedy turned to his second, his eyebrows up in dumb interrogation. In one brown hand he held a comb. Unconsciously he pointed it at the prone figure.

"Well, what do you know about that?" he asked.

Stanforth looked down at the man and pondered.

"Betty Halston? Betty Halston?" he muttered. "Who is she?"

"She was the girl John Argle was waiting for at the gap last night."

Stanforth looked at him with a puzzled frown.

"You've got away ahead of me," he said. "John Argle? Never heard of him." He walked over and with a tremendous heave picked Harris up and dumped him on his own bed. He loosened his clothing and sopped a wet sponge over his head. "Mr. Harris doesn't seem to like the idea of death," he observed. "It'll take him a quarter of an hour to crawl out of that faint."

He dabbed the sponge again and clicked his teeth.

"John Argle," he repeated. "No—I don't seem to fit him in."

"You weren't there. You missed it. Beardy Bill. That's who John Argle is. But you can keep that right under your hat. His name down here is John Argle. Don't blame him, poor devil. Came down here to get away from it all. And if I know him there's going to be hell to pay. He was sweethearting Betty Halston."

Stanforth let out a long-drawn whistle.

"Bill down here," he gasped. "And sweethearting the girl? Say, it was at the gap that you found the fake Star, wasn't it?"

"Just there."

"Gosh! This knocks the house over again."

Kennedy sniffed and finished brushing his sparse hair.

"Seems we'd better sit down and wait till the show gets started," he said. "We ain't invited yet. Like trying to do a sum with only half the figures written down."

Stanforth scrambled into his coat.

"C'm on, if you're ready," he said. "Better get down and see what's doing. What in thunder did they want to move the girl for? Idiots."

He went out muttering angrily, with Kennedy behind him.

"You haven't been in the library yet, have you?" asked Kennedy, catching up.

"No. Why?"

"*There's no windows,* that's all. It's an inner room, padded all round. Panelled in oak. A silence room. His lordship's private sanctum. Looks as though our red maniac doesn't need windows to climb in and out of. Stanforth, I'm ten fathom out of my depth."

They got through to the servants' quarters. Lord Gairlie was waiting for them in the passage from which the women's bedrooms opened. He was white and haggard, with drawn lines under his eyes and a tense look that told of nerves keyed up to the last note.

"Gentlemen, this is most appalling news," said Gairlie shakily. "Harris has told you, I suppose. Why isn't he with you? I told him to bring you back."

"He's in a dead faint, my lord, on my bed," said Stanforth bluntly. "Better send for a doctor. He's all in—and we shall have to have a doctor's verdict in any case. When was the body found?"

"A few minutes ago. Barson went into the library as usual, wheeling a vacuum cleaner. The only light in there, as you know, is electric, and he didn't notice anything until he switched the lights on. I gave orders for you to be sent for immediately. But for some extraordinary reason he had the girl brought up here first."

"M'm—where is Barson?"

"Attending to his usual duties, I imagine"

"I'd like to see him, my lord; send for him, please. Which is the room?"

"Here. Come in, will you? This is exactly as she was when they found her, except that she was on the floor, of course. Heavens! What's coming over the place? Robbery—murder—mystery—it's awful!"

Kennedy shouldered his way in. The dead girl was on the bed, very still and pathetic. One arm was flung up across her face as though to ward off a suddenly expected blow, and in her eyes was a dreadful look of shock and pain.

"Might—could it be—heart failure?" asked Gairlie, hoarse with emotion.

Kennedy did not answer, but Stanforth shook his head. "Not with that look in her face, poor lass," he said quietly. "That girl saw death coming before it got to her."

Kennedy was bending over her, examining the curious colour chang in her dress.

"What was the original colour of this material?" he asked, bending closer over it and fumbling for a magnifying glass.

The housekeeper supplied the information, stepping softly forward.

"A shade of dull purple, sir," she said.

The dress was no longer a deep purple. It was a stained, uneven red, verging off in places into streaks of vivid scarlet. The markings were twisted, and the colour varied several tones in patches. It was more like a garment that had been badly or incompetently dyed—two or three shades seemed to have run into each other, and the drying process seemed to have been achieved by screwing the whole thing into a ball and baking it.

Then Kennedy began picking out tiny pieces of glass from the fabric, infinitesimal pieces that glittered here and there, some so insignificant that they were little more than powdered glass. But they were there, driven deep into the very fabric.

Lord Gairlie touched his arm.

"Will you—can't you, please, let young Delayn out, now?" he pleaded. "After this it is humanly impossible for him to have been mixed up in this case. He was in a cell when this happened."

"I'm making no promises," said Kennedy curtly. "Candidly, I'm not so sure that we've got the right man in young Delayn. He *may* be mixed up in it. I don't know. But I do know he's not the principal. The real man is still in this house."

He eyed Lord Gairlie square in the face as he spoke and the millionaire wilted. If he didn't exactly look guilty, he looked doubly anxious, and the worry-lines seemed to deepen under his eyes. The change was not lost on the detective.

"If I could only get at the truth I fancy one or two people would be in for an uncomfortable time," he said. "This job seems to get thicker and thicker every hour."

"But surely there is nothing to be gained by keeping Mr. Delayn in custody?"

"Mr. Delayn stays in custody until either the magistrate dismisses his case or until I am in possession of such evidence as would justify his release. Up to now I haven't got it. He's in on suspicion of being connected with a robbery. This is murder."

Gairlie sighed and drew back, unable to look at the pathetic little thing on the bed.

In five minutes Kennedy had satisfied himself that there was no mark on the girl's body. So far as he could see there was no possible cause of death other than poison. And he was prepared to stake his professional reputation that poison was as far from the truth as anything else he could suggest. Kennedy found himself up against a brick wall. The girl's attitude, the look on her face, the very circumstances in which she was found, all pointed to death by violence. The tiny fragments of broken glass, the mysterious change in the colour of her dress, all went to prove that, without a shadow of doubt, Betty Halston had died anything but a natural death. Everything was there except the explanation. There was nothing whatever to account for the sudden cutting short of a life that was just beginning to open to the greatest adventure of all.

In a little while the doctor came.

Kennedy explained the circumstances and for twenty minutes neither spoke while the doctor was engaged upon his task.

Kennedy did not tell him murder was suspected. All the doctor knew was that the girl had been found dead.

In the end he stood up and looked with deep concern at the detective.

"You're from Scotland Yard, aren't you?" he asked gravely.

"Yes, sir. My name's Kennedy."

"Then I feel I can talk to you freely and in confidence. Mr. Kennedy, it is a dreadful thing to say but there is not the slightest doubt that this poor girl was murdered."

Kennedy half inclined his head. "My own conclusion, sir," he said, "Can you say how it was done?"

The doctor shook his head. "I must confess I haven't the vaguest inkling. At first I suspected cardiac trouble, but I happened to attend the girl professionally several weeks ago for a mild attack of influenza. And I can say without fear of contradiction that Miss Halston's heart was perfectly sound. I am absolutely at a loss."

"Poison?"

"Taken internally? M—no. She would have complained long before she got into that state. No, Mr. Kennedy, in my critical opinion this girl died *instantaneously.* No sooner had she seen death than it was upon her. She was dead one second after she realised she was being killed. Dreadful—horrible."

"Do you mean that you never *will* know what killed her?"

The doctor shrugged. "There will be a coroner's inquest, of course," he said." And I shall ask for a post mortem. That may reveal something. But as it stands this is the most inexplicable case that has ever crossed my ken."

Kennedy thrust his hands into his pockets. "Deeper and deeper," he muttered.

There was a soft knock at the door, and the footman looked in timidly.

"Mr. Kennedy, there's somebody in the hall who wants to see you urgently," he said. "He says his name is John Argle."

Kennedy thought hard for a moment and looked across at the doctor.

"It's her fiancé," said the detective. "Hadn't better let him come in here. John Argle is the type who would let right up on a job like this. Grim, restrained sort of devil—you know him, I suppose? He'd go berserk."

"Oh, yes, I know him. He has been in the village some years, I believe. A curious character. He seems to have no profession and remarkably few friends. Odd that he should be engaged to a vivacious girl like Betty Halston. Odd, too, that nobody should know about it. A secretive sort of man, apparently."

"Very," said Kennedy shortly. "I'll make an order that no one is to be allowed in this room until the police investigations are completed. If necessary I'll station a local constable at the door— "

He broke off on a word. The door was being pushed open. Quietly and very deliberately John Argle came into the room. Regardless of the two men he went right close up to the bedside and stood there, staring down at the face of his dead. He did not speak and for long seconds he did not move, but on his face there was a look of silent, all-feeling grief that sprang from the very depths of his soul. The smouldering lights in his eyes glowed red, danger lights that blazed a threat of a greater vengeance than lay in the hands of man, a threat that became infinitely more sinister by reason of the mountainous restraint that compassed it.

Kennedy went up and quietly gripped his arm.

"Steady, old man," he said gently in his ear. He walked towards the door. John Argle followed without the least resistance.

"Kennedy," he said, "I'm—I'm asking a favour of you. Don't often ask favours of anybody, but I want one now."

"Go right ahead, boy. I'm listening."

"I want you to concentrate on the rubies. That's all. This—this other thing," he pointed a finger dumbly at the closed door— "This is mine! *Mine!* You understand?" he blazed with a sudden rush of white-hot ferocity. "Mine! I'll get him! You keep off. You keep away, He's mine—and I'll get him."

In a second his flare-up was ended. The fiery rush of words died out the moment they left his mouth; and he was quiet again, utterly normal except for that silent glare of malignant purpose that glowed in the black depths behind his eyes. Kennedy did not answer. He turned the matter soothingly into a safer channel.

"I want to ask you a few questions, John," he said. "If you feel up to it."

Argle nodded, very slowly.

"It's about last night, when I met you at the gap. You were waiting for Miss Halston. Did she come?"

"No. She must have been too busy. Or else she would not disobey your order that no one was to leave the Castle."

"How long did you wait?"

"Until all the lights went out in the servants' quarters. About three in the morning, I think it was."

"You waited out there in the darkness until three."

"Yes. It was raining then, raining hard."

"Tell me, did you see or hear anybody in the lane while you were waiting?"

John Argle looked at him without emotion.

"Yes," he said tonelessly. "I did. And I'm not going to tell you who it was. So don't ask me. I saw him. He was crawling towards that gap in the hedge. I know him! He didn't see me till he was bending to crawl through. I thought it was you again, and I called out. He turned and ran like a dog down the lane."

"*Down* the lane?"

Argle nodded.

"Who was it, John? Come on, don't be a fool. I can find out if I have to measure every boot in the village. It was raining hard. There will be bootmarks there at the gap—"

"No, there won't," said Argle, with devastating deliberation. "I trampled them out as I came up. I came up to see her this morning, and the lodgekeeper told me she was dead. So I went round and trampled them out. Because *I* want him. And I'm going to get him"

Kennedy made a little impatient noise with his tongue against his teeth.

"Tell me, John," he demanded. "I can get him quicker than you can. You, at least, ought to know better than to resist the police in the pursuit of their duties. Come along now. Who was it? I demand to know."

John Argle pulled himself effortlessly from his grasp.

"I'm not telling," he said with flat decision. "Not if I was called up to the House of Commons and all Parliament demanded to know. You can do what you like about it. I'm having the first hour with the man who killed Betty."

Without another word he turned and pushed his way down the passage and disappeared.

Kennedy made no move to restrain him. He watched thoughtfully as his great figure went heavily round the corner. It was no use hammering at a man in that frame of mind—least of all at John Argle. That tremendous calm presaged a far more violent outburst to come, a storm that would be dangerous even to John Argle himself. But for the time being, he judged it better to leave John Argle alone.

He went back into the death room. Doctor Mabey was making out his report. When he had finished and was reaching out for his bag, Kennedy asked him to come down into the library.

"I'd like you with me, if you can spare the time," he said. They went down together. Harris, the butler, had recovered, and by Lord Gairlie's orders, was standing on guard at the door, still very white and shaky, and not at all happy. The whole thing had got on his nerves, badly.

Near him, standing to attention like a private with his sergeant, was Barson, the plateman, who had been sent for by Lord Gairlie.

The detective began a meticulous search of the room. He turned all the lights full on and went over the place with a fine tooth comb. And all he found were a few more tiny pieces of glass identical with those he had taken from the dead girl's dress. They were buried in the carpet near the fireplace, and extended over a wide area. For the rest, there was absolutely nothing to account either for Betty Halston's death or for the mystifying change in the colour of her dress.

Doctor Mabey pottered about on his own, and after a few minutes discovered traces of a further discoloration. It was the result of an accident. On the writing-table was a large blotter filled with sheets of green blotting paper. At least they appeared to be green—until he accidentally knocked the blotter to the floor. The blotting paper became dislodged and spread out over the carpet in a wide fan. Both Kennedy and he then saw that only the upper surface of the top sheet was green. All the rest were blue, even the underside of the top sheet. The only colouring of green was the upper side of that sheet.

"Any ideas?" asked Kennedy.

Mabey shook his head. "Not a glimmer," he said. "I am as much in the dark as you. It's most puzzling—most puzzling. But I don't lay claim to any special power of deduction."

Kennedy called Barson in.

"Where was the girl lying?" he asked.

"Just here, sir, near the table."

"What was she doing in here?"

"Just clearing up, sir."

"But it isn't her duty to clear the library, surely. That is more in the routine of the under-footmen?"

"Yes, sir, but she wanted the glasses, sir. Halston was stillroom maid, and one of her duties was to keep all the glasses clean and polished. You and his lordship had whiskies in here, and she was going all over the place looking for strays left about."

"I see. What time would that be?"

"Long after midnight—about two o'clock in the morning, I should think."

"Who locks up?"

"Mr. Harris, sir. But he didn't lock the library last night. Everyone was so late, and he didn't know whether his lordship would want to use the room again. I don't think any of the downstairs rooms were locked last night."

"All right, Barson, that'll be all. I think you were very foolish to touch things in any way until the police had investigated. I'll say no more. Damn foolish! But probably hasn't done much harm. You may go."

Barson went out, breathing a profound sigh of relief. And after a little while Lord Gairlie came in.

"No success, Kennedy?" he asked. It was obvious from the acute dissatisfaction on the detective's face that things were not going well with him.

"Very little, my lord." The Yard man was almost brusque.

Gairlie hesitated in troubled indecision.

"Have you—have you—that is, do any of your inquiries tend towards your taking a more lenient view regarding the arrest of Mr. Delayn?"

Kennedy eyed him square. Quietly, yet with steely force, he touched off a mine.

"My lord," he said, "why are you so anxious to get Mr. Delayn released?

Gairlie licked his dry lips and looked away, out through the door.

"Get Mabey away," he whispered. "I'll tell you privately."

Kennedy crossed to the doctor, who was still trying to elucidate the mystery of the blotting paper.

"Doctor," he said. "You might give Harris the once-over. He's only holding out now as a matter of honour. Very bad this morning. Half an hour in a flat faint."

"Indeed?" said Mabey, cocking up his eyebrows. "Dear, dear, why wasn't I told? I'll see him now."

He hurried out, and the door closed behind his broad, friendly back.

"Now, sir," said the detective, wheeling round. I'll trouble you for the full story—fairly told. I hadn't been four hours here before I realised that I was only working on half a case. The other half's still in the air. I haven't a ghost of an idea what it is; I'm all in. But this much I do know. The other half is in this house. Maybe in this very room. And you know *something* about it."

Gairlie was pacing up and down soundlessly on the thick pile carpet, in deep cogitation. Suddenly he stopped in front of the detective.

"Kennedy," he said sharply, "you're getting wrong ideas into your head. I know as little about this mystery as you do. It's worrying me out of my life. Good heavens—the servants are getting frightened out of their own shadows. They are coining all sorts of horrifying phrases about it. Only ten minutes ago I overheard one of them talking about the Silent Death. What's going to happen when the servants begin talking like that? Kennedy, this matter *must* be kept quiet until we've got to the bottom of it."

"Why?"

"It *must.* That's all I can tell you. It means ruination to me if it isn't. And I've got trouble enough on my hands as it is. If Delayn comes up before the magistrate it will cause a public scandal. The whole story of the broken engagement, of his bankruptcy, of the murder here—the whole wretched, sordid story would be out. Nothing could stop it."

"It's happened to others, sir. The higher you climb the further the flop. Rank doesn't pull a blanket over the law. Doesn't matter where murder happens, you can't keep it out of the courts."

Lord Grairlie mopped his forehead.

"It isn't that so much," he said, striving to make Kennedy see his point. "Scandal and publicity are bad enough in all conscience. But the effect on Change will be a thousand times worse. There are millions at stake in my concerns. Millions of mine. Millions of other people's money. All wrapt up in the single word 'credit.' If my credit went—and it would—the effects would be incalculable. I couldn't hope to hold out. Kennedy, for the sake of ten thousand homes in the North and ten thousand more in the South, you've *got* to drop your case against Delayn. You know he isn't guilty. You're only holding him as a hostage till you get the real thief."

"Then why did you call in Scotland Yard?"

"Because I want those rubies back. Bring them to me and I'll ask no questions. I won't prosecute. I won't even ask the name of the thief. But on the day you restore the Gairlie Rubies to me, I'll put a cheque for ten thousand pounds in your hands. *And I'll forget it*"

Kennedy looked up with a glint of antagonism in his eyes.

"Don't talk money to me!" he snapped. "You know enough to unlock Delayn's cell. And I want it from you in words, not bribes."

"I'm not offering bribes," retorted Gairlie. "I'm putting up a reward for the return of my property. There's the work of a lifetime wrapped up in the Gairlie Rubies. And I want them—before they're broken up."

"Well, if you want them back as badly as all that, give me the clue that'll put me on their track."

"How can I? I don't even know it myself."

"Yes, you do. There's something at the back of your thoughts that you won't let out."

"It wouldn't help you an inch."

"It couldn't do less. It wouldn't make the darkness any darker." Kennedy was beginning to feel his feet. There was a faint glimmering of light in the blackness that enshrouded him. His obstinate tone was beginning to tell on Gairlie. The millionaire was looking more and more uneasy. The detective's persistent hammering was shaking him.

Kennedy slid a finger into his pocket and pulled out the imitation Burning Star.

"Lord Gairlie," he said, "I could find out where that was made."

The peer gasped and sat up stiffy in his chair.

"A fairly simple proposition. This crystal is beautifully cut. Only an expert could have made such a copy. And there are not so many reliable firms in London that the man responsible for this could not be easily traced. An hour's tour of the West End jewellers would produce the man and the history of this copy."

Gairlie was again striding agitatedly up and down the room.

"That wouldn't do you any good," he said hurriedly. "It would only put you off on a false scent."

"What are you so worried about? What are you frightened of?" Having got him off his poise Kennedy was not letting him go. "Somebody has been laying a trap to get those rubies for some weeks now, hasn't he?"

"Yes—yes. I suppose so."

"Ever since last summer you have been losing red things from every room in the Castle—the inference is that whoever was responsible for the thefts were after something bigger than plum jam, table centres and raspberry toffee."

"Of course—I know."

"Well—having lifted the rubies, you'd think those thefts would cease, wouldn't you?"

"Naturally!"

"This morning my razor-case went—a red leather case. Out of my room. Looks as though somebody is still after something."

Gairlie ran his fingers through his white hair.

"I—I don't know what you're driving at," he said helplessly.

"Don't you? I'm wondering whether this fake was dropped accidentally—or just thrown away! I'm wondering whether if we found any more of the Gairlie Rubies, we should get the same nasty shock. I'm beginning to think it will pay us to put up the stiffest case against Mr. Delayn we can possibly invent. Maybe if we let the papers broadcast the whole show there might be an interesting communication made to Scotland Yard—from someone in the City. An insurance broker, shall we say? Or an assayer of valuable jewellery?"

Lord Gairlie collapsed in his chair.

"For God's sake, don't. I'll tell you. Only if you've any pity at all in your heart, keep the matter to yourself."

The detective nodded and pulled out his notebook.

"Damn lucky you didn't claim on the insurance, wasn't it?" he said waspishly. "There's no need to tell me. I know. Those stones were all fakes. That so?"

Gairlie put his head on his hands. "Yes," he said distractedly. "Sit down, Kennedy, and I'll try to explain."

Kennedy, satisfied with himself for the first time since leaving London, crossed to the door and gently turned the key.

"That brings us down to bedrock," he said. "Mind, I'm promising nothing. All I want from you is a straight deal. I haven't had it yet."

Lord Gairlie looked at him, haggard, a man beaten by circumstances, with the worn-out look of a man who had been putting up a fight against odds beyond his strength.

"Kennedy," he said heavily, "in having to make this confession to you, I'm the most humiliated man on earth. I'm degraded in my own sight. There's nothing in what I've done that I need be ashamed of, except that for nearly two years I've been acting a lie. Acting a lie to the world, to my friends, even to my wife. Kennedy, you think I'm one of the richest men in England, don't you?"

"I'd swop my little place in Brixton for this," agreed the detective. "I'd even risk changing incomes."

"My dear man, unless a miracle happens, I'm as badly smashed as young Delayn."

Kennedy stared at him, a penetrating look that read him through and through.

"*What?*"

"You don't believe it. Of course you don't. But I tell you that I'm at my wit's end how to carry on. Do you remember the Imperator Insurance smash a couple of years ago? Three millions of Gairlie money went when that crash came. Three millions. I had to draw my horns in. Enterprises in which I could have made fortunes were beginning to open up—and I had to let them go. Opportunities that a man would grasp at with thanksgiving came my way—and I couldn't take them. My capital was gone. The whole financial world wondered who was the anonymous loser who, when that crash came, could afford to lose three millions and not feel it badly enough to make a public protest against the criminal wickedness that had allowed it to vanish. I was the man. And I *dare* not admit it. The moment that knowledge leaked out there would be a run on me in a hundred different places. I'd have my back to the wall inside twenty-four hours—and no possible chance of fighting back."

Kennedy sat up and scratched the back of his head.

"Then you were the man who wouldn't lay a claim when the Imperator smashed?" he asked, "the man who dropped three millions when the Wizard cooked the books?"

"Yes. And it spiked my guns for everything else. I was in two others after that. Nothing like so bad, but any sort of blow is bad for a man who is tottering on his feet. I was nearly knocked out. Taxes have nearly slaughtered me. I was paying heavily on cash I had'nt got. I raised half a million on the rubies more than a year ago. I had them duplicated by the finest jewellers in Paris. The real jewels are in a safe deposit in the name of a group of London financiers. I cannot redeem them till my cheque for half a million and interest is honoured in their name. Even Lady Gairlie doesn't know that the jewels she wore last year were just so much glass."

"Bit tough." grunted Kennedy.

"I tried to keep them—God knows I tried." cried Gairlie. "I parted with huge blocks of some of the finest shares on the market. Sheaves of them—I let them go and turned them into cash, to keep other interests on their legs, a gambler's chance, and put every penny of what was left into a company exploiting a new method of making artificial silk. The process was commercially impracticable from the start. Our product costs considerably more than real silk. The chemists who drew out the formulas were hundreds of pounds out,"

Kennedy moved uncomfortably in his chair. Gairlie was putting a case that only an automaton could not feel sympathy for. The facts and figures of big business were away over his head, but the note of human tragedy that ran through it all vibrated in every fibre of his finer nature. But it was getting him no farther forward. Gairlie's confession only complicated things

"All this is dreadful for you, sir," he muttered. "But—but I can't see where it lands me."

"Kennedy that charge *must not go* through. I've told you all I know. Opened my very soul to you. And you've *got* to stand by me now. The theft has become almost insignificant from your point of view. But for me the showdown of the real facts means the end.

"I wouldn't care if I'd only been man enough to tell Lady Gairlie. But pride wouldn't let me. She thinks I'm the same tremendous moneymaker of the old days, the greatest industrial magnate in the kingdom Kennedy. I'd go mad if I broke her splendid faith in me."

Kennedy leaned forward and touched him imperatively on the arm.

"Had you any intention of claiming on the insurance company?" he demanded.

Gairlie looked away from him. "I—I don't know," he said miserably. "I was—I was considering the possibility. That's how bad things are with me, Kennedy. Three months more like this will break me. Three *hours* of a criminal charge against young Delayn will see me taking the coward's way out."

"Do you mean that?" snapped Kennedy, glaring at him.

Lord Gairlie clenched his hands till the knuckles shone white.

"I do." he said.

The Yard man climbed slowly to his feet. He was breathing hard and feeling as badly strained as Gairlie himself.

"It's the very devil of a hole," he said at last. He turned suddenly to the man in the chair, a beaten, cowed man, plumbing the very depths of self-degradation. "Lord Gairlie," he said, "have you any objection to my taking this story right to the Chief? The whole story, glossing nothing?"

Gairlie made a slight gesture of indifference.

"It's the only way out that I can see," went on the detective. "I'll have a conference with him and explain details. I may be able to do it on the long-distance wire; on the other hand, he may call me to London. The third possibility is that he will come down himself and take charge. In any case you'll have to prepare yourself to meet him. Only an order from headquarters can hold up the procedure at the local court now. And only the Chief can make it."

Gairlie nodded sombrely. "Quite; I understand."

Kennedy jabbed at his notebook for a minute and then looked up, alert and decided. He had got the full conception of his case at last and he was eager for action.

"This is the case now. As I see it," he said. "The thief still thinks the real rubies are here. He's still trying to lift them. And he's going to keep on trying. Thinks he can get the real ones. He's got the bit between his teeth—hasn't even stopped at murder. That means we can get him. I'm asking the Chief for reinforcements. Plain-clothes men from London. And I'll station a man in every room in the Castle. All night and every night, till we get him. That's the layout. And with the help of your staff, we'll hammer this matter out to a finish."

Lord Gairlie looked up with a glimmer of hope in his eyes.

"Does that mean you will advise the withdrawal of the charge against Mr. Delayn? "he asked.

"It means that if I have anything to do with it the whole case'll be withdrawn. I want to cancel the whole box o' tricks," said the detective decisively. "It's our great chance of getting at the truth about that boy. If he *is* mixed up in it we'll get to the bottom of it inside twenty-four hours after releasing him. The others will get into touch with him. He won't be able to keep away from old associations. They won't let him. He'll be an index finger pointing at the man we want."

"Kennedy, I'll never be able to thank you enough for this. If you succeed I shall be your debtor for life."

"You can thank me by squaring Delayn. He's a mettlesome young devil and somehow I can't see him eating out of my hand. He has spent a night in a cell. Won't be feeling exactly full of charity and admiration towards the police. You'll have to fix him."

"I'll do my best, Kennedy—rest assured of that," said Gairlie thankfully.

"Your stiffest job'll be to break a spot of unpleasant news," said the Yard man grimly.

"And that is—?"

"That he is still a prisoner in these grounds. Can't have him taking to his heels and cutting the ground from under our feet. If Delayn comes out, he stays here."

"It's going to be very difficult," muttered Gairlie. "You know what I mean?"

"No, I don't," said Kennedy bluntly.

"It means keeping the boy penned up here with—Lonora."

"Can't help it, sir. A job's a job. Can I use your 'phone?"

Lord Gairlie indicated the instrument standing in a little recess.

Kennedy put the call through, and while he waited for the connection he sent for Stanforth. For a solid half-hour they talked over the new developments, Kennedy giving his second every detail.

"It's our only get-out," he finished. "Delayn comes out and Lord Gairlie gives him the run of the place. You'll be his boot-heels, the back of his overcoat—everything else that's close behind him. I'm getting on to the Chief now. I'll bring him round to our way of thinking, and the rest will be up to us. Next thing I want to get hold of John Argle again and Dutch Uncle him into coughing up what he knows. That ought to put us on the right track. Delayn will confirm it—or clear himself. I'm asking the Chief for thirty men. I think he'll agree when he hears there's murder added to the count."

He turned suddenly to a ring on the telephone.

"Hello—is that you, Chief?" he called. "Kennedy here. Gairlie Castle. What? Yes, sir. Complications setting in almost every hour. There's murder crept into it. One of the maids here. Not the slightest doubt. Murder all right or I'll eat my hat. Not a clue as to how it was done. And, hello!... Those rubies were duds. Yes. Lord Gairlie himself has just admitted it. Copies. Real ones in a safe deposit in town. I recovered one piece last night. Dropped near a gap in the hedge. I'm asking for extras, Chief. I want thirty. I know it's a big order, Chief, but this is one of the toughest things I've struck. You see what's happening? The thief is still on the warpath. Still trying. And I want to nail him. I think so, yes. I'm doing my best, but you've no conception of the man's methods. He's a ghost. You can't see him. Can't hear him. Comes and goes like a shadow. And about as noisy. The only way to get him is to put a man in every room and wait till he shows up. Can I act as I think fit? Well, you must telegraph that order for Delayn's release. That's all right—there'll be no case. Lord Gairlie can fix that. But the court sits at eleven. It's half-past nine now. Right. I'll go along and see the magistrate and put it all square. Are you coming down yourself, sir? Eh? Await developments? That's all right, sir. And you'll send those men to get here after dark. A Flying Squad van will do fine. Thank you, sir. Goodbye."

He put the receiver down and nodded to Lord Gairlie.

"That's all right, sir," he said breezily. "The Chief is wiring the court immediately. I'll see the magistrate and the Chief Constable myself.

"Delayn will be out before midday."

V

Delayn returned in no sweet mood. The interview was short and volcanic. Delayn was aggressive, aggrieved, and full of heated demands for explanations; Gairlie apologetic, pacific, doing his best to smooth things over and yet break the news to him that he was still a prisoner in the massive boundaries of Gairlie Castle.

And when at last the cat was out of the bag Delayn took it in a way that astonished his host—just looked at him with eyes like balls of acid, and a look of wintry, frozen hostility on his face that made Gairlie shrink.

"I see," said Tommy. "Very charming of you, I'm sure." That was all. The expected bomb-burst of flaming anger did not materialise. Whatever pressure of emotion was working up behind that bitter mask remained where it was, bottled up and corked down.

"I'm sorry, son, it has not been my seeking," said Gairlie haltingly. "I'd send Lonora to the town house, but Kennedy—"

"Please don't distress yourself, sir. I understand perfectly." Delayn's voice was a chunk of polar ice. "I'm to be the decoy duck. Quite. I'll do my best to oblige you... *But not in the way you think.*"

He cut the conversation short there. The next thing that Gairlie saw of him was his back swinging out through the door.

Kennedy spent a profitless afternoon at the gap. He went down with callipers, artist's plaster, and measuring rule. The light was none too good, although the miserable monotony of the rain had ceased. The skies were leaden, and as heavy as though another downpour was due at any minute.

There were dozens of bootmarks in the thick, squelchy mud of the cart-track, and dozens more on the grass plot by the gap. But they were all John Argle's. The dour friendless figure had done his work well. He seemed to have taken a line from the centre of the lane to the gap, and deliberately trodden out every footprint.

Kennedy went over it all. But the callipers told him his own story, John Argle had beaten him. And John Argle was not to be found. Kennedy combed the village, and toured the adjacent town. Stanforth went out in the car through the neighbouring country. But Argle had taken himself off.

Coming back through the village on towards evening, Kennedy dropped in quietly at the local tavern. The first man he saw in the little taproom was Stanforth, sitting cheerlessly in a corner away from the window, smoking placidly at an old briar. No sign of recognition passed between them. Stanforth, having glanced momentarily at the newcomer, glanced away again equally casually.

And at that Kennedy's heart gave a jump. It was a sign that was older than the hills in their craft. Stanforth by his very indifference had said, plainer than words could speak, "Don't go—there's something in the wind."

A faint hum of voices drifted over a partition from another bar, bucolic voices of the labouring class, but their conversation was scarcely audible.

Stanforth tossed the local paper on the stained table.

Kennedy knew that sign, too. He nodded affably and picked up the paper.

"Good evening," he said. "Nights still get dark quickly, don't they?" He sat on the edge of the table, swinging a leg as he swished open the pages.

The landlord came round to the other side of his counter.

"Pleased to see you, sir," he said pleasantly. "Stranger parts?"

"Yes. Motoring through," said Kennedy. "Care to join drink, sir?" he turned to Stanforth.

"No, thanks," grunted Stanforth. "I have mine."

Kennedy turned to the paper. Stanforth puffed stolidly at his pipe. He did not even look at his senior again, contenting himself with listening to the faint tap of darts hitting into the dart board on the other side of the partition.

Kennedy found what he was looking for, a faintly pencilled note along the margin of an inside page.

"Listen to the conversation in ale-bar," it said. "Yokels telling queer stories of things at Gairlie Castle. Specially one with cold in head. Seems to know what he's talking about."

Kennedy made a neat spill of the margin, pushed it into the fire and lit his pipe. For the next five minutes he was lost in an intent perusal of the local paper.

Kennedy began to sort out the voices in the other bar. One was so quiet he could hardly hear it at all, one was resonant, full-blooded, and referred to by the others as Tom. Harry was the owner of a nasal voice—Kennedy docketed him away as an adenoid case—another, whose name did not transpire, had a trick of hissing his s's—the sign-manual of ill-fitting false teeth, declared the Yard man. Fred, of the cold in the head, wasn't talking just then. Fred was, apparently, an extremely good listener, who only spoke when he had something definite to say.

"And that bain't the only thing neither," said the adenoid case defensively. "You can laugh, but I know what I'm talking about. Only last week I said—you wait. There'll be murder up at the Castle before long I said. Mister Tom behind the bar'll tell you the same. He was here when I said it, and his wife called shame on me. Murder, I said, and I said it fair. Couldn't see no other way for 'tall to end up. Fred Tolleridge told me only t'other day—Fred what's second gardener in the greenhouse—he telled me he picked fifty tewlips one evenin' for table flowers, an' ten of 'em went before he'd got out of the room where he put 'em. Put 'em in a vase on a window table, he did, and then he walked to the door and turned to see how they looked—from a distance like—and when he turned round they was gorn. Red tewlips they was. And they was gorn. That's nigh on thirty times I've yeared tell of queer things like that up at the Castle. And I *knowed* there'd be murder 'fore it finished. Well, now they've *got* a murder, and mebbe Gairlie will take on to call in them Lunnon police. Smart chaps."

The quiet one admitted that there might be something in it. "But they won't never solve it," he added. "To my mind it's a haunt. And you can't never solve a haunt. My grandfer *swore* Castle was haunted. To my thinkin' he was right."

"What do you think to it, Fred?" The resonant voice put the question respectfully.

For some seconds there was only the soft "tat" of steel dart-heads sticking into wood. Then Fred said: "Lunnon police has already been called in. Two of 'em come down by car. 'Fore the maid was murdered that was. Lunnon police can't be no better'n Yardley. Couldn't stop the maid being killed anyway."

"Lunnon police in village?" queried Tom in surprise. "Well! They've kep' it mighty quiet. Two of 'em, you say?"

"Yes, Tom. One tall and t'other short. Short one's boss."

"Well," said Tom, in between scoring twenties with astonishing regularity. "If you ask me, there's more than one in *this* village knows more about them goings on than an honest man ought to know."

"Meaning who?" demanded Harry, pulling out the darts and calling the score. "Twenty, forty, and a double twenty—eighty."

"That big-bearded bloke for one," declared Tom. "Him who's always prowling about the Castle grounds after nightfall. What's he up to? Eh? Why don't he ever go up there in daylight? Tell me that. Allus after dark. Sometimes as late as midnight I've seen him slipping along on the grass. Allus on the grass. Never in the road. An' if you hail him he don't answer. Why can't a fellow give a civil 'Good-night'? Can't think why Yardley hasn't got after him before now."

"You mean John Argle?" asked the quiet one.

"That's who I mean. Who is he, anyway? Why don't he never come in here and have a social half-pint? Where do 'ee get his money? He don't never work. And he ain't got no one working for him. So how does he come by what he gets? Mr. Brindley, the grocer, tells me he allus pays cash for what he has. Mr. Talbot, the butcher, says same thing. Never owed anyone a penny, he hasn't, not since he came to the village three years ago."

"I've never seen him prowling round Castle grounds," said the quiet voice aggrievedly—almost as though he thought Fate was dealing unfairly in not letting him into all the inside secrets of the village.

"Well, I have," said Tom definitely. "I mind last year—late August it was—when the rain came on the cut corn and we was a fortnit late gettin' it in—me and Joe Steggles came down Boundary Lane every night after dark. 'Leven o'clock it would be, what with summer time an' all—some nights nigh midnight, 'fore we got into the lane. And every night, reg'lar as starshine, we'd see him, creepin' about an' slippin' through the hedge when he caught sight of us. A nasty customer in my opinion. And one that would pay Yardley to keep an eye on."

"It wouldn't." The statement was quite simply made. But there was definite knowledge in its very delivery. It was the voice and tone of the man who *knew*,

"What's that, Fred?" asked Harry.

"I'd look elsewhere, that's all," said Fred. "You've been comin' down Boundary Lane up to midnight. Well, I've been comin' down right up to two an' three of the morning. Champion

Nellie Bell has been in calf, and I've been settin' up with her. Day and night I've sat with Nellie, comin' back down the lane I've seen some queerer sights than John Argle a'settin' on the Boundary Stone a-waitin' for his lass. That's all John Argle was doing in the lane—a-waitin' for the lass who'll never come out to meet him again.

"There's someone else knocking around these parts who might well be watched by those whose job it is," went on the authoritative voice. "No names, no pack drill. But you know him. Sometimes he stands outside this very bar, turning a handle. Lives in the common lodging-house in the town. But he's got another place where he sleeps when he thinks fit, you know that little stone hut over by the quarry pits? Over there. I've seen him slipping in and out at all hours. And the night before them rubies were pinched I saw something else in the lane. Two hours after John Argle had given his lass the last kiss she ever got from him, I saw 'em—at the gap in the hedge—the man I mean—and *something else*! I was after them as quiet as a ferret. But they was gone like a shadow before I got there." Fred paused, like the good showman he was. Then very deliberately he said: "But they couldn't hide what I found—tiny little footmarks in the mud. Tiny as a newborn babe's, with five little toes and all, There in the mud, by the gap in the hedge!"

There was a long interval of silence in the outer bar. A piece of information like that required a deal of thinking out. Prints of a newborn baby's feet. It was certainly a puzzler, and yet profoundly in keeping with the rest of the baffling things that were happening daily—almost hourly—at the Castle. But there was not a doubt that Fred knew what he was talking about. As head cowman to the Gairlie estates they knew he had been up late o' nights for the last ten days, tending one of the finest beasts Lord Gairlie had ever raised.

"Reckon I don't quite understand you, Fred," said Harry awkwardly.

"You know who I'm hintin' at?" demanded Fred.

"Oh, aye. I know who you mean, and so do the others, I'll lay. Never did see any good in foreigners, and he *are* a bit of a slimy one. But I can't understand what you say about baby's feet, five little toes an' all. D'ye mean he tooken a baby up there in the cold rain without its boots?"

"No. I don't mean nothin' of the sort, Harry," said Fred stolidly. "I said: 'Tiny little footmarks *like* a newborn babe's.' 'Tain't necessary to have a baby up there, without boots on, to make tiny little footmarks, is it?"

"Well, to my way of thinkin', it *is*!" declared Tom.

"You can take it from me, Tom Pedder, it ain't. So far as I know, the man I'm hintin' at ain't got a baby, and never had one. But he certainly has got a monkey—that comes round with a little red hat when he plays the 'armonica."

There was a ready, half-excited assent to that last observation. Here was a new idea to work on—a plausible theory, with a grounding of fact and definite knowledge. They knew the whole gamut of what careful old Fred was suggesting.

José Latta was the man, the dark-eyed oily foreigner with the suspicion of a limp, caused by years of carrying a hurdy-gurdy on the hip. They knew him. He was often at the doorway of the "Castle Arms," his organ perched on the top of half a broomstick, and his bad-tempered monkey peeping in at the door, holding out its little red hat.

And there was mystery about José Latta. They remembered that, too. Quick, urgent voices spoke of odd things they knew, or had heard, of the nomad purveyor of music. He tramped his way from village to village, with that villainous monkey either perched on his back or holding his hand, padding along like a horribly humanised child. And, now they came to remember it, he always seemed to be in the vicinity when one of the inexplicable thefts occurred at the Castle.

First one remembered him plodding through the lanes when the card-box was stolen. Another recalled that he saw him camping by the wayside, sharing his supper with the monkey, on the evening of the night the red table-centre vanished. And he was playing at the "Castle Arms" itself three hours before Harris reported the loss of the red lacquer god.

A monkey, they argued, would be able to get almost anywhere. They were the most marvellous climbers on earth. And Fred had seen them both at the gap in the hedge. He had seen the little baby footprints left by the beast. Doubtless Latta trampled them out on his return journey. But these were the facts. Latta was in the habit of taking that monkey up Boundary Lane at two and three o'clock in the morning. They went through the gap in the hedge. And, a few minutes later, another astonishing robbery would occur at the Castle.

From that moment the truth became obvious. A monkey was tractable, trainable. A man, given patience and perseverance, could train a monkey to be attracted by red things. By giving it rewards of favourite morsels he could teach it to act as a retriever and bring those red-coloured objects back to its owner. The more they talked the more simple the explanation became. The perfectly trained monkey was the solution to the problem that had baffled them for months. What other explanation could there be? Why else should José Latta have a monkey? Why else should he crawl through the gap in Boundary Lane in the dark, silent hours? Why else should his visits coincide with the loss of red ornaments at the Castle? They nodded their heads ponderously at Fred, and admitted in their inmost souls that the native-born villager had stumbled on the clue, when all others, including Scotland Yard, had failed.

Then, having boiled it down to that, they came up against another snag. Admitting that José was the culprit and used his monkey as a wonderfully effective catspaw to further his nefarious schemes, how were the actual thefts committed?

"I was hall-boy at the Castle when I was a kid," said Harry quietly. "And if I remember rightly those rubies were stolen from her ladyship's boudoir, up on the third floor. That boudoir has got windows that are double-locked all the year round. There's a pair of six-inch steel screws driven through each. And there hain't a handhold for so much as a fly up them walls."

"There's enough for a monkey," averred the voice with the loose plate of teeth.

"No more than there is up the Nelson Column," declared Harry. "You'd want a fly to crawl up that. And whatever it is, José Latta's monkey ain't a fly, nor it can't get into locked and screwed-up windows."

"There's a window on the ground floor," said the decisive voice of Fred. "Nearly underneath the boudoir. Trailin' up at the side of it is a broken lightnin' conductor that runs almost up alongside them boudoir windows. A monkey could make that jump to the window ledge with one hand."

True enough. The buzz of eager approval carried that point. But Harry was not to be put off. He had found his point and he intended to stick to it.

"That lightnin' conductor is nigh eighteen feet above the top ledge of that window," he said firmly. "I've seen it dozens of times. An' I don't believe Latta's monkey or any other monkey breathing could jump that far in a straight line. And that bit of wire is so rotten by now it wouldn't support the weight of a monkey only half the size of Latta's."

That was something they hadn't thought of, and they admitted its equity. Eighteen feet was too much for any monkey to jump.

Fred waited till the buzz of argument died away, and then delivered his masterstroke. "Latta could take an eighteen-foot pole in with him," he said. "Mind you, I hain't saying I've seen him carrying no such object, I'm only saying it would be easy. A thin pole wouldn't weigh much, and he could carry that—and his monkey. Or he could hide the pole somewhere in the grounds. Lord knows there's places enough. Whoever goes in the big spinney, eh?—Hain't above a hundred and fifty yards from the Castle walls. He could crawl in, get his pole, stick the monkey on the end of it, an' h'ist the whole contraption up to the broken lightnin' conductor. Then up goes the monkey, hand over fist, and jumps across to the window ledge."

"Yes, and what then?" demanded Harry. "He still can't get into the room. Them windows is still locked and screwed."

"I agrees, Harry. *But the ventilation hole ain't.* A monkey could crawl through that hole where a man couldn't."

Stanforth groped for his hat. He stepped gently out of the bar and vanished through the swing doors. The landlord came in carrying oil lamps, for the night was falling rapidly.

Kennedy stood up, called for half a pint, and paid for it. He drained his ale at a gulp and went off into the night.

They met a few yards down on the opposite side of the road.

"What do you think of it?" asked Stanforth.

"Velvet!" breathed Kennedy, a note of exultation in his voice. "Gosh, it's neat. A trained monkey. Why in hell didn't I get it before? Sticks out a mile now!"

"Where do we go from here?"

"Ring up the chauffeur. Tell him to get down here with the car. We'll comb every village for fifteen miles around. Latta is knocking a *somewhere.* He's on foot—can't have got far. We'll get him tonight."

"A quick run through the locals?"

"That's it. We shall find him outside some village pub, grinding away at his hurdy-gurdy. Grinning his thanks for coppers thrown into a little red hat. A red hat. And coppers. Lord! And he's playing for a million. Surely I'll hand it to José."

Stanforth hurried off to 'phone. A few minutes after he had gone a great motor lorry came booming through the little village street. Kennedy spotted its cut and rig as it swept round the green by the "Castle Arms." He stepped out into the road and flagged it.

"You're from the Yard?" he asked, as the brakes brought it grinding to a standstill.

"Inspector Kennedy?" asked the driver, peering down.

"Yes. Who've you got there?"

"Thirty plain clothes. Woodson in charge. The Chief is coming down himself later on. That's his message to you, sir. Any orders, sir?"

"Yes. Go straight to the Castle. There's orders at the lodge to let you right through. Tell Lord Gairlie you've seen me and that I'll be with him before midnight. Looks like being a tough night."

The lorry-driver pushed in his gear. "The Chief will be down somewhere about midnight," he said. "Will that suit you?"

Kennedy nodded. "Yes, that'll do for me. Is he coming by car?"

"Yes, sir. His own. But he doesn't expect to get away much before half-past nine."

"You could recognise his bus?"

"I'd recognise the Big Blue a mile off."

"Well, here's what I want. Take this bunch up to the Castle. Give them my instructions. Then come back this way till you're about a mile outside the village. Wait for the Chief. When he comes, stop him, and tell him to make for Boundary Lane, about two miles up the road to the left. Halfway up the lane you will find a long oblong stone. Wait there in the shadow. Opposite you'll find a gap in the hedge. I shall come through it, about one in the morning. If not, tell him to wait till something happens. That all clear?"

"Yes, sir."

"If you should see Beardy Bill prowling about take no notice, and don't betray yourselves. He—"

The driver cut in in sheer astonishment.

"Beardy Bill," he gasped. "Good Gawd, sir, you don't mean to say *he's* knocking about round here?"

"Very much so. But Beardy Bill doesn't matter. He's John Argle in these parts. But whatever he does, don't let him influence your actions, I want you and the Chief to keep both eyes skinned for a wop. His name's José Latta. Plays an organ. It's a hundred to one he'll have a monkey with him. Follow him wherever he goes. And for God's sake don't give yourselves away. I want Latta to get right through to the Castle."

"Right. I've got all that," the lorry driver whispered. "Where do we go from there?"

"The Chief will know," said Kennedy grimly.

The driver clicked his teeth. "You bet," he said. He eased off his brakes and slipped back the clutch. The great lorry roared off towards the Castle through the heavily falling darkness. Kennedy waited, in the black shadows of a clump of overhanging trees, for Stanforth and the car.

"Apples, sir? Fine rosy apples, sir?" An old woman with a little fruit barrow, homing from some local market, proffered him the last remnant of her wares. She was passing slowly up the opposite side of the road, and the light of a single gas jet flooded down on her from an isolated standard.

As she plodded on there arose a mournful wailing from the porch of the "Castle Arms," the agonised moanings of a wind instrument with half the notes missing and the other half shockingly out of tune. It was José Latta, back in his haunts again!

The detective wheeled as the first notes droned out. In the faint light that came from the entrance of the tavern a swarthy figure stood. Kennedy got a complete view of him. He was a little below medium height, dressed in thick cord trousers and a ragged velvet coat. A gaudy silk handkerchief was knotted round his neck, a vivid thing of staring orange and green and blue, above the threadbare velvet jacket it added a splash of colour that struck a bizarre note entirely in keeping with his gipsy appearance.

He was grinding away at his organ, an oblong box perched on the stump of a stick, leering an oily grin at a labourer who went past him into the inn. At his side a Rhesus monkey bobbed and gibbered, holding out its little red Turk's fez with pathetically pleading gestures. Its stringy arm shot in and out, and every now and then the quaint little face peered into the hat in a search for coins, whether anyone had thrown any in or not.

The old apple woman was twenty or thirty yards up the road. Kennedy chased after her and bought a bagful of fruit; oranges, bananas and apples—*red* apples.

"Stanforth," he said, when his second arrived; "we've got Latta where we want him! He's up at the "Castle Arms," with his monkey! I've got some red apples here. Come on. We'll put that little brute through his paces right now!"

"Right," said Stanforth; "I'll go into the ale bar. Mustn't be seen together again. Work it when you hear me inside."

Kennedy passed on. In the porchway Latta looked up as the detective came by and jagged the leather thong. "Hey, Jacko!" he cried. The monkey caught sight of the stranger, hopped over towards him with its ungainly gait and thrust out the hat for alms.

Kennedy looked down at it, his hat on the back of his head, his hands thrust into his trousers pockets. Jacko waited, his beady eyes blinking up at the detective and his thin brown arms pushing the cap against his knees. When he saw there were no pennies forthcoming he began dancing a stumpy little jig, chattering away to himself and scratching industriously.

Kennedy laughed.

"Want to sell him?" he asked.

Latta smiled broadly and shook his head. "I no sella da monk," he said smoothly. "He makka da living for me. They pay for da monk—not for da music. No sella heem."

"Give you a fiver for him."

"He costa me more than that," said the organ-grinder placidly. "Me no sella heem—not for tenna da pounds."

Kennedy deliberately pulled out four rustling five-pound notes.

"There," he said gruffly. "Twenty. You can get another tomorrow for a couple of pounds. Selling?"

Latta twirled away at his handle and disdained a reply.

"H'm, pity," muttered the detective, stuffing the notes back. "Friendly little devil. Tell you what. Let me take him inside and make a collection for you. I'll get more than you can."

Latta smiled again and nodded profusely.

Kennedy took the thong and led the gibbering little thing into the saloon bar.

The inn had filled up considerably by now. The occupants looked up as Kennedy entered, leading the little monkey by the hand.

"Brought a little friend to see you," announced the detective. "Sit up and beg, Jacko; show the gentlemen how you earn pennies."

"Poor little beast," said one of the men. "Looks as though a good square meal would do him good."

"That's what I brought him in for," said Kennedy. He turned to the proprietor. "Got any biscuits there?" he asked.

The owner shook his head dubiously. "I've got some, but I think they mostly eat fruit—bein' natural-born in trees and livin' in trees."

"Fruit, eh?" muttered the detective. "Well, I've got plenty of that. Which does he like best, oranges, apples or bananas? Let's try the little beggar."

He pulled out an apple and a banana and held them out. The apple was probably the reddest variety known, a ripe, rosy Quarrenden, almost scarlet in its intense red.

"Jacko!" he said; "here, boy!" The monkey cocked up his bright eyes and looked at the proffered fruit. It seemed to interest him, for he threw his hat away and hopped a few paces nearer. Kennedy enticed him softly and held the fruit closer.

Jacko, rather suspicious of this wholly unusual generosity, eyed the gifts askance for a moment and looked up timorously at the detective.

"Take it, boy." Kennedy clicked his tongue gently at the pathetic little figure. Gradually getting the better of its diffidence, the monkey hobbled right up to the outstretched hands, paused for a couple of seconds in childlike hesitation, and then, in a single lightning action, grabbed the banana and leapt high to the top of the partition between the two bars.

The Yard man stood there with eyes wide open in sheer surprise, staring first at his empty hand and then at the shining red apple clutched in the other.

Up on the partition Jacko sat hunched up and contentedly peeled his banana, munching it in short, chumpy mouthfuls of thorough enjoyment.

In the other bar the dart players looked up at the sudden scuffle of tiny claws on the ledge above their board. Stanforth had pushed in a couple of seconds before the monkey made its leap, and the whole crowd stood staring up at the chattering apparition. Stanforth saw in a flash what had happened; the banana in the skinny paw was chapter and verse for every word of it. He gazed at it as though unable to believe his own eyes, dumb with unbelief. Something must have gone wrong. Perhaps the monkey had been frightened—perhaps Kennedy had only tried with a banana to begin with—perhaps the real test of the apple was yet to come—a dozen possibilities whizzed through his head in as many seconds. His fingers mechanically sought his pocket. They clutched a round, red apple and brought it out to the light of the yellow oil lamps.

The eyes of Fred were riveted on him in a tense expectancy. Those in that bar had neither seen nor heard what had transpired beyond that partition. But they all believed in Fred's theory, and they all saw the pulse-tingling coincidence of the stranger's entrance—with the red apple in his hand and the monkey perched above him.

Stanforth approached and held the apple high. The monkey jabbered fiercely, glared at it, and deliberately turned its back on him. Stanforth poked the monkey with the apple and whispered hoarsely to it. Jacko turned, eyed the red fruit for a moment, took another bite at the banana and chattered angrily. The perspiration of unbelief was breaking out on the detective's forehead. This was out and out heresy. In spurning the gift Jacko was committing sacrilege in his eyes. He jabbed him with it again and the monkey, in a flurry of rage, seized it and flung it down at Stanforth with all its force. It hit his bowler hat full in the middle, punching a huge dent in it. Stanforth was so astonished that he forgot to take it off and straighten it.

A slow exhalation of breath rustled round the bar. Dumbly Fred advanced and held up a handful of red matches. The monkey, screaming with temper at being interrupted at his meal, grabbed them and sent them hurtling across the bar.

"Well, dang my hide!" muttered Fred.

Stanforth stumbled out of the bar, his thoughts flying round in a whirling chaos in his head.

Kennedy was coming out of the other bar with his face as black as a thundercloud.

"Ken, what do you make of that?" gasped Stanforth weakly.

Kennedy did not answer. He just looked at him, and his eyes said all and more than his tongue could possibly have told.

VI

Nine o'clock boomed from the clock tower of Gairlie Castle. Kennedy and Stanforth were in the library, going over the plans for the night with Lord Gairlie. Kennedy, disillusioned but determined, was telling Gairlie of the arrangements he had already made.

"Whatever it is, sir, it isn't a monkey," he said emphatically. "Take that from me. We've tried it. And we sunk! Still, I'm after Latta. The wop's in it all right. Turned down an offer of twenty pound for the animal. See? Pulling my leg. Spotted me. Tumbled me. But I'll get him!'

"He has been seen in my grounds late at night," admitted Gairlie.

"He *has?*"

"Yes. My gamekeepers have reported him. I naturally inferred that he was after a bird or a hare. Poachers do pretty well in this neighbourhood."

"José was after higher game. Take it from me. And he isn't going to stop. Even knowing the Yard is on his heels. He's got guts. Now this is the way I argue. Whatever gets into Gairlie Castle is something with a brain. Something that can differentiate between colours. Something that can move about. Something very small and light. Knows how to do its job in silence. Can reach up to the electric light switch very well. I'm stationing my men in all the likeliest rooms tonight—to watch for that little gent. I want certain windows left open. All the staff you can spare will patrol the passages and corridors all night on all landings, Ceaseless patrol will be maintained. Outside, too. I want all your outside staff who know every inch of the grounds. How many men can you vouch for?"

"Let me see. You'll want the gamekeepers—the gardeners—and cow-men. That will be sixteen. Is that sufficient?"

"Fine! I want them outside, posted at regular intervals, so that there are always two or three in sight of each other. They will not only have to patrol the grounds continually but keep their eyes on the Castle windows, too. The Castle will be in entire darkness all night. Lights out at ten-thirty. After that not a glimmer of light is to be struck anywhere in the rooms. Warn the servants that the order must be rigidly obeyed. At the first streak of light in a window the outer guard will sound the alarm. One will remain outside immediately below the window in question to collar anything that tries to climb out. Another will yell to the inside patrol and wise them the room where it is. My men will all be armed. Arm those of yours that you can trust. All inside doors to be left open and all inside men will patrol in stockinged feet. If he breaks through a barricade band like that—he will *deserve* another pot of jam."

"I agree," said Gairlie. "This is something *like* a hit back at the brutes!"

"I'm putting a wax pellet under the knob of every light switch in the house," went on Kennedy. "Whoever switches on the light breaks the pellet. Switches will be filmed over with wax for fingerprints. Fine threads of silk across all the windows. Under the window frames I'm having thin wafers fixed. They'll break if the window's opened only half an inch. The rest will be organisation pure and simple. Just one thing more. Mr. Delayn stays in his room all night—with one of my men with him."

"That," said Lord Gairlie with a troubled countenance, "is going to be a little awkward."

"Not at all, sir," snapped Kennedy. "It's for his own good. Couldn't have a better alibi. If anything happens tonight he's clear."

"Would you care to explain that to him yourself?"

"Sure. That boy's as tractable as a child if you treat him the right way. Where is he?"

"In his room. He hasn't moved out of it since he left the police station. I don't think he has any intention of leaving it until you cleared this matter up."

"Oh?" said Kennedy with a sudden show of interest. "Dull work sitting in one room all day. What was he doing?"

"Reading. He's keen on applied chemistry I believe. He was absorbed in a treatise on that subject."

"Chemistry, eh?" ruminated the Yard man. A vision of a strangely discoloured dress, a watchcaseful of broken glass, and the white face of a dead girl floated before his eyes.

"That's a new one on me. Is he any good at it, do you know?"

"Took fairly high honours at it as a student, I understand. But I can't think that his studies have been maintained to any extent." A ghost of a smile flitted across the peer's face. "His friends are rather amused at the idea of Tommy as a scientific chemist," he said.

Kennedy eyed him closely, one eyebrow drawn down in a curving frown.

"But personally you are not so sure, eh?" he asked.

Gairlie paused for a moment, thoughtfully fingering his cigarette-case.

"Personally," he said," I think Mr. Delayn could do anything better than most men if he gave his mind to it. Some of his ideas, thrown at me off-handedly in their embryo state, have been highly successful in my own concerns. They have been improved and properly developed, of course, but the mere fact that he saw possibilities in certain processes where my own experts were blind to them was enough to convince me long ago that Delayn is throwing himself away at the tennis nets and on the cricket fields."

"H'm!" said Kennedy. "I think I'll go up and see him myself. Where's his room?"

"He's chosen a new one. In the attic, right under the roof. Says he won't be compromising anyone up there. He's a sensitive young fellow. Harris will take you up."

Kennedy grunted and followed the butler up four flights of wide, carpeted stairs to where a smaller flight led up to the darkness above. Up that they went, Harris switching on the lights as they climbed. The main living-floors of the Castle were left below, and utter silence reigned around them. The butler pointed to another staircase at the far end of the landing.

"That's the last floor, sir," he said. "The rooms there haven't been used for years. Mr. Delayn's room was specially cleaned out and warmed for him today."

"All right, Harris; I'll go up alone," said Kennedy. "Switch out the lights as you go down."

The butler turned and went back; Kennedy followed his progress by the sharp blacking out of the lights as he went down.

Kennedy pulled out his torch and silently climbed the last flight. Lord Gairlie had referred to it as the attic, but even the topmost floor of Gairlie Castle was built on a ponderous scale. To right and left a line of rooms opened out—a round score, ten on each side. At each end a winding staircase led up through a trapdoor to the flat roof.

In the transom above one of the doors a dim light shone; it was the room that Tommy had chosen for his home until the law and all apertaining to it gave him leave to remove himself elsewhere. Kennedy tapped gently at the door.

"Come in," growled Delayn. Kennedy pushed in and found him sitting there, his feet stuck out to the heat of an electric fire and a weighty volume spread out on a reading-stand under his eyes. He was propped in an armchair, dressed in an old coat and even older grey flannel trousers. Over in a corner was his bed, with a dressing-table beside it. That and the armchair and a table piled high with books comprised the entire furniture of the room.

"Oh, it's you, is it?" said Delayn, and turned to his book again.

"Yes. sir. it's me. I've got a bit of news for you."

"So've I for you." Delayn held up a pontificial finger. "Do you know it's possible to make a silk stocking out of a potato and a gill of sour milk?" he demanded

Kennedy shot him a doubtful glance.

"It's about tonight, sir," he said. "I'm asking you to stand by me and do all I say without sitting on your dignity. If all goes well tonight your name will be cleared."

"—And that, with a marrow and a pound and a half of flour, you could put the whole Gaiety chorus into silk tights?"

Kennedy leaned over, closed the book with a bang, and tossed it among the pile on the table.

"Got no time for fooling," he rasped. "If you're wise you'll talk sense."

Tommy raised his eyes despairingly to the stone roof. "Ye gods!" he breathed "I tell him the most beautiful discovery of modern time and he tells me to talk sense!" He peered at the detective. "Is my correspondence being tampered with?" he asked.

Kennedy shook his head. "No," he said. "Not yet!"

"Well if you'd glanced through my mail this morning you would have seen a letter from Hallorans. Ever heard of Hallorans?"

"No" Kennedy, like a much offended Buddha, was stuck right in front of him staring down.

"Fairly big firm, in their way. They test out other people's ideas—for a consideration, of course. Only drawback is

I haven't got the consideration. Wouldn't care to buy a real man-sized motorcar, I s'pose?"

Kennedy barked a high-powered "No! And I'll trouble you to listen to me." he added.

Tommy waved an airy arm. "About this footling mystery business?" he asked "Too busy—much too busy."

"Are you? Well, now; sit back and hold tight." Kennedy was rapidly getting hot under the collar. "You stop being busy right now and give the working hands a show. I'm putting a man in here with you tonight."

"I sincerely trust the brute doesn't snore. Hallorans have demonstrated conclusively that a little idea of mine, properly handled and marketed large scale—"

"Damn Hallorans," snarled the detective.

"On the contrary. God bless Hallorans. Nice, kind Haiti shall go up and see them tomorrow,"

"You won't!"

"I think I shall. Yes-s, I certainly think I shall. Tell you what—I'll take four-fifty, money down, for that car I'd hate to go up there without their consideration."

Kennedy stood up, fuming. "Are you going to listen to reason?" he protested. "Listen—I don't care a hell's rap about motorcars, Hallorans, potatoes or sour milk. And what's more—damn silk tights! I'm telling you one of my men is staying here with you in this room all night. And whatever happens—you won't be allowed to leave it! Also I want your word of honour that you'll put this light out sharp at ten-thirty. And that on no account will you switch it on again."

Delayn pondered the matter, and then shook his head vigorously.

"Couldn't dream of making such an absurd promise," he said. "I shall be reading hard and I shall want that light till at least three in the morning."

"I shall give my man orders to switch it out at half-past ten!" stormed Kennedy.

"And I shall give him orders to switch it on again at twenty-nine minutes to eleven."

"He won't do it!"

"In which case I shall biff him on the jaw and switch it on myself."

"*Will* you?" Kennedy suddenly went mad. He pulled out his revolver—a blue-shining Colt—gripped it by the barrel, and literally pounded the switch off the wall. At the first smash the room was plunged in a sightless darkness, a Stygian pall of utter black. He bashed away until the switch hung loose on the wire, and then, groping in the darkness, he pulled even that from its moorings wrenching away a yard of wire, so that the end of it dangled high above him.

He switched on his torch and shone it full on the placid face in the armchair.

"Laugh *that* off!" he snapped, making for the door.

Delayn shrugged regretfully. The door opened.

The light of Kennedy's torch snapped out, and from Delayn's chair came a sweet "Good evening. Don't slam the door as you go out. I'll spring you five per cent commission if you can find a purchaser for that car."

Kennedy went out, slamming the door with a crash.

He groped his way downstairs, feeling as cross as a bear. Delayn hadn't been fair with him. Hang it all, he had only gone up to the young cub out of sheer generosity. All he wanted to do was to put him right for his own guidance. Secretly he admitted, he had also intended pumping him about his scientific knowledge, particularly with regard to a certain instantaneous death not unconnected with a handful of splintered glass. Still, the young rip wasn't to know that. And even if he did there was no excuse for putting on highfalutin airs. He'd half a mind to go back and blaze it all out with him.

Stanforth knew the moment he saw him that something had gone wrong, and he formed a fairly shrewd idea that Tommy had proved a tougher handful than he had expected. Kennedy drew him aside.

"Listen," he said; "that youngster is kicking over the traces. Bit of a swelled head, I think. I'm not at all satisfied with the way he's acting. I've just smashed the switch of his light. He refused point blank to douse it of his own accord. I want a specially good man in the grounds below his window. One you can trust to keep his eyes on that window and not move. And I want you to keep in constant touch with him from inside."

"Right—I'll see to it. Lord Gairlie is making arrangements about food for the night. Hot tea and sandwiches will be available for all hands any time. Cans of tea will be passed round the outside men every hour; those who want it can have brandy or whisky as well."

"Good. Where's our crowd?"

"Down in the hall, waiting for you."

"Come on then; let's get at it."

They went down and collected their men. They were a fine hefty-looking lot; capable, competent, and all with that touch of rather heavy self-confidence that stamps the policeman. Kennedy gave them an extensive résumé of the whole case, right from the time the first red object was stolen from the Castle.

"And our job tonight," he said, "is to finish it. There are control points head of the stairs on each landing. Man in charge at the point will report at the central post here in the big hall. All patrols will report to his control point every ten minutes, having visited every room on his landing. Chief will be here at midnight. Either he, I, or Stanforth will always be available at the main post here in the hall. The patrol will carry on through the night, ceaselessly, each man going his rounds in an endless circle. There must be no bungling. Go for your man the moment he shows up. *And get him!*"

Kennedy had chosen his main posts well. The central position in the hall was visible from every landing. It was in the middle of the great bay beneath the dome-like tierings of landings that opened up from the central stairway. Anyone by leaning over the balustrades that circled the landings, could immediately see his controlling officer and signal any suspicious occurrence. The control points at the stair-head of each landing could look right down on Kennedy's table.

Gairlie, who joined the detective while he was posting his men, quietly approved of the whole scheme.

"I have a feeling we shall get the brute tonight, Inspector," he said.

"Get him or bust!" said Kennedy shortly.

Gradually the party grew thinner and thinner as Kennedy posted his men. By the time the top landing was reached only one remained. The detective took him up to Tommy's room and went in without knocking.

Delayn, by the light of a solitary candle, was still reading, his back turned to the door. He had made himself thoroughly comfortable with a pile of cushions at the back of his head. Perched on a soap-dish that crowned an unsafe-looking column of books, the lone candle guttered. He had stuck it so that its light shone from a few inches behind his right ear. He carried on unconcernedly reading, not condescending to look round at the detective's abrupt entry.

"Sold the bus already?" he asked.

"You'll stay in here all night," said Kennedy to his man. "Don't let that gentleman out of your sight," and he stressed the "gentleman" till Tommy's toes wiggled—"And don't let him get out of this room. Sharp at half-past ten douse the candle. Pitch it out of the window if he tries to light it again, and throw his matches in the water-jug. If he gives any trouble yell out for me. I'll come and settle his hash. Lock the door on the inside and put the key in your pocket."

"And I hope it keeps fine for you," cooed Tommy as the Yard man stalked out.

The detective hurried downstairs. The outside staff had been assembled, and without telling them too much of the inside details he gave them their orders.

"The moment you hear anyone in the grounds," he said, "freeze yourselves stiff. Don't make a sound. At the first movement, lie low and watch. He'll make for the windows. One of the gamekeepers had better shadow him—someone who knows how to keep dead quiet.

"As soon as he has got in, all of you concentrate under the window where he entered. Sound the alarm as soon as he's in. Let it rip! Then our bunch inside will crowd in on him. Or—if you see a sudden light spring up in any of the rooms creep to the dining-hall window and pass the word in to me. Tell me which room the light has appeared in—and leave the rest to me. Silence and speed. Those are the watchwords. Come outside and I'll give you your positions."

Kennedy took his men out to points about thirty yards from the castle walls. Then he strung them out in a long tenuous line that completely circled the building. He posted them in all the darkest, quietest spots in the grounds. Then he crept back to the house.

In the castle a vast oppressive silence reigned. One by one, at unequal intervals, he ordered the lights to be put out. Room by room flickered into darkness. By twenty past ten only the main hall and a few of the living rooms on the second floor were lit. Kennedy sent Harris round to put them out, an ordinary duty which would be his final task under normal conditions.

By half-past ten the Castle was in complete darkness. Stanforth was already well on his way with the wax-spray. Here and there along the landings the dim white of a face showed faintly luminous. Now and then a soft padding of stockinged feet, hardly perceptible on the thick carpet, came softly on the stillness. The whispered voice of a control man passing the "all's well" to the main hall sounded sibilantly.

Stanforth had covered fifty or sixty switches with wax, fixing the tiny pellets under the knobs as he went. He had reached the third floor and crept into a room which had not yet been dismantled from its state of emergency bedroom for the reception. That was one of the rooms that Kennedy had decided to leave open. The door and window stood wide. Beneath the window was a little occasional table. Kennedy's reason for leaving that window open was that a red lacquer box stood on the table within a foot of the glass.

The detective went over to the window, fixed the wafer at the side of the jamb, glanced out to see that all was quiet, and went back to the door. The switch was on the wall just inside the door. Quietly and carefully he began spraying it, squeezing gently on the rubber bulb, the hot wax coming out like a thin vapour.

Suddenly he switched his head round. The merest suspicion of a sound had come from outside the window. He waited, his head screwed round over his shoulder. Nothing happened, just the padding of a guard going the rounds on the landing and the echo of the wind sighing fitfully outside.

He turned to the switch again. A hand, a queer, deformed hand in a long black glove slid silently in at the window. It gripped the red lacquer box gently. The bottom of it scraped ever so faintly on the polished table top.

Stanforth whipped round and stared full at it.

For the space of a single second Stanforth gazed in a state of fascinated trance at the apparition, unable to take his eyes off the horrible thing. The odd deformity, half human, half animal, sent a feeling of nausea coursing over his body. It was a revulsion against the unnameable, the inexplicable, all that was hair-raisingly revolting. The tiny fingers, attached to the caricature of an arm, were short and stubby. The black cotton glove that encased it hung limp on the underdeveloped flesh. And half the fingers were left bare.

With something of a shock Stanforth realised that the fingers were white, a doughy, bloodless white, and that the fingernails were of the unmistakable shape and size of a human nail. They were pinkish, too, the only spot of colour visible.

Then from the side of the half-open window a single eye looked in. It was lifeless, and yet in some queer way, unutterably baleful. There was something octopus-like in its silent, unwinking stare, as though the cold soul of a fish looked out of its pulseless depths.

And in the next second the whole thing vanished, whipped into invisibility in the flick of an eye.

Stanforth started forward with a wild jump. An electrifying cry hurtled out of his mouth, and set the guard jumping into action outside on the landing.

Then he rushed back to the switch. Stockinged feet were pounding up the corridor, voices were barking staccato questions from the floors below—and the outer patrol had not been given the signal.

He thumped the switch down and began spitting out a torrent of white-hot curses. The light did not come. The wax had found a flaw in the switch and had insulated the circuit. Something hissed and crackled for a moment, and then a thin streamer of blue sparks shot out. Eight precious seconds had been wasted and still the outer patrol had seen nothing to make them raise the alarm.

Kennedy's voice sounded outside. "That was Stanforth's voice shouting," he cried, breathless from his flying rush up from the hall. "Where are you, Stan? What's wrong?" he yelled.

"Here! In here!" shouted Stanforth, kicking the door wide open. "Matches! Quick! This damned switch has gone!"

He rushed to the window and flung it high as others came pouring in at the door. He craned his head out as far as he could reach and stared down into the blackness of the grounds below.

Not a thing! Not a break in the smooth, unscaleableness of the giant wall. It streamed away below, sheer and bare as a worn cliff-face.

"Hi!" he yelled. "Guard! Below there! What the hell—" Hoarse voices called from the shadow, and footsteps came running out from the trees.

"Lights! Quick! Play on the walls!" Stanforth bawled his orders down. Lanterns began to glimmer in the grounds, hurrying towards the walls.

"What's the matter, sir?" inquired a voice tremulous with sudden alarm.

"Didn't you see it? Didn't you see anything climbing the walls?"

"No, sir; nothing passed us—and nothing went up the wall that we saw."

Kennedy thrust his powerful torch into Stanforth's hand from over his shoulder. Stanforth grabbed it and sent its beam glaring down the sheer fall of the granite wall. Sideways, down, and finally up overhead he swept the shining ray, playing it round in great curving arcs of light.

And there was nothing to show for it, absolutely nothing to account for that horrible black arm with the baby fingers, and the solitary eye that had glared in at him from outside the window.

"What was it, Stanforth?" hissed Kennedy.

"Tell you in a minute. Quick—get everybody out into the grounds. It can't have gone far. A black arm with a single eye behind it. That's all I saw. It climbed up to the window and stole the red lacquer box off this table."

"Rot!" said Kennedy.

"I know. But I saw it—and the box has gone. Rot that off!"

Kennedy whipped round. The room was jammed with his own men and a crowd of the Castle staff, all asking jerky questions of each other, and all unable to find answers.

"Out into the grounds!" said Kennedy. "Search the grounds from end to end. Don't leave a yard uncovered. Split up into twos and take your lanterns. Spread out from the house in a ring and go right on to the boundary fences, then back in a circle. I'll be out when I've got the hang of it."

In five minutes the whole crowd were out and scattering, the lights of their lanterns bobbing about like stars among the trees, gradually growing dimmer and dimmer and disappearing into the surrounding darkness. No sudden hail came from them; no shrill yell to tell of a discovery or an explanation of the mystery that got deeper and deeper with every second.

Stanforth watched them go with his hands propped out on the windowsill, smouldering red anger in his eyes. He was mad with himself. The great chance had come and he had let it slip. The odds were that the chance would never come again. He could not even excuse himself on the score of its utter unexpectedness. Barely half an hour from the setting of the guard the thing had happened. The very least he had expected was an attempt in the silent hours before dawn. And then there was that shockingly unlucky incident of the light. If that wretched switch hadn't failed he could have got the alarm out to the outside patrol before the thing had got away from the window. The shorting of the switch had been a calamity, just the kind of ill-fortune they had been struggling against ever since they started on the case.

Slowly the silence settled down again, grim and portentous in its very intensity.

"Well, Stanforth, what happened?" demanded Kennedy.

Stanforth looked ruefully at his leader.

"Darn little that I could see," he said. "I was standing there over at the switch waxing it. I thought I heard a sound, just a faint scratch outside the window. The place was in utter darkness, but there was just a dim half-light coming in at the window. Enough for me to work by, anyway. I listened for a moment and heard nothing more. I turned and got back on the job again.

"And then, a few seconds later, there came a faint scratch from the table here, and I wheeled round. There was a red lacquer box standing right here—you asked for it to be put there yourself—on the table within a foot of the open window. When I turned there was a hand already on that box and it was lifting it."

"A hand?" queried Kennedy.

"Yes, a hand. And I'll be shot if I can say whether it was human or not. It was the beastliest looking thing I've ever seen. There was a long black glove on it—it went right up the arm, but the fingertips were cut off, leaving the last two joints of the fingers bare. And the fingers were putty-colour, with little pink nails. The nails were human, I'll swear. Monkey's nails are black—and long—and—and, damn it, they *look* like monkey's nails and this one didn't."

"Did it look like a mask, say, a plaster cast, or something in papier mâché that might have been drawn over an arm to disguise a monkey's paw?"

"No, it didn't. The fingers moved. And they gripped; and somehow they looked natural—in spite of their colour."

"And it came from outside the window?"

"Yes; that's the living marvel of it. I tried to get the light on, but the blamed switch fizzed out. The wax had found a leak and insulated it, I reckon. What with making a rush to the window and trying to get that switch to work and shouting for the bunch, I must have lost eight or nine seconds. And the thing had gone by then."

"But that's impossible. There's nothing breathing that could have got back down that wall in even thirty seconds—not if it had a ladder there."

"Can't help it, Kennedy; I'm only telling you facts. It was there—and I saw it as plain as I could see anything in this blue night-glow. And it got the box, too. It kept its head long enough to do what it came for."

"That would only leave it one hand free for climbing."

"I know. I'm not trying to offer explanations. I haven't got any. All I know is what I saw. A hand and an arm with a black glove on it—and an eye that looked at me through the glass. It just seemed to stare in like a glass eye that had got a bit dull—and then it vanished—the whole contraption. Went out into nothingness like—like the blinkin' fuse when I jammed it on."

Kennedy took his torch and shone it carefully over the outer sill. Marked in the thin dust was the barely visible print of two hands, pointing outwards.

"No good," grunted Stanforth. "They're mine—where I leant out to give the alarm."

For several minutes Kennedy searched with the light over every inch of the wall within reach. And he found not so much as a scratch or a scrap of anything that would shed a ray of light on the mystery.

"Blest if I know," he said. "It beats me—beats me flat. The thing couldn't fly, anyhow; and that's what it seems to have done. Stanforth, this thing's getting on my nerves. I'll be thankful when the Chief gets here. Maybe he can get a line on it. I'm nearly through. Pst! Listen!"

Both men thrust their heads out of the window and leaned out, straining their ears. From somewhere a hundred yards to the right came a faint sound. It grew and grew, resolving itself into an immense pounding of heavy boots through the darkness.

"Hi! Hold up there," bawled Kennedy. He whipped out his gun and sent a shot crashing down.

Then a voice boomed up from the darkness.

"Come on—I've got him," it yelled, a stentor voice that welled up to them with all the vengeful fury of passion in its notes.

The sound of its progress thundered on into the night and grew fainter. And then from far in the misty distance came a long-drawn, blood-chilling cry that died on the silence and left it pulsing.

"My God, Stanforth—come on, boy," said Kennedy. "That was John Argle."

The two detectives leapt to the door and raced down the stairs. The main hall was still in pitch darkness. Kennedy groped for the switches and flooded the place with light. On the big table were half a dozen spare lanterns, and he seized one.

"This way," he cried, and made for the great main entrance. In a few seconds Stanforth was at his side, and together they ran up the gravel drive.

"It was over here—to the left of the lodge," breathed Kennedy. "That's where it seemed to come from."

"Over by the Long Coppice," said Stanforth. "That's on the direct line from the Castle to the gap in the hedge."

They rushed on in silence, saving their wind. The Long Coppice was nearly a quarter of a mile away from the Castle—a good sprint even for a man in first class condition. Kennedy was soon pumping hard, but Stanforth was slipping along on his lank legs breathing easily through the nose, and covering the ground with something less than half the exertion his leader was putting out.

When they had covered a hundred and fifty yards the fearful scream was repeated—it came right from among the gaunt trees of the Long Coppice.

In the midst of it there broke out a fierce animal yammer, a queer throaty sound that continued in a heat of passion. For full fifty yards of their rush it continued, and then it snapped off short.

"That was a monkey," panted Kennedy. "Little brute made the same noise up on the partition at the 'Castle Arms.'"

They reached the first belt of trees and Kennedy stopped, feeling for matches.

"Better have a spot of light on this," he said. "Don't like fumbling around for shrieks and screams in the dark."

Stanforth opened the glass of the hurricane lamp, and somehow they got it alight. They stumbled about among tree roots and bushes, getting further and further into the spinney and then found themselves rabbit wire.

"Better work along this way," said Kennedy, bearing off along the wire to the left. "The gap in the hedge is on that fine." For ten minutes they continued a fruitless searching and prodding about among the undergrowth. Then Kennedy, getting impatient, sent a hail bellowing through the trees. He repeated it again and again as they went along.

Other lights began to wink among the black trunks; acknowledging shouts answered him. The gunshot from the castle window was bringing the searchers back.

Suddenly Stanforth halted, holding up his hand for silence. From away on the right against the rabbit wire came a faint sound—the long, deep breathing of someone whose teeth were clenched; there was a slight hiss in it, of the breath going in and out through the teeth.

They hurried over, the lantern raised high. A few yards away they found him, John Argle, flat on his back against the bole of a tree, his face upturned to the night. He was almost insensible, his eyelids twitching with the first slow efforts of returning consciousness.

Kennedy went down on hands and knees and propped the lantern by the great bearded head.

"Good heavens, Stanforth, look at that," he said.

The virile head was badly bruised, and there was blood on the face and the harsh black beard. But it was not to that that Kennedy had drawn attention.

Sheer across the face from left to right was a streak of red lines. They were in perfect parallel and began right up under the hair, finishing on the neck below the ear. There were three of them, and their effect was ghastly in the sallow light of the solitary wick.

The two men bent closer and inspected them.

"Queer, isn't it?" grunted Kennedy.

"Sticks out a mile, I should say," replied Stanforth.

"Yes, I know—but where does it come in? I can't connect it."

Kennedy opened Argle's collar and eased his head from its painful strain over the tree-root. The man's breathing became calmer, the tenseness slid out of it, and he relaxed.

"He'll be round in a minute," said Stanforth. "I want to know how he got that bash across the face. There must be a pretty hefty giant knocking about to give Beardy Bill a smash like that."

"I wouldn't care to tackle him anyway," grunted Kennedy.

Argle moved and opened his eyes. He stared dazedly at the two men and tried to collect his scattered faculties. The brooding, resolute eyes looked fearlessly up and a deep frown crossed his face. Then slowly remembrance came back into his eyes, and their dark depths glowed with sudden fire.

"Oh, it's you, is it?" he growled. "Well, did you get him?"

"Get who?" asked Kennedy.

"The man I was chasing."

"We haven't got anybody yet—but he won't go far. He's still in the grounds and the patrols are closing in."

Argle looked acidly at the detective. "If you haven't got him now, you'll never get him," he announced. "He's got away. You can lay your longest drop on that."

"Who was he, anyway?" demanded Stanforth.

The hard, bitter frown came back on John Argle's face and he faced round savagely at the detective.

"You find out the same as I did," he rasped. "I've got first claim if they string me up for it."

"Don't be a dam fool. Come on—who was it?" cut in Kennedy.

"Somebody you couldn't find. Leave it at that, Kennedy. I'm glad couldn't get him. That's all I've got to say."

"Argle, you're only laying up trouble for yourself. You're making yourself an accessory."

"I'm laying up bigger trouble than you think," came the venomous answer, and the grim eyes turned wickedly sullen. "That brute got my girl—and I'll get him. I'll make him squeal too—before he goes out.

Kennedy clicked his tongue in sheer desperation.

"How did you get those wounds on your face?" he demanded.

"Hit my head on that damn bough," said Argle pointing upwards,

Kennedy glanced up. It was a walnut tree that Argle had fallen under and a great down-drooping branch projected from about eight feet up the trunk to within barely a yard of the ground.

"How did you get into the grounds?" asked Stanforth.

"Never you mind," snapped the injured man. "I was in, and that's all that matters. And I saw what your men didn't. I saw him—the swine—coming from the back of the servants' quarters. And I set out to shadow him. But down there by the fountains he heard me. He slipped on to the grass lawns and doubled back. I lit out after him. Could hardly see him in the darkness and I followed his sound. Suddenly he shot round and headed across for the Long Coppice. That's on the way to the gap in the hedge and I knew he was making to get out and away. So I pelted after him again. And some blame fool shot at me from the Castle windows. I shouted and kept on. He led me right on this way and I was within ten yards of the swine when I banged my face against that bough."

Kennedy straightened up and looked down at him. He was feeling hotly resentful. Argle had secrets and inside knowledge that he wasn't sharing, All the argument in the world wouldn't shift the man. He had worked himself into that state of heated unreasoning resolve where nothing would satisfy him but the accomplishment of his set objective.

The detective leaned down and touched the three long scratches.

"Those weren't made by the bough of a tree," he said.

"I didn't say they were," retorted Argle.

"Those are scratches—the marks of a monkey's paw."

"I know. I'm not arguing about it."

"José Latta has been here. It was José Latta you were chasing."

"Not me, Kennedy. I'm not telling. If you want to know who I was chasing, you should have been here."

The first arrivals of the returning searchers were gathering round, and Kennedy, exasperated, made a sign to them.

"Pick him up and carry him back to the Castle," he said. "Stanforth, you and I'd better take a run down to the gap and see if there's anything doing there."

He turned and went off without a further word. As they reached the hedge the moon began to show for the first time that night, a thin scimitar of white against the blue-black sky. They crawled through the breach and emerged on the deserted lane. Kennedy went across silently to the boundary stone. A face peered from behind it as he approached.

"All right, sir?" whispered a voice.

"Yes. Anything to report?"

"Nothing at all, sir. There hasn't been a soul in the lane since I took up position here."

"Haven't seen José Latta and his monkey anywhere, I suppose?"

"Not a sign. But I heard a shot in the grounds, sir, about half an hour ago—and I heard screaming twice—from over there near the big spinney. But my orders were to remain here, whatever happened, and keep an eye on the hedge."

Kennedy nodded. "We've missed him all right," he said to Stanforth "I fancy the beggar has some other way of getting in and out of the grounds, all right," he said, turning back to the sentry. "You wait on here till the Chief comes. There'll be someone else with him, and they'll come up the lane from the village. When they come bring them straight through to the Castle. We've seen all we're going to see tonight. José has slipped us."

They made their way back through the grounds in an aggrieved silence.

The big spinney loomed ahead, blotting out the view of the distant Castle. They made a detour to skirt it, and as they emerged round the end Stanforth suddenly started forward at the run.

"Gosh," he said. "They're still at it." Three lights were full on in the second story of Gairlie Castle, shining steadily into the night. And as they looked a fourth and a fifth snapped on.

"Run," hissed Kennedy. "We'll get him yet."

The two men jumped into a flying effort of speed. Stanforth let himself go. He heard Kennedy's labored "Don't wait for me—get on ahead," and he opened out. Kennedy was some seconds astern when he made the wide steps of the entrance. He took them three at a time, and went on into the main hall, almost cannoning into the butler as he swept through the door.

"Whoozat?" he gasped, holding him by the lapels and peering at him.

"Me, sir—Harris, sir—the butler, sir," stammered that worthy with a rush.

"Who's upstairs? Anyone gone up while we've been away?"

"No, sir, no one. I've been keeping guard here."

"Then who's fooling with the lights upstairs?"

"There isn't anybody up there, sir. I've had my eye on this door—never left it, sir, and no one has come past me."

Stanforth left him and made for the stairs at a run, catfooted in spite of his breakneck speed. If he had muffed things once that night he wasn't going to muff them again. Somewhere up there was the wholly unauthorised Something they were hunting for, the cool-brained, impudent Something that had worried, amazed, and exasperated them since the hazy days of the late summer. The wall-eyed cheek of it stung his professional pride to its deepest quick. That the brute should attempt to come back after the hullabaloo of the last half-hour made him literally prickle with wrath.

The lighted rooms were down at the far end of the second landing, a section of the house that had, until then, escaped the attention of the ft marauder. He tiptoed to the first room he came to. There was no light in there and the door was partly open. He pushed it wide and peeped in. He strained his eyes into the darkness and listened, with every fibre in him tuned up for the slightest sound.

Nothing happened. He switched on his torch and played it rapidly round, a quick searching glare that sought out every possible hiding-place in two seconds. Nothing. He withdrew his head and tried the next. Nothing again. And the windows had not been interfered with in his absence. He crossed over and inspected the wafers by the light of his torch, and they were intact. So was the wax pellet under the switch of the electric light.

He went out and stood on the landing, immobile and silent, in a tense attitude of listening. All was quiet as the tomb. There was not a sound or the scratch of a sound from anywhere in the dark building. The main hall was as silent as the tiering, echoless upper floors.

And then, from the opposite side of the balustrade came a tiny bump. As a sound itself it was infinitesimal, but in that vast oppressive silence it sounded on Stanforth's expectant ears like a bag of flour falling on a muffled drum. He started across the landing. The bump had come from a room on the other side, almost opposite.

He crawled round towards the door, already forming the conviction in his head that that bump was the slight sound of a light body dropping to the floor from the window. He had reached the end of the balustrade and was turning, when assurance became doubly sure. The room from which the bump had come leapt suddenly into a fullness of light. The door was open a foot, and the light poured out in a flood. And right at the moment when Stanforth's hopes were running to the topmost pinnacles again, the silly, inane tragedy came. He was within three yards of the door when it happened. A frightened, querulous voice piped up from the darkness below.

"Mr. Stanforth, can you hear me? There's another light come up on the second landing." It was Harris, shaky and scared, down in the main hall. In a second the light was out and there was a scamper of padded feet across the room.

"Damn!" snarled Stanforth, and leapt at the door. He hit it with a full-shouldered charge that nearly toppled him off his balance. As he stumbled through his hand fell with a bang on the switch inside the door. The flood of light jarred on his brain as his gaze flashed to the window—a tall, double-lighted window with a big table in front.

Heavy plum-coloured curtains draped that window, thick folds that fell in a fine sweep from the fat brass pole sheer to the floor. They went divided down the centre from top to bottom, and during the day were drawn back by thickly braided bands caught up at the sides.

But the bands were now dangling, and the curtains were just swinging together. They closed almost at the same second that he crashed the light on. In that tenth of a second he caught sight of a tiny back view, a dwarfish, deformed little back, that seemed to brace up and launch itself through the window into space. It was only a momentary flash of light, but it burned itself on his brain with all the fiery intensity of an acid. The thing—whatever it was—and even having seen it he couldn't say with any hop of conviction what it was—was very small;

certainly under three feet, probably nearer two, he thought, but it was hunching for a spring and he couldn't with certainty.

But what he did see was that it was clothed entirely in the same black cotton stuff that he had mistaken for a long glove an hour before. It was like an overall suit, dead black, and it continued up over the head, with tiny slits cut for the ears like the pantomime dress of King Rat. From the cut of it, it was possible that it continued right across to cover the face as well. The feet were cased in Chinese shoes, black and soft and tight, with a heavy white felt sole at least an inch thick.

And over and above everything he saw that there was neither tail nor anywhere that a tail could have been coiled in that tight-fitting fleshing of black.

All that he saw in the brief fleeting sight of it as the curtains closed behind it. He floundered forward to get round the table, clawing it on one side. The window shut with a bang from outside as he heaved at it and he hissed curses at the table, the window, and everything else connects with it. The thing had slipped through his fingers again.

With a mighty shove he got the table clear and flung the curtains aside. They closed again behind him, and he swore again in sheer temper as the light was cut off. He tried to hold them apart with his feet while he struggled with the badly jammed window. Precious seconds were racing themselves off the clock. And in the midst of it the realisation thundered across his brain that in switching on the light he had obliterated the only definite they had—the fingerprint on the wax film on the switch. He heaved and strove at the window in a frenzy of desperation.

The thing was stuck tight. For a moment he half thought he had been driven between the two frames. He pulled out his torch again, flashed it on and inspected it. But there was nothing there. Neither was the horrible little apparition anywhere visible.

"Devil take it," he muttered, and tore off his coat. He propped the lit torch on the sill, put the heels of his hands under the window ledge, and thrust upward with a jolt that came from every muscle in his back. The window went up with a smash and he leaned out, peering down in to the gloom.

But he knew, before he got that window up, that it was useless to look for that amazing visitor. It was altogether too elusive. It seemed to be able to disintegrate itself into the very darkness, to dissolve into the air. Once before it had played that unbelievable vanishing trick on him, and for the second time almost within an hour he was floundering about in a morass of doubt and puzzlement. The walls were bare, as bare as the tenantless void of an ocean on which there is no sail. It was empty, and its very emptiness seemed to be ringing with silent laughter at him. He was nonplussed, every inch of him. He took off his hat and mopped his damp forehead.

"God bless my soul," he breathed. "I'll be seeing spooks in a minute. If I wasn't sane—and sober—"

He caught sight of the rear-guard of the search party straggling round the far end of the house.

"Hey," he shouted. "Seen anything below there?"

"No, sir," came an answering voice.

"Nobody passed you—going your way?"

"Nothing here, sir."

"Something about knee-high, dressed like a hobgoblin?"

"*Eh?*" came the astonished query.

"Oh, go to blazes," rumbled Stanforth to himself. The very tone of the man below was answer enough.

He drew his head in and searched the room. There were soft dull patches on the highly polished surface of the table, diminutive little things, the size and shape of a baby's shoe. Evidently the queer apparition had walked across the table when it got in at the window. The switch clue was obliterated, the wax being rubbed right off by Stanforth's own flailing hand. He went into the other rooms and searched. The silk threads and the wafers were intact save in one, where both were broken. It seemed as though the strange visitant had got in there and then gone to the other rooms via the landing. Why it should have got out again and climbed in at the window where Stanforth and Harris detected it was a puzzle that he gave up. It was beyond him. Thank heavens, the Chief would soon be there. The responsibility of thinking it all out would then be off his hands.

The switches in the other rooms were helpful. There were faint markings on them which ought to be of valuable assistance when properly developed and photographed. But, so far as he could tell, they did not look like any fingerprint that he had ever seen. He locked all the rooms to prevent other hands defacing the marks, and went out to the landing.

Kennedy, blown to his last gasp, was toiling up the stairs with Lord Gairlie.

"Anything doing?" he panted.

"Gone," said Stanforth acidly.

"Quick—try Delayn's room," said Kennedy.

Stanforth went up, switching on the lights as he went. There was no light in Delayn's room, and by the time he had found the door Kennedy was on the landing. He went in with his torch on—and shot out again.

"Delayn's gone," he gasped.

Kennedy sat himself on the edge of a projecting baulk of timber. He was blowing like a bull and the perspiration stood on his forehead in glistening beads. Lacking Stanforth's rubber lungs, it took him some time to get his wind back.

"What happened?" he gasped. "I saw another light come on while I was running."

Stanforth detailed the whole affair to him, right down to a minute description of the weird little thing he had seen leaping from the window. Lord Gairlie had joined them, and listened with increasing amazement to the detective's story.

"Kennedy, might I suggest that we have all lights on for the rest of the night?" he asked. "The women are almost hysterical in the servants' quarters. They are all huddled in the big common room, too frightened to sleep—too frightened even to go to bed."

Kennedy nodded. "Nothing else for it," he said. "Means we are finished for the night. Can't be helped."

He turned to Stanforth. "Tell Harris to put all the lights on," he said. Outside patrols go back to their posts and carry on. Inside guards stand fast. All doors and windows to be wide open and continual patrols kept up on all landings. And—just keep your mouth shut about what you saw in the room. If the women get to hear about *that* we shall never hear the last of it. They'll drive themselves silly with fright."

Lord Gairlie looked his gratitude. "Thank you very much, Kennedy," he said. "I know what it means to you, and I appreciate it fully, I'm dreadfully sorry about Delayn," he added. "I never dreamed he would break his parole."

"He didn't," snapped Kennedy. "He withdrew it tonight. Said he was going to Manchester or somewhere. He's done it, too. Young fool. He's only piling up suspicion against himself again. Carey was watching him. Good man, too. How'd he get through?"

He went over to the deserted room and gazed round. Lord Gairlie held a lantern high, and Kennedy slipped his torch out. The room told its own tale. The window was wide open. Kennedy looked out. Immediately below was an ornamental coping that gave onto the lower battlement a few feet down. A good athlete could have climbed over the battlement to a great square rain pipe which ran down the wall and was lost in a rich growth of ivy thirty or forty feet from the bottom.

"Simple as eating duck to a chap like Delayn," commented Kennedy.

As they went out, Carey returned, hot and flustered.

"Well; what happened?" snapped the detective ominously.

"He—he got away, sir. Couldn't help it. There was a dreadful going on downstairs. Mr. Delayn was asleep on his bed. Had been for half an hour. When the row started he didn't even turn in his sleep—even the revolver shot didn't wake him. So I thought it was all right to leave him for a bit. Doors were opening and shutting all over the place. I could hear our men shouting and calling out, so I went to lend a hand."

"You let him bluff you as easy as that!"

"Couldn't help it, sir. He seemed to be sleeping like a babe. When I got back he was gone and I rushed down to see if I could trap him on the wall."

Kennedy growled something sulphuric under his breath and left Carey stammering apologies to his uncompromising back.

The Chief arrived soon after one in the morning, a tall, stiff, soldierly looking man, with keen grey eyes and a nose with something of the hawk's beak about it. He wasted little time in getting down to the bones of the matter. In five minutes he, Kennedy, Stanforth and Lord Gairilie were in conference in the main hall, the Chief munching sandwiches and sipping scalding coffee, while all three detailed their stories from their own angles.

He spoke only at rare intervals, and then only to shoot a quick, searching question at one or other of them—questions which showed that in a few brief minutes he had got a thorough grip of all ramifications of the complicated case. He was particularly severe on Stanforth, the only one who had actually seen the queer creature.

"Quite remarkable," he said at last. "And entirely new. Like nothing that has come within my experience."

He took out a pencil and began to sketch, taking his directions from Stanforth. At the end of five minutes he had made a detailed drawing of the object as Stanforth had seen it. He studied it closely.

"Unique," he muttered. "And it tells so little, too. Still, it's something to work on. The points of suspicion are: Latta undoubtedly—a servant possibly—and Delayn, well, just a shade. I'll make up my mind about Delayn within five minutes of meeting him. This is really a most interesting case, my lord," he said, turning to Gairlie. "It means that a new criminal brain has arrived, a brain which functions on new lines and conceives fresh methods. If you will extend to me the courtesy of a room I would like to stay on for a little while and take charge myself."

"I shall be only too delighted," said Gairlie thankfully.

"I'll make a full investigation in daylight," said the Chief. "Meanwhile I'll get a little sleep. You fellows had better turn in, too. Can't burn the candle at both ends. The patrol can give us a call if anything more happens."

VII

Lonora slipped early out of bed—she found sleep as elusive as the odd creature that infested the rooms.

The guards were still on duty when she got down, for the dawn was still young. But they were preparing to end the patrol as soon as one of the detectives appeared to give the word. During the day only the outer patrol was to be maintained in the grounds.

Lonora went along to her father's room to get the later news of the night's happenings. The sudden declension of Tommy came as a shock to her. She wandered out into the grounds to think it over. It was raw and cold, but at least the air was fresh and invigorating after a night of badly broken slumber.

A hundred yards from the front of the house, on a terracing of flowerbeds, was a statute, a fine copy of Rodin's "Thinker." It was poised on a base of fem-clad rocks, among which little rills of water trickled. She could see it mistily in the distance, the great bent stone body, the elbow on the knee, and the massive head propped by the chin in its hand; the living, petrified embodiment of brooding, concentrated thought.

Suddenly she blinked and stared at the statue. There seemed to be something odd about the "Thinker" that morning. Somehow he wasn't looking so huge, quite so tremendously omnipotent, in his world of introspection. And—and—"Good gracious!" she muttered. That's what it was, of course. Rodin's "Thinker" was wearing a shirt!

She hurried forward and then stopped dead in utter astonishment, Rodin's "Thinker" calmly uncoiled itself from its pedestal, shook itself, stretched the stiffness out of its joints, and groped among the wet ferns for its coat.

Quite unperturbed at her presence the apparition waited till she caught up to him. He stood facing her, oddly calm and cool, a figure of immense depth of chest and breadth of shoulder, with a black beard and a livid claw mark across his face.

"Who on earth are you?" she demanded.

"I'm John Argle," he said. "Tell your dad I know who's playing tricks up at the castle. Tell him, too, that I'll get him before he does!"

John Argle made his announcement with all the flat calm of a man who, having pondered the subject well, says, "It looks like rain, I think."

For several seconds Lonora stared at him, not quite sure that she had heard aright. "You? You're John Argle!" she said at last. "Then you're the man who was badly knocked about last night, and was brought into the Castle half dazed."

"Yes, miss; that's me."

"What business have you in these grounds? How did you get in?"

"Missy, there's more ways of getting into Gairlie Park than climbing over the wall or walking through the lodge gates."

"What are you doing here?"

"I'm looking for someone."

"Who?"

"The man who killed Betty."

"What business is it of yours?"

Argle took a long sheath knife from his pocket and slid his thumb reflectively along its razor edge. Idly, almost unconsciously, his great thumb caressed the shining blade. Then his gaze travelled slowly to hers; he sought her eyes and held them, staring into her very thoughts with his own dark pupils expanding and glowing, smouldering up from their chill calm to a molten fire of unquenchable hate. Lonora stared back in a trance of fascination, half of fright and half of horror. She read in that bitter, wicked look all the hates of a million centuries, sublimated and crystallised into one tremendous demand for vengeance. She could see it there, ruthless, relentless, implacable.

Without a word he put the knife back into his pocket.

"*You* had better start talking about the weather, miss," he said.

But Lonora shook herself out of the miasma those merciless eyes had induced.

"You are aware that the police are already engaged on this case—that they are up at the Castle now?"

"Oh, yes; any amount of 'em."

"And that I can call them and have you arrested?"

"Not you, miss. Kennedy wouldn't arrest me any more than Stanforth would. They know me."

"But you are trespassing."

"They wouldn't arrest me for trespass," he chuckled wickedly. "There's no felonious intent!"

"How do you come to know Kennedy and Stanforth?"

"That's neither here nor there, miss. I do, and that's all. I know the Chief, too. He landed here about midnight. Him and the driver. I saw 'em out in the lane. Creeping up quietly by the hedge. And for an hour they sat, back of the Boundary Stone. Then they came in through the gap and went into the house."

Lonora looked at him in utter perplexity.

"I haven't the vaguest idea who or what you are," she confessed, "But I certainly think you owe me some explanation. Don't you?"

"No, miss; I don't. My business is *my* business—and those who don't poke their noses into it don't get their noses pulled."

"What were you doing on that pedestal?"

"Just waiting—and looking."

"Not a very remunerative occupation, is it?"

"You think not? Well, you take it from me, I saw more last night than Kennedy and Stanforth and all the gamekeepers put together. And if that walnut tree had only been ten yards farther east I'd have got him!"

"What has become of the statue?"

"I took it down. I'm using the pedestal as a watching post. A lot of people came past last night and never noticed me. I'll do it every night, too, till I get him."

"Where is the statue?"

"Down there in the rose clump."

"Hadn't you better put it back?"

"Yes, miss. I was going to. Just thought I'd hang on for another five minutes, to see if I could see anything when the light got stronger."

"Who helped you to cart it down there?"

"Helped me?" John Argle looked at her in mute surprise. "I'll show you who helps *me*," he said.

He turned and picked his way over the terraces to a thick clump of rose trees that grew in a wide circle at the bottom. And then Lonora was presented with a spectacle of such sheer colossal strength as she had never dreamed possible. It seemed incredible that such tremendous lifting power could have generated in a single human form.

John Argle took a stance across the statue—an unwieldy doubled-up thing that lacked all semblance of a decent grip or handhold—braced his feet firmly on the cropped turf, and bent down. He gripped it under the crook of the bent arm and the bowed head, and, with the muscles of his huge back constricting under his coat like flat snakes, slowly straightened himself. And as he came into the upright, Rodin's "Thinker" came up with him. With the same deliberate purposefulness he turned, and carrying the thing in his arms like a fantastically overgrown baby, walked steadily to the pedestal. There was no show, no pompous exhibition of braggadocio in the consciousness of his strength; just the bald, undeniable accomplishment of something he had already said he would do.

Lonora watched him with popping eyes. He got to the pedestal, and with a slight hitch of the hip, cocked the statute on the broad surface and balanced it there. Then with a clean jump from the rocks, he was up beside it, straightening it on the slab. When he had finished he stepped down, softly rubbing his hands.

"Good morning, miss," he said quietly and slouched off towards the Long Coppice.

And thereafter John Argle seemed to vanish as mysteriously as did the Castle marauder. Kennedy, who wanted him badly, hunted for him high and low. All his accustomed haunts in the village, and they were few enough, were sounded without avail. John Argle had taken himself off for reasons best known to his grim, dour self, and it seemed that only John Argle could find him.

The Chief was early astir. He had a quick breakfast with his host, at which they were joined by the two inspectors and Lonora, who related her adventure of the morning.

Lord Gairlie leaned across to the Chief with a look of puzzled inquiry. "Tell me," he said, "who is this John Argle?"

The Chief shook his head and laughed quietly.

"That's not for me to say, sir," he said. "He is in a somewhat difficult position, and it's not to be wondered at. His secret is his own. I should ask him yourself. He's quite a good sort at heart, and it is more than probable he would tell you quite frankly. But I should be breaking confidence badly if I betrayed it."

"I shall certainly ask him the moment I see him," declared Gairlie. "The fellow has a confounded impudence helping himself to the run of the grounds. How is it that the patrols didn't detain him?"

"Probably too quick for them," said the Chief dryly. "But you will be seeing quite a lot of John before this case finishes—or my estimate: the man is sadly astray."

But if John Argle had succeeded in removing himself from sight, there was someone else who seemed to have wiped himself off the face of the earth. And that was Jose Latta. He effaced himself. The constabulary of the whole county was out on his heels. Mounted men went out through the lanes and byways, prying into every likely hiding place for miles around. Latta was known to the police throughout the shire, and his apprehension was hourly expected. The countryside was scoured, searched and watched in every parish, but no news of his detention came through. Latta had wiped himself off the map. The strains of his wheezy organ were heard no more at the wayside inns.

The Chief and Kennedy went out in the afternoon to the little stone hut on the brow of the quarry, but though certain interesting evidence came to light there, the man they wanted was not on view.

The place was unhealthily airless and dark—Latta had caulked up the ventilation with old sacks and nailed boards across the apertures where the windows had been. The floor was littered with refuse, and the only article of furniture was a broken deal table in the corner, on which stood the organ-grinder's domestic effects. A kettle, a battered frying-pan, a tin bowl and some old crockery composed the lot. A billycan hung by the stone fireplace, across which were two iron bars. Latta's commissariat was equally elementary. A few stale crusts, some packets of soup powder, a broken bag of flour, a long string of onions, a tin accommodating a mixture of salt and pepper, and a piece of mildewed corned beef. That comprised his entire larder.

Kennedy pulled the bar out of a grate and prized away the boards covering the window. A broad beam of light fell athwart the cabin and lit up its darkest comer. It was Latta's sleeping quarters, as primeval an arrangement as the rest of the establishment. A heap of straw and dried bracken was strewn on the bare boards and over them a red horse-blanket, probably stolen, was laid.

A smaller heap of rough straw at the foot of it, littered with scraps of stale food, was presumably Jacko's resting-place.

"Filthy hole," commented the Chief.

Kennedy pointed to the head of the pallet. There were *two* pillows there, canvas bags stuffed with dried leaves. And on the far one was a bundle of tiny clothes such as one would put on a child of three.

The Chief leaned forward and poked at the bundle of clothes with his stick. There was a tiny woollen jacket, a blue knitted pullover, a romper suit and several vests and children's underclothes.

"Satisfied?" he asked, turning with a queer little smile to Kennedy.

"No!" muttered Kennedy, and went down on hands and knees beside the pallet. He threw off the rug and the old clothes and turned back the straw. Under the compress of the old bracken and stuff beneath, the rest of the evidence stood revealed. Practically everything stolen from Gairlie Castle during the past few months was lying there. The crimson table centres, the card-box, three red vases, a valuable piece of old blood-red. Italian majolica, several red ornaments, Delayn's technical treatise, Kennedy's own case of razors, and a whole assortment of things that had never been missed at all at the Castle. But one thing they searched for specially and failed to find and that was the red lacquer box which were stolen in Stanforth's presence the previous night. That particular box was not there, though they hunted for it high and low. Under the pillows at the head of the bed were more clothes, cut on the same lilliputian pattern, but of a different style entirely. These were miniature man's clothes, serge and tweed, with shirts and shoes and collars and ties to match. There was a walking stick, too, eleven inches high—and the whole miscellany was offset and left doubly puzzling by two hats and a cap that would have fitted a quite ordinary head.

"Satisfied yet?" queried the Chief.

"Not yet, sir," grunted Kennedy, throwing armfuls of the bracken out of doors. "Just let me get this filth cleared away. Then I'll have another go. Coming up interesting, isn't it?"

"Decidedly so. Floorboards and firegrate now, I presume?"

"That's the ticket, sir" Kennedy was busy with the firebar again, tapping it gently over the floorboards. He found a location almost immediately, a board that struck a hollow note. He thrust the edge of the bar between the planks, wriggled it into position, and prised the board up.

The Chief stepped over the hole, and bending down, peered in. The remainder of the spurious Gairlie Rubies lay there in a neat nest, winking up at them. Kennedy dived his hands in and pulled up a double handful of the glittering things.

The corsage, the tiara, and the great necklace shimmered in his fingers like blobs of living fire.

"That's the chunk of evidence I wanted," said Kennedy with a satisfied nod. "That pins it right down to where we want it."

"More than enough for me," agreed the Chief. "'Phone for the warrant to be made out as soon as we get back. Possibly he is already detained by now."

"One thing's certain," said Kennedy. "Latta didn't come back here last night, else he'd have cached the red lacquer box. Looks as though he's winded us. Taken to his heels. In that case, we're in for a weary search."

"These clothes," said the Chief, stirring them over with his toe. "They could very well be worn by a trained monkey—don't you think?"

"Quite possible, sir. But if it *is* a monkey I'll lay a thousand to one it isn't Jacko."

"Is it feasible that he has two? He is cunning enough to play his little game like that—roam round the countryside with one by day, and raid the Castle at night with the other—the specially trained one."

"M'm—yes—it's a possibility," admitted Kennedy. "But it don't seem to fit in with my opinions somehow. No monkey ever wore a hat as big as that or boots as little as those. Monkeys have got long flat feet; those shoes are small enough for a Chinese woman."

"You see what I'm driving at, Kennedy," said the Chief quietly. "This weird collection of clothes may be purely a bluff. Exactly the kind of thing a shrewd criminal brain like Latta's would plan. You remember how he spoofed you with the monkey in the 'Castle Arms.' That was done deliberately. He hoodwinked the villagers and got them all talking about the monkey. You fell for it. Depend upon it, the monkey is connected. Otherwise he would have abandoned it."

Kennedy scratched his head. "Blessed if I can see it," he muttered.

"Look at it this way. Latta is clever enough to think out a new criminal device—a method by which some of the best brains of the Yard are completely baffled. He has the nerve to carry out his ideas; even had nerve enough to attack again in the midst of that wild uproar last night, with sixty armed men on his heels. On the top of all that—what? All this accumulation of evidence which we have found here. The rubies, the spoils of his long raids at the Castle, the baby-clothes, the grown-up apparel. Do you think Latta would dream of leaving all this damning evidence lying about here for anyone to find—unless he was deliberately throwing dust in our eyes? Would anyone but an idiot—or a super-craftsman—hide stolen goods under a loose two-foot plank? Would anyone but a maniac—or a master—leave such an astonishing clue lying about as those weird clothes? Of course he wouldn't. He's simply hitting us in the nose with a particularly smelly red herring. Doing his best to send us scampering off on another false scent, wasting our time and energy. Do you see now?

"What I can't get over," said Kennedy, struggling against the Chief's cold logic, "is that Latta *has* got something with him, something small and strong, and able to get about of its own accord. And it goes up to the Castle with him and gets in at the windows. Stanforth saw it."

"*Does* it get in at the windows? It doesn't get in at the boudoir windows. They are double-locked and had not been opened. It didn't get in at the library windows, because there are no windows in the library."

"Well, sir, there's two pillows, and a separate place for the monkey."

"Naturally. He wouldn't lay out a dummy for us with the clothes and fail to corroborate his evidence. Pack up all that stuff and bring it back to the Castle for examination. Our job now is to concentrate on José Latta."

But the concentration of the drive against Latta was not so simple as it sounded. The afternoon came and went without news of the organ-grinder. Neither he, nor his organ, nor his monkey were seen anywhere in the whole run of the county. The police scouts were doubled as the afternoon wore on and still there was no result. And then the aftermath of dusk had gripped the countryside again, leaving the Castle a sentinel of gloom awaiting immobile for the fresh fears of a new night.

The guard went on duty again an hour after darkness had fallen. Silent figures stole out one by one. They melted into the black darkness and became one with the night.

Inside the patrols picked up their positions and began their silent sentry-go. All through the night it continued, a ceaseless passage of sentries from point to point, from door to door, from landing to landing.

Midnight struck, and the Chief decided for a few hours' sleep. Lord Gairlie had had camp beds made up for the three of them in the main hall, close up to their job.

"You turn in, Stanforth," he said. "Kennedy, you carry on till four. Then call me and I will relieve you."

Kennedy sat out his lonely watch at the big table; going up on the landings at every half-hour to take reports from the controls there, and every now and then he made a silent crawl round the watch points outside. Every man was on the alert, wide-eyed and watching from behind the back-sight of a gun.

"Looks to me as though he's too fly to try anything tonight, sir," whispered one from a deep hole under a box hedge.

"Kick that idea out of your head," hissed back Kennedy. "That's what he wants you to think. Keep your eye skinned raw."

At four o'clock he called his Chief and crawled to bed with his clothes on.

The Chief took a cold water wash and pushed his head under the tap. The country air had rammed sleep into his eyes. He made a quick tour of the inside patrols, and putting on an overcoat, went out to get a freshener of cold night air.

Quietly he made his way round by the rose garden to a point where there was no patrol within twenty yards of him on either side. He had noted that as the weakest link in the chain, and he sat down on a garden seat, partly to cover the hiatus, partly because he wanted to have a hard, uninterrupted think.

He had been there for about ten minutes, silent and motionless in the darkness, when there came a faint sound from somewhere behind him. He listened. The sound was repeated; the stealthy rustle of footsteps over the wet grass.

The Chief screwed round silently on the garden seat and peered into the dark. The sound ceased and an ominous silence hung over the gloom of the rose bushes, as though the unseen walker had suddenly sensed the detective's presence and had come to a dead stop where the shadows lay faintest.

Suddenly he saw him; a doubled-up patch of utter blackness at the end of the clump of rose bushes. It was a man; a well-set-up figure of a man, judging from the bulk of his outline, and he was down on one knee, apparently tying a bootlace. In a little while he got up unconcernedly and began walking again, heading almost directly for the right of the garden seat. The Chief waited for him without the flicker of an eye, just turning slowly enough to keep him in full view as he came up. The man seemed to be making for the gravel path—an offshoot from the main driveway that led directly up to the great entrance doors of the Castle itself, and from the line of his approach it was obvious that he was actually making for the Castle.

He was picking his way with deft care and he seemed to know his way about with remarkable ease. Twice he stepped over the ends of garden beds that were practically invisible, and once he made a slight detour to avoid the iron cover of a hosepipe connection. The Chief eyed him fixedly.

The figure looked uncommonly tall and workmanlike, and seemed to loom bigger and more primed with strength the nearer it got.

And there was another nasty thought trickling through the detective's mind. Whoever the strange visitor was, he seemed to have an inside knowledge of the organisation of the outer guard, for it was apparent that he had deliberately chosen that weak point at which to break through.

The unknown was within three yards of him when the Chief pulled his bluff. He suddenly snatched his hand to his hip and hissed out a sharp

"Hands up!"

The figure jerked back for the fraction of a second in sheer astonishment.

"Put 'em up!" commanded the Chief.

The visitor seemed to collect his scattered facilities in a single flying grab.

"Not darn likely!" he muttered, and made a headlong plunge past the detective, with the sudden kickstart of a man trained to the minute. But as he went hurtling by the Chief jumped after him, thrust out a firm hand that gripped like the claw of a hawk on the flying instep, and braced his whole strength backwards. The intruder pitched over on his shoulders and turned a complete somersault with the detective still hanging on like a leech. There was a convulsive pull from the prone man's foot, a vicious tug that tore the boot free and ripped bits of skin from the restraining hand.

But the Chief went at him with a Rugby tackle, collaring low and falling with his weight. And as he fell he sent up a shout that brought answering bails booming through the darkness.

"Let up, you fool!" snarled the voice, and with a tremendous heave he writhed round on the ground and got a grip on the detective's shoulders. Much to his amazement, the Chief found his body being turned; slowly, but with inexorable sureness, his hold was broken and the stranger sprang to his feet.

Sounds of running footsteps were flying from right and left through the darkness. The unknown, with a final shove at the clawing hands of the Chief, took to his heels and ran.

"Over there! To your right!" yelled the Chief, rolling to his knees. "Shoot at him—stop him!"

The running feet swerved off in the direction of the streaking figure. One firing from the hip, sent a gunshot shattering and echoing among the trees. The running man began doubling and twisting at terrific speed in and out among the flowerbeds. In five seconds he was lost to sight, swallowed up in the encompassing blackness.

"Quick! To the Castle! Surround the walls!" The Chief was running as hard as he could lift his legs, and the others came pounding along in his wake. But the intruder was in ahead of them. He had cut across by the statue of "*Le Penseur*" and as he careered by the "Thinker" chuckled softly to itself.

Other units of the guard were hurrying in from distant points, shouting to know what the firing was all about. They joined in the chase and went rushing on towards the Castle. Once they saw him, and only once, a black figure pelting along at a whale of a pace towards the Castle steps.

And there they lost him. They spread out in a wide chain and surrounded the building, eyes continually on the move and guns at the ready. But there was neither sight nor sound of him. He had reached the walls a good hundred yards ahead of the hunt, and the moment he reached them he vanished. The patrols inside, alarmed by the firing in the grounds, were on the alert, and both Kennedy and Stanforth were up and doing. Kennedy was standing just inside the entrance doors, a service Webley in his hands.

The Chief rushed up the steps. "Anyone come in during the last minute?" he demanded.

"Not so much as a fly!" declared Kennedy.

The Chief turned and pelted down the steps.

"Lights! He's climbing the walls!" he yelped.

But they were too late. There was a black figure going up the ivy, hand over hand, as cat-footed as a monkey. It worked along to the right, and when the hold of the ivy on the wall petered out, it fastened on to the great square stack-pipe that carried the storm-water from the eaves to the drains below. Then, swinging out fearlessly above the abyss of shadows, it made a foothold on the lower battlements, balanced itself precariously for a moment, and ran along the foot-wide parapet, jumping lightly over the deep embrasures as it came to them. And by the time the sickly glow of the lanterns shone out far below it was beyond their range by a hundred feet, a vague, unseen blot of invisibility high up against the ceiling of the night, reaching up to the coping overhead and swinging up to it with agile ease.

There was no more sleep in the Castle that night. The entire male staff was turned out and set to work on a continuous hunt through the rooms. The Castle was searched from cellar to roof. Not a corridor was left unpatrolled, not an apartment was left unvisited for more than ten seconds at a time. To aid the search all the lights were switched on and the whole Castle swam in a blaze of radiance. It was done as much to assist the outer guard as those inside. With a stream of light pouring from every window it was impossible for the intruder to get back the way he had come. The whole sweep of the walls on all sides was sufficiently illuminated to show up even a pigeon or two that nested on the battlements. No living thing could have got out of one of those windows or crawled back down the walls undetected.

For an hour the search went on, and then Stanforth came flying down the stairs. He beckoned to the Chief. "Quick, up in the attic," he whispered, and then went leaping back up the stairs again.

Up went the Chief, toiling up the endless flights; up and up into the silence that reigned at the top of the house. He breasted the top flight and emerged on the dusty, cobwebby sweep of the attic landing. Stanforth his torch shining down at the floor in a wide circle of light, was motioning him from the far end. He picked his way among the beams and out-jutting timbers to where his assistant stood, making signs for silence, in the last doorway on the right.

The Chief approached, and Stanforth switched his light into the room, directing it square on the bed in the corner.

The Chief peeped in. Sleeping there, calm and serene as a babe, was Tommy Delayn. His clothes were all neatly folded over the back of a chair, and he had laid out a change of linen for the morning. And—impudence upon impudence—his boots were calmly stuck outside the door to be cleaned. Troubled by the glare of light on his face, he stirred in his sleep and half turned over.

Muttering unnameable things under his breath, the Chief shook him roughly by the shoulder. Delayn sat up blinking. Stanforth had followed the Chief in, and the light of the torch was full in his eyes.

"Wha—what's the game?" he growled.

"Are you the fool who passed me in the grounds an hour ago?" snapped the Chief.

"Wooden be 'tall surprised," said Tommy sleepily! "Highly probable because I don't think *you* would ever pass *me*. And for the love of mud take that darned light out o' my eyes."

Stanforth still stood there, his torch full on, its beam directed square on Delayn's features. Tommy leaned up and, with an irritated sweep of his fist, knocked the thing spinning across the room.

The torch was smashed against the opposite wall and in the pitch darkness that fell Tommy turned over to go to sleep again.

The Chief shook him.

"How did you get in?" he demanded.

"Floated up the wall," came the semi-somnolent answer.

"Why?"

"Hate waking the servants at this ungodly hour. And my way saves wearing out the carpets."

"Where have you been?"

"To London, dear—to see the Queen. G'way and lemme sleep." Delayn coiled himself up comfortably under the blankets.

"My son, I'll have a few words to say to you in the morning," snorted the Chief angrily. "Stanforth, you'll stay here with him for the rest of the night." He stamped to the door.

As he went out a soft voice from the bed murmured: "When you get down, tell Kennedy that things have improved so much that I'm thinking of buying another car. You might tell Lord Gairlie that, too."

For the rest of the night Stanforth sat on a chair at the foot of the bed while the minutes ticked slowly by. Tommy slept peacefully. From his easy breathing and quiet stillness in the bed, no unpleasant dreams disturbed his slumbers.

Daylight came, and with it the cessation of the vigil in Gairlie Castle. The guards were withdrawn and crawled away to get a few hours needed sleep.

Delayn woke as the clock was striking seven. He yawned and stretched and clambered out of bed.

"Hallo!" he said, blinking at Stanforth, "What's doing?"

"Finished with that bed?" growled his guard wearily.

"Sure. Hop on!"

The detective flopped himself down and was asleep almost as soon as his head touched the pillow. Delayn grinned and reached out for a pair of spring developers.

Lord Gairlie was at breakfast with Kennedy and the Chief. A secretary was opening a huge batch of mail, passing the more important ones over to him. While he was reading one with frowning eyes and a troubled face, an express telegram was brought in. It had been hung up at the village post office overnight, having apparently arrived very late.

Gairlie opened and scanned it. The frown increased and a harassed look came into his eyes. He turned to the secretary.

"Have you a letter there from 'Silk Limited'?" he asked, and passed the wire over to the Chief. "I'm afraid I shall have to leave you for a while," he said. "Read that."

Reference to letter, it ran; *imperative you come to London immediately. Urgent. Board meeting called for midday. Signed Lister.*

"Lister," he explained, "is executive manager at Silk Limited, the most dreadful failure with which it has ever been my misfortune to be connected."

Gairlie rustled the telegram. "This is dreadful," he said. "The factories stand there idle—half a million sunk in plant alone. We've been staving off for months hoping our chemists would find the way out. But this means that Lister can hold out no longer. I'm in the worst stewpan of my life."

"Here is the letter, sir." The secretary passed it across. It set Gailie's pulse jumping, so vastly different was it from what he expected. He pushed back his plate and read it through, calling hurriedly for a big cat to be got ready with all speed.

My Lord,

I am writing in some urgency, and I trust a certain disjointedness will be excused.

This morning I received a visit from the representative of a firm styling itself "The Untearable Silk Manufacturing Company." There is no such firm registered at Somerset House, neither does it appear in any of the trade directories. He seemed a most unusual young gentleman, with apparently not the faintest idea of business, but a certain assurance of manner that induced me to listen to him. When I taxed him with the extreme anonymity of his alleged firm, he calmly assured me that quite apart from not being in the trade directories, it isn't even in the telephone book. He also added that it hadn't got an address yet, either, but that the defect would be remedied as soon as he had collected a few partners.

He explained that up to the present he alone was "The Untearable Silk Manufacturing Company," and added that he was desirous of doing business with us. Against that he displayed a quite unique ignorance, and seemed surprised to know that Silk Limited could not possibly do business with a non-existent company.

Subsequently he produced a small roll of silk, and handed it to me for inspection. I may say at once that it is really wonderful stuff, an entirely new fabric, that has not yet been released to the general market. That he assured me, was his own production. I know every artificial silk in the world, and I can positively state that the silk he handed me is something new. The quality is superfine, and, I am quite sure, will take dyes perfectly. He calls it "untearable," and to all fair limits it is a justifiable description. It is delicate and fine, and what is infinitely more to the point, it is double-woven. *This means that the fabric will not "ladder." I tested it severely, and though, under pressure, a thread broke here and there, there was no sign of a continuation of the split. A tear simply remains a tear, the same as in a serge or a worsted.*

Naturally I was intensely interested, and interrogated him at great length. It became apparent that although he had but a child's conception of commercial methods, he was a master of the chemical end. His formulæ were all convincingly logical, and I could find no flaw. This process, fully developed, will turn out a better silk even than the raw sample he showed me, and it will be thirty per cent, cheaper than any artificial silk now on the market. *This is a tremendous statement, but according to the documents at present in my hands, it is more than feasible.*

I asked for his business reference, for it was obvious that the fabric had been made by an outside firm to his specifications. He gave me Hallorans, of Manchester, a very likely connection indeed.

I immediately secured a first option on the production of silk on terms to be agreed. Also I have wired Hallorans for full details. If their reply is what I hope, I will telegraph you, and would advise you to hold yourself in readiness to come to London at a moment's notice. The gentleman in question—he gives his name as Mr. D. Lane—is willing to attend any meeting we may convene. But I think the board should meet first and discuss the whole position. I have retained his test roll of silk, together with his formulæ.

I am, my lord,
Yours faithfully,
J. J. LISTER.

Lord Gairlie put the letter down with a shaking hand. His face had drained white. Lister was a shrewd man—he would not put his name to a letter like that unless he had conviction to back it up. If this hope held good, salvation was holding out both hands to him. The reaction after months of strain told on him badly. He sat back trembling.

"Anything wrong, sir?" asked the Chief in alarm.

"Good heavens! No," said Gairlie quietly. "It looks as though everything is going to come right at last."

Gairlie re-read the letter. In ten minutes he was speeding to London in a fast car.

When he arrived at the handsome buildings in Cornhill his fellow directors were awaiting him, and he went straight into the chair.

At the head of the table in front of him he found a neat pile of documents—all perfect typewritten copies of the formulae and various papers which Mr. Lane had left, alongside them a roll of raw silk. As to the quality of the silk Gairlie did not pretend to be able to form a judgment; but it certainly looked as good as any of the raw silks that he had seen.

He opened the meeting without any beating about the bush by calling in the factory manager to make a statement.

Lister was a dapper little man with a sharp, almost perky quickness of gesture and mannerism of the London sparrow.

"Gentlemen," he said, "you are all acquainted with the gist of the matter that has occasioned this meeting, for I wrote you all the same letter, These are the further details. Last night I received a telegram from Hallorans, of Manchester, confirming The Untearable Silk Manufacturing Company's connection with them in a professionally experimental capacity. They mentioned that further particulars were being mailed that night. I have received them since. Briefly, from what Hallorans say, Mr. Lane's claims are, if anything, too modest.

"The vendor's experiments with Hallorans have extended over a period of months. And the process is finally perfected.

All that remains to do is to set about the manufacture of the fabric exactly as it stands. I stayed in the office throughout the night working on these specifications. Gentlemen, these formulae are not only workable, they are flawless. Any of you with technical knowledge will realise that the whole thing, has been worked out with undeniable skill and astonishing ingenuity."

"What is your candid impression, Lister?" asked Gairlie.

"That we should buy this process whatever the cost. If we turn it down we shall be flying in the face of Providence. He is asking £100,000 flat for the sole manufacturing rights, a seat on the Board, and ten pert cent of the net profits. My lord, it's cheap at the price. Dirt cheap. The young fool doesn't know. There's millions in this. Other firms will gnaw their own gums when we put this silk on the market. It's the biggest, surest winner you've ever known."

"How soon can you make a full investigation, with all tests, and prest a detailed report?" asked Gairlie.

"A matter of forty-eight hours, sir. I've already mastered the system and I fully understand the process. The rest is simply proving out on our own plant what Hallorans have already done. According to Mr. Lane, the process will be cheaper by thirty per cent, than any other artificial silk yet manufactured. I would say that, manufactured on a big scale, the percentage will be nearer forty than thirty. Gentlemen, it is my studied conviction that this fabric will give us a monopoly of the artificial silk world."

Lister opened a little travelling case that he had placed on the table. He shot out of it an assortment of little rolls of silk of beautiful colours, some extremely pale and delicate, others rich and full toned.

"Gentlemen, those colours were infused into the substance before it was even made into silk," said the manager quietly. "Look at the colours. Look at the sheen. Real silk, untouched, hasn't a quarter of the luster of that. It is the dyeing that breaks down the lustre of artificial silks—in our case much of our standard output will never see the dyer's vats. Those rolls arrived this morning from Hallorans. They represent Mr. Lane's final experiments."

With such a report from their head technician, the question of further proceedings was never in doubt.

The head of Silk Limited drove back to Hampshire with a greater peace in his soul than he had known for many a weary month.

Evening was falling when the gates of the Castle loomed ahead, a peaceful evening full of quiet hush and faint sweet scents. He stopped his car at the gates and got out. A quiet walk up the great drive would be a pleasant prelude to dinner and the news of the day's events at the Castle.

Gairlie turned the first bend in the drive, where the great quarter-mile of double chestnuts gave way to a line of giant oaks. The Castle was visible through the trees, a dim patch of grey, picked out here and there with the yellow glitters of lighted windows.

Leaning against one of the oaks, one hand idly on a hip, was a deep-chested figure of a man. He was staring hard in the direction of the Castle his back turned to Gairlie, motionless, like a figure carved in stone, At first Gairlie thought it was one of his gamekeepers out on a silent prowion his own, but there was something so totally unfamiliar about the broad uncouth shoulders that he crossed over towards him.

The figure turned and touched a low-drawn slouch hat that seemed to cover all of his face except the end of a blunt nose and a massy black beard.

"Good evening, sir," he said quietly. "A grand evening for finding what we're looking for."

Gairlie surveyed him with a slight frown.

"You are the mysterious John Argle, aren't you?" he asked.

"Yes, sir, that's me."

For a few seconds Lord Gairlie eyed the man reflectively. Then, very suddenly, he asked: "Who are you? Nobody here seems to know much about you, except that you manage to exist without much physical effort."

"Well, there's nothing much wrong with that, sir. A man can keep himself to himself without bein' counted a sinner for it."

"Oh, quite. You've every right to preserve as close a silence as you wish about yourself. I admit. I'm simply asking you out of curiosity. Your actions entitle me to some sort of an explanation surely? You appear to trespass in here at your own sweet will; you remove a statue from its pedestal, occupy its place all night, and replace it in the morning; you break in when you think you will, and are heard flying through my woods at dead of night, and are brought into my house half unconscious. Tonight I find you almost hidden among the trees, staring at my house as though you were contemplating something decidedly unpleasant—on the whole, I think I'm entitled to know what it's all about, don't you?"

Argle looked away over his shoulder. New lights were springing to life in the rooms of Gairlie Castle, and he watched them for some seconds as I though making mental notes of their positions.

"No," he said, after a long silence. "I'm doing no harm to your property, except treading down a few blades of grass."

"I'm not objecting to your coming in here. Don't think that. But there is something unexplained—unsatisfactory—I might even say dangerous—about your presence here. You admit that nobody in the locality knows much about you and yet there are some, to my definite knowledge, who apparently know quite a good deal about you."

"Friends of yours, maybe?"

"Yes and no. There are, for instance, Messrs. Kennedy and Stanforth. They seem to know you fairly well. You also appear to be known to the Chief of the Criminal Investigation Department."

"Oh, *them*," said John Argle, and all the disinterest was back in his voice. "Oh, yes, I know *them* all right."

Gairlie eyed him squarely. "Have you ever been in prison?" he asked.

Argle took out a much-burned pipe and began filling it.

"Never been in front of a magistrate in my life," he announced.

But Gairlie was not to be fobbed off with a half answer.

"I asked you if you had ever been in prison," he repeated.

John Argle nodded off-handedly, and thumbed a plug of tobacco into charred bowl.

"Oh, I see," said Gairlie, a burst of understanding breaking across his brain.

"No, you don't," said Argle, deliberately striking a match. "That's where you're wrong, sir. That's what they all think. And they're as wrong as you."

"I'm sorry—I naturally thought—"

"I know you did. And I'd already said I'd never been in front of a magistrate. If you know law, you'd have knew what I meant." He puffed away stolidly at his pipe.

"Well, then, if there's nothing unpleasant about it, what's your objection to telling me?"

"Unpleasant?" Argle puffed his pipe and pondered the word. "Ain't sure," he declared. "Word gets around, you know, sir. And it ain't nice to be known to the police the way I am."

"John Argle, word will never get around from me," said Gairlie quietly.

The grim figure looked up at a wood-pigeon, high in the dusk, making frantic efforts to escape the relentless swoops of a peregrine falcon that had cut it out from the sanctuary of the trees.

"Well, I don't mind telling you, sir, if you put it like that," he said "Not that I've got much to be ashamed of. But mind, it's just between you and me. I've had to shift diggin's too often about it already."

Lord Gairlie bent his head forward and John Argle whispered softly in his ear.

Gairlie slowly pulled himself upright again.

"So that's it, is it?" he breathed.

"Yes, sir, that's it. And now you know why I keep myself to myself and—come in here o' nights to do a bit o' thinkin'." The bearded lips cracked into a humourless grin and John Argle, raising his hat for a brief second to intimate the complete termination of the conversation, turned back and leaned against the tree, staring at the silhouette of the fast-fading Castle.

Lord Gairlie, his face a mask of sudden understanding, thrust his hands back into his pockets and resumed his walk. He understood then why neither Kennedy nor the Chief himself would have much to say about John Argle, understood why they accepted him in such good faith the moment they met him, and realised fully why he had seen fit to change his name.

And, clearest of all, he understood the real reason for the fierce desire burning in his breast like a white-hot coal, the ferocious determination to run to earth the man who had murdered Betty Ralston.

IX

The inquest on Betty Ralston revealed nothing. The doctor himself conducted the post mortem, and a government pathologist came down to investigate. But their combined evidence at the adjourned inquest took the sum-total of knowledge not more than one inch further.

Doctor Mabey assured the coroner that there was nothing which, within his knowledge, could have accounted for her death. The suggestion of heart-failure was ruled out. Had there been anything unsound about Betty Halston's heart he would have discovered it long ago. And the post mortem showed that the heart was as sound as the doctor's diagnosis. All the other organs were equally virile. Analysis had revealed no trace of poison. Both he and the government pathologist had applied every test known to medical science, and the result was nil.

The only possible clue, and that a very faint one, was in the condition of the lungs. The lung tissue appeared to have been slightly scorched, but the defect was so slight that it was purely a matter of speculations as to whether the injury was of recent origin or not. It was simply that the finer fibres were withered, a condition which might quite conceivably have been caused by continual cigarette smoking.

Death, in his opinion, had been instantaneous. The heart had stopped on a full beat at the height of contraction, and the ventricles were empty. Life must have ceased so abruptly, and the heart became so instantaneously rigid, that it had not relaxed a fraction after its last beat.

The coroner put the question: "In your studied opinion, was death natural or not?"

"Decidedly not," said Mabey. "I am convinced that Betty Halston was killed by some outside agency, the precise nature of which I cannot identify. I tend to the belief that the condition of the lungs is not unconnected with it. The rest is just mystery."

The jury brought in a verdict of "Wilful murder against some person or persons unknown."

Latta continued to be as elusive as the shadow of a ghost. He was neither seen nor heard, and slowly the conviction grew that he had fled the country. Nobody had caught so much as a glimpse of him, since that fateful night after Betty Halston died.

The only one who was still definitely convinced that the man was still lying low somewhere in the castle precincts was the Chief himself.

The Chief believed that Latta was a man, who, once having got his tentacles on to a proposition, would never let go. And his surmise was vindicated in a tragic way when the Silent Death stalked through the halls of Gairlie Castle for the second time.

It was Harris, the butler, who brought the news. He was going the rounds of the rooms one night—nearly a month after the first murder—taking hot drinks to the guard on duty. He opened a door on the second landing, and the tray dropped with a crash from his shivering fingers.

The big table in the centre was of dark old Jacobean oak. And between that table and the fireplace, flat on his face and motionless, was the prone body of a man.

Harris knew the man well. It was Ferguson, one of the men sent down from the Yard when Kennedy first came on the scene. Harris had discovered in him a common link of union, for each had come from the same hometown; and a keen friendship had sprung up between the pair.

The butler, with his eyes popping in his head, stood in the doorway, half-fearfully whispering the fallen man's name. The crash of the falling tray had jerked into life the nerves of the patrol on the landing. Hoarse breathless cries were calling from the main hall. Harris stepped forward a yard, treading heavily on broken glass. It powdered under his boots with a sharp crackling noise, and he stopped dead, swallowing at a dry lump that had somehow got into his throat.

Instinctively he knew that Ferguson was dead. There was death in the stiff poise of the head, death in the stiffness of the tense body and the out-flung, inert hands. And something that was deep-rooted in the very fabric of him warned him to keep away. There was tragedy and horror in that lifeless thing on the floor.

Hurrying footsteps sounded along the corridor, muffled on the thick pile carpets,

"Hey! Harris! Anything wrong?" A man's strained voice barked the query ahead. In that atmosphere of apprehension such things as suddenly crashing trays jarred raspingly on nerves already worn to shreds.

Harris backed out to the landing as the first of the hurrying guard cannoned into him. Speechless, the butler pointed a stubby forefinger at the body on the floor, and looked bleakly at the guard. The man peered in and staggered back. "My Gawd!" he gasped. "They're at it again!"

Then turning, he stuck his head over the balustrade. Kennedy, directly underneath, was forcefully demanding to know what in blazes all the row was about. Over in the corner the Chief was just rolling off his camp bed, rubbing his eyes.

"What's up, Milligan?" demanded Kennedy.

"Come up at once, sir—Ferguson's got his," called the guard.

Stanforth was already hustling up the stairs. Kennedy followed, suddenly grim and full of urgent action.

He pushed in through the door hot on the heels of Stanforth, stepping wide over the broken glass. They saw the prone body, stretched out as flat as though it had died in falling—and fallen so stiffly that not even a knee had bent.

The Chief was beside them almost before they realised it, down on one knee, turning the body over. There was no mark on the chalky face, no wound or scar that would have told how death had come to him.

"It's—it's the Silent Death again." quavered Harris fearfully.

The Chief wheeled on one knee.

"Get *out*," he snapped. "Get out and stay out! And if you open your mouth about this to the women servants I'll flay the living hide off you."

But there was no need for Harris to open his mouth. The news had gone through the house like a whirlwind. Frightened groups of servants were gathering in the corners of the landings, whispering fearfully among themselves. Half-formed fears, repressed for weeks, sprang up anew. Gairlie Castle was a house of death. The ghastly Thing that haunted the castle walls and scaled impossible heights without effort was spawn of the devil himself. It was neither man nor animal nor anything else that could stand in the light of day, and to see it was to die. First Betty Halston and then Ferguson.

Kennedy sent hurriedly for Lord Gairlie.

The Chief stood up and sniffed the air.

"Smell anything?" he asked, and sniffed again.

"There's a bit of a queer, sweetish smell," admitted Stanforth. "But I think it's natural to this room. There's a sandalwood box over there on that cabinet—I think that's got something to do with it."

"No," said the Chief softly. "Something sharper, more pungent. Do you get it, Kennedy?"

Kennedy shook his head. "Afraid I don't, sir," he said. "But I've been smoking all the evening."

"Faintly sulphurish, Kennedy, like the after-whiff of a match that has just been struck. Get it now?"

"No, sir, I don't," said Kennedy truthfully.

"H'm! Queer—very queer indeed. I could swear I get a tiny irritation of the nose if I inhale deeply."

He steered away from the fallen figure and surveyed the room. The windows were shut and the clips fast locked on the inside. He tried them all, and it was obvious that the windows had not the remotest connection with this new tragedy. Two of them were so caked with paint that they refused to open at all, the other two only came open after a violent effort.

"Anybody gone for the doctor?" asked the Chief, closing the windows.

"Yes, sir, Doctor Mabey has been 'phoned for," said one of the patrol.

"When was this man last seen alive?" asked the Chief.

"I saw him myself at eight o'clock," said Kennedy. "When he went on duty. I detailed him for this room myself. Ferguson was specially keen, and I've always had a good man in here ever since we adopted the system of stationary guards. This room is on a direct line with the section where things are most likely to happen. The library is almost immediately below and the room exactly above this was where Stanforth actually saw the Black Arm creep in."

"This room has been visited before, hasn't it?" inquired the Chief.

"Yes, sir. It was from this room that a red wooden cardbox was stolen two months ago. And just before the theft of the rubies a bunch of tulips disappeared from that window seat."

Kennedy was kneeling by the body.

"Gosh! That's odd." he breathed. "His tie, sir! It's changed colour while we've been talking. Look—it's turned red!"

"Devil take me!" muttered the Chief. "It was a sort of dullish brown when I turned him over."

"And look here!" Kennedy was bending low, examining the ends of the trousers under a magnifying glass. Presently he felt in his pocket for a tiny pair of tweezers. He picked something out of the fabric and held it to the light.

"Glass!" he said. "There's a lot more here. Splintered and driven into the clothing."

The Chief went out to the landing, where all the guard on duty on that floor were gathered.

"Who was the last man to patrol this landing?" he demanded.

"I did, sir, myself." It was Mavis, the man in charge on the second landing.

"How long since?"

"Barely twenty minutes, sir. I opened the door and looked right in. He gave me the O.K."

"Was he all right, then?"

"Quite, sir."

"What was he doing?"

"Sitting on the edge of that big table there—staring hard at the window." The Chief took Mavis inside and closed the door.

"Now look here, Mavis," he said. "This thing is getting out of perspective. Unless we get to the bottom of it—quickly—we shall have more trouble on our hands than we know what to do with. Now *think*—and answer these questions as clearly as you can. To begin with, your table at the head of the stairs is not more than twenty yards from this room, is it?"

"No more than seventeen full paces, sir. I've tried it."

"And this door was open?"

"Yes, sir. About a foot."

"Very well, then—in the silence that has reigned in this house for the last month you would be practically bound to hear any noise in this room, wouldn't you?"

"Couldn't very well help it, sir."

"*Did* you hear any sort of a noise whatever, during the last twenty minutes?"

"Not a sound, sir."

"Think. Think back. The sound of a window being opened, the faint tinkle of fine glass breaking—it would be no more than a vague little 'pop'—you would surely hear that from where you were, with your ears tuned to catch the faintest sound?"

"I should have heard it all right, sir, if it had happened, but I didn't hear anything."

"Not even the sound of a falling body?"

"No, sir—not a thing."

"But Ferguson is a big man. There would have been a heavy fall when he went down."

Mavis looked helplessly at his Chief. "I can't help it, sir," he said worriedly. "I didn't hear a sound. I'd say so, if I had."

The Chief turned away with a harassed look. There was absolutely nothing in the room that could give him the faintest clue to the enigma. The windows he had already discounted. Betty Halston had met her death in the library, which was entirely innocent of any kind of a window; and from that it was obvious that windows played no part in this campaign of silent murder. Against that there was the unshakable testimony of Mavis, one of the steadiest men in the whole contingent. Mavis had heard nothing—the guard had seen nothing. It was impossible for anyone to get in through that door without being seen. Anyone or any *thing* crawling along that landing would have been instantly visible to a dozen pairs of eyes. Mavis would have had him—or it—in view the whole time. The puzzle became more and more baffling.

He went over to the fallen man. The same traces of shock and sudden horror were there, printed on the dead features at the moment of death, that were present on the face of Betty Halston. There was the same acute dilation of the eyes, the same look of quick fright and stiffening of the muscles, as though to brace against a sudden, unexpected blow.

Very carefully he unfastened the dead man's tie and took it off. It was just an ordinary tie such as one could purchase in almost any haber-dashers, and it had been tied in an ordinary sailor knot. He held it under the glare of a table lamp.

The oddity about it was that only parts of it had changed colour—those parts that were exposed to the light when the tie was actually being worn. The method of wearing the tie could be traced in the thick creases. The part that went under the coat collar, the broad tails that were hidden by the waistcoat and the parts of the actual knot itself that were covered by the outer fold, were still intact so far as the odd discoloration was concerned. All these parts were still of a soft chocolatey brown. It was only the lengths that were visible to the eye when the tie was in use, that had changed colour. Those lengths were now a deep uneven red, streaked across by the watermark lines of the pattern.

The Chief ran his fingers through his hair. "What colour was Betty Halston's dress?" he asked.

"Plum colour," said Kennedy. "And if you ask me, the same poison that killed Betty Halston killed Ferguson. Same poison discoloured her dress and that tie. There'll be scorching of the lung tissue in this case same as in hers."

"Mabey said that the scorching might have been caused by excessive smoking," commented the Chief.

"John Argle himself told me the girl had never smoked in her life," said Kennedy bluntly. "The other girls told me the same, and they ought to know. They worked with her."

"It has been obvious to me since the first case that this is the crime of a poisoner. I'm not disputing your contentions. They coincide with my own. But what I want to get at is, who is the murderer, how did he gain access to this room, and how was the poison administered?"

"Toughest mystery I've ever known in my life. Seems there's a way of getting into these rooms we know nothing about. How could anybody get into that boudoir up there and get away with the rubies? I've been taught that there's only five ways into any room on earth. Through the door, window, floor, walls or ceiling. But that ruby job has got all that beat. I've sounded every inch of those walls, tapped every foot of the floor. Taken up trestles and gone over the ceiling from end to end. And there's not a hollow in the whole place. And we know for a fact that things have been taken out of these rooms with a guard posted at the very door. Things have disappeared in the three minutes that have elapsed between the visit of one patrol and the next—"

"Stanforth saw something climbing out of a window," suggested the Chief.

"That's only one instance, sir. It didn't get out of a window when Betty Halston was murdered. Or tonight when it got Ferguson. No. That window theory doesn't work. Whoever did this job—and all the other jobs—has got ways and means of getting in and out that we know nothing about. And I've tapped for secret passages till I'm sick of sound of a hammerhead."

"Wasted labour," said the Chief. "Lord Gairlie and I have scrutinised the plans of the whole Castle with a highly skilled architect. Every room, every passage and corridor. We've gone over the blueprints with measuring rule and callipers. There isn't a single wall or apartment of this place not accounted for in those plans. *And there isn't a wall, anywhere, thick enough to hide a secret passage.*"

He sent for members of the outer guard and questioned them closely. One man, a gamekeeper, had been stationed directly opposite that window and within forty yards of it. The detective concentrated on him.

But again he met with the same amazing blank. The man's eyes had never left the windows he had been detailed specially to watch. They were all lighted, and he could not possibly have failed to see anything trying to open them. So far as he was concerned it had been another blank night. Nothing had got past them in the grounds—nothing had been seen on the walls. With absolute conviction he swore that nothing had even for one single second marred the clear silhouette of that lighted window. "At least," he amended, "nothing from the outside. Sometimes Ferguson himself came and peered out into the dark grounds."

"Did he seem all right then?" asked the Chief.

"Why, yes, sir, he always waved us the O.K. though he couldn't see us. It's the arrangement between us."

"When was the last time you saw him at the window?"

The gamekeeper pulled out a huge chronometer. "About twenty-five minutes ago, sir," he said.

The Chief glanced at his own watch. "We've been here a quarter of an hour," he said. "You saw him alive and well twenty-five minutes ago. That brings it down to ten minutes." He checked up suddenly. "All right," he said. "Go back to your post and pass the word round that the most rigid watch is to be maintained for the rest of the night. Someone, or something, has got inside the cordon. And it must not be allowed to get out." Doctor Mabey arrived a few minutes later. He came in with Lord Gairlie, who had been doing his best to pacify the servants.

There was a knock at the door and Delayn came in, breathing hard and with his collar torn. Word had got through to him high up in his attic of the tragedy down on the second landing. His relieving guard had brought the news, and Delayn had immediately jumped to the door. The restraining hands of two policemen had tried to stop him. One had been collared by the heels and sent into a flying back somersault, the other had gone rocking against the wall with the most astounding thump on the chin he had ever experienced in his life.

"Say," Tommy demanded. "Am I supposed to be under arrest in this house—or am I not?"

The Chief's eyebrows went up. "Why? What's wrong?" he asked.

"Because if I am I'll trouble you to have me trotted off to the police station. And if I'm not you'd better advise your squad to keep their hands off me. I've had enough of it. Is there any reason why I can't leave my room if I want to?"

"Yes. After lights-out, I think it better in your own interests that you remain under surveillance."

"Well, I'm not standing for it," came the heated reply. "And you'd best tell your men so. I've had to get rough with a brace of them up there, and I'll tell you this, the next that lays hands on me will come to in hospital. Either I'm under arrest or I'm not. And if I'm not I'll go where I like. *When* I like. See?"

He stood in the centre of the room, a picture of wrathful indignation, trying to adjust his burst collar.

The Chief went over to him, and laid the hand of pacifying remonstrance on his shoulder. "Sh! Not quite so hot, my boy," he said. "My men are simply obeying orders. They've no right to restrain you by force, but you see one of their colleagues has been murdered, and naturally they are a trifle sore—and keen to get the murderer."

"And they aren't the only ones," flared back Tommy. "The whole crowd of you have been looking on me with a watery eye ever since those wretched rubies were lifted. I can't move without one of your men detaches himself from the mob and follows me around like a faithful hound. For a month I've been penned up in an attic room twelve by twelve, and every night there's one of the guard sitting at the foot of the bed counting my snores. I've even had the special treat of a night in a police cell. All of which is very interesting and as it should be—providing you're guilty and haven't anything else much to do. And I have! I've got a heck of a lot to do. And all this footling surveillance doesn't tend to help me. I've been trying to untangle this job myself."

"*You* have?" said the Chief shortly.

"Yes, I have. Seems to me neither you nor any of your assistants know anything about chemistry. Neither do I, perhaps, but I certainly don't know less than you do. And I've had the presumption to put my own little scrap of knowledge into use."

"Indeed," said the Chief. "Perhaps you would care to explain?"

"That's what I came down for," said Delayn, gently rubbing a sore knuckle. He looked over at the doctor, still busy on his knees by the dead policeman. "Mabey," he said. "You understand more about this than the Chief, perhaps you would be good enough to check me and tell me if I'm wrong."

Doctor Mabey stood up, brushing the tips of his fingers.

"Certainly," he said.

Delayn picked up the dead man's tie and examined it critically under a tiny watchmaker's microscope.

"If you remember," he said. "There was a similar discoloration to this in the dress Miss Halston was wearing when she was murdered. Now before a dye changes colour some chemical change or other must take place in the elements of which that dye was composed. For instance, contact with an acid, or certain alkalines. Acid on certain blues will turn them red. It was obvious to me when I saw Miss Halston's dress that it had come into contact with a very powerful acid. Both the dye used in colouring her dress and the dye that made this necktie brown were of vegetable origin—not aniline. You'll notice the aniline dyes on the rest of the clothing have been impervious to the action of the acid."

"That tie," said the Chief. "Didn't change colour till after we got here—ten minutes after the man was murdered."

Delayn nodded. "It is an old tie. Probably has been fingered to hundred times in the action of putting it on and taking it off. A certain amount of grease has been rubbed into its surface.

The acid would take some few minutes to break that protective film. My point is that the acid, in only having effect on dyes of a vegetable nature, has thinned out the field of speculation considerably."

"Reduces it to about four possibilities, I should think," agreed the doctor.

"Precisely. The chief corrosives. There are one or two exceptions, but I think they are right off the map. Suppose we accept the fact that death in each case was caused by a discharge of highly powerful acid. It becomes obvious that it must have been used in a highly vaporous form—I would suggest tremendously volatile gas. That again reduces the field, Mabey?"

The doctor nodded vigorously. He was beginning to follow the line of argument, and mentally he was warming to the young man.

"You should know, sir. You were present at the post mortem. You detected a slight scorching of the finer lung tissues. Proof again. Now a corrosive acid, powerful enough to kill in a single breath, would after a few minutes even have an effect on silver, wouldn't it?"

"It would indeed," said Mabey.

Delayn bent down and unfastened Ferguson's watch-chain, He laid it on a clean handkerchief and held it out for inspection.

"It is an indisputable fact," he went on, "that a man's watch-chain is never cleaned from one year's end to another. Mine, I know, has never been, and I don't suppose anyone else's has in this room. It is a trick of market hucksters to sell certain types of Silver Revivers. You may have seen them. They borrow your discoloured watch-chain, dip it in a tumbler full of their patent Reviver, leave it there for a couple of minutes, and when they lift it out the chain is sparkling and as brilliantly new-looking as when it was hanging in the silversmith's window."

"Yes, I know the gentry," said the Chief grimly.

"Well, that preparation of theirs is nothing but a fierce acid. It eats away the dirt and incidentally the first covering of silver. A new virgin stratum of silver is exposed, and the chain is practically as new—except that two or three shillingsworth of pure silver is left in the acid for the benefit of the huckster."

"I get you," said the Chief. "Then if you are right that watch-chain should wipe clean?"

"As a new pin," declared Delayn.

He took the chain by the clasp and rubbed the whole length of it vigorously with the handkerchief. At the first stroke the film of dirt came away in a long green stain. In a few seconds the chain was shining bright, clean as only pure silver can be, save in the interstices of the links where the linen could not reach. And there the grime showed up in a contrast so sharp that it seemed almost black.

"Pretty fair reasoning," commented the Chief. "It practically gives the *cause*, but—"

"Just a moment," said Tommy. "In a few minutes I'll be able to tell you the exact description of the acid used. I've laid a trap in every room of this Castle, and if my theory is right, I'll have the final proof under your nose just as soon as I can put the tests through."

The detective pricked up his ears again. Delayn was announcing himself as an exceptionally thorough young gentleman, besides a remarkably competent one.

Delayn tossed the chain over to the Chief, and stooped down fumbling under the table. Fastened underneath by a couple of pins was a thin strip of paper about two inches wide by eight inches long.

"See that?" he said, holding it out. "That's a plain piece of litmus paper coated with a thin receptive veneer of my own. Litmus paper is this has turned red—undeniable proof that a corrosive acid has been discharged in this room. Certain qualities of it are absorbed in the veneer. In a few minutes I'll be able to tell you exactly what discoloured this litmus, and incidentally, what killed Betty Halston and Ferguson."

"I'd like to come up with you—if you can work with a stranger at your elbow."

"Certainly. Makes no difference to me," said Delayn.

They went up together to that dull cheerless room where Delayn had passed the solitary monotony of the last four weeks. Its character had changed considerably since the night he had made his risky trip to town; via the window, the rainpipe and the ivy.

There were rows of bottles half full of highly coloured chemicals, boxes of powders and crystals, basins and pots and mortars and test tubes cluttering the whole surface of the bench. There was a small retort and several spirit lamps, and a brazier. Immediately under the window was a clean marble slab. And just overhead, nailed to the wall, was a locked poison cupboard. The whole place looked—and smelt—far more like a practical laboratory than a young man's bedroom.

"Come right in," said Tommy, switching the lights on.

The Chief pushed the door to behind him. Delayn was climbing into villainously filthy smock-coat.

"Fairly sure about that poison already, aren't you?" asked the Chief.

"Yes. Almost certain it's hydrocyanic—easily the most deadly vapour poison known to science. A single whiff, properly administered, would kill a horse stone dead in the tenth of a second." He was cutting the strip into four little two-inch squares and laying them on the slab.

"Is there any smell to it?" asked the Chief suddenly.

"Yes. Not very pronounced, but extremely persistent—and penetrating."

"Slightly sulphury?"

"M'well—Yes. Personally I should say a nearer resemblance would be to say that hydrocyanic smells like bitter almonds taste—if you get what I mean."

"You've got it!" said the Chief. "That's what I could smell down there when I first went in. Bitter almonds. Not a doubt of it. It irritated the top of my nose, particularly after a deep breath."

"That was the remnant of the vapour in the air. Thank God it disperse quickly."

"How does it get into the room? Any idea on that?"

"Not a single one. That end of it seems more like a miracle than ever. One thing is obvious; it is contained in a glass shell. Not a bottle—something like a glass bubble, I should think. It would burst bomb-fashion, blowing its container almost to powder. If it was a bulb, say, six inches in diameter, that would be quite sufficient to kill anyone within a radius of some yards. The victim would be dead before he hit the floor."

"That's what seems to have happened."

"On each occasion. How the murderer got into the room is a puzzle. But it seems as though the unfortunate victims had found out the secret: and met their death before they could even raise an alarm. The murderer must have flung the bulb full at them."

He took one of the slips of litmus paper and smeared it with a chemical from a bottle. The thin veneer immediately decomposed and after a few seconds the mottled red tint faded, and the strip returned to its original blue.

"That was a drop of peroxide of copper," said Delayn. "There only one more test I need make. If I can persuade these other pieces to give as a tiny suspicion of Prussian blue you can take it from me that these murders were committed with hydrocyanic and nothing else."

He took the three pieces of paper and soaked them in a shallow dish of distilled water, dabbling them about with a scalpel. He took a thin phial from the poison cupboard and uncorked it. After a minute or two he took the litmus strips out of the dish, squeezing them as dry as he could with the scalpel.

He held the phial up to the light, and the Chief caught the spelling on the label, Caustic Potash. Delayn saturated the solution with it. Then he added a mixture of ferrous and ferric acids.

Almost immediately the deep, unmistakable tint of Prussian blue shot through the liquid. He poured it into a thin glass jar and held it against the bulb of a lamp. The mixture was as blue as the deep blue sea.

"Satisfied?" asked the Chief.

"Absolutely," replied Delayn. "Both Betty Halston and Ferguson were murdered with hydrocyanic acid."

Doctor Mabey had finished his examination when they got down again. And again it was the same dreadful story of utter perplexity and sheer inability to state with any assurance the cause of death.

The same tale was told at the inquest. The same adjournment was made. The same request for a post mortem was put through.

And after three days the same verdict was returned: "Wilful murder against some person or persons unknown."

Five days had elapsed since the murder of Ferguson, and during that time the Castle had been turned upside down without revealing a single further clue to the mysteries hanging over the place. The outer guard had been strengthened till there was not ten yards of the circle without its watchful sentinel. The inside patrol was reduced to a skeleton, three men on each landing, keeping up a ceaseless sentry-go through the hours of darkness.

Out in the grounds the ring of guards was almost unbroken. Every single unit could *see* his next in the line on each side of him. Words were passed from one to the other round the entire ring.

And the marauder got through again. With every man tuned up to the last ounce of concentration, with never more than a ten yards gap to wriggle through, the thing came again to the

Castle. No one saw it; no one so much as glimpsed its passage. But it came. And it went. And it left its deadly mark behind it.

One night a red dictionary was missing from the library. It was there at midnight when Lord Gairlie's secretary used it. She distinctly remembered leaving it beside her typewriter when she finished work. The loss was not discovered until the next afternoon. And Harris couldn't remember whether the library door had been locked overnight or not.

Stanforth assured him that it wasn't, for he had looked in there himself several times during the night. And he had seen nothing wrong. At four o'clock he had gone off duty and his relief could explain the mystery no further. The dictionary had gone, that was all that was known. The outer guard had seen as little as had the men inside.

Another night a red inkstand vanished, a recent acquisition, a gift from a friend in India. It had only arrived a few days before, and Lady Gairlie had had it put on a writing table in a room on the first landing. The room was illuminated all night and was visited occasionally by one of the guard. The ornament had stood on a table behind the door, and as the guard had merely glanced in to make sure the room was empty, it was excusable that he should have failed to notice its absence. The maid who came in next morning was the first to discover its loss.

The Chief was at his wit's end. He candidly admitted to Gairlie that he was as far from the solution as when he first came down.

"It amounts to this, my lord," he said helplessly; "some of these men, at least, will have to go back to duty. For five weeks now I've had them down here and we are no further forward than if we had stayed in London."

Lord Gairlie was silent. He was not surprised at the Chief's words. He had seen the trouble coming all along. The surprising thing was that the Chief had held on so long. Personal pride was responsible for that, of course. For the last three weeks the retention of the guard at the Castle had been the result of the Chief's own fight against the higher command in London. He couldn't possibly go back after that exceptional lapse of time and present his Commissioners with a report that contained nothing but a dismal story of complete and utter failure.

At the same time neither could he keep such a powerful contingent in Hampshire indefinitely. The hard-luck tale would have to be written, the penning of it never so galling.

Nevertheless, the quiet decision evoked a surge of uneasiness in the landowner breast. He looked out through the wide swing doors of the great house to where the first warming sunshine of March flooded the countryside in its tawny brilliance. Gairlie could see it all slipping from him. He could not hope to keep the Castle open while such grisly things continued to happen. It was like tempting a burglar with an unprotected jeweller's shop. With the guard still in possession he felt he had some justification for carrying on.

But with the main body of police gone the thing took on a different light. Gairlie thought of the toll of death the curse had levied upon the Castle and he could not help feeling that any further death would be laid at his door. If he shut the Castle up, locked, bolted and barred it, there could be no further loss of life. The thing couldn't kill what was not there.

"I hope I haven't given you too painful a blow?" the Chief said solicitously.

Gairlie turned away. "No, Chief; I've been half expecting it," he said. "What else can you do? But—it puts me in a dreadful quandary all the same." He looked out again at the sunny-bright countryside. "Frankly," he said," it means selling—this."

The Chief showed his extreme surprise. "But—but why, sir?" asked. "I understood from various conversations with you that financial clouds were lifting."

"Financial considerations are only one reason," replied Gairlie. "Silk Limited is on its feet again—or will be as soon as we can get it going—and Silk Limited was quite the worst of my troubles. The process is patented and protected in a hundred ways, and the inventor refuses to depart from his terms. He only seems to deal through his legal advisers. Trust the lawyers to butt in! Still, we are on the deal of our lives if we can only clinch it—but a hundred thousand needs some raising in these days—especially on the hush-hush terms that I require it."

"A hundred thousand!" The Chief whistled.

"It's worth half a million if he did but know. And on the terms has laid down it looks as though he will make that much *a year* out of it. Mr. D. Lane is no fool. Or his lawyer isn't, which is worse. Fifty thousand has already been paid as a guarantee. I've got to find the other fifty thousand before the month is out or I lose my option—and the greatest money-maker of a generation."

"Can't you increase your capital in the company?"

"That would halve my own profits, and I'm looking to Silk Limited to recoup what I've lost in the last five years."

"I'm sorry to hear this," said the Chief gravely. "Won't the lawyers give you a little grace?"

"You should know what lawyers are. And if they did? Fifty thousand would be just as hard to raise in three months' time as now. My position won't be any better than it is now, for years—except through Silk Limited. It's my only hope of salvation—of getting back to where I was. This new invention will sweep the market. And I've got to hold it. My only hope is selling out here. It will be awful—like losing an only child. Your decision to withdraw the guard here finishes it. It either means selling out or closing the place. If I closed it down it would simply be eating its head off."

The Chief looked at him, more grieved than he could say.

"It *is* an impasse, isn't it?" he muttered.

"I—I suppose," said Gairlie haltingly, "there is no likelihood of your altering your decision to withdraw your men?"

The Chief shook his head slowly. "The matter is more or less out of my hands," he said. "I am responsible to a rather autocratic board, you know, and their later communications to me have not been any too suave. I am summoned to a conference in London tomorrow. And I know what that means: 'Show results or return the men.' And I've no results to show. We haven't even been able to prevent murder."

His voice trailed off to a murmured undertone. Turning, Lord Gairlie saw the reason. Lonora was coming down the great staircase, smiling a bright "Good morning " as she came.

"Hallo, dad," she said cheerfully. "You're looking awfully glum. What's wrong? Any more horrors been happening during the night?"

"No, my dear," said Gairlie; "not exactly horrors, but an accumulation of difficulties has rather—er—come to a head, and I'm a little worried."

"Oh, you men make me tired!" she said. "Here's the most glorious day we've had for months, and here you are, cooped up indoors, getting morbid over your troubles. Come out and have a breath of fresh air. Excuse me shanghai-ing him like this, won't you, Chief—but he needs it." She caught him under the arm and dragged him imperiously out into the sunlit gardens.

* * *

Gairlie did not mind. He rather liked being taken charge of by his daughter. It was a pleasant antidote to his morose thoughts.

She halted suddenly by a great marble terracing that sheered up from the carpet beds.

"Now, dad," she said; "what's the trouble? Don't try to bluff me. You're nearly worried out of your life, and I want to *know!*" She seated herself with flat decision on the broad stone coping and faced him.

Gairlie looked into her eyes and turned away. Down below the terraces a burst of new crocuses were bobbing their heads to the tiny wind ruffles; daffodils bowed their heads demurely, basking in the life-giving sun.

He jerked his arm towards the dancing daffodils in an ill-assumed attempt at jocularity.

"The flowers seem to be coming along beautifully, don't they?" he said "Have to prepare ourselves for a spate of spring poems in the magazines if this sort of thing keeps on."

Lonora looked at him intently. She was not going to be side-tracked as baldly as that.

"Now," she said severely, "you're trying to revoke. And I'm afraid I can't allow that. The daffs have been in full bloom since Monday—and you've only just noticed them."

"Really, my dear, I've been awfully busy; you've no idea—"

"No, you haven't. You've simply been worrying your head off over something that you are keeping to yourself. And it isn't fair. And for you to try to fob me off with a sudden interest in spring flowers is—is almost laughable."

Gairlie made a little gesture of helplessness.

"How can I help being worried with all these terrible things happening around us?" he said. "The robberies are bad enough, but these murders are too awful for words. I'm positively dreading the night."

She shook a scolding finger at him.

"Daddy, that won't wash," she said. "You've known all about that for a long time. This is something new. It isn't the rubies, because you've got them back. And it isn't the robberies and murders, because you're already doing all you can to put a stop to them. No. It's something personal, and I want to know what it is."

Gairlie put one foot on the broad white coping and rested his elbow on his knee. There was a slow yet sudden change in his manner, as though he had just acknowledged to his inmost soul the rectitude of his daughter's attitude.

"Lonora, my dear, I *am* worried, dreadfully worried," he said. "And my greatest worry of all is wondering what you will think of me—when you know. But you've had quite enough unhappiness yourself. I should only be a brute to add to it."

Lonora flicked an imaginary speck of fluff off her sleeve; it was plain that her determination was not altered in the slightest.

"And you think I'm going to be satisfied with that, do you?" she said with a hard little tightening of the chin. "If it's as serious as you suggest the very worst you can do is to keep it to yourself. I dragged you away from that policeman so that I could have this talk, and I'm certainly not going to be put off now. Good heavens! From the look of misery on your face anyone would think you were contemplating bankruptcy!"

Gairlie looked down suddenly, horribly aware of a great lump in his throat. Her last sentence dinned on his brain like a thousand hammer-heads wielded by an army of satanic imps, shrieking with devilish glee.

"Daddy dear, please! Mother is as worried as I am. Sit down quietly and tell me. We have a right to share your troubles as well as your joys. Life isn't all success, and there's no shame in defeats now and then. Come along and tell me."

Gairlie grasped at the proffered straw as something to pin his thoughts to, something to force into use as a beginning.

"So—so mother has noticed it, too?" he muttered.

"Yes, you dear, silly old thing. You don't think you could keep such a mood as yours from her, do you? She was up at the head of the stairs this morning watching you talking with the detectives. You are *always* talking to detectives these days. I shall be glad and thankful when they've all gone away. Mother sent me down to you."

Gairlie swallowed at the detestable lump in his throat.

"My dear," he said in a strained, grating voice that he scarcely recognised as his own, "I've been trying to keep this from you for months. I've resorted to every subterfuge a man can invent to hide it. Two weeks ago I thought I'd succeeded. Today I know I've failed. It has just been a weary putting off of the evil day."

He stopped, fumbling for words, and she kept silent. There are times when the gift of silence is priceless, and Lonora had grasped that blessed truth.

"You—you said just now that I looked like a man contemplating bankruptcy," he said with an effort. "Would it—would it surprise—or hurt you very much to know that that is what I have been doing for over a year? Contemplating bankruptcy. God, it's awful! And it's true! This morning I've had news that makes it not merely a possibility of the future but an established fact of the present. Broke—for a paltry fifty thousand. That is the perfectest hell of it."

Lonora's face went deadly white. For Gairlie, broken and bewildered, to admit that to his own daughter meant that every avenue of hope had already been explored, every possible chance of averting catastrophe been plumbed to the bottom—and found empty.

She gasped at the sheer unexpectedness of it, at the stunning collapse it portended. "Good heavens!" she breathed, and sat back on the coping staring at her father. After what seemed to him æons of silence, she burst out: "But—but, daddy—it can't be true!"

Gairlie looked at her dumbly. In a moment she was beside him, her arms round his neck, pouring into his ears a passionate torrent of sympathy.

"Fifty thousand!" he muttered. "A man who controlled millions going down to the dust for a paltry fifty thousand!"

Lonora, her arms hugging him close to her, made him look up into her eyes. "Daddy," she said, "won't any of your friends come forward and stand bond for that?"

Gairlie shook his head. "I have already drawn on my friends for every penny my credit can stand," he said. "My dear girl, apart from borrowing more, it's—it's due, and long overdue, that some of my borrowings were paid back."

Lonora's cheeks were blanched, but in her eyes was a light of high determination. It meant humbling herself to her knees, but she did not falter.

"Well, *I've* still some friends," she said quietly. And without another word she turned and left him, speeding up the wide steps of the castle entrance. Her mother stood pale and anxious at the head of the steps. She ran up to her and gripped her arm. "Mother—I *must* see Tommy—*at once*," she said.

Lady Gairlie started back in a maze of unbelief. For five miserable drawn-out weeks those two unhappy young people had played their pitiful game of hide-and-seek. They had chosen, by tacit consent, different hours for taking a breath of fresh air in the grounds. Meals were served as far apart as they could possibly be. Ever since the arrival of his laboratory paraphernalia from London, Tommy had buried himself in his little attic under the roof. His sporadic visits to town were always scrupulously stage-managed by Harris, who prospected ahead and gave him the word when it was safe to voyage down the great staircases. For with such mountainous barriers between them it was impossible to meet. A meeting would have been a disaster, and Tommy had no intention of allowing it to happen.

And Lonora, on her part, had been a flitting figure of which one caught only vagrant glimpses. She spent most of her time in her mother's rooms or out in the greenhouses, where her hobby of orchid cultivation helped to pass the difficult time.

Yet here she was, after hurrying up the drive in a state of suppressed agitation, *demanding* to see the man she had painfully avoided for over a month. Lady Gairlie could scarcely believe her own ears.

"You *what?*" she repeated, looking at her daughter with a puzzled frown.

"I want to see Tommy, mother. I *must* see him. It's most awfully important. *Please* don't ask why—just be a good chum and tell him I want to see him." The words tumbled out of her mouth in a breathless rush. By sheer force of will she took her mother in through the doors and across the great hall. Lady Gairlie still protesting that the whole thing was most unseemly, but being half led, half dragged to the stairs. On the first landing, Lonora kissed her mother impulsively. "You dear," she whispered. "Tell him I'll be in the morning-room." Lady Gairlie, worried and unsettled, went on alone.

X

Up in his little attic room Tommy was hard at it. The window was open wide to the air and the electric heater was going full blast. So also were the brazier in the corner and the half-dozen spirit lamps in a row on the bench.

A most villainous smell pervaded the place. It was of extraordinary pungency, as though a mixture of old leather, perished indiarubber, and last year's onions were being slowly burned in a dry crucible. It proceeded from iron bowls and thick earthenware vessels perched precariously on the tops of the lamps, the brazier and the heater.

There came a gentle knock at the door and Delayn turned.

"Hallo!" he growled. "What is it?" He went to the door and flung it open. A swirl of eye-biting smoke streamed out, and Lady Gairlie jumped back in astonishment.

"Goodness! What is it—a fire?" she gasped.

"I'm awfully sorry," said Delayn quickly. "I'd no idea who it was. No, there's no fire; only a little smoke and perhaps a lot of smell. A new idea I'm working out. Cast leather. Soles from the mould. Pretty good, eh? But they do kick up a bit of a whiff, don't they?"

Lady Gairlie smiled faintly and dabbed her eyes with a handkerchief, "It is a little overwhelming," she said unsteadily. "I *do* hope you're not too busy?"

"Well, I've just reached a rather critical point in a series of experiments," said Tommy. "Why—did you want to see me specially?"

His own eyes were almost blinded by the penetrating fumes, and he could not see his hostess's perturbation in the shadowed gloom of the landing.

He kicked the door open behind him. "Please come in," he said. He went in and switched on an electric fan to disperse some of the worst of it. Then, without a further word or sign, he went round his entire apparatus, turning off the burners one after another. Slowly the seething boil of the mixture stilled and finally ceased. He went right up to her and stood, red-eyed from the heat and smoke, looking down at her.

"What is it, Lady Gairlie?" he asked quietly.

Lady Gairlie looked at Tommy with quick remonstrance.

"You've broken your experiments," she said.

Delayn waved the matter aside. "I can start them all over again later on," he said. "They're of small moment, anyhow. There's something wrong. What is it?"

"Tommy, Lonora wants you; wants you badly."

A look of incredulity shot across Delayn's face.

"What?" he jerked.

"She—she is in dreadful trouble downstairs—almost in tears. She begged me to come up and tell you."

Lady Gairlie did not even see him go through the doorway. She heard the faint bump of flying boots, but that was after he got to the stair-head. In twenty seconds Delayn was tapping softly at the morning-room door.

Lonora stood by the open windows, looking frankly at him as he softly closed the door behind him. Delayn was aware of a sudden catch in the throat when he saw her. She looked so unutterably lovely standing there. The sunlight cast a vague shadow across her face, throwing into a finer more subdued relief the smooth lines of her features.

She came towards him holding out her hands, half shyly, half gladly. A meeting that might have been made intolerable with a false word or look was gently broken down with something marvellously approached the normal.

"Hallo, Tommy," she said softly. "It's so nice to see you again."

"I think I should have said that," replied Tommy quietly. "You're looking awfully sweet today, Lonora." He took her hands and squeezed them reassuringly. "It *was* nice of you to send mother up," he said.

She looked at him with a shade of guilt in her eyes. She was uncomfortable, driven into a comer by circumstances which nothing within her power could have prevented. The position, she realised, was unbearable.

Tommy was speaking again, opening up the way for her. Bless her for that. Still holding her hands, his quiet voice barely audible even in the hush of the room, he seemed to lift the barrier of diffidence gently aside.

"I want you to tell me just what the trouble is, dear," he was saying. "Mother told me—a little. Don't be frightened. Tell me—what's wrong?"

Her eyes met his quickly, burning bright. "Tommy, you dear," she said; "you don't know how difficult it is."

"It shouldn't be, Lonora, between old friends. At least we understand one another. The trouble is that you're trying to find an easy way of saying something painful. Believe me, dear, there never is an easy way. Why not take all you want to say, put it into one sentence, and throw it at me?" He smiled a grim little smile. "Let *me* sort it out afterwards," he said.

She looked up at him suddenly. "How many millions do you think dad is worth?" she asked.

Delayn gazed speculatively out of the window.

"Dunno, I'm sure," he replied. "Four?" He reflected for a moment on his unwilling host's various companies. "Yes; four, I should think. Probably nearer five. Five if the market's on the bull, anyway. But I haven't studied the financial columns lately. Since my little pile went phut I haven't been able to work up an interest, somehow." He wasn't looking at her, and her own head was bent.

"Four—or maybe five?" she pondered. "Yes, that's about what I thought... Millions of pounds, you mean? Not single pennies. Millions of pounds. Good heavens! What can I say now?"

With a sudden jerk he put his fingers under her chin and tilted it up so that her eyes met his, full and square.

"Well, that's the worst over," he said flatly. "There's some faint suspicion of the rest glimmering in my head. Totally incredible and unbelievable. And I expect I've got it all beautifully addled."

"But—but, Tommy, can't you *see?*"

"I'm afraid I can," he nodded. "I hardly know whether to laugh or faint. I shall laugh, I think. Gosh! It's farce reduced to tragedy. Tell me, when did this happen?"

She shook her head. "I don't know," she said vaguely. "I'd never even imagined it. It must have been slowly coming for some time."

"Well, when did you first hear about it?"

"This morning; less than half an hour ago. He was worried and harassed. I thought the police were beginning to get on his nerves. I took him out into the sunshine—and he told me. I made him."

She turned and tried to move away, but he held her—held her hard.

"All pretty definite, I suppose?" he said, and marvelled at the naturalness of his own voice. Gairlie gone down! All the pomp and pride of the House of Gairlie, humbled, beaten, grovelling in the hell that he himself had gone down to, only five damnable weeks before! His brain could only faintly grasp it.

"Not—not actual bankruptcy, surely?" he said after a long pause. Gairlie might have come a whale of a cropper, but even he couldn't accommodate a complete knockout.

Lonora was fighting back tears of absolute self-degradation. "He said that he is smashed unless he can get hold of fifty thousand pounds."

Tommy whistled. "Lord Gairlie—bust for a mere fifty thousand. Rot! Absolute piffle!"

"Tommy, he's borrowed everywhere! He—he's at the end of his tether."

Tommy whistled again. Her last words had explained away whole rows of incredible mountains.

And then the dawn broke. "My God! And you've come to me?" he gasped. There was a long, ferocious silence. She was going limb in his arms and he carried her to a broad couch beneath the window and sat her down. Almost in a dream he patted her shoulder.

"Fifty thousand," he said in a screwed-up sort of voice. "Yes, I think I can manage that, Lonora. Just about; if I can get up and see my footling lawyers before they splash it around among my own benighted creditors. Gosh! I shall have to whizz, though."

He hopped to the door.

"Hey! Harris!" he bawled. "Put me through a London call. Gilbraith and Gilbraith, solicitors. Tell 'em I'm coming up by car and they are to do nothing till I arrive. And have my car got ready. Hustle!"

Tommy found himself back behind the couch again, patting the trembling shoulders as a fondly, foolish nurse might cosset a child. "There, there," he said fatuously. "So that's all finished and done with." It was a ludicrous thing to say. But somehow it seemed to fit in.

"I'll—er—just take a little run up to London and—er—see to it, and then everything will be all right, won't it?" He patted her again, but she gripped his hands, and her quivering lips just touched them.

"No, Tommy; it won't be all right," she said tremulously, "Everything will be all wrong—horribly wrong. I—I never dreamed you could do it yourself; it never even entered my head. I had a vague sort of idea that perhaps some of your friends—I've met so many of them, and they all seemed able to—to be able to discuss finance in business terms—I thought perhaps you could arrange it as a business matter—Daddy even said that he would get rid of the Castle—and—oh, Tommy, it seems *all* wrong!"

"Oh, I don't think so. I'll put it all through my lawyers. It'll all be on a purely business footing, if that's what's worrying you. Dad gets his fifty thousand, I get my receipt, and the lawyers work out the repayment terms among themselves. What could be fairer? Perhaps it would be just as well if dad didn't know the actual lender's name. Be rather difficult for him, don't you think? Yes, I think the lawyers had better do it."

"But. my dear boy, he will insist on knowing. And—and I shall tell him."

Delayn stood up and coughed.

"Shouldn't do that," he said jerkily. "Mean to say—we've both of our points of view. You see—you don't understand the gorgeous bit of comedy wrapped up in this. Perfectly frightful thing to say, I know. But there it is. I could tell you in one word what he wants it for. And that's what makes it such a yell! I even know *who* he wants it for!"

"You do?"

"Yes. Me!"

Lonora screwed herself round on the couch and looked up at him.

"I'm afraid I don't quite understand, Tommy," she said.

"Certainly is a wow," admitted Tommy. "Pity he didn't tell you more. He must have mentioned Silk Limited?"

Lonora started. "Yes, he did," she said. "That was the name of the company."

"And he wants the money for the second half of the purchase right to make Untearable Silk—to pay the inventor for his patents and copyright."

"Yes. Yes."

"Well, I'm the inventor. Isn't it a shriek? Good enough for a farce. And, you see, the whole core of the yell is that this fifty thousand I've got is the fifty thousand he's already paid me for the first instalment. I'm D. Lane. Did he mention D. Lane?"

Lonora shook her head in a way that betokened a lost soul struggling hopelessly out of its depth.

"Well, that's who I am to dad. Mr. D. Lane, of the Untearable Silk Manufacturing Company, no address, London. Doing business through the farm's representatives, Messrs. Gilbraith and Gilbraith. Dad has already paid me fifty thousand. I thought that lump would just about square my own dad's debts and leave me a bunch of tenners on the credit side. But now he wants it back to pay it back to me again. See? Sounds a bit intricate, but it's as easy as breaking an egg really. And it's the laugh of a lifetime."

"But—but, Tommy—"

"It works out like one of those chess problems in the weeklies. 'White to move and mate in six.' Dad pays me fifty thousand. That's the first wad. I give it him back. He pays it me back again. That's the second wad. He's all square except that he still owes me fifty thousand, which he can pay back out of the first year's profits. Saves watering capital and prevents profit-sharing with strangers. I get my fifty thousand back in time to pay out my creditors before they shove me in jail—and, all told, there's no spilt milk for anyone to cry over."

Lonora was looking at him through a blurred mist of tears. Two trickled down her cheeks, one on each side of her nose.

"Bless my soul, dear, what's the matter now?" gasped Delayn. He went round to her, and she pulled him down beside her, so gently that he scarcely felt the pull. There was a choking sound in her throat. She tried to strangle it by burying her head against his shoulder. And her arms were round his neck, holding him tight, as though afraid ever to let him go again.

It's a most embarrassing job for any man to take almost heartbroken "Thank you's" from a girl. His imagination did not compass the fact that in admitting the invention which her father was chasing with every nerve and sinew that was in him, he had made good in her eyes to a degree that swamped even a world's championship at Wimbledon, or a double century against the fighting Australians. Here was a new Tommy, an undreamed of Tommy. A Tommy who had plunged gamely into that other great sport, the vast world of commercial enterprise, a world that is peopled with keen, experienced brains, and impregnated with the fiercest spirit of competition known to humankind; and not only plunged into it, but emerged at the other end with a glittering prize in his fingers. It was a Tommy she had never suspected, a Tommy that was laughed at by his own friends. She hadn't a word to say. She just held him and pressed him to her.

Harris tapped at the door and announced that the car was waiting.

"Splendid fellow," thought Tommy. He was profoundly thankful that she had spared him the intolerable ordeal of thanks. He worshipped her for it. But anyhow, he argued, it was the kind of thing Lonora was bound to have done.

She clung to the lapels of his coat and looked with brimming eyes into his.

"Is—is that all, Tommy?" she asked in a tiny little voice—little more than a whisper.

Delayn did not answer at once. Then he said, "Yes, I think so—dear."

Her fingers whitened and she whispered: "Are you sure? Five weeks ago you were—were going to—Tommy dear, make it easier for me—you know you've—*you've a right to now.*"

Delayn stood up and gently pushed her back on to the couch.

"I didn't think you'd ever want me to buy you, dear," he said. "We won't talk of that again, please. When things are more settled and—and other things have proved themselves—yes. I'll talk to you then." He stooped and kissed her. "I'll be back before nightfall," he said. "Don't tell dad a word of this."

He turned and hurried out to his waiting car.

Delayn chased off to town, and by sheer persistence and immovable obstinacy won his way with the Gilbraiths. The new agreements were through. They provided Tommy with £100,000 flat, a seat on the board vendor's shares up to £20,000 and 10 per cent, of the yearly profits. Delayn was made for life. The only job was to get Silk Limited started, and he convinced the Gilbraiths that his way was the only way.

He stayed to see the documents drawn out and dispatched. Then he sent Lonora a wire.

Everything O.K. Loan gone through. Tell dad. Tommy.

His car hummed back over the white road, singing to him a song of speed and power and a new world opening its doors to him in a sunburst. There was not a single cloud on his whole wide horizon. Not a single shadow—until he got to the gates of Gairlie Castle.

And there the overhanging shadow of fear declared itself again. The lodgekeeper came out to open the great gates for him, and there was something in the set pallor of his face that made Delayn lean over from the driving wheel and stare at him. "What's wrong?" he demanded.

The lodgekeeper came over, as though fearful of being overheard by some omnipotent Something in the very air. He jerked a bony thumb over his shoulder and thrust his white face up against Delayn's ear.

"Another murder, sir—up at Gairlie," he said. "It's getting too bad to bear—that's the third. An' there'll be more yet if they don't close it down and leave it in peace." He peered down at the hedges beside the gates as though even their bare roots might harbour the horror. "Seven more of the servants left the moment the news got out. An' I don't blame 'em, either. There was some talk this morning of all the police going back, but I reckon this new job has scotched all that. It ought to, anyway."

"Who is the victim this time?" demanded Delayn.

"Mister Harris, sir, as inoffensive a man as ever trod earth."

"Not—not Harris, the butler?" gasped Delayn.

The lodgekeeper nodded. "Yes, sir—*him*," he said. "And a wickeder thing I never heard of. Old Harris wouldn't of hurt a fly. But he's gone. Just the same as the others went. Why don't they close the place down? Shut it up and give the Thing time enough to die off? Sending men to their deaths it is. Thirty years Harris had been at the Castle. Butler for over twenty years—and now they've killed him. Killed him stone dead. And who's the next one on the list? We'll all be wiped out if we stay here. All the lot of us, one after the other. We—"

Delayn silenced him peremptorily.

"Easy! Easy!" he said. "For heaven's sake get hold of yourself. When did all this happen?"

"Soon after you had gone, sir. About eleven o'clock, it would be. I know it were about then, because the Chief had just gone out in the master's car to the station. Going up to London he was, catching the eleven ten. So he'd be gone through the gates somewheres about a quarter to. And just after that the Chief's own driver comes racing down the drive hootin' for the gates. Coming like hell he was, and blinding at me because I couldn't get 'em open without he had to stop. He were driving the Chief's car as I sung out to ask him what the hurry was all about. But he wasn't stopping to tell me. He was halfway down the road before I knew he was through. Seems he was rushin' to intercep' the Chief before he boarded the train. The master had sent him out as soon as the murder was discovered. But he just missed him by about as long as it took me to get them damn gates open. The train was just working up speed when he hove in sight of the station; the master's car was just settin' out on the way back. Now he's up in London, and his lordship's fair dancin' mad. An' no wonder. They wired to catch the train at Paddington, but he never replied. So it looks like he never got it."

"Where did all this happen?" demanded Delayn.

"In the library, sir."

"The library again! Good Lord!"

"The master had been in there, sir. Only went out five minutes before, or he'd have been gone himself. He'd been in there talking with Mister Stanforth. When they went out. Mister Harris went in to clear up—glasses and siphons and such-like. The other detective, Mister Kennedy, he saw him go in. He reckoned he'd been in there about five minutes—you can see the library door from the big table where he was sitting in the hall. Well, Mister Kennedy, he wanted some matches for his pipe, and he got up and went to the library—there's always any amount of match-stands in there. The door wasn't closed, mind you; hadn't been closed since Harris went in. But when Mr. Kennedy looked in, there was Harris lying dead on the floor, with a duster in his hand. Looks as though he'd collected all the glasses like, and was just going round wiping the odd bits of wet off the table. And before he knew what was happening he was a dead 'un. And so we'll all be if this carries on much longer. The end of the master's cigar was still smoking in the ashtray, so you can tell how quick it was."

He stopped, and the look of nameless fear crept back into his eyes.

"The master told me to tell you when you came in, sir," he muttered apologetically.

Delayn did not reply. He eased his foot from the clutch-pedal and turned the car into the great drive. The trees swished by as he raced her to the Castle.

Lord Gairlie met him at the entrance, a haggard figure with a face bearing traces of a tragedy that was rapidly becoming too heavy for one pair of shoulders to bear.

"This is terrible news—terrible news," he said sombrely. "The lodgekeeper told you, I hope? Three in five weeks—God! It's driving me mad."

"Bad luck, sir," replied Delayn. "I suppose no further clues than ore?"

"Not a thing. Not a single thing. Just dead! That's all. Kennedy and Stanforth are up there now. They can't even get on to the flimsiest sort of clue. It's getting more hopeless with every day that passes. How they do it, eh? How? *How*" He clenched his hands and shook them above his head in a wild access of helplessness. It was a gesture of genuine grief, coupled with mad rage against the wanton slayer.

"The Chief is still in town, isn't he?" queried Delayn.

"God, yes. He's gone up to a conference. Think of it—he's gone to arrange for the withdrawal of the police protection here, and the moment he gets out of sight—this happens."

"Can't you get him on the 'phone?"

"Kennedy is trying to. Go up to him, will you, my boy, and see if you a can think of anything. I've racked my brains till I'm nearly crazy."

"They found my litmus paper?"

"Yes, under a chair close by where Harris fell. It was as red as blood."

Delayn went through to the library. He pushed open the door and went in. The dead man had been lifted on to the table and a white sheet covered him. The litmus paper, dumb witness of the dreadful means employed to commit the murder, lay on the top of the sheet, a strip of sullen portentous red. Kennedy stood by the 'phone in the corner, thumping the receiver bracket. Stanforth came over, gloomy, troubled, and looking as though he would have thrown the whole thing up for a row of beans.

"Bad business this, sir," he muttered. "Can't seem to get our teeth into it anywhere."

"It *is* an unholy mystery," agreed Delayn. "Things seem to be going from bad to worse."

"There must be an explanation somewhere," growled Stanforth. "But I'll be shot if I can dig down to it. I'm not sure the staff here aren't right. They just call it the Silent Death, and leave it at that."

"Kennedy, I believe, was in sight of that door from the moment Harris came in here?" said Delayn.

Stanforth assented. "Yes. He couldn't be anything else. You know his table—right opposite this door. Staring him in the face all the time."

"And he actually saw Harris go in?"

"Sure. And he says that right from that moment he was looking hard in this direction. You know how a fellow gets sometimes on a job like this—a bit glum and upset? Well, that's how he was. He was sitting at that table with his chin in his hands, thinking his head off. And all the time that library door was stuck flat and square in front of his eyes. Can't get away from that, can you? He was like that for some minutes, just sitting and thinking and staring. And then he put his pipe in his mouth and began fumbling for some matches. He hadn't got any, and he starts walking the twenty odd paces to this very door that he'd been staring at for six or seven minutes. Now, sir, could anything or anybody have slipped along that great hall and got into this library without him seeing it? It just couldn't be done. The way we've been this last few weeks has stretched our eyes and nerves out till they're damn nearly bursting. We whip round if a mouse squeaks in the wainscotting, we turn if the wind swings a lamp so that a shadow moves on the floor. At night we're keyed up so high that—dammit—we can see in the dark. And yet *something* got through! Somebody managed to run the blockade of Kennedy's eyes, and I can't believe it. I won't. It just couldn't happen."

"And yet," said Delayn quietly. "It did, eh?"

"Yes, of course it did," said Stanforth fiercely. "For the tenth time since we came on the case the impossible happened. Harris was stone dead on the floor there when Kennedy pushed the door open."

"You found glass fragments again, I suppose?"

"A square yard of them. All in one patch this time, bar a few that were blown across to the opposite wall. It all boils down to this—somebody got in here, *somehow*, and threw that gas bomb at Harris, and then got out again the same way as he got in. And I can't believe it."

"Couldn't the assassin have concealed himself in here before Harris got in?" hazarded Delayn.

"Lord Gairlie was here himself for pretty well half an hour before Harris came in. I was with him myself. He sent for some whiskies and cigars and we sat here talking over the case, robberies and murders and all. Everything. Take a look round the room yourself, sir. Is there anywhere a cat could hide without being seen in a single look? Is there anywhere a man could hope to get without being seen the moment you entered the room? You know there isn't. Not a curtain nor a piece of furniture anywhere that you can't see all round. Those bookcases are flat against the wall. There's not a window in the place and the lights were all full on. Lord Gairlie was sitting in that armchair by the fire. But I wasn't. I was standing up half the time, walking up and down while we talked. And if anyone was concealed in that room then, and I didn't see it—you just prove it to me, Mr. Delayn, and I'll resign right now. I'd sooner sell pipe-lights on Westminster Bridge than call myself a detective. All I can say is that if anyone *was* in here—he'd fixed himself up so that no human eye could see him! And I reckon Kennedy'll say the same from his end out there in the hall."

"You're hinting at some marvellous new invention, I suppose? Invisible clothes or—"

"Not on your life," snorted Stanforth. "Hard facts and harder proofs. That's the order of our training at the Yard. And it doesn't include invisible clothes or marvellous machines that only function in the brain of a lunatic. No, sir, the criminal brain is only cute, it isn't wonderful. There's nothing more in it than meets the eye of everyday investigation. But in this case it's got us on our blind spot. The explanation is as simple and commonplace as two and two—only we can't find the numbers on the board. That's all. When I say human eyes couldn't see it, I mean that it's so simple we couldn't see the wood for the trees."

"Then you still don't believe in miracles?"

"No, I don't," the Yard man snapped. "I've seen too much. You can teach a youngster criminal investigation the same as you can teach him arithmetic. Clever criminals don't invent new methods, they only produce new twists of the old. This case is just as bald-faced as the others—if we could only light on that damned new twist! But we can't!" He turned and dug his toe into the carpet, vicious as only a man can be who, knowing his own strength, knows that someone is making a fool of his weakness.

Kennedy was having trouble with the 'phone. There appeared to be something radically wrong with it. For a couple of minutes he had been pumping the receiver handle, getting into momentary touch with the local exchange, barking his right number, and cursing at being disconnected from London. Then London came on again and he howled the Yard's number at the operator.

"Hey!" he yelled. "I want Scotland Yard—you had me on two minutes ago and then some fool began messing about with the line. What? You just plug me in and keep me through! Yes—hallo—that you, Chief? Been trying to get you all afternoon.

Harris is dead! Can you hear me? I say Harris is dead! Yes—soon after you—Hallo—hallo! Confound—" He thumped the receiver again, pounding it up and down and getting violently red in the face. "Hallo!" he shouted. "Hallo!—Yard! Hey! Damn!" A sudden silence had closed down over the wire. It was noiseless, not even the faint sputtering of a faulty connection, not even the still fainter murmuring that told of the line still open to a distant exchange: just a painful, omnipotent blank.

Kennedy turned with a deep-voiced snarl:

"This line has been cut!" he said.

XI

The Chief had not enjoyed his conference with the Powers of the Yard. Shorn of polite officialdom their fiat had amounted to the bald ultimatum that twenty-nine men could no longer be spared wild-goose chasing at Gairlie. The case had been a complete police failure. The Chief's arguments in favour of a continuance of at least another fortnight were going for nothing—when they received powerful and totally unexpected backing in the shape of Kennedy's interrupted 'phone call reporting the death of Harris. That altered matters. The ultimatum was scrapped in favour of a terse "Carry on."

* * *

The Chief went back by car, waiting for nothing.

He found an air of gloom hanging heavy in the great halls of the Castle, a gloom shot through and through with fierce helpless rage.

Stanforth was looking more bitter than ever.

"D'you know what I'm going to do, Chief?" he rasped.

The Chief raised an eyebrow.

"I'm going into that library myself tonight. And I'm going to stay there till I've found out!"

The Chief's eyebrows went up a notch. Stanforth was looking at him, hot-eyed and belligerent, a man demanding fight with every fibre of him. He was a man, too, who had mastered a very human fear of the unknown and was ready to battle with it—in face of the knowledge that three had already paid the penalty for discovering its secret. There was just one little advantage that gave him confidence—the fact that he had *seen* it. For one fleeting moment he had glimpsed it; and he knew what he was up against. And whether it was man, monkey or devil, he was ready to have a go at it. And in his own dogged view, the only way of coming to grips with the horrible thing was to beard it in its own den.

But the Chief wasn't seeing eye to eye with him. It was one thing to lose a man by sheer accident of professional risks, but it was another thing entirely to have a man deliberately challenging death by stepping on its trailing coat tails.

"Stanforth, you'd better have a hot whisky and go to bed," he said. "Get a good night's sleep for once."

"I tell you, Chief, I'm game to try it," said the detective. Hang it all, what's the use of carrying on like this? All the watching and waiting in the world doesn't prevent the thief having his way. We are as far from a solution as when we started. For heaven's sake let me have a shot at it. I know I may have to wait hours or even days for it to show up, but what does that matter? I can wait in the library just as well as out in the hall."

The Chief shook his head. "Can't be done, Stanforth," he said. "I admire your pluck, but you are simply asking for trouble. And, judging by what has already happened, you'd get it."

"But Chief, the odds are all on my side," persisted Stanforth. "I've seen it; I know what to expect. And I'll promise you the little brute won't get away a second time. I've got a gun, and I know how to use it. If that little devil doesn't sling its hands up at the first shout I'll plug every chamber into it. Over and above all that I've read up every word about hydrocyanic. (There's a whole shelf of books about poison gases up in Mr. Delayn's room). 'When in danger of coming into contact with hydrocyanic, shut your eyes and hold your breath and run from the infected area.' That's what the book says, Chief, and I reckon it's easy. If I can't hold my breath long enough to fix that little brute, I'll eat my hat. That is, if he gets the chance to fling one of his bombs—which he won't."

The Chief was thoughtful for a while, working out the pros and cons. The way Stanforth put it made it all sound very logical and possible—but still at the back of his brain there persisted the little crawling devils of doubt. He was apprehensive of the whole affair. If Stanforth went into that room, deliberately and with the Chief's concurrence, and failed to come out, there would be the very deuce to pay, and he knew it.

And yet there was a golden chance held out, the possibility of forcing the issue. If the job was to be done at all, Stanforth was by far the best one to do it. He was primed with a knowledge the others did not possess. If anything happened in that library and Stanforth was able to keep his end up and hold it, with just a flicker of luck they might be able to clear up the whole case in one swoop. And it was time the luck turned. The raider had had it all his own way too long. Stanforth was right; it was far better to go out and attack than to sit back purely on the defensive.

"Why not give it a run, Chief?" Stanforth argued. "There's nothing to worry about. I won't be fighting a lone hand. We can make arrangements that will make me as safe in there as out here. The whole crowd of us will be in it—and I'm blest if I can see that little midget getting the best of our bunch. It's the chance of a lifetime. If we can solve it from the library end we've solved the biggest half. Two murders have been committed in that room. It's got some method of knowing when anyone's there—I'm certain of it. And it will come again—depend on it. With a guard in there watching and waiting, it will be challenging it to come out and have another go. It never shows itself when there's two in there. It's my belief it only carries one of those poison bombs at a time. And if that's so I reckon I stand more than a fifty-fifty chance of getting my hands on it."

The Chief turned to the other man.

"What do you think, Kennedy?" he asked.

Kennedy scratched his chin and did his best to stay on the fence. It wasn't exactly a fair point for him to give advice on. Stanforth was the man whose head was going into the noose, and he felt it was hardly up to him to urge him to take such a risk, even though he himself would have done it. It was like taking a friend into the dentist's and advising him to have it out without gas.

"I think Stanforth is right. The crux of the mystery seems to centre on the library," he said slowly. "There's no possible means of getting into that room except through the door. Not that we know of, anyway. And if the murderer can manage to get through such a barrage as we could put up, then it's time we threw up the case. Don't like the idea at all. But when it's all boiled down to facts, it does give some chance of getting to grips with it. Something's got to be done. We could carry on for months and get no further. Solve the mystery of that library and we've as good as solved the rest."

Stanforth cut in again eagerly. "What's the odds?" he said. "We stand just as much chance of being picked off in our own rooms as anywhere else There's an element of risk in even living in this house. I don't see that the risk is any greater in there than out here. Let me try—anything's better than this never-ending watching."

The Chief gave a bit of ground.

"What—exactly—do you propose, then?" he queried.

"Get Lord Gairlie's permission to shift every bit of furniture out of that room," he said. "That will give me a clear view all round the four walls; and definitely prove the room is empty before I go into it. The door can be left open. Kennedy and some of the others will be right outside the door, looking in say at every sixty seconds. The rest of the men will be strung out round the hall and along the walls leading up to the library door. And if anyone can get into that room through that lot, I'll eat my whole uniform, let alone my hat."

The Chief looked across at the stout oak of the library door.

"Sounds fairly thorough," he said. "And the next?"

"I'll keep on the move inside so that the men out here can hear me, as evidence that I'm still O.K. And I won't even give him the chance of walking round in a continuous circle. I'll keep shifting my direction, chopping and changing about all over the shop. He won't be able to time me at any given spot. There won't be two seconds gap at any time when my eyes are not in range of any particular wall. And I'll have my gun in my hand all the time. Every now and then I'll whistle, and the moment I hear or see anything I'll yell. Will *that* suit you?"

"Yes, with one thing more," said the Chief grimly. "Kennedy, get me a hatpin, an ordinary steel hatpin, and a reel of strong thread."

Kennedy hurried off without a word to the servants' wing. When he got back the furniture was already being carted out of the room of death and stacked in the great hall.

The Chief took the hatpin and drove it horizontally into the jamb of the door on the inside, so that the black, shiny head pressed hard against the upper panel, like the automatic foot drumstick of a jazz drum. Then he knotted a long length of thread to the head of the pin and tugged it gently. The head tapped on the panel with every tug. The other end he tied to Stanforth's wrist, so that no matter where he was in the room he had only to flick his wrist to give the watchers outside the signal that he was still all right.

"Satisfied now, Chief?" said the detective, when the last piece furniture had been piled in the hall.

"Yes," said the Chief. "And I'll be here with Kennedy. In you go!"

Stanforth lit a cigarette and went in. The door closed behind him, so that only a Chinese of light shone through.

For many seconds there was a tense, unbearable silence in the area outside the door. Eyes were strained on that Chinese of light as though it were the last connecting link between them and the man who had gone in to face death alone. It was a world of silence that was beaten down into utter immobility. The Chief found himself listening for even the faint sound of breathing—and failing to find it.

Someone shuffled uneasily and half turned to scan the opposite wall. The faint noise was like an explosion of sound. Three or four of them whipped round with their guns at their hips, startled eyes staring at the man who had moved. Even Kennedy, immobile as a sphinx, let his head switch round in a sudden single movement.

A few muttered whisperings came from the other end of the file. Somebody was advocating more lights. Though the main floodlights were on down the centre of the hall, there were a few ornamental group lights that were not burning. Their absence threw faint shadows in the corners. Nothing in the ordinary way, but in that atmosphere of nerve-tingling expectancy little things like that seemed to stand out with stark malignancy.

Kennedy held a whispered consultation with the Chief. His eyes with snake-like flickers from the Chinese of light to the distant shaded corners.

"Might as well have them on, sir," he said. "There's no object in giving even a doubtful point away on this game. Can't see that it'll make any difference—I can see the whole place from here. But you never know."

"Were those lights out when Harris went in?" whispered the Chief.

"There were no lights at all burning, sir, except those over the entrances to the long corridors up there at the other end. It was broad daylight.The front doors were open to the sunshine."

"Were there any shadows along this wall?—Any doubtful patches where such a little apparition as the thing that could wear the clothes we found in the hut could find shelter in slipping along, say from the dark corridors to this door?"

"May have been a bit darkish in places, sir," replied Kennedy. "Light enough though for me to have seen anything that *moved.* Still, I don't see why we should give away chances. We want all the light and all the help we can get."

The Chief nodded. "Quite," he said. "Get them on—get there off on. I can't conceive anything getting past this cordon."

Kennedy made a sign to a footman standing nervously by the table in the centre of the hall. The footman came over and stopped some yards from the door, eyeing the Chinese of light as though is was something sinister. Kennedy beckoned him closer, and he tiptoed fearfully up. "Get all the lights on," said Kennedy in his ear. "Every switch in the place. Give us every light you've got."

In a little while there came a sharp click of switches, and new bursts of light sprang up in the dim corners, flooding the place till the whole hall swam in white radiance. In that merciless glare not so much as a mouse could have moved without detection.

Sixty feet away by the far wall a grandfather clock ticked the seconds ponderously out. In the oppressive silence the slow, metallic tick-tock, tick-tock came over as clearly as though the clock were just inside the great oak door.

Then with a suddenness that made them jump, the pin-head struck the inside panel. It was the first sign Stanforth had given, and it jolted them badly. It was like a drumbeat from the very halls of doom.

The Chief put his face against the crack of the door and whispered: "Are you all right, Stanforth?"

With a deep breath of relief they heard the quietly confident answer: "Sure—everything O.K." One of the men, in the sudden easing of the strain, struck a match to light a cigarette, and Kennedy felt his scalp prickle at the sudden scrape of noise.

"God, this is awful," he breathed.

The Chief nudged him back to a sense of realities. "Won't happen yet," he grunted. "We're letting it get us on the jump. Thing isn't likely to have a go till it's sized up the new lay of the land. Stanforth's all right for an hour, I should think. Mightn't happen at all tonight—or ever!"

Kennedy shook his head. "Not so sure," he whispered back. "It's as slippery as an eel. Might try to catch us on the hop with a quick rush. All be over in two seconds. Don't like it at all."

He leant forward and pushed the door open a foot. "All right, old man?" he asked in a breathy hiss.

Stanforth had been standing in the middle of the room. Above his head a group of electric lights blazed, flashing back from strings of glass prisms. In each of the four corners green-shaded reading-lamps burned. They were perched on brackets screwed into the wall, but attached to long flexible coils so that they might be placed anywhere at the occupant's convenience.

Stanforth was round like a flash as the door opened. Obviously not only his nerves but his faculties were on the very razor edge of fierce expectancy.

"Oh, it's you, is it?" he growled. "Why the hell didn't you give me a warning? I might have slugged a bullet into you. For the love of mud sing *out* before you mess about with that door."

He spoke viciously. On a task that filled every scrap of his senses it was not easy to cool down to normal at a moment's notice. All the time his eyes were flicking from wall to wall, from corner to corner, from floor to ceiling, there was not a square foot of space in the whole room that his eyes were not continually scanning and re-scanning.

Kennedy essayed a reassuring smile, but it was a ghastly effort, a humourless grin that exposed his teeth like a death's head.

"Sorry, Stan," he apologised. "Couldn't hear you moving. Just wanted to see if things were all right. You said you'd give us a signal more frequently."

"Been getting my bearings," said Stanforth irritably. "Trying to fix suspicious spots in my head. But damned if I can make anything out yet. All right. I'll give a knock every half minute. Can't whistle. Tried to, but my tongue's as dry as a rag. Be all right in a bit."

Kennedy withdrew his head with an easier feeling.

"Seems all right, sir," he said as he pulled the door to.

"Send and ask Lord Gairlie to come here," replied the Chief shortly. "Ask him to bring the plans of the ground floor—the sections concerning this library and the rooms around."

A few minutes passed, leaden things, slower and even more dragging than the ticking of the soulless clock across the way.

Stanforth was moving about with more freedom inside. They could hear the soft scuff of his boots on the carpet, and every now and then a loose board squeaked faintly as his weight came on it. The listening men found themselves waiting for that little squeak, counting on it as a definite proof of their man's continued welfare. At erratic intervals came the abrupt tap of the black pinhead.

Lord Gairlie came down with the plans and the Chief studied them. From them it became clear that one side of the library was actually part of the castle wall. In an earlier century it had had some other use than as a quiet study and storehouse for precious books, though what that use was and why the room was built windowless was unknown. The point that mattered to the Chief was that the far wall of the library was the man castle wall, and that immediately beyond was the wide sweep of the grounds. Just to cover even that vague chance, he sent two reliable men out to patrol that wall outside.

Kennedy tapped at the door and looked in again. Stanforth was still all right. Kennedy informed him quietly of the new covering move outside, and Stanforth muttered his agreement.

Half an hour passed, a half hour of tense silence, broken only by the shuffle of Stanforth's moving feet and the sharp tap of the pin on the panel.

And then, just when the unbearable strain was beginning to wear off—it came. There was just the faintest little "plop," from inside the room, followed by a strangled gasp. Then a revolver shot crashed out and the Chief and Kennedy flung themselves against the door as there came the sound of a heavy fall from within.

It had all happened in less than a second from the first little "plop" to the impact of the detectives' shoulders on the door. But in that moment the whole of the guard in the hall were galvanised into sudden vaulting life.

It was electric. Kennedy and the Chief were at the door in a single swaying leap. There were four others within two yards of the entrance, and they were on the jump before the shot rang out. One same concentrated sweep of movement seemed to communicate itself to every man there.

The door swept round and cannoned heavily against the wall, jarring the partition wall with such force that one of the reading lamps fell from its bracket with a crash. The crowd were at the door, a group of white faces staring in at the scene inside. Kennedy, with the force of his collision with the unresisting door, went sprawling on his face into the room. To that sudden plunge he probably owed his life, for the fall shook him so that for several seconds he lay there, gasping, while the invisible, colourless something that might have slain him drifted by over his head.

The Chief caught just the faintest whiff of it as he stumbled forward into the room At the first breath he staggered back; the faint, hardly perceptible aroma of bitter almonds was there in the air; the thin, illusively dreadful taint of hydrocyanic.

"Back!" he gasped. "Back, all the lot of you!"

He pulled a handkerchief from his pocket and stuffed it over his nose and mouth. There was a violent pricking going on in his lungs where the slight touch of the dispersing vapour had scorched the membranes, and the breath-catching grip of it had made his eyes water badly. It was like sniffing a super-strong solution of ammoniated spirits of salts.

Hydrocyanic, being a highly volatile gas, disperses rapidly. It also tends to rise, which was the only reason why Kennedy did not stiffen out like a log where he lay.

Stanforth was lying in a huddled heap by the edge of the carpet. Above him a wisp of smoke hung faintly in the glare of the lights: the sharp tang of cordite stung the air. Overhead, towards the panelled ceiling, a jagged hole showed in the white of the wall. The room all round was panelled in carved oak almost black with age, but between the top of the panelling and the edge of the ceiling was a deep frieze of white plaster. Dotted along the frieze were some fine old pieces of willow plate, and it was in the centre of that frieze, between two blue plates, that the bullet had struck. It had torn a big hole, for the soft lead of the bullet had expanded on impact, and a powdering of fallen plaster lay on the floor under the hole.

The Chief went in, and turned the body over. Stanforth was quite dead, his forefinger still gripping convulsively on the trigger of his revolver.

And beyond that there was nothing; nothing except that faint scattering of minutely shattered glass on the floor. There was one piece lying close to the dead man, the largest piece they had ever found. It was nearly half an inch square and it was eggshell thin. But the rest of it was almost powder, as fine as grains of sand. Some of it was blown into Stanforth's clothing; and there was the same look of shock and fright in his face that was so marked a characteristic in the other cases.

Kennedy was picking himself slowly to his feet; his sullen, angry eyes turned on the body of his partner. For ten years those two had worked together, a double-harness team as sound as any the Yard had known. Many of the riskiest jobs in the department had fallen to their lot, and neither of them had ever been known to shirk the issue. Gunmen and hard cases, drug traffickers with strings of a—med bullies at their heels, murder jobs with the murderer ready to do another the moment the hand of the law showed up—all sorts of touchy cases where the first law was courage and the last was self had come their way and been taken in their stride as part of the daily grind. And long, lanky Stanforth had always taken his share of the heat of the day without a murmur or a growl. And now that was all over; over and done with. The most reliable double-harness pair in all headquarters was broken, back-pegged, finished. Kennedy was groping through a blind fog of vengeful hate and vague unbelief. That partnership had lasted too long.

"Dead, is he?" he asked as he stood up. It was as much as he could do to look at the Chief. Somehow that fallen body mesmerised his eyes.

The Chief did not answer. He waved the crowd back and shut the door. "Damned awful, isn't it?" he said at last.

Kennedy stared at his partner. "I'll—I'll strangle the swine when I get him!" he burst out. "I'll get my fingers on his throat and—and—" He stopped suddenly and turned away.

"Bah—what's the use of talking!" he growled. "He's gone—and—say, Chief, where do we get off now? We're as far as ever we were. And We've lost another; one of the best I've ever known. For God's sake how did it happen? How much longer is it going on? If we don't get our claws into something soon I shall go stark staring mad."

The Chief was staring up at the hole in the frieze. To him the mystery seemed to concentrate on that revolver shot. What was Stanforth firing at; was he firing at anything? There was not a clue of any sort. He went over to the body again. Death had been as instantaneous as a flash of light. All the evidence of instant and complete annihilation was there in the face. He stooped to take the revolver from the lifeless hand. The finger was gripping the trigger so stiffly that he had to twist the gun half round to disengage it.

"Do you think he saw anything, sir?" asked Kennedy dully.

"No. I believe the firing of that shot was purely accidental. He probably saw the bomb coming—or heard it bursting. (That, I imagine, was the 'plop' we heard.) It was either the sight or the sound of that glass bulb that made him gasp. When it burst he was immediately enveloped in the smothering fumes. The sudden contraction of the muscles caused the gun to go off. He may even have been dead when he fired. Self-preservation would make him fling his hands to his face: it is an instinct older than the hills. That accounts for the bullet going right up there."

"You don't think anyone tried to get at him through the ceiling?" suggested Kennedy.

"That ceiling is only eight inches thick, and there have been two men posted in the room above since Stanforth went in."

The door was suddenly flung open and Delayn entered in a state of eager excitement. In his hand was a fat bunch of paper strips. They were litmus papers, and two out of every three were dull red.

Delayn made a wide fan of the strips and thrust them under the Chief's eyes. "What do you make of this, Chief?" he asked.

The Chief took them with newer seriousness on his face.

"Go on, boy. What happened?" he said quietly.

"Well—just nothing—except that!" Delayn nodded towards the strips. "I've just collected them from some of the upstairs rooms. Looks as though there's been a hydrocyanic explosion in pretty well every room in the Castle! I haven't tried the third or fourth floors yet. All these papers are from the floor immediately above this. I put them behind picture frames, underneath tables, at the back of ornaments, and over half of them record the discharge of hydrocyanic. What do you make of it?"

The Chief examined them closely. Delayn had done the thing thoroughly. Every one was neatly printed with the number or description of the room in which it had been secreted. He hunted for the one from the room overhead. There it was: Number 3, First Floor—and it was almost crimson.

For a few minutes the Chief was silent.

"Looks pretty bad, sir," said Kennedy in an undertone.

"Yes," muttered the Chief. "It's getting worse and worse. It must be a maniac—an absolute maniac. Looks as though these poison discharges take place blindly, with the perpetrator unaware of the effects of his action."

"Then these deaths are accidental?"

"More or less. He's aiming to kill, but he isn't always sure there's a victim in the room when he explodes his bomb. That leads to another line of thought—a dreadful one. These bombs may be hidden in the room hours even days, before they explode. There may be another chemical aamixture in them which slowly increases the pressure till bursting point is reaches."

"Sounds feasible," muttered Kennedy. "That would account for red litmus slips, and explains the wanton killing of Betty Halston and Harris."

"Then," cut in Delayn, "there may be dozens of these damnable things concealed in the Castle at this very moment?"

"Obviously," said the Chief, with a worried frown. "It means the whole place must be searched at once. And there's the possibility of the foul things going off at any moment. What's the best antidote for this gas, Delayn?"

"There would be a grave risk at any time. He's using his gas in its most powerful form. The only safeguard, and it is certainly not guaranteed is alkali in strong solution. I would suggest it soaked in lint sopping wet and tied over the mouth and nose."

"Have you any in your room?"

"Heaps. I'll go up and mix the strongest solution I can make."

"Then make half a dozen masks, too. You'll help in the search. It's best to have someone who knows a little about the technical side of it."

"Certainly; who are the others?"

"Kennedy and myself and any others who care to volunteer."

* * *

Twelve days had slipped away since Stanforth's death. Days that were crowded with alternate surges of hope and despair, of temporary promises of success and the stings of continued failure. The search had revealed nothing. Not a bomb had been found; not a single thing even remotely resembling a container of lethal gas. All the most likely and unlikely places in the Castle were delved into, turned upside down and explored to the last inch. The only new piece of evidence vouchsafed in the hunt was that the servants' quarters bad remained immune. All the litmus strips scattered through the staff rooms were as blue as when they were first attached.

The inquest revealed nothing more than was already known. It was simply a repetition of the other three. The same evidence was given, the same symptoms explained by Doctor Mabey. Death was due to hydrocyanic poisoning by inhalation. As to how it was administered he had nothing to say.

Even the Chief's evidence, given with all the quiet force at his command, failed to bring in a verdict against José Latta. The Coroner, sitting with a jury called from the town in view of the intense local feeling against Latta known to exist, ruled out much of the Chief's assertions. He held that such evidence was not for his consideration but for the ears of a magistrate. The result was that the same verdict was returned—wilful murder against some person or persons unknown.

Inquiries were put on foot as to the history of José Latta. The immigration officials were called in; their vast organisation began to swing into action.

Latta's history, so far as could be traced locally, was uninteresting. He was an ordinary itinerant Italian, who for years had earned a precarious living in the neighbourhood. He was native to no particular village, but tramped around, skimming a few coppers from day to day as he passed. The strains of his wheezy organ were liable to be heard at any tavern door in the countryside, and his little monkey was known to children from one end of the county to another. And that was as far as the information went.

Latta, so far as the very efficient local police could trace, was just a usual Italian organ-grinder of the type that just seems to happen naturally in a locality every now and then.

And then the immigration people got on the right road. From somewhere in the expanse of their mighty web a single loose strand had appeared. To their experienced eyes, that was suspicious. The vigilance and supervision of incoming aliens is so complete that a broken link shouts aloud of something gone wrong in the chain.

They followed the strand and traced it right back into Italy, the old Italy that lies at the heel of the boot and looks out over the blue waters of Otranto.

Right through to Torre Cavallo they traced it and ran it to earth in the old castle that stands on the crest of Pinta della Contessa, looking out to sea.

A great sheaf of information was unfurled. It was put into a sealed portfolio and dispatched to the Home Office. The Home Office sent it to Scotland Yard. And Scotland Yard sent for the Chief.

The Chief went up in his own car. The whole dossier was spread out on his table in chronological order, and he went through the papers rapidly at first, then with increasing care.

At the end of it all he stood up and looked at the Commissioner…

"Extraordinary!" he said.

The Commissioner cast an imperious eye over the documents.

"But, you'll admit, fairly conclusive?" he said.

"Absolutely watertight!" said the Chief. "As thorough a job I've seen for years. At least, from that end. The chain is as complete as an endless cable. Link by link it's all there. But, as I say, only from the Italian end."

"You doubt if this man is the José Latta of Torre Cavallo?"

"Hardly that. He may be; probably is. But the connection on this side is not fairly established. I mean the necessary binding element between the events at Torre Cavallo and Latta's campaign at Gairlie Castle."

"My dear Chief, I should think the rubies would be link enough. It's a cause—a motive. It works, even by the most elementary rule of thumb."

"Yes," grunted the Chief. "But if Gairlie has never been to Italy, if none of the rubies ever came originally from Italy, where's the link?"

"Not satisfied, eh?" queried the Commissioner.

The Chief did not reply for a while. Silently he collected the papers and replaced them in the portfolio. Then he said grimly: "I didn't say so. But I'll be able to tell you tonight—after I've had half an hour with Lord Gairlie."

He drove back to Gairlie with the whole dossier out on his knees, poring over the documents again and again until the whole story was printed on his memory. When the car pulled up at Gairlie he had worked it out its logical conclusion, and was impatient to talk the matter out with his lordship.

Lord Gairlie was in and the Chief sent a message to him asking for an interview in a few minutes. Meanwhile he took the dossier through to Kennedy and gave him a full résumé of the affair. Kennedy went through the papers with the Chief at his elbow making explanatory notes as he progressed.

"How does it strike you?" asked the Chief when Kennedy was through.

Kennedy breathed gently. "I'd say there was enough here to hang Latta without anything else. That's if he's the same man. But—it all depends."

"Exactly," agreed the Chief quietly. "His lordship is coming along in a minute, and I'm going to try it. You'd better be here too. You can make notes of his replies if he tries to wriggle. With a story like this he may take a bit of nailing, but if it's all on the level he'll come out with the straight story—if he's wise."

They talked for a few minutes, almost in whispers, and then Lord Gairlie came in.

"Good evening, Chief," he said. "Sorry to have kept you waiting, but glad to see you again. Had a pleasant journey?"

"Yes, my lord, and, I think, a most profitable one." There was an incisiveness in the Chief's voice that made Gairlie look at him with a sharper interest.

"Not more bad news, I hope?" he asked quietly.

"On the contrary. Certain information has come into my hands, which may or may not throw a light on the series of mysterious occurences going on here for the last few months. Inquiries outside this country have recently produced results that, to say the very least, demand further inquiry. And it is in respect of those results that I wish to solicit your help."

"Certainly, certainly," said Gairlie, pulling a chair up beside the two men. "Won't you smoke?" He held out a leather cigar-case.

The Chief took one in silence. He paused with the cigar halfway to his lips. "This help that you can give me will probably take the form of a questionnaire from me to you," he said. "Have you any objection?"

"Not the slightest. I'm only too glad to be of any assistance, though I cannot see what—"

The Chief struck a match and poised it in front of his cigar.

"I need not tell you, sir, that you need not answer a single question unless you wish," he said. "If you do, you will be doing so simply to please yourself, and to help me clear up this mess."

"Quite; I understand."

Lord Gairlie was looking at him oddly. The Chief seemed to have become vaguely antagonistic. There was something unfriendly in the little hard inflections in his voice; there was a warning in them, an official hint that the free and easy companionship of the past weeks was only an assumption, and that behind the friendly mask was the face of Authority.

The Chief puffed at his cigar. Kennedy had already got his glowing with an unhurried stolidness that franked his own personal peace of mind.

Gairlie leaned forward and put a hand on the detective's knee.

"Precisely what is the trouble, Chief?" he asked. "Nothing unpleasant, I hope?"

"That depends, sir," said the Chief. "In the first place, have you ever been in Italy?" The Chief fired the question at him direct. If he expected it to cause Gairlie any uneasiness he was disappointed.

Gairlie, raising his eyebrows in slight surprise, murmured, "Why, yes. Several times. I have big business interests in both Rome and Milan."

The Chief waved his cigar. "Further south, my lord," he said. "Say, right down by the Strait of Otranto."

"Yes, I know it well. Lady Gairlie and I wintered there once."

"When?"

"I think it would be about nineteen hundred and eight or nine. Wait a moment and I can tell you exactly. Lady Gairlie was not well and I took her straight to Italy, Lonora was still a baby—three, I think. Yes; that was it, nineteen eight."

"Where did you stay?"

"Moved about a good deal. There are some beautiful little villages down on the southern littoral. But Brindisi was our headquarters for all mail. Every couple of weeks or so we went back there for shopping and all that sort of thing."

"H'm! Brindisi, eh? Did you ever get down to Torre Cavallo while you were there?"

Gairlie looked up sharply. "Torre Cavallo?" he replied. "Yes, I did go there once or twice."

"Something happened there, didn't it, my lord?"

"N—no; I'd hardly call it that. But—"

"Well?"

"The only thing about Torre Cavallo that I remember is that it was there that I got hold of the Burning Star."

"That is the big pendant stone, isn't it?"

Gairlie nodded. "Yes, the original of the one Kennedy found at the gap in the hedge."

"Fairly important stone, isn't it?"

"Biggest in Great Britain," said Gairlie decidedly. "It is reputed to be the biggest in the world, but I think that claim is exaggerated a little. There are stones in some of the Maharajahs' royal regalias that are possibly far larger than mine."

"But at least," went on the Chief, "the Burning Star is the biggest in England?"

"Undoubtedly."

"And extremely valuable?"

"It alone is insured for twenty thousand pounds."

"Is that your assessment of its value in the open market?"

The peer shook his head thoughtfully. "Hard to tell," he said. "So much depends on market conditions. If a collector really wanted it he would go to considerably more. Rubies that size aren't picked up every day."

"Would you sell it for twenty thousand?"

"Certainly not. I could dispose of it tomorrow for more than that. One collector, an extremely wealthy American, cables me an increased offer every six months or so."

There was a touchy uncomfortable silence for some time. It was as though the Chief had been fencing and was slightly puzzled to find that his foil pierced nothing but air. Gairlie's answers had come straight and sure. His admission of the origin of the Burning Star had come unasked. It was the one big fact that he had offered voluntarily, all the rest had come as a result of direct questioning. And it was the one point on which the Chief had expected to have to drag out of him by sheer persistence of cross-examination. He was unsettled. Gairlie wasn't acting as though he had anything to hide, and yet, almost as though he was on a shrewd defensive, he wasn't giving away an inch.

"You see what all this is leading up to, don't you, sir?" The Chief looked across from under half-lowered lids.

"Candidly—I don't," answered Gairlie without hesitation.

"Well, equally candidly—just *this*. Where did the Burning Star originally come from—*and*—how did you get hold of it?"

Gairlie's hand was going out to take his cigar from the ash tray. Halfway there it stopped dead. Kennedy screwed his eyes round and looked at him. Lord Gairlie's hand shook and he had white under his tan.

For a moment the peer looked at the Chief steadily with an intent scrutiny. The question had come to him knife-like and hard. There was no disguising the timbre of it. It was the voice of Authority, and Gairlie realised vaguely that the police were in possession of facts that in some way told against him. Something had happened back there in Italy and he was struggling to get his wits to bear on it.

He admitted that the stone had come to him in a remarkable way and that in the getting of it he had won the prize of a lifetime—and dirt cheap. But everything had been perfectly legitimate and above-board, The only snag that he could recall was the price he paid and the fact that such a large stone should have existed in the apparently open market without his being aware of it. Still, the Star had been offered to him openly and without any show of secrecy and he had bought it, marvelling the while at its cheapness.

"You remember the incident?" It was the voice of Authority again hinting that the law does not brook being kept waiting for an answer.

"Perfectly—perfectly," said Gairlie in an uneasy voice. "I can even remember the names connected with the sale. I believe I still have one or two documents—letters and such like—that passed between us. I have the receipt in any case. Shall I ring for it?"

"Where did that stone originally come from—*and*—how much did give for it?" There was steel and acid in the Chief's voice and something more, too, that was just a little merciless. Gairlie got the picture of him then as very much the high officer of the law, which, having got its teeth into something, was not letting go until it was satisfied.

"I haven't the least idea where the stone originally came from," Gairlie bluntly. "I gave a thousand pounds for it."

"A thousand pounds. H'm. Something less than a twentieth of its value. Bit of a bargain, wasn't it?"

Gairlie smiled faintly. At any other time he would have plunged into the story with all the collector's exultation in having wrested a plum from the tree. He would have revelled in it as he had done a hundred times before, swelling with pride at having brought off a successful coup in the byways of the collector's world.

"A bargain in a million," he said simply. "It only happens once in a lifetime. I don't expect it to happen again."

The Chief shifted in his chair and crossed one knee over the other. "Hadn't you better tell the whole story—in your own words?" he suggested.

"If you wish it, Chief. It's quite simple. Its only point being that it was a genuine transaction and not a spoof: for really by the time I got the stone I fully expected to find it a fake."

"Yes—well?"

"I was staying at the Hotel Vittoria at the time, a nice little place looking out on the Strait at Torre Cavallo. In the afternoon I received a call from a person giving the name of Emmanuel Calaghi."

"Who?" interjected the Chief suddenly.

"Emmanuel Calaghi, an Italian, an extremely well-spoken man, with the most engaging manners. He spoke English fluently."

"Make a note of that name, Kennedy," grunted the Chief.

Gairlie waited while Kennedy wrote, and then continued: "He was a somewhat remarkable individual in that he appeared to know a great deal more about me than I thought was known in the little town. For instance, he knew that I was Lord Gairlie, though we were travelling as Mr. and Mrs. Bulmerdine, my family name. He knew that I was an extremely rich man, which in those days was blessedly true. Furthermore he knew that the collection of rubies was my hobby and that I had already amassed a number of unusually large specimens. I naturally admitted all this, but requested him not to make my identity public. He assured me that he had no such intention, and coming quickly to business, asked if I was open to buy a decent ruby if it should be offered. I replied that I was always ready to buy a good stone provided it was up to my quality. He then told me that he knew of a hundred and forty carat stone, flawless save for a minute air-cloud in the base, and that fault so tiny that it was only visible under a microscope.

"I was astonished, very naturally. A hundred and forty carat stone is a tremendous thing in the jewel world. But he assured me that there was such a stone and that it was for sale. If I would name the price I was prepared to go to he might be able to bring off a deal satisfactory to both of us. It appeared that he was not the actual owner, but an intermediary. A commission agent or a friend, I can't say which, for I never saw him again."

The Chief nodded to Kennedy to jot that statement down.

"I told him that I couldn't possibly do business on those terms. I couldn't make him an offer for something I hadn't seen. I should want to see it first, to handle and test it, quite probably to send it to London for assessment and report—for I was not such an expert in ruby values then as I am today. Nowadays assessors come to me for an opinion, sometimes even for advice. I asked him if he had any conception of the value of a flawless ruby weighing a hundred and forty carats. Quite frankly he said he hadn't, but that no doubt he could get the stone for me, and if I would insure it in his name, I could have it for a few days' inspection before making an offer.

"That was an eminently fair proposal, and I accepted. He said that he would either bring the stone the following day or send someone to me to account for his absence. A little delay might arise owing to the fact that he thought it advisable to get police protection—a very sensible precaution, I thought.

"I was keenly interested, as you may imagine. It was like dipping one's hand into a bran tub and bringing out the finest prize in the whole tub. I asked him for some particulars about the stone. Where had it come from? Who had first brought it to Italy? Who was the owner? Why wasn't it insured—for had it been insured I should certainly have heard of it.

"But on all these points he was non-committal. The ruby, he said, had been in the possession of a certain local family for generations. Its existence had not been divulged because there were certain incidents connected with its coming out of India that the family thought best should remain hidden. It is my belief that the ruby had been hidden away somewhere when it was first stolen, and had only just come to light again; the descendants of the old marauder in faraway India had suddenly unearthed it and wished to turn it into good silver lire. That was only my impression, of course, but it persisted.

"I was so eager, and yet in a way, so incredulous about the whole thing, that I asked for the name of the vendor in confidence. He regretted his inability to give it to me at that stage, but declared that before the deal went through he would put me in full possession of all the facts I required. The only thing he asked was that I would telegraph my bank in England to send funds out to meet my cheque so that a quick sale could be effected.

"In view of the fact that he was receiving police protection I assented for it was obvious that none but a fool would call in the police unless everything was on the square. Calaghi, perfectly satisfied, bowed himself out. That evening I went to the post office and wired in my own code two hundred thousand lire to be telegraphed to the local bank. The lira in those blissful days hovered with beautiful stability around twenty to the pound sterling. In sending for ten thousand pounds I was allowing for a certain Latin tendency to exaggeration.

"Lady Gairlie returned in time for dinner, and over coffee on the veranda we opened our letters. You can imagine my mystification when I opened one with an Italian stamp and found a repetition of the offer just made me by Calaghi."

The Chief cocked his ears up and leaned back in his chair.

"That letter," he said quietly, "was posted in Brindisi. It was signed Carlo Valotti. Yes, continue."

Lord Gairlie stared at him. "How on earth did you know that?"

"Quite all right, my lord. You just carry on. I'm beginning to sea light. You don't speak Italian, do you? Not enough to read the local paper?"

"Oh dear, no. Just enough to carry on a one-sided warfare with the waiter at our table; sufficient to order dinner, and that's about all."

The Chief nodded. "That's to be regretted," he said. "Had you been able to read you would never have got possession of the Burning Star. Emmanuel Calaghi came to you on October tenth, nineteen hundred and eight. Isn't that so?"

"Somewhere about then."

"You can take it from me, sir, it was. On the morning of October the eleventh Emmanuel Calaghi was found in his house at Torre Cavalle with a Mafia knife stuck in his back."

"Good God!" whispered Gairlie.

"And the police have been hunting for Carlo Valotti ever since," added the Chief grimly.

Lord Gairlie looked dumbly at the Chief, wishing with all understood a half of what was passing in the detective's mind. His thoughts began to swim, tumbling pell-mell over each other in a broken compote that became more and more distracting as fresh thoughts tumbled amongst them.

At last, after what seemed half a night of waiting, the Chief took a tiny slip of paper from his pocket and scanned it, then put it back in his pocket. That was all. The simplest of actions. But somehow it seemed so enormously full of malignant portent, that Gairlie's nerves jumped up on edge.

"Well?" said the Chief. It was a short, clipped off little syllable more pregnant with command than any bawled out order.

Lord Gairlie ran a finger round the inside of his collar. Somehow it had gone surprisingly tight.

"Really—I—er—things have taken such an extraordinary twist that I—er—er—I'm rather out of my depth. I—er—I hardly know what to say. I assure you I was entirely ignorant of such a dreadful crime hidden behind the purchase of my Star. Honestly this is my first intimation of so tragic an affair. I bought it in all good faith, accepting the story at the story's worth. Emmanuel Calaghi dead—murdered—I can scarcely believe it."

"Well, *you* never saw him again, did you?" said the Chief.

"No, I—er—why for all I know, I might have been the last man whoever saw him alive!"

"You were!" said the Chief flatly.

Gairlie went white. For a fearful moment he thought the Chief was accusing him.

"Calaghi had been dead many hours when the body was discovered," he went on." Medical evidence put it as sixteen. What time did he leave you?"

"About—four o'clock," jerked Gairlie.

"Four o'clock in the afternoon to eight next morning is sixteen hours. And Calaghi's body was *carried* to his house. There was a blood trail right from the Hotel Vittoria to his front window, a lattice thing open day and night. The murderer just carted him along and put him in there. Four o'clock in the afternoon, broad, blinding sunlight, and nobody saw it. Uncanny, you think? Not very. You owe it to that fact alone that a warrant didn't go out for Mr. Bulmerdine! Mafia. That's the power of it. Or was then—before the war. You can bet your life that scores of people saw, possibly including the police. And they also saw the Mafia knife. That's quite enough for any south-born Italian. Probably it was because Mafia was at the back of it that Valotti wasn't taken red-handed next day. He was marked. That I know. You bought the Burning Star three days after the receipt of that letter from Valotti?"

Gairlie admitted it.

"Valotti was given that long to clear. The warrant wasn't issued until the fourth day," the Chief went on. "Still, that's neither here nor there. You had got to the point where, after Calaghi had gone, you received a letter from Brindisi, signed by Carlo Valotti. Continue from there. You don't happen to have that letter now, I suppose?"

"As a matter of fact I have. I kept it as a souvenir of the event."

"I'd like to see it afterwards, if you please. What did Valotti say?"

"In the letter?"

"Yes. Was it in English or Italian?"

"English. Very bad English. He said that a Signor Calaghi would be calling on me, probably had already called and would have explained all about his mission. He assured me that the stone was now out of Calaghi's hands and had been entrusted into his keeping. If it was convenient he would call at my hotel at midday, when he would be in a position to produce the stone within an hour. If the hour was inconvenient, would I please a note in the foyer for him, mentioning any time suitable to myself, and the deal could be put through with expedition and dispatch.

"Well, in view of the fact that Calaghi had already said he might have sent a representative who would act for him, I saw nothing suspicious in that. The whole thing seemed to fit itself in quite clearly, and to be perfectly honest, the possibility of there being any sort of criminal intent at the back of it never even entered my mind."

"You saw him at midday?"

"Yes. He seemed a pretty ragged specimen; but then, none of the coastal Italians are anything more than picturesque."

"You saw him alone? Lady Gairlie was not there?"

"I was quite alone. I wanted to give Lady Gairlie a pleasant surprise when I put the stone into her hand."

The Chief nodded. "Yes. Go on."

"He spoke English a little better than he wrote it, though he was difficult to follow. He explained, in a version of the story that differed very little from Calaghi's, that the jewel was in bad odour in the household concerned. There were internal jealousies at work in the house, different branches of the family claimed it, and yet none dared put it on the market and make public the history that lay behind it. If I would buy the stone and make no mention of the vendor's name I could have it quite cheaply.

"I pointed out that as I did not know the vendor's name I could not very well divulge it. Valotti seemed relieved and said that his instructions were that he was not, under any consideration, to divulge the name. The gem had lain hidden away and practically forgotten so long that it was just as well not to disturb the dust of old bones. The stone could be sold quietly and taken out of the country—and nothing more would be heard of it. All that was asked of me was a promise not to open my mouth about the affair while I was in Italy: and on reaching England I would not give the story to the Press or even say definitely where I originally bought the stone.

"I promised on condition that the stone was worth purchase, and that I received a written receipt for my money. He appeared perfectly satisfied with my promise, and when I asked him the tested weight he replied without hesitation: 'One hundred and forty-two carats—English jeweller's weight.' I was incredulous, amazed! If you have any conception of the collector's fervour you will understand. I was mad to see that stone. I asked him when I could see it. Without another word he pulled something from his tattered pocket and tossed it on the table—the living pulsing Burning Start!"

Lord Gairlie checked up for a moment, his eyes alight and glowing. For him the moment was born anew, that first nerve-stinging moment when his eyes first beheld the Burning Star in all its marvelous beauty.

"Can you—can you imagine what I felt like just then?" he asked, staring excitedly at the Chief. "A dream come true. A silly, foolish, hopelessly unattainable dream—such as all collectors carry in their inmost hearts, come true before my eyes. A reality. The biggest, most astonishing ruby my eyes had ever beheld. And never since have I seen one so big or so perfect. I picked the stone up tremblingly. I knew just a little about rubies, even then, though not nearly so much as I know now. And even to my half-tutored eye it was obvious that the thing was genuine; as flawless a stone as I have ever seen. I took it out on the balcony, the better to examine it under the fierce light of the noonday. I had my glass with me, and I went over every tiny facet of it. You know the stone? You have seen the copy. It is shaped like a monster loganberry. I had stumbled on the absolutely exquisite and unbelievable.

"I wheeled on him and demanded the price, aware in my heart that the ten thousand I had cabled for would not be nearly enough. I was prepared for almost any exorbitantly impossible price, for I was not unschooled to the ways of the Latin, and I expected at least an hour's hard bargaining, with possibly not a little bad language before the deal was through—and I was quite ready to go to a good deal more than its strictly commercial value, for I was buying never to sell again.

"Judge my utter amazement when he took a foul-smelling cigarette from his lips and quietly murmured, 'Twenty thousand lire.'

"I knew I couldn't possibly have heard aright, and I repeated my question. 'Twenty thousand lire, signor,' he repeated, and blew smoke rings among the glass beads of the candelabra.

"'Twenty thousand lire?' I gasped. 'You mean pounds, surely.' But he shook his head, quite unconcernedly. 'No, signor. Twenty thousand lire. The price is little—ah, so tiny—but that is all that is asked. Not many people like you come to Torre Cavallo, and that ruby, he buy your silence too. That is why he is cheap. He is no good to the one he belong to. If he keep him he just lay there in the little drawer. Year after year. No good to the one he belong to. No good to anyone else. If he sell him for the big price he must go to the big sale. And then—trouble! Ah, such trouble! Six, eight, ten of the family all claim the share that is not theirs. The feud break out again. But now, he forgotten. For man year no one ask about him. He is still in his little drawer, and there he stay forever. But soon you will pay for him twenty thousand lire. And then you will go away and forget Torre Cavallo, forget Emmanuel Calaghi, forget Carlo Valotti. Maybe you forget all Italy and come no more here. Ah? Yes? '

"'Look here,' I said. 'I must send this stone to Rome and get it valued. I want to find out where the trick is. You understand? If the stone is real I will buy it, and pay anything you ask in reason. If not I shall take it straight to the police station and tell them this story. Do you agree?'

"He nodded his head violently. 'Yes, yes, I agree,' he said without the slightest embarrassment.

"I sent one of the bank messengers by car right away to Brindisi, where he caught the afternoon train to Rome. The bank told me the the right jewellers to go to, and I wrote them a note. The gist of it was: Is this a genuine ruby, and if so, do you know its history?'

"The man was back in a couple of days with the stone. The jeweller's reply is in one of the bureaux in the library now. Their answer was that it was one of the most beautiful rubies they had ever seen, certainly the largest. They were surprised to see it, as, up till then, they were quite unaware of its existence. To their knowledge there was no such stone in all Italy, unless it had been hoarded away for generations in some unknown private collection.

"All that completely bore out everything that Carlo Valotti had said. I was beginning to feel a bit of a cur forever having doubted the poor brute.

"Valotti called and I discussed the matter with him. You may perhaps be amused at the idea, but I was actually arguing with him to take more for the thing. But twenty thousand lire was his price, and twenty thousand lire was all he would take. That and secrecy. Those were the terms and I paid them. I got the cash from the bank and he gave me his receipt."

The Chief was silent for a long time, staring hard at Kennedy. His brain was racing along over details he had just heard with lightning rapidity. Then he muttered in a suppressed voice: "God, you were lucky, my lord." He leaned forward and looked Gairlie right in the eyes. "You left Torre Cavallo the same day, didn't you?" he said.

Gairlie nodded. "Yes, almost within an hour. I was eager to take the Burning Star somewhere where it could be properly set. We had a sort of footman-chauffeur with us."

"Ah! You went by car!" The Chief breathed the words as though light had dawned on him. "Yes, of course! And you owe your life to that—certainly you owe twenty thousand lire and the Burning Star to it."

"But—but—I don't quite—"

"The Mafia had marked you down for twenty thousand lire... visiting Englishman whose consul might kick up a bit of a stink, the job had to be neatly done. The usual methods wouldn't work. So they played the ruby trick on you—and for the first time in feudal history the Mafia lost. And they lost because there was a renegade in their own ranks. Calaghi was the leader of the Mafia for a hundred miles round. That is their talisman—the symbol of their chieftainship. And you've got it! But you see—the Mafia, or what's left of it, has traced you even to here. You were to have been interviewed a few days later by one who would have represented himself to be the Chief of Police. He would have hinted at the transaction, informing you it was a stolen gem. You, to save scandal, would have had to give it up. But Calaghi turned. He wanted the full price. He was ready to clear with your good money in his pocket. Someone in the hotel—the waiter, maybe—was also a Mafia agent. He overheard. Calaghi died. You got the stone. The sudden departure took them by surprise. The 'Chief of Police' generally catches you in the station. *But they're on your trail my lord.* Carlo Valotti had a crinkled scar on the lobe of his left ear, I think!"

"Yes, that is so."

"So has the man who has been chasing that ruby ever since. Carlo Valotti is José Latta!"

Lord Gairlie sat back and stared. "I—I can't believe it!" he gasped.

"You will!" replied the Chief tersely. "Times and dates don't lie. The Home Office has ways of its own of ferreting out facts abroad. Valotti got clear without difficulty. Fifteen days later José Latta landed at Southampton."

"Indeed!" said Gairlie in surprise.

"Yes. From the S.S. *Printano*, an Italian tramp steamer whose last port of call was Brindisi. He spent years trying to get on the track of the Mr. Bulmerdine who all unwittingly had given him the slip in 1908. I've turned up the records at the Yard. Latta, under one alias or another, has done several spells of hard labour and two of penal servitude. He has been deported twice. But this is the interesting point. Every conviction against Latta has been for housebreaking—and in every single case the house broken into was owned by a Mr. Bulmerdine! He apparently turned up all the Post Office directories in the kingdom, took the names of all the Bulmerdines he could find, and then waiting his opportunity, broke into their houses, searching for his precious stone. Apparently he did not understand the British peerage. We have only just been able to connect this up, for Latta has been convicted under all sorts of fictitious names. The vital proof, though, is that in every case where a man named Bulmerdine has had his house broken into, the criminal answers to the description of José Latta. If you want further evidence, my lord, you have it in your own eyesight. You are the only one among us whoever saw Carlo Valotti. But you've seen José Latta hundreds of times. Don't *you* see the resemblance?"

"Y-yes," muttered the peer. "Now that you call it to mind, of course, I do. But, of course, I never even thought of it till now—never dreamed of connecting the two. This was all years ago—and—and one inherent Italian is so much like another. The organ and the monkey and—well the general incredibility of the whole thing—I—"

"Quite, my lord, I can understand perfectly. But facts are facts and now you've got them all. The Burning Star was their religious stone. The trick itself is old; there are dozens of similar cases pigeon-holed at the Yard. The victim keeps silence for his own sake. On the face of it the deal looks slim and he wouldn't like the facts to become public. Looks as though he was trying to beat some poor devil out of a fair price for his treasures. But some have smelt a rat, and have given the yard the fact in confidence. I quite believe the Burning Star has been offered to a good many other unsuspecting English visitors to Torre Cavallo. But you, on a sheer fluke, got away with it. I can only offer you a thousand congratulations—and advise you to keep both eyes skinned for the vengeance of the Mafia."

XII

Aching days passed like lead-weighted years. To Lonora they were appallingly empty, as monotonously similar as nights spent in a hospital ward. Tommy had become an enigma. She could scarcely think of him without a feeling of troubled suspicion. A thousand times a day she vowed to herself that if Delayn did not wish to trouble himself further about her she certainly was not going to worry. No man on earth is worth a heartbreak. She was not going to run after him, or even harass her mind with the thought of him. She told herself so bluntly, not without a touch of the old Gairlie asperity.

And yet the battle went on despite her determination. It partook of the nature of a baffling series of questions—without answers.

Why hadn't Tommy spoken to her after that last meeting—after once having broken the ice? Why hadn't he been decent about it and let the old sweet routine return? Did he no longer care for her, now that he had discovered her father's financial instability? Was he still keeping out of her way on account of his own alleged insolvency? If he really was in monetary difficulties, how could he afford to lend her father fifty thousand pounds without apparently feeling the strain?

The fifty thousand, she knew, had gone back to him almost by return of post—did he consider fifty thousand too insignificant a sum on which to offer his hand?

Lonora was in her own orchid house trying not to think. Gairlie was mooning along morosely towards the hothouses, intending to have a quiet talk with her and get her to confide in him. Not that he really knew what was at the back of it all—and if Lonora couldn't talk to Delayn and ask for a plain statement of affairs—*he* could!

He was rounding a clump of peony bushes, already showing a mass of green leaves, when he heard hurrying footsteps overtaking him. He turned to see Delayn coming up almost at a run.

He waited for him and just as Delayn was about to burst out with something which was apparently of high import, he took him under the arm and steered him back the way he had come.

"Ah! Delayn," he said, "I want to have a serious talk with you—a very serious talk. Several times this matter has been on the end of my tongue, but the only time I am able to get a word with you seems in the precence of third parties. And that, you'll admit, is difficult."

Delayn checked up and stared at the peer.

"Well, what's wrong now?" he snapped.

"Why are you still staying in Gairlie Castle?" The question came as a soft-nosed bullet. Delayn stopped and jerked his arm from Gairlie's grip.

"Oh, so it's like that, is it?" he growled, and his eyes screwed up with nasty little glints shooting from behind them. "Like *that*! Well, in the first place, because I was forced to—even at the expense of a night in a police cell. And in the second place, because, having had to stay here a month against my will, I brought my laboratory paraphernalia down here, and with my experiments in their present stage, it is highly inconvenient for me to break off and go."

"Oh, indeed," said Gairlie. "I would hardly have expected that from you Delayn."

"Exactly what do you mean by that, sir?"

"I mean that to make your supremely ridiculous chemical experiments an excuse for keeping my daughter in this intolerable position, is to say the least of it, rather caddish, don't you think?"

Delayn flushed. "Haven't given that end of it a thought," he declared acidly. "I had it rammed down my throat for a month and now I'm taking the daily dose because I've got used to it, that's all! And as for my supremely ridiculous experiments—take a look at *that*!"

He slipped off his running shoes and stood in his stockinged feet, holding up the soles to the peer's inspection. "I've run twelve miles a day in those every day for five weeks," he said. "Look at 'em, not even started to wear yet. *And* on gritty gravel! By the time I've got my mixtures fixed to my liking and marketed the idea—Soles from the Moulds—I'll be able to lend you another fifty thousand; also the result of a supremely ridiculous experiment."

Gairlie gasped and staggered back.

"And that's not all," went on Delayn. "By midnight tonight, I'll have the whole solution to the mystery of Gairlie Castle neatly folded up and put in an envelope for your clearer understanding."

Delayn turned, a waspish, venomous glare in his eyes. But Lord Gairlie grabbed him by the arm and swung him round, his grip on the sleeve.

"Boy—did you say that *you* were responsible for that fifty thousand loan?" The peer's face wore a look of frozen unbelief, and the tone of his voice was sheer incredulity made vocal.

"I did," said Delayn. "I'm D. Lane, *alias* The Untearable Silk Company. The process you are exploiting now is mine—and I *don't* peel my spuds before I turn 'em into silk socks. My lord, you can take it that I'm not leaving until my finances are in such a condition that I can approach Lonora regarding a matter that has necessarily been in abeyance for some weeks.

Meanwhile, I'll go and find the Chief, or Kennedy, or someone who can help me along another line of business."

Gairlie sat heavily down on a seat, watching the retreating figure of Delayn, who was striding off towards the Castle. Of all the shocks he had ever suffered, this was the most tremendous. He was bereft of words—almost of thoughts. Delayn a master chemist, the man responsible for the "miracle" that had happened to Silk Limited—bitterest of all—the man who had come to his financial salvation! He couldn't credit it. All he could do was to sit and stare at the diminishing figure. He was flabber gasted.

Delayn went on into the Castle. The Chief was sitting at the big table writing what was destined to be his last report from the Castle. If the last few days had been unbearable to Gairlie and Lonora, they had been sheer gall to the man from the Yard. His last fortnight was slipping slowly but surely away. There would be no appeal against the decree of the higher command. Two weeks they had given him in which to clear up his case, and he had had to fight even for that.

Day by day the precious hours had drifted away and with every hour his last hope grew fainter. He felt like a man waiting for a mountain to move of its own volition. Somebody sat on the edge of the table beside him, swinging a leg. The Chief glanced up to see Delayn, still a little flushed after his interview with Lord Gairlie.

"Busy?" jerked the younger man.

The Chief pushed his papers back irritably. "Have I ever been busy since I came down on this confounded case?" he rasped. "I'd like the chance to get busy. It would be a comforting change."

"Well, you can have that chance right now."

The Chief's eyes flickered.

"Go on," said he cheerlessly, "I'm not stopping you!

"John Argle has bobbed up again." Delayn took a cigarette from a neat gold case and lit it placidly.

The Chief watched him like a stoat sighting a rabbit.

"John Argle, eh? Well, that's an item certainly." He was fencing to find the opening that Delayn had apparently found. "But where does that take us to?

"With the thin end of a wafer of luck, Chief, it's going to take us to the end of this case."

The Chief pressed his lips into a straight, unfriendly line.

"Been having a word with him?" he asked softly.

"Hardly," Delayn smiled. "But I've heard him talking."

"Oh? Talking never struck me as being one of John's accomplishments."

"Well, he's talking now," said Delayn grimly. "And he's saying a mouthful, believe me."

"Do you know who John Argle is?" the Chief asked suddenly.

Delayn nodded. "Yes," he said. "I've often wanted to meet one. Interesting devils, aren't they?"

"They are when you can get 'em to talk," grunted the Chief. "But mostly you might as well try to start a political debate with a defunct oyster. Talking, is he? Where?"

"Down at the 'Castle Arms.' He's half tight."

"Not on your life," said the Chief. "Argle doesn't drink."

"Go down and take a look," said Delayn.

The Chief fingered the pages of his report. John Argle down at the "Castle Arms," slowly getting tight? Very slowly his fingers twisted on his report. There was a rustle of tearing paper. Delayn watched him. In a little while there was nothing but a small heap of minute squares of paper, torn out of all recognition.

"Go on, boy, I'm listening," the Chief said.

Delayn jerked his thumb over his shoulder. "I was down there ten minutes ago, called in for a tank of cider. Argle was in there—with half the village staring at him goggle-eyed. He'd put a five-pound note on the counter, and was telling the whole shoot to drink with him. 'Drink up, boys,' he growled, 'Drink to my health and a mighty quick passing! I'll be up for murder this time tomorrow. As God's my judge, they'll be swinging me. Damn good joke that! And all them horrors up at the Castle, they'll be *finished* before the night is out. Finished and done with. I've found what I've been watching for for weeks. Saw it with my own eyes an hour before dawn this morning. And by God, I'll get him tonight—him and his little ghost, too!'

"He was leaning against the bar, Chief, drinking double whiskies. And boss told me he hadn't stopped for an hour. Fifteen doubles, he said, and beyond loosening his tongue he might as well be drinking ice-cream sodas."

The Chief was reaching for his hat. "Come on, son," he said. "I know how to make John open his mouth just one inch more." He was halfway to the door before he finished speaking, with Delayn hurrying along in his wake.

Argle was still propped against the bar when they reached the inn. Ked-eyed, bitter, regardless of the newcomers, his deep voice boomed: Ominously through the room. "Saw him with my own eyes," he declared. "The man who murdered my girl. And as there's a sky above me, I'll kill him stone dead tonight. Man, god, nor devil will stop me. He killed Betty—and though I swing in hell through an eternity for it, I'll smash the living heart of him tonight. And you blighters, take my tip, and stay as far away as you can get from Gairlie Castle tonight. There'll livin' hell let loose there when midnight strikes. Go to bed early an' pull down the blinds. There'll be bullets flying round there—aye, and worse."

He suddenly ripped from his pocket a great blue shining Colt and swept it round the circle of white faces. "G'wan. Drink to me—an' a quick passing. A long drop and a stout rope—that's all I—What in hell's name—"

There was a knife-like movement of a hand over his shoulder, a sharp twist and a backward wrench. Argle heaved round, his hands going out for the throat of the man who had done it. His blazing, smouldering eyes lit full on the figure of the Chief, standing coldly in front of him, tipping the bullets out of the open gun.

"Argle," he said icily. "Come outside."

Imperious as an emperor he took the man by the sleeve and piloted him out through the crowd of frightened locals. Out in the glare of the sunlight he wheeled on him. Argle blinked in alcoholic uncertainty at the masterful face.

"John Argle," said that masterful face, "I want to know what you've seen—and I want to know *now.*"

"I'd sooner swing," came the thundery answer. "Go an—"

"Listen," said the Chief in a steely whisper. "Tell me what you know *and your name will never be mentioned in the case.* You understand what that means? You won't even be called as a witness. If a name should be called for—you'll be simply John Argle and your evidence won't be required. Now—doesn't that satisfy you?"

"My God!" Argle's eyes lit up. "Come here," he grated. "Lemme whisper."

Argle took the Chief away to the side of the road. Delayn could not hear a word of the conversation. All he saw was the huge bulk of John Argle whispering earnestly to the detective, gesticulating in short vehement gestures that intensified the urgency of his words.

The Chief listened with slowly growing wonderment on his face. And when Argle was finished he stepped back and stared at the grey mass of Gairlie Castle rising amid its trees.

"Don't you believe it?" demanded Argle.

"Believe it!" The Chief was trying to puzzle out by what trick of brain-fog he had missed seeing the solution himself. "Believe it! Lord! It's as simple as A B C. Why in the name of all that's marvelous didn't we tumble to it?"

"And you're standing by what you said?" Argle was out for his pound of flesh—and he wasn't giving up an ounce of it.

The Chief turned to him. "Yes, Argle; I'm not going back on a promise. But I'm making one condition, and you'll have to abide by it."

"And that is—?"

"That you go back to London by this afternoon's train. You must never come near Gairlie till the case is over in the courts. You understand? If it gets around that you have been concerned in this case I shall be in the hottest water of my life. The only way you can help me is to go and hurry yourself in London and forget that you ever lived in Gairlie village."

"All right, Chief," said Argle. There was a deep note of untold satisfaction in the rumbling voice. "I'll do whatever you say, so long as you don't let me down—but, my Gawd! I'd like to get my hands on him to night. I knew it was Latta, knew it was him all along."

"Well, all right. You've no grumble. You get the last laugh. And you're welcome to it—bloodthirsty old devil!"

The Chief beckoned Delayn and the two of them hurried back to the Castle leaving John Argle staring after them till they were out of sight. Then with a heavy slouching gait, he turned and made his way to his own little cottage.

"How do you sleep at night, Delayn?" asked the Chief suddenly.

"Pretty heavily, Chief, why?"

"Would an ordinary noise wake you—a noise, say like rats scampering, or stealthy footsteps prowling about at night?"

Delayn shook his head. "Don't think so, Chief," he said. "I'm generally asleep as soon as my head hits the pillow, and I sleep like a dog till the alarm goes off."

"There's no fireplace in your room, is there?"

"No—just a little electric radiator."

"Have you ever heard any queer sounds up there in that attic of yours when you've been working late?"

"Well, there are a good many queer sounds on the top floors of an old castle like Gairlie. All the cisterns and things are just out there on the landing."

"No, my son. Higher up. On the roof."

Delayn stopped dead and eyed the Chief. "So that's it, is it?" he breathed.

"Sure as God made little apples," grunted the Chief. "Odd, too. Both Kennedy and Stanforth searched the roof. It was explored thoroughly the first week I came down here. And they never found a thing. Not even a footprint. But that was just after a night of heavy rain, so there wouldn't be much left in the way of dustmarks. Still, I'd have thought you'd have heard something, right away up there."

"Not a sound. That roof is about two feet thick. You could hold a dance up there and never hear a sound. Did Argle actually see anything?"

"Saw him at dawn this morning, peering out from behind a chimney. Argle was up a tree in the spinney just below. Tells me he suspected the roof from the beginning, which was why he adopted his own lookout in the grounds. Latta gets up the wall behind the servants' block, where the ornamentation in the masonry gives him foot and hand-hold all the way up. Looks as though he has been camping out up there ever since the death of Betty Halston. Remember that night Argle was brought in half unconscious. That was when he saw him climbing back down the wall. He gave chase, and was going to knife him when he hit the bough of the tree. He actually got his hands on him once, but the monkey flew at him and nearly clawed his eyes out."

Delayn was walking beside the detective in a state of suppressed excitement. "My aunt!" he breathed. "There's going to be a lively time tonight."

"There is!" agreed the Chief grimly. "And it will be up to you as much as anyone else. Your particular job just now is to observe a profound silence. Kennedy is the only man who need know anything at all until nightfall. If this leaks out before we're ready, or if Latta gets suspicious, he'll clear out like a shadow and we'll never be able to pin him down. We both carry on as though we knew nothing. We are waiting for nothing—expecting nothing. Just the usual arrangements will be made. But as soon as the servants have retired for the night things will begin to hum."

They entered the Castle and sat down to an unhurried lunch.

Kennedy came in later, and the Chief took him on one side and gave him the whole lie of the land.

And from then on it was a painful, nerve-racking idleness, waiting for the end. When night fell the Chief issued an order that no one was to go into any room, on any consideration. Otherwise the arrangements continued exactly as usual. The staff were dismissed to their own rooms and told that they would not be required any more that night. The rest of them, Lady Gairlie and Lonora included, were told to stay out in the main hall. Some of the rooms were lit in the ordinary way, but no one was allowed in them.

When all was silent as the grave the Chief rose. Kennedy and Delayn rose with him. "Got those masks, Delayn?" asked the Chief, and he nodded.

Together they crept up the long flights of stairs to the Castle root.

On the top landing they halted and the Chief gave his final instructions.

"Absolute silence until Latta is actually sighted," he said. "I will take the position by the side of the wall at the servants' block. If he arrives at all he will climb the wall there, but my impression is that he is up there already. I doubt if he has left the roof for weeks. Kennedy, you will take the far end of the other wing, and Delayn will be in the centre. We first explore the whole place—got your guns handy? Good. Our squad below is carrying on as usual, and the outer patrol are all at their posts. I've sent to tell them all that something will be happening tonight, and that they must keep their eyes skinned on the roof. Eight of the inside guard are coming up here in half an hour, and will wait under the trapdoors for a signal. The rest are going the rounds of the doors and windows on the floors below. After the search, if we find nothing we go to our positions and wait. If either of you see Latta or that brutish little thing he carries with him, follow him until the other two can get up to you—or he does something that nails him. Then pounce on him and hold him, whatever happens. Is that all clear?"

The others assented, and the Chief mounted the spiral staircase that led to the roof. All three wore rubber tennis shoes blacked over, and they made no sound on the iron stairway. Slowly the Chief raised the trapdoor, and there came a rush of cool air blowing on their faces through the aperture. He waited a few seconds and pushed it higher; then, quietly as a cat, he crawled through. One by one the others followed. Delayn was last, closing the door back soundlessly. Kennedy and the Chief were on all fours crouching in the black shadows of the battlements.

They crawled across and got into the sheltering lee of the wall, out the land. The roof was flat. Viewed from where they were, it looked like a huge courtyard, bounded along the edges by six feet of battlemented walls, and broken here and there by great sections of squat chimneys.

They were in the middle of the central block. Just in front of them was the great plate glass dome of the dining-hall far below. On either side the great wings stretched out into the night, the flat surfaces unbroken save for the squares of chimneys and ventilator stacks. Down below in the grounds all was sheer blackness. The only light there was came from the single glowing window in the lodge beyond the drive. The lights of Gairlie village glowed dim in the distance.

The Chief moved away, hugging the cover afforded by the rising wall. The others followed him like black shadows. Right along to the far wall they went, to the outermost end of the servants' wing. The Chief squiated down the wall where Argle had seen Latta climbing. Taking the perpendicular sight from the top it was easy to see how the little Italian had been able to make the ascent. But the wall was bare—and down at the bottom two men were watching, hidden in two great ashbins within ten yards of the spot where Latta would have to begin his climb.

The three of them began combing the roof, yard by yard. Every nook and cranny of the battlements, every sheltering square of chimney stacks was searched and scoured with a fine tooth-comb. Nothing could have evaded that meticulous search, nothing could have escaped its thoroughness. They carried masks, made of black wool impregnated with alkali, in their hands, ready for action at a moment's notice.

By the time they reached the central dome again the Chief on ahead a few yards, and the first clue had fallen to him. They saw him beckoning them from the biggest of the smoke stacks. Latta, lulled by long weeks of immunity, had grown careless. He had left evidence lying about. Stowed away among the chimneys were stores of foodstuffs. But of Latta himself there was neither sight nor sound.

They passed on right to the far end of the opposite wing. Here and there they found other traces of the marauder. There was a green baize bag with a cord attached which looked as though it might have been carried tied to the waist. In a box in another stack was a little black overall suit of of knitted wool, and beside it along coil of thin but beautifully made manila rope.

"See?" whispered the Chief with barely restrained excitement. "That little horror never climbed a wall in its life. Latta *lowered* it from the roof. Dressed in that black overall—the hood goes right up over its head—the thing would be invisible from below. That's why Stanforth never saw it. He thought the thing had leapt sheer out into space. So it did—but it didn't go *down.* The moment it leapt Latta hauled in the line as hard as he knew how—he could haul in a little thing like that with one hand. My God—it's all as clear as day now. He simply waits his opportunity, lowers it down, and it gets in at the windows. If it's what I think it is, it would have strength to open any window in the Castle—"

"Yes—but the rubies. It couldn't open *those* windows. I tried them myself. They were jammed tight with dried paint. It was as much as a full-grown man could do to open them. Had to heave like the devil before they gave an inch."

"That little narrow-hipped brute came in through the ventilator hole. That aperture is built into the thickness of the outer wall—two feet at the very least. It could hide in the tunnel and wait till the coast was clear. The room was brilliantly lit; it could look through the spinning electric fan and see everything that was going on. The moment the room was empty—there was its chance. The jewels were lying there, open and unprotected. It moves the fan standard to one side, climbs through and jerks the cord. Latta lowers it to the floor from the room above. It crosses to the table, puts the jewels into the baize bag at its waist, goes back to the wall, signals to Latta, who pulls it up the wall to the aperture again. In that soft, woolly suit and felt shoes that could be done absolutely soundlessly. It squeezes back into the tunnel, replaces the fan standard in the centre of the shaft, tugs the rope again, and Latta hauls it up to the roof. Total time, something under two minutes. They've probably been practising the trick for weeks by night. I wouldn't be surprised if they could go through the whole evolution in under sixty seconds."

Delayn suddenly jagged the Chief's arm and whispered: "Down!" All three instinctively ducked as though pulled down by elastic. "The wall—over there," hissed Delayn.

A head had appeared over the battlement, a black silhouette against the misted black of the horizon sky, crowned with a battered felt hat. It was Latta all right. All unsuspicious and apparently far from expecting danger, he made not the slightest attempt to conceal his movements. He threw a leg over the coping of the battlement and climbed over. Clinging to his neck pick-a-back fashion was the unholy little apparition Stanforth had seen.

He was talking to it viciously, savagely, upbraiding it for some real or fancied fault, and the little horror answered it back in a deep guttural voice, fiecer than that of his master!

He swung it off his shoulder and it dropped to its feet. A second later the monkey topped the parapet and jumped over beside him.

"Pah! You ruin us!" snarled Latta. "How many times I tella, you? Hey? A dozen times I tella you not to wasta the bomb. How many you throw, eh? Ugly fool that you are—how many you throw down the damn chimneys?"

"All I like!" growled the little brute. "When there is a fire in the room and the smoke comes up I throw the bomb down. Someone is there. I kill him! When I smell cigar smoke coming up the ventilator I throw one down there! I kill 'em all!"

The pygmy held its ground with the insolence of a heavyweight champion facing a weaker adversary, and the cock of its head was precocity run riot.

Latta was nearly mad with rage. From the welter of his abuse it emerged that, unknown to him the dwarf had been amusing itself flinging, bombs down the chimneys and ventilators and the stock was pretty well exhausted. Latta held out a large oblong box and opened it. "Here, look, pig! Zis is the last! The last! Fool! And we have not gotta the rubies yet. For two pins I—"

"Hands up!" snapped the Chief, pulling out his gun.

Latta had the dreadful glass bomb in the air as though he would hurl it at the little pygmy. He wheeled with a yell of amazement and Delayn saw the arm go back for the throw. Quick as thought he fired from the hip. There was a crack and a crash and Latta with a bullet through his hand and the pieces of the shattered bomb falling about him, fell in a heap on the roof.

What followed happened in such a breathtaking hash that it held them rooted, unable to move. The moment Latta was down the little pygmy was on top of him. It flew at the organ-grinder's throat like a whelp at a rat, a streak of black in the darkness, its tiny fingers clawing at the neck with all the indomitable strength of frenzy. It snarled unutterable things from the depths of its throat, mouthing them out in a semi-dementia that made the scene horrible beyond its ordinary vileness.

In the dim light they saw that it was dressed in a perfectly cut lounge suit, with tiny brown boots beautifully polished and a stylish little felt hat that might have fitted a baby. Grovelling there on the prone man's back it was a shocking travesty of a fashion plate, almost nauseous in its completeness. In its mad attack its hat rolled off, showing a neat little head of soft flaxen hair brushed back in the very latest masculine mode, And, dancing round them both, chattering wildly in fright and dismay, careered Jacko, the monkey.

Twice the little monkey darted in, laying a pathetic paw on the immaculate little shoulder, pulling anxiously, almost beseechingly, at the little berserker. And each time the pygmy, pausing for a second in its onslaught, seized it by the throat and flung it against the parapet. Its strength seemed incredible. The monkey cannoned against the masonry as though it had been flung by a fully developed man.

Then Latta called his bluff. His sudden collapse had been a sheer blind to take his foes off their guard. Knowing the deadly properties of his weapon, he had held the bomb high. And he shut his lungs the moment he saw the flash of the discharging gun. Coincident with that came the impact of a red-hot sword point in the centre of the palm of his hand. He dropped in a heap, his sound hand feeling convulsively in his hip pocket for his gun. The wind dispersed the gas in a silent puff.

And on top of him then came the pigmy the moment it saw its tyrannical master go down. For some seconds Latta held his bluff, and then, when the vicious fingers had made the whole world swim before his bulging eyes he let up. With a rabid snarl he suddenly wrenched over and fought back shaking the little man in his hands like a rag doll. Jacko, screaming with helpless rage, ceased his insane dancing and flew at them both.

"For God's sake, get hold of them!" hissed the Chief. "They'll be murdering each other!"

"Lights!" cried Kennedy. "Why the hell didn't we bring lanterns? Can't see a damn thing!"

Delayn jumped forward and dragged the pygmy off by sheer strength. It clawed and bit and screamed like a maniac, but Delayn held on and hauled it clear. Latta was rearing to his feet with red murder in his eyes. Delayn wheeled and pitched into him, knocking him flying.

He himself went over headlong with the force of his impact, and when he picked himself up Latta was on his feet again struggling to get an automatic out of his pocket. But the long grip handle had got tangled in the tattered lining, and before he had wrenched it clear Delayn was at him again. With a superhuman heave he pulled the gun out and up behind the Italian's back. One hand was round the swarthy neck in a merciless hold that choked the breath out of his body, the other was clamped on the gun, his forefinger feeling for the trigger.

Kennedy was coming up at the run behind them. "Hold him! Hold him!" he yelled.

"Stand clear!" shouted Delayn. "Look out, men! The gun!"

Kennedy heard and understood in the same pulseless second. He flung himself flat in mid-career, slithering along on his stomach on the slippery roof. Delayn's finger had found the trigger. Without a pause he jagged it back.

A sequence of jarring red spurts spat into the darkness from behind the Italian's shoulders and a murderous stream of bullets shot out far over the dark grounds. Kennedy, scrambling up again, reached up and savagely wrenched the empty revolver away. He flung it with a clatter against distant battlements. Ten yards away there arose a tremendous commotion under the roof, and then the trapdoor was flung violently open, and a stream of police erupted on to the roof from below. "Thank God they've got lanterns! Gosh! Look at that pygmy!" Kennedy rushed to help the Chief who was endeavouring to separate the monkey and the apparition. In the méleé the monkey had attacked the dwarf in an access of rage only possible in a maddened simian.

Latta tore himself free with a fierce effort. Fighting like a maniac he made for the parapet where a rope dangled. Seeing its uselessness—the grounds were agog with shouting guards—he suddenly turned and flailed in at Delayn with both arms going like windmill sails. Delayn side-stepped and ducked a wicked swinging right and clipped up a smash to the jaw as the organ-grinder blundered by. It brought him up with a jerk, his head going back with a snap.

Latta spun round and shook himself, coming back like a whirlwind. He was yelling mad, stark flaming rage running over in a riot of fury.

Delayn stepped back and flicked out a long snake-like left to steady him; He liked them best that way—the roof and the night and the macabre setting faded over far skylines.

The Italian plunged in snarling fearful things in his own tongue. Again Defayn's left flicked out full in the teeth and pulled him up dead. A tenth of a second later the right came over and cracked home on the point. Latta went over in a crumpled heap, out to the wide. One of the guard grabbed him and slipped the handcuffs on while the organ-grinder was still drifting through the misty aisles of dreams.

Delayn wiped a spot of blood off his cheek and turned to see the brief, unstoppable tragedy that occurred by the great central dome.

The monkey and the pygmy were fighting like polecats, swaying about over the roof in a blind surge of animal frenzy. The Chief had the pygmy by the neck trying to shake it clear, but it seemed to have got out of all control. The monkey, too, not recognising friend from foe in the fury of its pitiful little soul, snapped and bit at the detective's hands. Their actions were so amazingly volcanic and sudden that they tore themselves free as often as one or other of the guards got a hold on them.

And then the pygmy slipped, falling forward with all his weight on the monkey. The great dome was just behind. Jacko screamed, a long-drawn terrified squeal that echoed far away into the night. There was a rending crash of glass as they fell against it. The lead-work caved in, locked together in a clawing embrace of death, they toppled through. The pygmy made a despairing clutch at the side of the dome, but the glass smashed away in his hand and they went down, turning over and over in the air on the awful plunge to the bottom.

The Chief stared in through the jagged hole. The two little bodies were huddled there on the great carpet. Their arms still tightly clutching each other, smashed and mangled, they lay there without a quiver. In a little while Doctor Mabey edged in beside the group of servants staring in silent horror, and they saw him go forward and turn the little pygmy over.

Kennedy turned away. "Where's Delayn?" he asked. "My heck! That boy knows how to serve out a right-hander to the jaw!"

But Delayn had vanished. Down below in the great hall he had seen Lonora, shocked and frightened, trying to soothe Lady Gairlie, who was nearly fainting with the sudden horror of it all. And the moment he had seen that he had dived for the trapdoor.

The Chief was over by the parapet gazing down at the point where Latta had first appeared. Eight feet down was the coping and parapet of the secondary roof, the top of the big set of bulging bays that ran sheer down the whole height of the Castle. Under the near wall of that bay was a natural opening, a sort of concealed hollow under the battlements above. Search here revealed a heap of old bedding and yet more foodstuffs. Evidently Latta had prepared the place long ago, probably when he first began his raids on the Castle.

"Come on," said the Chief. "Let's get down, I want to see what Mabey has to say about that ghastly little dwarf."

* * *

Down below they found the doctor ruminating wonderingly to himself. The body of the extraordinary little thing was up on the table and he had straightened out its twisted limbs.

"What is it, Doctor? What do you make of it?" asked the Chief, going up close.

"A cretin," replied Mabey; "without doubt—an astonishingly perfect example. I've heard of them even smaller, but never one so perfectly developed."

"A what?" asked the Chief in a puzzled voice.

"A cretin. It's an abnormality of growth occasioned mostly by a lack of iodine in the air, or even in the soil itself. Iodine is the natural element which controls the action of the thyroid gland. The thyroid is undoubtedly the most interesting of all the human glands. Among other things it provides the nutriment for the growth cells. Its action produces a variety of effects according to climatic circumstances and so on. In England chiefly in the Derbyshire hills and the Cotswolds, iodine is notably lacking. But there the resultant disability takes the form of goitrous neck. Guite is purely a tremendous inflammation of the thyroid gland.

"But there are certain valleys in Switzerland—and in the Urals too. I believe—where the trouble takes the form of pure cretinism that you see here. In the museum at Zurich there is a specimen only sixteen inches high—the most perfect specimen of cretinism known to medical science: that is, if one may use such a term as 'perfect' in describing the horribly imperfect. In the case of this little thing here, the body, head and limbs are perfectly formed. Only the eyes continued to grow after, I should say the age of six. That is the horror of the ailment; you have the virility and brain and cunning of a man in the body of practically a baby. The tremendous size of the eyes would account for the repulsive sight Stanforth saw at the window. From that angle Stanforth would see only one terribly exaggerated eye, without any true glitter of virility in it. A curious turn for cretinism to take.

"Some of the Swiss mountain districts, particularly the heights above Brienz, are absolute breeding-grounds for cretins.

"Not all like this, of course. Some grow perfectly normally to, say, twenty or twenty-five before the growth ceases. But dwarfs are common. It used to be ascribed to the inter-breeding of the mountain folk; but medical science has proved conclusively that lack of iodine is at the bottom of the trouble."

"You think his brain developed, then, Doctor, in spite of his stoppage of growth?"

"To a very great extent, yes. But there would be certain blanks in it. He could talk and reason; he would probably have a very excellent memory, but in some things instinct would take the place of intellect."

"So that even though its brain wasn't quite normal it would be trainable? I mean it could be trained to recognise similarities?"

"Yes. But in what way?"

"I'm referring to the extraordinary chain of robberies of red objects of all descriptions—boxes, flowers, slippers, ornaments and goodness knows what. To me the thing seems to have culminated in the theft of the famous rubies. Would it be possible to train this little dwarf into laying hands on anything it came across of a red colour provided its stunted brain could not assimilate the fact that the rubies were the primary object?"

"Most decidedly. I should say that is the explanation. Such emphatic cretins as this are as liable to sudden whims and freaks as a lunatic. This particular specimen, for instance, would be liable to ungovernable fits of rage. On provocation it would go practically insane."

"I can believe you!" said the Chief feelingly.

"But most of the time it would be entirely amenable. Its strength would be out of all proportion to its size."

"It could force open windows?"

"Easily. It could understand electric light switches, and would know all the first principles of self-preservation. And under normal conditions it would be a very tractable little creature."

The Doctor was completely vindicated in his statements next morning when José Latta, after refusing to say a word in his own defence, broke down. For some hours he had denied all knowledge of the robberies and all responsibility for the murders. Then the Chief confronted him with his proofs and he broke into tearful confessions.

He was the Carlo Valotti of Torre Cavallo, and the original intention was to swindle the supposed Mr. Bulmerdine out of twenty thousand lire. Unfortunately Calaghi had turned renegade and set out on his own to get the stone's full value and then decamp. Calaghi was murdered—Valotti had perpetrated that deed himself—and the Burning Star having been innocently taken over the frontier, he, José Latta, was deputed to get it back. Then came the war and the gradual loss of power by the Mafia. Latta dared not return to Italy without the jewel. He had stayed on and finally located Gairlie in Hampshire.

He had recruited the cretin, who was the son of an old Mafia bandit born in exile in Switzerland. The cretin's name was Ruga Carippo, and he was over thirty years old. For months they had camped on the wide roofs of Gairlie Castle, Latta training the pigmy in its exploits, which were always carried out in the early hours of the morning. Carippo could not appreciate the significance of rubies, never having seen them. He could not visualise anything from a spoken description.

So Latta had commenced the "red" campaign, until finally the rubies were lifted. He lowered the little chap, whose weight was less than thirty pounds, from the castle roof down to any window where access was possible. Sometimes he went right in, but his scope was limited by the rope he had to trail behind him. The actual theft of the rubies was done in just over a minute. The signal to haul him up again was a single jerk on the rope.

When the rubies were found to be fakes Latta foresaw police action. He stocked his secret retreat with food, and save for occasional forays for water, stayed up there. In case of emergency he had got a score of globes and filled them with hydrocyanic. He himself had used the first one. For over an hour he had listened to Lord Gairlie talking with Kennedy in the windowless library, the sound carrying perfectly up the ventilator shaft. Thinking Gairlie was getting on the right track he had gone over to the bay roof retreat, got a bomb and pitched it down. During that time Gairlie had left the library and Betty Halston had gone in to clear up. Then the worst tragedy of all came; the cretin, having seen its master do it once, had become imitative and had pitched bombs down the chimneys and ventilators every time he suspected a presence in the room below.

Delayn, with Lonora clutched close to him, listened to the whole narrative. When it was over and Latta was led away, cursing the lifeless body of his helpless little dupe, he took her out to the fresh sweet glory of the morning where nothing but cleanness and health filled the air. There was a medley of bird music and in the air was a nectar, a wine-warm urge towards the brilliance, the bloom and beauty that is waiting for young lovers in that sunny bright land of dream-days. Neither spoke a word for many minutes. There was no need. Each knew the other's thoughts to the last and finally blessed letter. Lonora turned and looked up him at last, and held out her finger. Tommy fumbled in his pocket.

"So that's all right," he whispered. And she laughed her reply in the sheer joy of being alive.

* * *

The hand of the prison clock crawled over the face of time towards the dreadful hour of eight. Outside the gates a huge crowd waited, for the mystery of Gairlie Castle had thrilled the land from end to end, and the court had been packed to suffocation throughout every hour of the trial and appeal. Two warders were standing with the doomed man. One mentioned to him as the door was pulled open.

José Latta stood up, sullen, morose, vicious to the last.

Down the long corridor lights glimmered. In their fitful rays he saw the executioner approaching side by side with the chaplain, the pinioning belt swinging in his hand. He drew nearer... nearer... he entered the cell. Without a word or a sign he stared at the stubborn face of the murderer.

José Latta gasped. He was looking full into the smouldering unforgiving eyes of John Argle, public hangman.

THE SILENT SIX

The terrible vengeance of a criminal, praised by the *Referee* as "An extraordinarily clever tale, in which the interest never flags."

I

When Damon Grey crawled back to the world from the utter blackout of a number in a cell, he stood debtor to himself for eighteen terrible years on the audit of life. The profundity of it dazed him; the magnitude of it appalled him. For the first time in eighteen years he breathed the sweet, forgiving wind of freedom, drank of it deeply—and scarcely knew it.

The awful emptiness of the years that had gone, the grinding crushweight of the dead routine, and all the numbing atmosphere of the changeless penal day, had crept into his mentality. He found himself listening for, and missing, the tramp of boots in the prison yard, the staccato rasp of a warder's voice. A third of a lifetime—flung away and burned in the fires. It had deadened him.

Eighteen years! They had dragged their way across his life with such dreadful deliberation that the scars of their passage had scored his soul.

His sole excuse for existence had centred on the one bright star—to be allowed to walk again in the cities of men, to taste again the unconsidered but exquisite little joys of life, to read newspapers—to get back to some comprehension of world-news, its life and its doings, to relieve his yearning eyes with a different sight, to speak, and be spoken to, on the common level.

And, chiefest of all, there was the great recompense to be made to that dear, sweet woman who for eighteen years had been married to nothing but a memory and a hope.

It had been a killing interlude for a man of the nature of Damon Grey. Eighteen times that damnable bell above the chapel-house had jangled a glad new year at him while he waited for Justice to decide that its acid had burned sufficiently deep. Eighteen sweet-scented springs, with their toy green shoots and their life-promising winds blowing free across the solidified sea that hemmed him in, had come and gone since the day the judge's eyes had bored into his from under a square of black cloth, set diamondwise on his head.

On that day, as on each preceding day, he had stood in the dock and faced the Bench, stony-eyed and silent. He had gazed coldly at the law with a glitter of silent contempt flickering up now and then in his eyes. And he had kept his steel trap of a mouth shut tight.

Lawyers had teased him, judges had commanded him, K.C.'s had fulminated at him, counsel had fretted and fumed about him, but never a one of them had shaken his terrific calm or broken his wintry silence.

Only once had he opened his mouth, and that was when, towards the end of the trial, Sir Henry Rumbold, K.C., prosecuting for the Crown, at him and thundered:

"Answer me! Did you or did you not, on the night of the thirteenth, murder Clifford Reese?"

And Damon Grey had spoken. Witheringly, and with biting scorn snapping up in every line of his face, he said: "Your wig isn't on straight! You look a perfect fool in it."

The tension in the court had been so tremendous that a squeak of laughter had ripped out and, as abruptly, ceased. And Rumbold had actually put the offending wig straight with a mechanical gesture of his podgy hand.

Damon Grey critically manicured his nails while the law finished blatherings above his head. He was perfectly content in the knowledge that, whatever had happened on that unfortunate night of the thirteenth, his five friends would have acted precisely as he was acting now. Any of them would have shut his mouth and kept it shut. If he opened it at all, it would merely have been to hit the law on the nose with a red-hot herring.

That had been their creed and faith ever since they had first banded together. Silence! If something went wrong while a job was being done; if a scheme miscarried and one of them was caught, then he alone took whatever the law chose to mete out. Never another one stood in the dock beside him. The pact of silence held good in front of the gallows as surely as in front of a safe. The very thought of confession or King's evidence had been expunged from their lexicons.

It *had* been an unfortunate night. He admitted that to himself as he deftly trimmed a cuticle. And they had all been in it. All the whole six of them. Pity that gun went off the way it did. Reese was too fat to get out of the way of it, anyhow, but there was no need to have shot him. They could have got clear away before he could have called in the police pack. Damon Grey had fired; he admitted that, too. But he had fired at the light. And in the sudden emphatic blackness he had stunned himself falling over a chair. Another shot had cracked out as he crashed. He remembered the gasp of the man, just before his own head hit the table-leg. He had stayed there, unconscious—with a gun in his hand—and the dead man sprawling at his feet. But the other five had got away. And the bond would hold.

He could take all that was coming. The other five would look after the little woman at home. That was as good as law to the Silent Six...

From out of the high-strung silence that gripped the court a measured voice came drifting over to him... "anything to say why sentence of death should not be passed upon you?"

Just for a second the high resolve went faltering out to an awed vision of a short flight of wooden steps leading upward to the cold grey of a dawning.

He cut his thoughts off desperately short. The law had got him anyway; no use losing his nerve at that juncture. He looked hard at the judge and murmured: "Well, *your* wig's on straight, anyhow."

They carted him away with the sentence still rushing through his cars. He lodged no appeal and asked no privilege: simply sat and waited for the day that never dawned.

He rather guessed that something had gone wrong when a Scotland Yard man came into his cell and asked him roughly two hundred questions. Although he answered each with a stony stare and a wall-eyed silence, he knew that the Home Secretary had smelt a rat.

For the Scotland Yard man asked him a lot of questions that showed that law and order had begun to put two and two together. They had deduced that Damon Grey was not a lone adventurer along the highways of educated cracksmanship. They suspected the existence of a highly organised, highly specialised combination of clever brains, of which Damon Grey was merely a component unit.

But they got little satisfaction and less assistance from Damon Grey. From then on he just sat and waited for the commuting of his sentence.

There came no word from the Silent Six. He did not expect it. But he wished he could have got word through to them. That Scotland Yard man was unsettling. It was not nice to have volleys of interrogatives fired at one about such things as the Great Bank of England Swindle after so long a time.

But there was no doubt about it. Scotland Yard had got every one of their greatest coups neatly docketed and filed away. And what was more, they had connected them all with the activities of the unknown coterie of which Grey was a very executive member.

And some of those cases really were remarkable.

There was the case of the Royal Diamond. That was a coup, if you like. Cool, calm, deliberate audacity, a level-headed weighing up of every single chance, an analytical insight into every possibility, and then the putting into execution of a perfectly conceived plan, each man working with his nerve and brain on an icebox. They actually hid the stone in one of the detective's pockets while the guests were being searched, and picked his pocket for it afterwards in the foyer.

Then there was the case of the Rockingham Emeralds. It was brilliant; but from the point of view of the Silent Six the theft was only partially successful, for one of the Silent Six was apprehended.

It will be recalled that the Rockingham emeralds were stolen. Seventy thousand pounds' worth of frozen green fire flicked out of existence in their transit from ballroom to orchid-house. Richard Kann was arrested one hour later for driving his new-fangled motorcar to the common danger. It was disastrous. The Rockingham emeralds were found in the knot of Richard Kann's necktie.

Kann stood his ground, as Grey had done. He took five years without a quiver. And the gang looked after his kiddies, for that was the law of them all.

There was nothing bizarre or theatrical about them, nothing sentimental or melodramatic. It was just the business arrangement of a business organisation. They were out for risky gain, and mutual safety was more than a binding part of their creed; it was a safeguard. Whatever profits the rest made while Kann was under the black arrow, a sixth part was earmarked to the bank account of his wife.

Damon Grey was in slightly different case there. He had no children. Only that precious little girl-wife who, dear to him and sweet beyond words, had been growing old, too, with the passing of the years.

Well, he would make it all up to her with every day that was left to him. It was dreadfully impossible, but he would do his best. There was money standing to his name in a bank that was still financially sound. And the gang must have added considerably to it at one time and another. He knew they were still in existence. Old lags, recidivists, brought him stories when they came back for further spells of imprisonment, stories of brilliant swindles and robberies carried out by men of great daring. And he recognised in them the hand of his old associates, noted the organising genius of Rackway, the nerveless, almost insolent, preparation of Leeds, the executive boldness of Grayne, the utterly audacious covering work of Kann and Lindrum.

And, all unknown to him, the long years had worked a metamorphosis in the soul of Damon Grey. When the prison gates finally opened to him there were two starkly contrasted possibilities about the future conduct of the man they released. They were locked away inside him, and the oddity was that Damon Grey himself was unaware of the existence the second.

One was that he would take himself and his wife away to some quiet little corner, far away from the glare and blare of life, somewhere where he could find rest and forgetfulness. The other was that a reaction would set in, and Damon Grey would become a human devil.

In all fairness to the man who subsequently shocked the medical faculties of the world by his apparent ability to kill any man at will with nothing more criminal than a sudden attack of heart-failure in a perfectly sound heart, and who exasperated the police of the whole kingdom by their complete inability to get hold of any sort of an explanation for the mystery, it should be said that when Damon Grey came out of Dartmoor he had not the faintest intention of ever becoming the relentless killing-machine he certainly became.

Rest and forgetfulness! His soul craved for them.

Nearing fifty he was when they released him. His hair was shot white at the temples, his feet had accepted the dragging gait of the exercise yard, and his shoulders were out of the square—quarry-work is back-breaking work, and it leaves its inheritance on joint and sinew.

But though the first creep of age was upon him, there was a potency about him of the rare sort that makes men turn their heads in the street. It was as though a virile, terrific force was bottled up and corked down somewhere in that clean, lean frame. It showed in the raw tan of his health, in his sure, deliberate movements, in the tense, piercing marbles of his eyes, in the delicate sense of quiet delight with which he did even the smallest thing, from looking at a sky-sign to going down in a Tube lift.

It was a cold grey day when Justice released him. He was profoundly thankful his wife was not at the station to meet the train. Dear woman! Trust her to know and to understand. He wanted to see a decent tailor before he met Iris.

After an hour at a Ready-to-Wear Service, he went to his bankers. They welcomed him with cordial dignity.

That was where he got his first shock. His account was exactly as he had left it eighteen years before. Except for the interest which had accrued slowly through the years, not a penny had been added.

Grey's eyes contracted wickedly when he saw the figures—forty-four thousand pounds—and the neat figures of the interest added year underneath.

The manager looked at him nervously. Damon Grey, for some reason that was entirely beyond his fathoming, had suddenly frightened him. He couldn't tell why, but it was so. A live rail looks exactly the same whether the power is on or off.

But there was no doubting that the power, the sinister, baleful Something, had suddenly shot into the soul of the quiet, icy man beside him. His lips, as he looked at him, were pressed up into a thin line like a pair of locked contacts. But actually it showed nowhere, not even in his eyes.

He just snapped the book shut and dropped it in his pocket. Then for a long half-minute he regarded the bank manager. And the bank manager felt as though two red-hot gimlets had bored sheer into the hidden thoughts behind his brain and were picking them over one by one in an unhurried search for the one he wanted.

Damon Grey tapped his pocket.

"Is that account all square?" he asked.

"Why—yes—of course it is," said the bank manager hurriedly. "Of course it is—certainly it is. Why? What—"

"That's all."

"But, Mr. Grey, you surely don't—"

"Thank you. Good day."

Grey went out into the cash department and wrote out a cheque. He looked suspiciously at the pound notes, till he caught the cashier's wondering eye upon him. Then he shrugged, filled up his wallet, and went out to find Iris.

A taxi took him to his old address. As the cab reached the familiar surroundings, misgivings began to stalk through his hopes. The neighbourhood had changed. It had gone back, slid back down the social scale. Instead of the once proud air of fashionable taste and propriety, the place was faded. There was an air of dingy gentility about it, a look of striving to keep up appearances that was positively painful.

At his own house, past which an occasional horse-bus had been wont to jog every now and then in the years gone by, a stream of red motor-giants roared and rushed. It was dilapidated.

Damon Grey jerked at the bell-pull.

A slatternly woman with wet hands and fishy eyes opened the door. She eyed him for a moment with bovine placidity. The female of the species being more deadly than the male, she was able to preserve a serene nonchalance despite the pimpling of tight-knotted curlers all over her head and the sackcloth apron caught up into its waist-string at one corner.

Grey raised his hat.

"Can I see Mrs. Grey, please?" he asked.

"Mrs. who?"

"Mrs. Grey—Mrs. Iris Grey."

"Never heard of her."

"I beg your pardon?"

"I said I haven't never heard of her. Speak plain English, don't I?"

"But I understand she lives here."

"Do you *reely*! You understand wrong, then."

"But hasn't she a flat or a room in the house at all?"

"No, she ain't."

Grey's foot whipped into the doorway as the woman slammed the door. He put his two hands against it and gave it one short, sharp shove that sent her stumbling back down the alleged hall.

"Don't do that again," he said.

"Well, what do you want?" she said balefully, wiping her hands on the sack apron.

"I want a little information concerning a Mrs. Iris Grey,"

"Well, I don't know nothink about her."

"How long have you been living here?"

"Six years—since the war."

"And she wasn't here then?"

"No. And who the hell are you, anyway, questioning me?"

"I'm the owner of this house!"

"Oh!" The woman was appeased and half scared at once, "Never knew I had a landlord," she murmured, still wiping her hands, "Thought we was a company."

"You pay your rent to an estate agent?"

"Yes, sir." The "sir" dropped in as naturally as a raindrop falls to the ground.

"Are you in arrears?"

"Well—er—you see, sir, times is very—"

"How long?"

"Nine weeks, sir; but—"

"Well, now look here. You know this neighbourhood pretty thoroughly?"

"Yes, sir."

"In two hours I shall be back. Meanwhile you will make inquires around here; people, and shops, and tradesmen, and suchlike—anybody whose knowledge of this locality goes back eighteen years. Find me somebody who remembers Mrs. Grey—somebody who remembers where she went when she went away—and I'll receipt your rent-book right up to date. Find me someone who can tell me *where I can find her now,* and I'll give you the whole house, title-deeds, rental, filth, and all. Good day."

One glaring look he gave her—a look that shot out of his eyes like a stone from a catapult. The woman blinked, and the next she saw of him was a striding figure down the road hoisting a commanding finger at a taxi.

He drove back to the bank, and his interview with the manager was short and fierce.

"Have you paid out any money to Mrs. Grey during the time I've been away?" he demanded.

"No, I don't think so—I'm quite sure we haven't."

"Did she open a separate account?"

"No—at least, not in that name. Had she done so your accounts would have been bracketed together in the ledgers."

"Did she ever come to you asking for help?"

"Oh, dear me, no."

"Do you know where I can find her?"

"I'm afraid I haven't the slightest idea, Mr. Grey. I rather thought she went away soon after you—er—left the neighbourhood. Haven't you got into touch with her yet?"

"I'm trying to, now."

"H'm! I rather lost track of her after her baby was born."

"You—*what?*"

The bank manager jumped. The last word had fairly sizzed at him.

"I—good Lord, Mr. Grey! You don't mean to tell me you didn't know she had a baby? Dear little kiddie; chubby little soul. Born eight months after you—after you went away. I remember—the wife mentioned it once or twice."

Damon Grey did not go suddenly white or even look as though that dreadful second possibility had dawned in him. He just stood where he was and stared at the bank manager. His head began to spin. Awful thoughts, terrible thoughts, went flying through his brain; burning thoughts that seemed to shrivel his blood with their heat.

"Iris—a mother—a baby—a child of mine. Good heavens!" he gasped.

The manager went to an ornate sideboard and splashed him out a brandy and soda with shaking fingers.

"Drink this, old man—awfully sorry," he said. "Never dreamed you didn't know. Thought they allowed you letters and—and all that."

Grey pushed the drink aside and mopped his forehead. His mind was stumbling through the dead profounds of his foggy inability to grasp new thought readily. Down there in Dartmoor his thoughts had all been orderly, labelled, precise. His views on life and things outside were set and rigid. He was a man who knew exactly what he thought and how many thoughts he possessed; they had been cell-mates with him too long.

And now that new events, new thoughts, new verities were springing up all around him, he found himself mentally unable to establish their proper orientation with anything less than a violent effort.

"She—she didn't write," he said quietly. "I asked her not to. Begged her not to—unless the need was urgent. I couldn't bear the sight of her handwriting in that—that hell on the moors!"

There was something terribly wrong somewhere. He sensed it with every fibre of his being. And that was all he did know. His brain was in a whirl, on fire. He, Damon Grey, a father! His wife, poor pitiful little girl of all his hopes and dreams and prayers—a mother! And the hellish tragedy of it. Eight months after the law had thrust him into the darkness. Not even time to whisper shyly in his ear that his greatest hope of her might soon be realised.

Damon Grey, with a light in his eyes like the green glimmer seen below the water when a shark turns far down, thrust his hands deep into his overcoat pockets and went out into the grey gloom of the afternoon.

The woman in Grey's old house was as mercenary-minded as she was shabby-souled. Long before two hours had sped she had found someone who remembered Mrs. Grey. She was a worn woman, cast in her own mould, but a decade fadier, and weightier by some inches all round. She kept the little dressmaker's shop at the corner, where, as she explained, she used to "gown the titles, in pore Mrs. Grey's time."

Her name was "the Miss Herris," and she was the well-head for all the news, gossip, and scandal of the locality for the last thirty years. Her memory for such data was positively poisonous, retentive as a dictaphone. It clutched at the details avidly, sorted them, filed them, and pigeon-holed them away in her catacomb of a brain. And she could trot out any given detail, or yard of details, at a moment's notice.

She had the whole thing off pat for Grey. There was no doubt about the accuracy of her information—nor the outspoken qualities of her serpent tongue.

"Yes, I knew Mrs. Grey," she said. "And I know you too. You're Mr. Grey. You're her husband. You were had up for murder eighteen years ago. Shot a man named Clifford Reese, you did, caretaker of a jewellery warehouse."

Grey stood and listened to it without a flush, without a word. Straight and full in the eyes he held her and waited. He knew it was coming. And it came.

"Your missus died when she had her baby."

Damon Grey winced, ever so slightly.

"She only lived a week after it was born," said the Miss Herris smoothly. "Starved she was, pore soul. The vicar tried to make her write to you, but she said she could manage without. Said you had asked her not to because it would only make it harder for you—with mem'ries of 'er, by post."

Grey gripped his mental self with both hands and held on.

"Where—did she die?" he asked quietly.

"She died on the other side of the river, in a poorhouse—in Lambeth. But she was near dead when they got her, so they couldn't do much. Died the same week in the infirmary, she did. Pneumonia got her. The marvel to me is that the kid lived at all. Its mother never had enough food to keep her body and soul together for six months before she took to her bed. One of 'em 'ad to die, so the doctors said. And it was the mother who went, pore soul; couldn't do no otherwise—she'd gave her life to the kid."

"Did the—kiddie live?" Grey forced the words out through jaws that had gone as hard as stone.

"'Ow do I know? They put it in a foundling school. People said you'd never live to finish your sentence. They said the shock would kill you—you being sensitive like. But I can see you ain't. Funny how wrong ideas go round about people, ain't it?"

And the lady who in her time had gowned the titles stuffed her gratuity into her purse and departed with the finest crop of new gossip she had for years.

During that fragment of time the reaction had set in in the soul of Damon Grey. The metamorphosis occurred. He was no longer the silent, reserved bit of prison wreckage, seeking some quiet corner wherein he could spend the rest of his days. His friends had sold him. The Six had betrayed the great allegiance that he himself had kept to the last tormented letter.

Damon Grey had aged during that recital. The years seemed to have taken a heavier hold upon him. The drawn, tired lines round his mouth seemed to have deepened and intensified; the wintry look in his eyes was barren, desolate. But every single inch of him quivered like overstressed metal.

He went out to a telephone, looked up a number, and put his call through.

"Who's speaking?" came a voice at the other end.

"Is that Rackway?" Grey's voice was like the distant mutter of thunder.

"Yes. Who is it?"

"It's me, Damon Grey. Get hold of Lindrum, Grayne, and Kann, and Stephen Leeds. Find them. Get them together. And then tail them! Tell them *I—am—coming*!"

Rackway's voice was cultured to a quiet smoothness. It had in it all the suave polish of the man with an education behind him. It was a voice that was disciplined to perfect and continual control. But even over the wire the sense of shock that suddenly charged it was unmistakable.

"Grey? Damon Grey?" he gasped. "But—but—surely, man you—"

Grey snapped him off on a word. His own steely voice cut in.

"I have nothing whatever to add. You understand that? I want no explanation from any single one of you. My address is, and will continue to be, the Grand Imperial. My suite number is four. You will telephone me at your earliest convenience."

"But, Grey, listen! When you—"

"Good day."

The receiver went on with a deliberate click, unmistakable in its stark finality.

Rackway pounded the instrument, but the operator came on to say that the line was cut off from the other end—a public call-box.

He hung up his receiver and wiped his forehead. The air had suddenly gone chill around him. An awful sense of apprehension was crawling alive in his heart. He experienced that same feeling of helpless nausea that afflicts the flesh when the eyes are compelled to look downward from a great height.

He read a relentlessness into that voice over the phone that was positively frightening. It seemed to be nothing more than a coldly deliberate threat, coldly considered and as coldly decided upon.

He sat down at the big library table and put his finger on his secretary's bell-push. But it was not until after a long interval of calculated thought that his finger pressed down on the button.

All thought of his usual afternoon's activities had slid out of his mind. Usually, in his role of outside broker, he would have spent a busy hour just then telephoning and dictating letters regarding certain Stock Exchange business of the day. For Rackway, whose keenest senses were all for his clever and audacious coups in the higher circles, camouflaged his life very successfully with daily incursions into the exciting realms of stock and share manipulation. But all that had gone. His mind was turning on the Damon Grey complication with lightning rapidity.

Rackway's intuitions were peculiarly fine-drawn. He absorbed facts and situations with a comprehension that was instinctive. And in this sudden bolt from the blue he sensed a more real danger than any he had faced in his life.

He was no coward. He had worked on the wrong side of the law too often to take fright at sudden emergencies. But in the dramatic return of Damon Grey he felt himself up against something that was right outside his normal grip. Grey's mood was awful, implacable; the mood that drives a man along a preordained road in utter disregard of the hangman's noose hanging like a grey shadow at the end of it. The voice that had come to him over that phone, as metallic as forged steel and as cold as a Polar wind, was the voice of a man who had looked at death and grown weary of it.

His secretary came in and took a seat opposite him. He looked at her for a long minute, full in the eyes, without speaking.

Candidly, she was worthy of an even longer inspection—and the accusation of rudeness could be fairly forgiven.

This is a very fair picture of Lorna Rennie, except that the picture is dead, pulseless, and merely an attempt to put into words the untranslatable:

Rather a small face, but intensely pretty; sweet, if you like, and with a sweetness, too, that seemed to be one with a tiny village in the hot suns of summer, of an innocent idyll among the honeysuckles, stocks, and rambler roses; of the dainty colourings of a fragile bit of Dresden china; of a Jane Eyre; of all that is trustful and delicately chaste. Eyes of fairest powder blue, that on occasion could light up with a quick fire of delight and become as full of shining colour as speedwell nodding in the sunlight; eyes that could fill with shadows and make a man catch at his breath for very shame of having clouded them; that were a complete and ever-speaking record of the thoughts and emotions behind them; the kind of eyes that, behind the footlights, fill the stalls with the same faces night after night, and raise men's glasses to a clink and a wish in the clubs. And, just above them, eyebrows that might have been put on with a single stroke of a master-painter's brush; a thin, curving sweep with the arch, no more, no less than perfection would have it. The colour of her eyes was a delightful offset to the faint pink of her complexion, and her lips were not too red. They were sweet lips, and there was character in them, but they were not so red that the tongue of feminine envy could sneer and say: "Lipstick."

There was the hair, too. It clustered over her head, and there was a sheen of spun floss in it. It seemed to cuddle her head, to make men's fingers itch to touch it and feel it softly in their finger-ends.

The connoisseur would say she had but one drawback, and even that would be gone all too quickly. She was, or appeared to be, not quite old enough! She was too young to ravage the soul of any but the real lover or the aged sinner. At first glance one would instinctively say: "Oh nowhere near twenty yet!" But after a few minutes in her company, or after a privileged look into the blue deep of her eyes, one would not be quite so sure. There was too much character, too strong an indication of judgment and maturing common sense for the epithet of "flapper" to have any justification whatever.

Rackway's eyes fell to her neck, a neck that was poised, white, and demure as a swan on the water, upon shoulders that were at once competent but entirely feminine. A neat gold locket on a spider-web chain was looped round that neck.

"Ah! Fresh jewellery today, Miss Lorna," he said with a touch of quiet banter in his voice.

Lorna half bowed her head.

"As you see," she said. And she was devilishly polite and dignified.

"Rather precious, is it?"

"Very precious indeed, Mr. Rackway."

"Another little present from Master Dickie, eh?"

"Mr. Ricks certainly did give it to me. You rang for me, did you not?"

Rackway took the cut without turning a hair. Lorna, with her pen poised over her notepad, waited with a bold effort at unconcern. But unconcern is not easy when maidenhood finds itself confronts with a passionate lover whose span of life has already passed into its second half. The love of the palpably ageing for the sweetness of the still gloriously young is not a nice love. It never can be a nice love. There is something distorted, diseased, something abnormal about it.

And it is more difficult still when the girl knows perfectly well that the love offered is as true and as genuine as any ever offered to a girl. There was no disguising the fact. Hildon Rackway was all too obviously madly in love with his charming secretary. In love to such a sincere degree that he was mastering it—holding it in check—lest his mad longing should precipitate a crisis.

For he was not blind to the fact that Lorna Rennie did not reciprocate in the slightest degree. She respected him, and admired him for the several very excellent traits she had found in his character, not the least of which was his unfailing courtesy to her. But farther than that her heart had neither the inclination nor the power to go.

She watched him sitting there, faultlessly dressed, immaculately groomed, his eyes upon her with just a suspicion of a smile in them; but behind them, buried deep, but welling up in spite of restraint, such a look of hope and yearning that a girl would be blind indeed who could not read it. Lorna Rennie knew that Hildon Rackway would have mortgaged his soul a dozen times for her. And his was not the desire that dwells in the heart of an old roué.

His love was there: it showed in a hundred ways. He had lightened her duties till she had scarcely anything to do at all. He had raised her salary time after time, till she knew she was receiving from him more than treble the normal wages of even a highly paid secretary. Every morning saw fresh-cut flowers on her table, expensive fruit in her room. She had her own maid.

But a girl of Lorna Rennie's nature loves once. And Lorna had already found her love. In Dickie Ricks she had found what sympathetic old people would call a perfect match and know deep down in their hearts that they were right.

Dickie Ricks was cut out for her from the time his life began. Handsome, careless, courageous, humorous, ready for a rag or a serious talk in the same breath, witty and clever beyond the average, Ricks was the type of clean-living youngster on whom the hope of the race depends.

And Rackway had quickly found out about Dickie Ricks. Almost at once he realised the hopelessness of his own case; for no man, having seen that young couple together, could ever have mistaken the inevitability of such a union of heart, soul, and spirit. Ricks was dark; Rackway was thinning on top. Ricks's step had a spring and a joy in it; Rackway's was no longer lissom, and there was nothing but hope in it. Ricks's race was only just beginning; Rackway's was nearly run. Ricks could talk with the fires of youth all alive and aflame within him; Rackway's was the speech of a man already looking down over the hill towards the sunset.

Rackway sighed and looked away. Even sweetness can be bitter sometimes.

"Would you mind taking down a few letters?" he said. "Thank you very much. Are you ready?"

To Chief Inspector Harnden, Scotland Yard.

Sir,—This is to acquaint you with the fact that I do not expect to remain living very much longer. If I die unaccountably, or from any suspicious cause during the next few weeks, Damon Grey will have murdered me. Damon Grey was released from prison recently. I am quite sure he will kill me.

Faithfully yours,

"And I will sign it when you have typed it," he added.

Lorna had started to her feet, pale with fright and horror.

"But, Mr. Rackway, you are surely not in earnest!" she gasped, unable even to finish the dictation.

"In earnest, little lassie?" he said. "Oh. yes. Type that letter and keep it always by you. When I am dead, post it to Scotland Yard."

Lorna looked at him helplessly.

"But—you must be joking, Mr. Rackway," she protested.

"That is the last thing I would do with you, Miss Lorna," he returned gravely. "No; these instructions to you are very definite, and I must ask you to carry them out to the letter. Damon Grey is, or was, a friend of mine. He has a bitter grievance against me for something that happened years ago. I thought him dead. That is the candid truth. But it seems he has come back. Damon Grey will, without a doubt, endeavour to kill me. If he succeeds, you will post that letter to Inspector Harnden without a moment's hesitation. You will tell the police as much as you know; it may help to prevent Grey committing other, equally serious, crimes."

The girl gazed at him, striving to solve the riddle of his extraordinary statements. For a moment she thought him slightly unbalanced. But she saw in his face a look she had never seen there before—and she had studied that face rather closely at one time and another. The lines in it seemed to have hardened, to have become more set and heavy. He looked careworn, as though a load that had been borne mentally for many years had suddenly become physical, too heavy for his powers.

That there was some secret behind his life she had rather guessed; but his occasional moods of taciturnity she had put down to business worries.

Not that she knew what his business was. All she knew was that he was interested in certain matters connected with the Stock Exchange that his four most important business connections were gentlemen named Lindrum, Grayne, Kann, and Stephen Leeds—all middle-aged men who came to his flat every now and then to play cards and talk.

With an effort of will she forced herself to sit down again, and she finished the shorthand note with a hand that trembled badly.

"If the danger is so very real—couldn't you—couldn't you tell the police now—before he does you any grave harm?" she suggested quietly. "Surely you can get police protection?"

"No," he said slowly. "There are other complications which you would not understand."

He drummed his fingers on the table. "Take down this telegram and send it to each of the usual four at once. Let me see, now; how shall we word it? Er—'Come immediately. Suggest rendezvous eight o'clock at my flat. Urgent.' Yes, that will do, I think. Send that to Kann, Lindrum, Leeds, and Grayne without delay."

"Thank you," said Lorna. "Have you anything else?"

"Not just now. I shall require you later on in the evening though if you will be good enough to stay. Would you mind?"

"Not in the least, Mr. Rackway. I will wait in my room for your bell."

Rackway waited until the door had closed behind her, and then picked up the telephone receiver. He gave the Grand Imperial number and asked that a message should be taken to Mr. Damon Grey, suite No. 4 to the effect that his friends would be waiting for him at eight that evening.

After a couple of minutes the voice of the hotel porter came on to say that Mr. Grey would be there on the stroke of the clock.

Rackway put his receiver down as though it had suddenly stung him.

II

Rackway's four telegrams were answered on time and in person. He waited for his visitors in his library, and before eight o'clock sounded the four of them were with him. Rackway's flat was in a beautiful old house in the secluded soul of Grosvenor Square, and its appointments reflected the taste of its owner.

The five of them were seated in old leather-cushioned chairs round a great mahogany table. The light from a single crimson-shaded lamp fell on them with a ruby luminance and lit up splashes of fire on the cut-glass decanters and glasses. A solitaire diamond blazed in the centre of the host's white shirt-front.

There was Lindrum, short and stocky, with confidence and ability cut into every line of him. There was Stephen Leeds, who looked as though an immaculate tailor's model had come to life in him. He wore clothes as though he was made for them and not they for him. He spoke with the easy accents of Oxford drifting through his voice, and his address was as sound as Rackway's. His circle was the highest flights of the social world. He did all the pioneering work for the Silent Six. It was from Leeds that their initial information came. He surveyed the land ahead and tested the possibility of every scheme before the rest of the six so much as discussed the matter. His information was reliable to the last final letter, whether it concerned the location of jewels, measurements of rooms, or the positions of burglar alarms.

His speciality was cards. With fifty-two cards in his hands Stephen Leeds could make a certificated oculist go and get his eyes tested for myopia. He lived in the best hotels, where his uncanny ability to do invisible things with a card-pack between the shuffle and the deal brought him in lucrative extras.

There was Richard Kann, the American, who looked as though it would not matter a tinker's cuss to him whether Judgment Day caught him halfway through his next meal or never came at all. He it was who had stood scapegoat over the Rockingham emeralds affair, and in connection with which case he had taken five years' penal servitude without batting an eyelid.

And there was John Grayne, taller than either Lindrum or Kann, and not yet aware of the existence of nerves. He looked to be afflicted with less temperament than a Hindu Buddha, and there was a trifle less excitement to be gleaned from his eyes. His was a poker face, mask-like, utterly uninformative.

But John Grayne could play the violin like an angel. He had the same bewildering command of fingerwork on violin strings that Leeds reproduced on the cards. Hostesses counted it an honour to have the great John Grayne playing at their receptions. And that, of course, made the *entrée* for the Silent Six. There were plenty who said that if John Grayne were given choice of his violin and the most beautiful girl in the world, John Grayne would hold out both hands to his violin.

Rackway swallowed a brandy and soda while the cigars went round.

Leeds was the first to speak. He knew there was something weighing pretty heavily on Rackway's mind, but he wasn't in the least anxious about it. They had been near the wind before—and worry didn't worry.

"If there's nothing more important on hand," he said in his easy drawl."I've a little thing I came across last week that rather looks promising. Lady Barberton's place: quite a sound proposition. Perhaps you—"

Rackway motioned him to silence.

"There *is* something more important on hand," he said. "It is this: Damon Grey has come back from Dartmoor!"

The four of them looked at him with puzzled incredulity in their eyes.

"Oh, but that's absurd," said Leeds after long seconds of utter silence. "Damon Grey died in prison years ago."

"Damon Grey did not die in prison," said Rackway quietly. "Damon Grey was through to me on the phone fifteen minutes before I sent those telegrams."

"Say, but we got it from a warder that that guy kicked the bucket in the prison hospital," put in Kann. "I got the wire myself from a warder I knew when I was crackin' rocks in Dartmoor myself. Sure, he's dead."

Rackway glanced at him. "Damon Grey will be here in this room at eight o'clock," he said.

The other four looked uncertainly at each other; Rackway's manner was beginning to tell on them. Then Kann murmured: "Well, about it?"

"Just this," replied Rackway. "Damon Grey has become the bitterest devil on earth. Had you been able to hear him as I did, you'd understand He's murderous."

"But—but why?" Leeds's voice was querulous. "We couldn't—"

"We ought to have made definitely sure," cut in Rackway. "Surely you realise that? We are at fault. That warder's statement should have been verified—a simple matter. Grey hasn't come out looking share of whatever income we have made during these last eighteen years. I don't think the money end of it has ever entered his head. *But*—we let his wife die while he was in Dartmoor."

A tiny rustle went round the table.

"The hell we did!" Kann spoke with steely quietness. It was as though he breathed out the words in a single gentle breath. Kann knew the thoughts that arise in a man's soul when the prison walls close about him, knew the intense magnifying power of isolation and enforced silence. He knew how, when in prison, a single hope can grow and grow until it exceeds all bounds of normal thought and becomes an all-consuming ambition, a religion.

Rackway nodded a mutual understanding at the American.

Grayne puffed at his cigar. Lindrum, with a strained look of uncertainty, slid his own shining automatic on the table and looked a mute inquiry at Rackway.

Rackway shook his head. "Better wait and see," he said. "You can take it from me—he's vicious!"

Leeds moved uncomfortably in his chair.

"I don't see how we could help it—about his wife," he protested "How were we to know she couldn't draw on his bank account? How were we to know she was starving? She never wrote, never said she was ill, never even let us know she was in difficulties."

Rackway held up his hand. "Neither did Kann's wife," he said."But Damon Grey took the trouble to find out! He did that himself. I don't suppose his own wife knew of our existence. Did yours, Kann?"

"My wife doesn't know anything about any of you," said Kann shortly. "I make it a rule of life never to tell a woman anything she need not know. She thinks I'm an underwriter at Lloyd's."

Sharp at eight o'clock there came a knock on the door. Lorna Rennie entered, white-faced and frightened. She hurried over to Rackway.

"Mr. Rackway—your visitor—it's Damon Grey himself," she whispered agitatedly. "What can I do. He thinks you're expecting him. He—"

She broke off and turned her head hurriedly. The door had opened again, silently and without haste. Without a word, Damon Grey came into the room.

There was a little gasp in the room when he entered—a tightening of the atmosphere that could almost be felt. They looked at him, that friend of other days, whose loyalty had turned to hellish hate, whose very presence there was a menace and a defiance. It was Damon Grey all right—Damon Grey come back to demand a reckoning.

Kann at least looked at him with a sort of super-personal keenness. He knew the intensity of his own thoughts and feelings when the world opened its gates to him anew, knew the pure delight of living again after moribund years in a grey mausoleum, and he looked for the signs in the other man.

But there was nothing to see in the face of Damon Grey, nothing but the grim purposefulness that seemed to have taken up a permanent abode there. He stared at them, an inscrutable image cast in rigid flesh and bone.

"Good evening, gentlemen," he said.

Rackway cleared his throat.

"We—we've been expecting you, Grey," he said awkwardly.

Grey's eyes went to the gun on the table.

"So I see," he said.

The tension in the room went up notch by notch in the silence that fell.

Leeds tried to ease it by an attempt at nonchalance.

He screwed round and looked up at Damon Grey. "Rackway tells me you consider you have a grievance against us," he said.

Grey turned a frosty glance upon him.

"You amaze me," he said.

Rackway jumped in with both feet, flat and square. He couldn't stand the strain of that cool devil standing there, without a single emotion on his face, without a single fear in his soul. "What did you want to see us for?" he demanded.

"I know you're bitter; I knew from the tone of your voice over the wire that you don't propose joining up with us again on the old footing. That being so, why have you called?"

Grey eyed him without moving a muscle.

"I wanted to tell you that this organisation will automatically disband itself as from today," he said levelly.

"Will it indeed?" said Rackway. "And why?"

"Because I say it will."

"And the alternatives are?"

"I can't think of any," replied Grey. "But there are two ways of disbanding, one of which you will certainly take."

"And those ways?"

"The first is that you go to Scotland Yard tonight and voluntarily confess your crimes."

"I—you—*what?*" stammered Rack way,

"I see no reason why you shouldn't enjoy the same delightful experiences that I have done for this last eighteen years."

"But—man—you're mad!"

"Saner than I was when I went to prison for you. You have no excuse for what happened while I was a number. I want none. You're merely going to taste the hell you made me suffer through the best years of my life."

"Failing which?" asked Rackway quietly, and Lindrum's eyes slid down to the automatic.

"This organisation will break up just the same," replied Grey. He spoke without a sign of emotion, as though he was merely having a pleasant chat with them. But Lindrum had seen the devilish wickedness that had begun to smoulder in the cold eyes. He made a flying grab for the gun and got his fingers on it.

Damon Grey ignored him.

"There are letters lodged with my solicitors that render me bulletproof," he said, addressing himself calmly to Rackway. "Those same solicitors must see me, personally, in the flesh, twice every twenty-four hours. On the day I fail to present myself to them they will proceed with the letters to Scotland Yard. The contents of those letters are such that you would all be under lock and key within twenty-four hours, even though you briefed every K.C. in the kingdom to defend you. Lindrum's revolver doesn't even amuse me."

Rack way gulped.

"And supposing we neither disband nor obey your ridiculous ultimatum?" he asked.

"You will disband without a shadow of a doubt," said Grey grimly.

"And why?

"Because your names will become nothing more than component parts of an inscription on a tombstone. I shall eliminate you—as surely as you're sitting there. It's Dartmoor—or death—for the crowd of you."

The silence that fell was as tinglingly full of strain as the tense little interlude that falls between the flash and the crash in a thunderstorm. It was prickly, alive.

Rackway pushed his chair back from the table. He had to do something to break up that silence. The look on his face was as hard as stone. There was something of the undentable quality of granite in it. Grey noted it and made a mental entry of the conviction that Hildon Rackway would be a man who would kick like a mule before he died.

Lindrum scuffled his feet and looked uncomfortable; Leeds stroked the back of his right ear and seemed to be pondering the matter from a disinterested standpoint. Rackway met him eye to eye.

"That—that is as good as threatening each of—"

"Threatening?" Grey slid the word back at him and nearly his features cracked for the ghost of a moment. "I'm not threatening you—I'm telling you!"

He let his eyes travel from one to the other of them, as a naturalist might inspect a series of new specimens in a case.

Of them all Kann was the only one whose face betrayed no sign of his thoughts. There was neither fright nor animosity in his eyes. He carefully damped down one side of his cigar where it was burning uneventfly. Having corrected the fault, he glanced up at Grey.

"Why?" he asked impassively.

Grey's forehead twitched. "Because I want to see the whole crowd of you treading the road I trod," he said. "Because I want to live here in London—in comfort, in *freedom*—and to know that you devils are all down there in Dartmoor, living the hours and the days and the years as I lived them. And, you swine, I'll leave your women to starve and die, as you did!"

Lindrum looked uneasily at the others, and then, as though deciding on his own line of action regardless of the rest, he stood up and addressed himself quietly to Grey.

"Look here, Grey," he said. "Let us talk this matter out in a sensible sort of way. It is utterly absurd of you to talk about murdering the whole crowd of us; it can't be done, you know. You aren't thug enough to attempt it, for one thing, and we wouldn't be such fools as to let you, for another. Now, suppose we have a settling day. We can draw up some sort of an account that will show you exactly how we have fared since you went away. We will pool your share out to you. And—"

Damon Grey, who had been watching him through unblinking eyes, suddenly let up on his iron control. He whirled round on Lindrum in a red-eyed passion. A long-pent torrent of hatred crackled at the man whose thoughts only ran to currency.

"Money! You skinny-souled son of Midas, do you think I care a damn for your money?" he burst out. "Do you think that money or anything else in the world, except your own skins, could buy what I've paid for—or stall off what's coming to you? Do you think that the soul of a woman, beaten and broken into hopelessness, is discussable in terms of cash? Do you think that your wads of paper can bring back to that poor little body the life you drained out of it? Eh? You murderers! While I was down there, holding on to my sanity till the years passed by, you let her starve.

"You thought I'd never live to get through it, did you? And so you betrayed her—let her slip through the fingers of life, left her to an empty cupboard and her own tormenting thoughts, to crush the spirit out of her and rob her of the strength to live. You murdered my wife just as surely as though you had shot her with poisoned bullets. As though her loneliness wasn't awful enough, you—Bah!

"Couldn't you see that it was only the thoughts of *her* that kept me alive down there in the moors? All that I prayed for, planned for, dreamed for, all that I held dear in the world was centred on that little woman of mine. She was life itself to me down there—my last bribe for existence.

"The rest of the world didn't exist. And you let her die! You hounds—you let her starve to death; she, with another precious little life slowly drawing nearer to its birth every hour! And you think you can rattle a money-box under my nose; think you can buy me off with your filthy money. You—you who pulled a gun on me!"

He suddenly checked up in his welter of words and swayed back from the table.

"Lindrum," he said in his old steady voice again, "you'll get yours—you'll get all that's coming to you for pulling that gun. There isn't a single one of you here with the pluck of a rat—or you'd have downed me long ago. And you, Lindrum, have got less than the rest. And I shall take you first. You haven't the necessary yard of grit to go along to a police officer and tell him the whole story. You will be alive tomorrow, but not after nine o'clock. I shall poison you. You won't know anything about it or how it happened. All you'll know is that you'll get a sudden violent pricking pain somewhere up in that cavity where your heart used to be. And in a few moments you will be an erasure on the book of life. Good evening."

He turned suddenly, opened the door, and was gone almost before they realised he had stopped speaking.

III

Lorna Rennie went back to her room with a head that was whirling around in a hopeless jumble of doubts and dreads. She was trying hard not to be frightened, but her hands were trembling in her lap. And she found herself listening with a sort of half-fearful expectancy for the sounds of something terrible to crash into life in the room she had just left.

Stark under her eyelids she saw the picture of that group in the library. It persisted there like some dread premonition of tragedy, vague but immovable.

Almost subconsciously her hand went out to the telephone receiver. She lifted it and gave a number.

"Hallo!" she said. "Is that Dickie?"

"Yes. That's the only girl in the whole cosmic system, isn't it?"said a voice at the other end.

"Dick, how soon can you get round here?"

"In two minutes nineteen seconds. Per motorbike. I've timed it several hundred thousand times."

Lorna laughed quietly. "Well, come round and see me now, will you, Dick?" she asked.

"Like a bullet. I've just put in a new plug. With a spot of luck I'll knock a second off the record."

"All right, old man—but be as quick as you can, please," said Lorna. Dickie Ricks came in very shortly afterwards. Lorna was relieved to see his strong young figure enter the room. There was a cheerful self-reliance in the lines of him.

He sensed something seriously wrong the moment he saw Lorna.

"What is it, little one?" he asked, sitting on the edge of the table and swinging a leg.

Lorna looked at him a trifle shamefacedly.

"It—it's about Mr. Rackway," she began.

"That blighter been pestering you again?" he demanded, a battle glint shooting into his eyes.

"No. Don't be silly. Mr. Rack way doesn't pester me. If you did know, he's been awfully nice to me ever since I came here. And—and I'd be most dreadfully sorry if—if anything happened to him."

Dickie Ricks stopped swinging his leg.

"Just what *is* the matter with you, Lorna?" he asked.

"I—I'm rather afraid of something happening in the library tonight—something awful."

"Come along; out with it. No ghosts or hobgoblins knocking about the place, are there?"

"No—but, you know, I've always told you I thought Mr. Rackwaynad something on his mind that seemed to worry him—something that made him reserved and unwilling to talk at times?"

"Yes, I remember you saying something about it, once or twice."

"Well, this afternoon he sent for me and—and he dictated a letter to me—a most extraordinary letter." She looked up at him keenly. "This is absolutely *entre nous*, Dickie, mind; not a word to a soul. I wouldn't tell even you, but I feel worried out of my life. And if anything happens in that library tonight I shall be up to my ears in inquests and police-court horrors."

"For the love of mud!" said Dickie.

"Not a word, then?"

"Of course not; what do you think I am—a loudspeaker?"

"No, but I know what you men are when you start yarning."

"But about this letter—"

"It was—he—that is, I had to write to an officer at Scotland Yard. And if Mr. Rackway dies unexpectedly he wants me to post it. In it he told the officer that he expects an attempt to be made on his life within the next day or two. He is in danger from a convict, a man called Damon Grey, He said that if he dies it will be Damon Grey who has killed him."

"But—Lorna—he hasn't gone dotty, has he?"

"No, he's as sane as you are."

"I don't know so much. A man who would fall violently in love, at his age, with a girl who continually intimates her objection to such attentions must be a bit crummy on the crust. You're worrying yourself into hysterics about a possibility that doesn't exist."

"Doesn't it?" said Lorna with a significant nod of her head. "Well, Damon Grey called this evening, anyhow."

"What?"

"He's in there now—in the library with Mr. Rackway. And all the others are in there too. And they're all looking as nervous as cats. And—and they were all *expecting* something to happen in there. And when Damon Grey came in he looked awful—terrible."

"Phew!" said Dickie.

"Dickie, I believe Mr. Rackway is in the most terrible danger."

"Wouldn't be a bit surprised. He has probably asked for it, too. Anyway, he doesn't get much sympathy from me, the old satyr. I don't like the man. Never did. There's something fishy about him. He's got eyes that tell lies when he's telling the truth."

"Yes, but then suppose anything really does happen?"

"I don't see how we can do anything in the matter. We can't stop it."

"Dickie, you wouldn't be so flippant if you could have been in that library a little while ago."

"This—this chap Grey. You say he's a convict?"

"That's what Mr. Rackway said in his letter to the police people. But he doesn't look a bit like that, really. He's got rather a fine face—if only it wasn't so terribly grim."

"Well, I'll stay with you until *he* goes, anyway! I don't particularly mind you being made love to by someone old enough to be your father, but I draw a very distinct line at you being in the same house with convicts."

He got off the table and went to the door.

"You stay there," he said. "And remember, if there's any trouble, ring for the police at once. I'll go along and see what's happening. Jove! I don't like the sound of that voice."

He tiptoed along the hallway and stood outside the library door.

Inside he heard the voice of Grey whipping the Silent Six with the bitterness of his tongue. He heard the jolting, bitten-off sentences he flung at Lindrum.

"And I shall take you first. You haven't the necessary yard of grit to go along to a police officer and tell him the whole story. You will be alive tomorrow, but not after nine o'clock!"

Ricks listened with tingling ears. The grim voice went on:

"I shall *poison* you! You won't know anything about it or how it happened. All you'll know is that you'll get a sudden violent pricking pain somewhere up in that cavity where your heart used to be."

And then came the vicious threat: "And in a few minutes you will be an erasure on the book of life."

The door was suddenly pulled open, and Dickie Ricks was face to face with Damon Grey.

For a moment they both stood stiffly immobile, staring at each other like two animals meeting unexpectedly in the wild, surprised, but with every nerve suddenly keyed up as taut as wire, Ricks saw two eyes, piercingly alive, glaring at him in the gloom.

Damon Grey, as rigidly unemotional as a statue, had halted as abruptly as though he had collided with a wall Ricks could but faintly see him, could barely discern the virile face, the grim doggedness that was stamped into every feature, but he sensed, in a single electric flash, the driving, dynamic force locked up in the man confronting him. Grey's hand was still on the door-handle behind him. With a slight slow motion of the wrist he pulled the door to. Ricks was almost startled at the loud click of the catch as it shut.

Grey's voice cut gently into the silence. Still with his hand gripped tight on the door-handle, he thrust his head forward a few inches and said! "And who might you be?"

Ricks drew a deep breath and straightened up

"My name is Ricks—Dickie Ricks," he said.

Grey looked at him pensively, as though turning the matter over in his mind and weighing up the full portent of each word.

"Ricks, eh?" he muttered, and the unfriendly glint increased in his eyes. "And where do you fit into this business?"

"So far as I can see, right here, where the door opens!

"Is that so? Don't you think you would be wiser to turn round walk, and keep on walking?" There was a purring, solicitous note in Grey's voice that made the very air tingle. "Don't you think it would better for you if you went quietly away and forgot that tonight happened?"

"I don't think so. I happen to have rather a retentive memory."

"For faces?"

"And places." Ricks gave him as good as he got, straight-eyed and undismayed.

Damon Grey nodded, a brief gesture as though to say that was Rick's funeral entirely.

"Well, look you here, Mr. Richard Ricks," he said. "You—"

"Excuse me. Dickie Ricks is my name. Dickie, just like that—see? Rather odd, I know. Parental whim, or something like that—but that's how I got it."

Grey half turned his head to listen to a low hum of voices that had suddenly broken out in the room behind him. Ricks could hear one in particular, a hoarse, excited whisper that cut persistently into the drone of the others. He guessed it was Lindrum's, and that Lindrum was being persuaded to do something against his strong inclinations.

Grey turned to the matter in hand with a suspicion of a smile of amusement in the corners of his mouth.

"How long have you been standing there?" he asked coolly.

"About four minutes."

"Four minutes too long, my son. A most unwise four minutes."

"I don't think so. A most interesting, a most unusual four minutes."

"Then you heard a good deal?"

"Quite a lot. Much more than a man might reasonably be expected to forget with the facility you suggest."

"Such as?"

"Well, one doesn't usually hear a threat of wholesale murder, delivered in the tone that brooks neither argument nor inference of jest, such as you used—I mean, one doesn't hear that sort of thing every night of one's life, does one?

"Nothing more than that?"

"Oh, yes. Lindrum is going to be the first to need a coffin, is he not?"

"He certainly is. There is nothing more sure in all heaven and earth, Mr. Ricks, Mr. Dickie Ricks—than that Lindrum will cease to be frightened of death by this time tomorrow night."

"So I gathered. Your voice is rather penetrating when you're menacing people. He is to be poisoned, I believe?"

"He is. Are you interested?"

"More in you than in Lindrum. Your method struck me as being rather downright. Mr.—er—I didn't quite catch your name?"

"That's very reasonable. I didn't say it." Grey's tone was as wintry as a dawn wind in December.

"You have a name?"

"I have. William Brown."

"Very fair, but neither William nor Brown. The wrong colour, in fact. I understand it to be Grey—Damon Grey." Ricks's cold audacity was as brazen as Grey's.

Grey's eyes never flickered. His assumption of the attitude of complete mastery of himself and of the situation never faltered. He just looked at Ricks and muttered:"So!"

For a few seconds the duel of sheer willpowers went on in utter silence, save for the rumble of voices behind the door, each of them striving to make the other turn tail and quit. Then Grey took Ricks by the arm and said quietly:"Come outside—somewhere where we can talk, before these fools come out. You've got bone in you, my son. Bone! And I'd hate to have to add your name to those of that crowd of murderers in there."

Outside, Grey piloted him over towards the gardens, with his muscular fingers still clasped on his arm. Ricks could feel the gripping strength of them through the cloth of his coat.

They walked in silence for a half-circuit of the railings. On the far side, where the gloom of the overhanging trees intensified the darkness around, Grey suddenly stopped and wheeled on him.

"You from Scotland Yard?" he demanded.

Ricks laughed under his breath.

"Not!" he said laconically.

Grey looked a little relieved. "Well, where *do* you come in on matter?" he said. "Are you one of the crowd?"

"Which crowd?"

"The Sile—that crowd I just left."

"Don't know them—except by name."

"Well, what were you doing outside that door?"

"Listening. It's a habit of mine. But, as a matter of fact, I was sent for. My sole object for being in that house was to protect someone."

"Rackway?"

"Not on your life!"

Grey pulled himself up short as a burst of understanding suddenly broke upon him.

"Oh, I see!" he said with a long breath. "Like that—like that—ah, yes!"

He looked up and down the deserted square. An occasional taxi had been swishing along, but just then the whole square was empty, and only the distant rumble of traffic broke the stillness.

"Tell me," he said gently. "Rackway is very much in love with the little secretary, is he not?"

"Yes." Ricks bit the word off as though he had a rabid grudge against it.

Grey continued in a dreamy, reminiscent voice that seemed to be contemplating distant vistas of peaceful delight. "Suppose you yourself were in love, Mr. Ricks—Mr. Dickie Ricks. Suppose there was someone in this world to whom you could lend your soul and not care whether she made or broke it, someone who was to you the sole difference between sunshine and the night, who was to you what heaven is to the angels, would you—would you take it very much to heart if, say, all that was suddenly blotted out?"

Grey waited a little while, but Ricks had nothing to say to him, and Grey carried on.

"Supposing you had a little coterie of friends—you understand, say, several people whom you really understood to be your friends in the very strongest bond that is understood in the word, and for whom you were prepared to make a—a rather serious sacrifice. Suppose something happened among you and a scapegoat was required. Suppose you made the sacrifice—a sacrifice that was to eat away the only years of your life that can really make marriage worthwhile. And supposing if, after nearly twenty years of hopeless hope in a prison cell, you came out again to find that the sacrifice had been turned into a joke against you. Suppose you found, in a brutal way, that she had died in the direst extremity that can fall to woman's lot to suffer—would you count it much a crime if you pet the fear of God into those friends before you killed them, as I undoubtedly shall kill them?"

Grey looked closely at the younger man all the time he was speaking. The pent-up bitterness in his voice was alight and flaming in his eyes. His words were a maledictory stream of passion so ferociously controlled that it seemed to be affably intended.

Ricks remained silent. He just returned the other man's gaze and let him do the talking. He knew he had got Damon Grey, to a certain extent, in his fingers; although, as Grey was then, he was quite as capable of putting an end to Ricks as any of the others who had incurred his hatred.

Grey's voice softened a little as he waited for Ricks to answer.

"You're young," he said. "You can appreciate the heartbreak of a hope, of a dream kicked out of existence. You can still see the colours in the rainbow; you still believe that some day you will stand where the rainbow ends. I, too, I am young. My God a young man in an old man's body. My passions have never burned out in the fires of love; they burned out inside me, fed on themselves, burned and sank and died as the years crawled on. But the hot loves, the splendid hopes and desires of youth—they never died! They lived, stayed alive in me potent and virile, marking time in me from the day I first faced the judge—while my body grew old and older all around them. Do you understand now? Do you realise now how much chance Henry Lindrurn has of living—or any of the others of that ring of devils?"

Ricks coughed and made a slight motion of his head towards the upper end of the square.

"There's a policeman standing over under that lamp," he said.

And Damon Grey crawled back into his cell of ice like a tiger to its cave when the sun comes up.

"The police, eh?" he muttered. "You would talk to me of police after—that?"

"Well, murder is still murder, isn't it?"

"No. I'll demonstrate it to you if you like. Go over and fetch that constable; go over and bring him here. Tell him all you heard tonight. Tell him every word I said, write down every threat I made, and tell him what the others said. Then go with him to Rackway's flat, and go in and explain all about it to them in there. And I'll promise you you'll make the biggest fool of yourself you've ever made in your life. Listen to me. Neither Rackway nor Lindrurn, nor anyone else in that library, will say they even know my name. They are too scared. They think they'll be able to put me off. They will deny you—flatly and utterly. They'll swear that they never heard of Damon Grey in their lives—nor of you, either. Go on. Go over and fetch that constable."

Ricks tried another line of argument. He had come to the conclusion that Damon Grey was either pitifully mad or diabolically sane. And of the two he rather fancied sanity.

He adopted the conversational tone with him, pointing out another defect in his campaign as matter-of-factly as could Grey himself.

"Supposing I inform the authorities," he said; "for you realise I shall have to do something in the matter? Supposing I tell that policeman. And supposing each one of your friends disowns me, and tells him I'm mad, and then, within twenty-four hours of my warning, your first murder is committed. How would you expect to continue? You would be arrested on suspicion."

"And released as soon as the inquest was held," said Grey gruffly. "A post-mortem on Lindrurn will show nothing more than sudden heart failure. A thousand police officers and a million doctors could not prove me guilty. And in any case you won't call over that policeman, or convey information to the authorities. Not out of any affection for me, but for the sake of that little girl Rackway is so extraordinarily devoted to. You wouldn't make any unpleasantness for her. As I say, you're too young."

There was another little silence, and then Damon Grey said pensively:

"Over and above which, if I thought there was the smallest possibility of your doing any such thing, Mr. Dickie Ricks, you would be the first one to contract heart failure! I would kill you like a rat. And there is no safeguard against the way I kill! By merely putting on your hat you might die. By merely taking it off you might no longer be alive. By handling a cigarette, or a match, or buying a paper, or opening a door, or doing any one of the million little things that go to make up the daily action of life, you are dead. Lindrum tomorrow will be too frightened to eat or drink. He thinks I am going to poison him. He *knows* I am going to poison him. And he will be frightened out of his life of touching food. By eight o'clock he will be in a blind panic, scarcely daring to breathe, let alone eat. But it will not be from food that I shall get him. His greater danger will lie in the cutlery he uses, in the plate he puts his food on, in his serviette, in the handle of his mustard-spoon, in the handkerchief he wipes his perspiring forehead on. And I could get you in just the same way—here and now. You would never know it was administered. All you'd know is that your heart would suddenly begin to race. The heart action would accelerate to such a tremendous extent that your constitution could not support the rush of blood. In a minute you would be dead. No, I don't think you will have anything to do with the police. Good evening, Dickie Ricks."

The grim, sinister figure nodded his head almost imperceptibly, wheeled on his heels, and walked quietly away in the direction of the Grand Imperial.

Ricks stood for a long time staring after him. The whole episode was over and done with in ten swift minutes: Grey had simply opened a door and walked into Ricks's life. In doing so he had opened a door and walked into Ricks's soul.

For Dickie Ricks was still in the first throes of young love: to him the world was simply a place planted in Creation by a benignly smiling Providence for the happy convenience of young lovers, a garden bounded by romance and bordered by hope, sunlit with happiness, tinted with blue.

He rubbed his chin reflectively. Something would have to be done about it. The question was—what? Grey had fogged him up, and he wanted to think himself clear again. He began walking quickly up and down the square. Several people came out of Rackway's house. He counted them one by one—four of them.

Grey's induced miasma was wearing off and he was getting back to himself.

"This will never do," he muttered irritably. "He's trying to bluff me—trying to get on my nerves. Kill a man by fingering a door-handle or touching a handkerchief? Mooncheese!"

He went quickly in through Rackway's gate and rang the bell. The maid showed him into Lorna's room.

Lorna was sitting down staring moodily into the lifeless heat gas fire. She rose eagerly as he entered.

"Dickie, I've been waiting for you," she said hurriedly. "What happened? What was all the trouble about? What is that man Grey going to do? Why is he so dreadfully bitter against Mr. Backway? What—"

"Whew-w!" said Ricks, and screwed his fingers into his ears. "Steady, m'selle!" lie expostulated.

She drew another chair up to the fire.

Dickie sat down. "Lorna," he said quietly, "I think the sooner you clear out of this place the better. I'm very much afraid there's tragedy in the air. And I wouldn't have you mixed up in it for all the Rackways and secretaryships in the world."

Lorna's colour had come up in a great rising wave.

"Dickie!" she said. "Do you really think he is going to kill Mr Rack way?"

Ricks answered her bluntly,

"Candidly," he said, "unless something or somebody stops him, I think he will kill the whole blessed crowd of them."

Lorna gasped. "You're joking," she said.

"Not with you, little girl. Damon Grey is capable of carrying out every threat he's made. That crowd your boss works with played Grey the wickedest trick one man could play another. And Grey will take his revenge out of them as surely as the compass-needle swings to the Pole."

"I—I can't believe it, Dick. I daren't. And—and how on earth do you know all this?"

"I've been talking to Damon Grey."

Lorna look at him in blank incredulity.

"*You* have? You've been talking to Damon Grey?"

"Yes. I had a most uncomfortable ten minutes with him. The man is a hopeless fanatic. He isn't nursing a grievance so much as nursing his revenge; he has put it in a shrine and dedicated himself to it. He is as cold-blooded as a pike—and as vicious."

"But—what about the police?" asked Lorna.

"The police? Neither Rackway nor Lindrum nor any one of them dare go near an officer of the law. Grey has got them hard up against it."

Lorna was nonplussed. So far as she was concerned, such things as murders and poisonings happened only in the columns of newspaperdom, somewhere outside her orbit altogether. That they could suddenly jar into her own life and whirl her and her own private affairs into their unpleasant vortex was a possibility so remote that she had never even considered it. She shook herself and rallied her wavering convictions,

"I don't believe it—I *won't* believe it!" she said.

"All right, m'selle," he replied. "Let me know what you think about it after nine o'clock tomorrow night."

IV

Damon Grey called a taxi when Grosvenor Square was left behind. His course took him into the heart of the West End shopping centre. But he was having no dealings with those mammoth palaces. He mistrusted them. And besides, there was only one shop in all London where he could get what he wanted.

He drove as far as Piccadilly and paid off his taxi there. From the Circus he walked up Wardour Street into the old Berwick Market, into the very soul of the cluttering slumland that lies off the main way like scum penned into a backwater and held there by the swift, roaring rush of the big river.

Through the maze of stalls and barrows, blazing with silks and glittering with brass in the light of the hissing naphtha flares, he slowly picked his way, avoiding the pavements with their standstill throngs as though they were plague-ridden. Then out of the market streets and into the byways, little cramped side turnings where the buildings huddled close to each other and deepened the gloom to impenetrable blackness.

Solitary gas jets flickering uneasily here and there cast pools of sickly yellow light for a yard or two around them, intensifying the squalor and the gloom.

He stopped outside a tiny shop window. It was unlit, save for the pallid nebula of dismal light from a lonely candle somewhere inside the shop. The name above the window was barely decipherable under a generation of unwashed grime.

Grey struck a match and held it above his head. In the quick flare he spelled out the name:

BANDRANA RAMADAN
HERBALIST AND TAXIDERMIST

The window was curtained, a thick pall of dust-covered crimson velvet about two feet back from the glass, leaving a narrow bay between it and the window. In that bay were a couple of dirty glass-covered specimen cases, some bunches of herbs, a tray of coloured beans, and a bowl in which two dead goldfish floated.

Grey pushed the door open, knocking on it as he went in. In the corner near the candle an old man was reading a book, his back turned to the door. He was a weazened, wrinkled little figure, with clothes that hung about him in thick creases as though carved in old smoky wood. His hair, beneath a tight Punjabi turban, was white and rat-tailed. A girdle round his waist pulled his skinny figure in like a thin hourglass.

A little to his left was a bit of mirror, the only really clean thing in the whole dingy shop.

Bandrana Ramadan did not move when Damon Grey entered. Except for a sudden snake-like flick of his eyes from the book to the glass, there was not a movement in the old man's body.

Grey walked up to the herb-littered counter.

"Good evening, Ramadan," he said gravely.

The Hindu turned and came over to him slowly.

"Good evening to you, Mr.—Smith," he said. His voice was soft, gentle, barely audible, but it carried perfectly. "It is good to see old friends again. You have been travelling?"

Grey shrugged. "Yes," he said quietly. "A not very interesting journey."

"So I heard. SoI heard. And what can I do for you?"

"I want seven ounces of powdered abani root."

Bandrana Ramadan's eyes contracted to narrow slits,

"Powdered abani root?" he purred.

"Yes, Seven ounces. And a bulb-and-bottle sprayer. You can get me those?"

"I can get you the sprayer, Mr. Smith."

"You can get me the abani root, too, Mr. Ramadan."

"Ah, I fear not. Times are not what they used to be. Things have changed since you went away. New laws have been thrust upon us and the old ones are enforced. Much as I would like to—I—"

"Nevertheless you will give me seven ounces before I leave this filthy hovel tonight."

Bandrana Ramadan sighed, and he raised his eyes pathetically ceiling-wards.

"Alas, Mr. Smith, I fear you must be disappointed. I gravely doubt whether seven ounces of abani root exist in this city. It is too dangerous to traffic in such things these days."

Grey let his gaze travel slowly up the wall behind the Hindu to a little glass case, shabby and dirt-encrusted. Inside was a tiny stuffed marmoset; it was peering out of the case with little beady eyes fixed mischievously on the scene below.

Grey indicated the case with a nod of the head.

"I see you have still retained little Jennie," he said off-handedly.

The Hindu blinked. "I could not sell her," he said.

"Not in eighteen years, Ramadan? Indeed, trade must be very bad, very bad. Come—I will buy her."

"But no. I don't think little Jennie is for sale, Mr. Smith."

"Just for old sake's sake. I will give you a fair price. Or shall I ask the first policeman I find to come in and rip up her little skin? The police never discovered the ultimate hiding-place of the Duke's—"

Bandrana Ramadan looked nervously around, quick little furtive glances that whipped across from left to right with rapid flicks of the eyes.

"Not so loud, Mr. Smith, not so loud," he begged, with an imploring touch of the hand. "The matter can be discussed—but you are most indiscreet—most indiscreet."

"Maybe so. I've been through a slight hardening process since we last met," said Grey. "Over and above which, I have little time to waste. Abani root requires eight hours' boiling, if I remember rightly. It leaves me little time to gossip here."

"Just so, Mr. Smith—wait a moment, please, only a moment." The Hindu crept shakily out of the shop into a little inner parlour. Grey caught a glimpse of it through a screening curtain. It was a villainous-looking litter of hanging snake skins and festoons of dried herbs. The ceiling was completely obscured by masses of roots and herbalistic impedimenta pendent from it. The whole place was like a naturalist's lumber-room—with the overpowering odour of a myriad aromatic herbs drenching it through and through.

The dealer pulled the curtain across the doorway behind him, and Grey heard him foraging about in the room, lifting boxes around, and then came the bump of a trapdoor closing.

It was several minutes before he reappeared. When he did he was carrying a small metal box and his hands were gloved. He laid the box on the rackety counter and murmured: "Will that be all, Mr. Smith?"

"Yes—if the sprayer is in that box, too," said Grey.

"The sprayer will be sent you in the morning, sir."

"The sprayer will be sent to me tonight," Grey assured him. "Suite No. 4, Grand Imperial."

"Very good, Mr. Smith."

"How much do I owe you?"

"Nothing at all, sir. I don't know you. You have never been in my shop or had dealings with me in any way whatever. I have never seen you."

"Quite," said Grey amiably, and went out into the night.

The old Hindu watched him go and stared at the closed door long after he had gone. His smoothly working thought processes informed him that someone would die a peculiarly inexplicable death before many hours had sped, and that a new hiding-place was urgently needed for the Chessington Diamond.

Grey hurried back to the Grand Imperial and went up to his room in the lift. On the way up he gave the attendant a ten-shilling note.

"In an hour's time or thereabouts," he said, "a messenger will bring a small parcel for me. I want it brought up to my room. Knock on my door and leave it on the mat outside. Don't, under any consideration, disturb me. I shall be very busy writing."

"Very good, sir."

Grey shut himself up in his room, and for many hours he was busy with a little crucible that boiled and bubbled over a small spirit-lamp. The powder was a greenish, unhealthy-looking colour, and he boiled and reboiled it in pure alcohol. Every now and then he added more spirit from one of several bottles beside him, trying and testing the hot liquid to various reactions in small glass test-tubes.

After nearly eight hours' continuous boiling and stirring he added a few drops of dark blue liquid from a tiny phial, and the mass in the crucible seethed to a green effervescent scum.

Damon Grey blew out the flame of the spirit-lamp up stretching his cramped muscles.

When the liquid had cooled he strained it several times through ganze. Then he pulled on a pair of thick flesh-coloured India-rubber gloves and put a small pad of lint over his nose. There were only a few thimblefuls of liquid as a result of his night's work, and he measured them with extreme caution in a graduated glass. He brought in the sprayer, unscrewed it, and poured the concoction in, standing it under running water to get thoroughly cold. While the water was running he poured several drops from two different bottles into a tiny tube, added a single pellet of soft yeasty-looking stuff, and shook the thing rapidly till the pellet had dissolved. Then he poured it drop by drop into the container of the spray.

He held it to the light and watched it critically. Slowly the mixture changed in colour from a light green to an even lighter, but slightly cloudy blue.

Damon Grey sighed with satisfaction, locked the sprayer away is his dispatch-box, and hung the windows open wide.

Dawn was breaking over London, chill and grey. The fresh air stremed in, and Grey breathed it deeply.

In a few minutes he cleared away all traces of his night's work. He put all his tubes and phials and bottles, his spirit-lamp, and crucible into an attaché-case and locked it. There was a man in Hounslow who had charge of an incinerator, and who, for a half-sovereign, would allow him to thrust that case into the furnace without asking a single question or trying to remember the incident.

The whole of the experiment had been carried out on the marble top of the washstand. He washed the whole stand over with hot running water and wiped it over carefully with a dry sponge.

Then, with a final critical glance round, he partly closed the windows and went to bed.

He slept until seven o'clock in the evening, when he turned out, dressed leisurely, and called up Lindrum on the phone.

Lindrum was not at home. Without a sign of surprise he rang up Rackway, and Rack way was in.

"That you, Rack way?" he asked quietly. "Is Lindrum with you? Grey speaking."

"We are all here together!" came the defiant reply.

"So good of you. I'll be with you, too, as soon as I've dined. Tell Lindrum that he will be a dead man five minutes after I enter your house, will you, please? Thank you."

Rackway hung up his receiver with a hand that was not quite steady. The four others looked at him, silent, Grayne with his eyebrows raised in a mute inquiry. Across on the other side of the table he caught a quick glimpse of Lindrum's lace, white and set, fixed on him with a look of tense earnestness.

"Was—was that Damon Grey?" he asked. He sat rigid in his chair, his hands locked together under the table, his shoulders hunched,

Rack way nodded.

"Yes," he said. "Speaking from his hotel, I think. He says he will be here as soon as he has dined."

"Was that all he said?" Lindrum's voice was abrupt, staccato. His mental strain showed in his taut muscles and in the glitter of his eyes.

Rack way shrugged, and crushed a cigarette stub into an ash-tray.

"Yes, that was all—no more than that," he said.

"Nothing about me?"

"Oh, no—just his usual ridiculous self."

"That's a lie." Lindrum flung the words at him bitterly. "It's a lie—and you know it. He—"

"Listen here, Lindrum," said Kann. "There's only one thing to do in this matter, and that's to go through with it. We're all in the same boat; and if one sinks we none of us swim. The obvious thing is to stand by each other. You won't be let down. Grey will have as nasty a reception as ever he had in his life if he cuts up rough. There are ways and means of disposing of a dead body other than putting it up for identification on a mortuary slab. I've got an alibi fixed for tonight that the Attorney-General himself couldn't shake. And I reckon we've all done the same little service for ourselves. Personally, I'm in Bedford at the present moment—and can prove it to the extent of eight reliable witnesses. Grayne is in his own home entertaining a few friends, all of whom are prepared to swear their lives away to that effect. I don't know what your own arrangements are, but I should guess they're pretty well as watertight. Any clever lawyer can prove black's white, but the cleverest prosecutor on earth can't prove it's butter—because it ain't."

"Yes, I know, but—"

"There's a lead box in Rackway's lumber-room," continued Kann calmly, "a lead box that would hold, say, a body comfortably. And down at Wapping Steps there's a motorboat—a motorboat capable of, say, running a lead box fifty miles out beyond Sheerness and coming back without it. And between this library and Wapping Steps is a motorcar with a closed-in tonneau. I can't see what the hell you're all het up over." He drew pensively at a cigarette. "Taking everything by and large,"he said, "I can't see what's to prevent us paying a little visit to Grey's solicitors after we have seen to Damon. They will have a safe in their office—a safe that would probably be prepared to reconsider its maker's flattering guarantees after we've done with it. Oxy-acetylene is rather a speciality of yours, isn't it, Leeds?"

Rackway smiled. "His new pipe went through a six-inch piece of test steel last week like so much lead," he said. "Quite a nice little contraption. Looks like a weekend suitcase. And it doesn't jink when you lock it."

But it was obvious that Lindrurn had got into a bad state of nerves during the day. He was living on them, eating them.

"That's all very well," he snapped. "You can do all that after he has made clay of me. He has sworn to get me tonight, and he will. What's the use of pretending we're as safe as houses? We're not! You're all right—your turn hasn't come yet. I'm the fool standing the rub."

Rackway looked at him shrewdly, and there was a tinge of regtwt'i his voice.

"I'm sorry you take it that way, Lindrurn," he said. "I thought you had more grit than that. But perhaps you're right. We can't quite look at it from your angle. Your job is to cut and run while the door is still open. Put as many miles as you can between yourself and Damon Grey. Beat it!"

But Lindrurn didn't. He hadn't the courage to. His never had gone. He wouldn't admit it and he didn't realise it, but it had.

"God! What's the use? He'd get me just the same," he muttered.

"Lindrurn, give me your gun," said Rack way. His voice was cold, commanding. He held out his hand for it, and Lindrurn passed it ever without a word.

"There's just one more thing," said Rackway, and looked round of his friends. He pressed his secretary's bell. "No need to drag her into this," he observed.

Leeds shrugged his shoulders.

"If she isn't in the house she can't be a witness," he said unconcernedly. "Send her out on a long errand somewhere—or tell her to go along and have an evening with her sweetheart; I suppose she's got one? Pretty kid like that—got a dozen, I expect."

Rackway shot him a glance that might have been made on blue steel.

Lorna Rennie entered with notebook and pen.

"Letters, sir?" she asked.

"No," he said. "I want you to settle a little bet for us. Take a box at the Majesty tonight and make a note of the exact time the curtain it rung down. Will you do that for me, please?"

"Rather a pleasant duty," laughed Lorna.

"That will be all, then, thank you."

She went out, but certainly not to the theatre. She went straight to her own room, where Dickie Ricks was waiting with uncompromising curiousity.

"Then that's all settled," said Rackway relievedly. "Do you feel a little less worried now, Lindrurn?"

Lindrurn looked up and snapped:"No, I don't!"

He grabbed the phone and called up his own house. His maid answered it.

"Hallo—has anyone been ringing for me tonight?" he asked.

"Yes, sir. A Mr. Damon Grey—about half an hour ago."

He slammed the receiver down.

And half an hour later the door opened. Calmly and without a trace of emotion, Damon Grey walked in.

"Good evening, gentlemen," he said. He closed the door behind him and advanced into the full glare of the lights. A terrific silence crawled across the room. It was as though all sound had been drawn out of it. The five of them stared at him without even the rustle of clothing to break the deathly silence. Even Lindrurn, whose face had gone as white as chalk, subdued his breathing into inaudibility.

Damon Grey looked them over, his face as expressionless as a block of stone.

"Good of you to accord me so full a gathering, gentlemen," he said quietly. "Perhaps you will also do me the further honour of remaining seated while this matter is being disposed of."

He glanced at his wristwatch. "Rather earlier than I thought," he murmured. "Lindrurn, you still have a couple of minutes yet to live—won't you make the most of them?" He held out his cigar-case, but Lindrum shied away from it as though it were bulging with the ten plagues of Egypt.

Grey made a little gesture of unconcern with his hands. "As you will," he said. "They're quite good—Bock y Ca—and not at all dangerous." He selected one and lit it with profound care.

Lindrurn's eyes went avidly to Grey's hands as they manipulated the matches. He suddenly sat up in his chair, stiff and rigid, as though he had been half electrocuted. Damon Grey's hands were encased in thick india-rubber gloves.

Lindrurn jumped to his feet with his face twitching.

"Look at him! Look at him!" he yelped. "Gloves on his hands. Rubber gloves. What's he wearing them for? The murdering devil. What's he going to do?"

Grey smiled at him tolerantly.

"Seems rather distraught," he mused. "That, of course, is to be expected. Conscience makes cowards of us all—even apparently of my once nerveless friends of the Silent Six. I'm sorry to see you giving way like that, Lindrurn; sorry, and rather shocked. At one time I had rather a high opinion of you. Especially do I recall one incident—the Walmsey affair. Do you remember it? The time we were surprised by the butler and you feigned unconsciousness? You pretended to run, if I recollect, and tripped over near the fireplace, went down with a most fearful smash. You shammed unconsciousness until the butler had passed you. I was hung up by my coat-tails, half in and half out of the window. You grabbed the poker, did you not? And nearly cracked his skull with it as he raised his revolver to shoot me. Now, that was rather cool, I thought. So cool and brain-steady that it is pitiful to see you now. The way you grabbed that poker from the grate and leapt—all in the same action, silent, alert, deadly—ah, my dear Lindrurn, that was an action worthy of the Silent Six."

Grey's voice dropped to a ruminative note. "We kept that poker, if I remember rightly, as a little souvenir. One of many such. Ah, yes, of course—there it is, over there in the grate."

He walked leisurely across and picked it up, a heavy brass thing with a massive handle of hammered copper. He examined it reminiscently for several seconds, trying its weight and swishing it through the air, as though dealing a blow at some imaginary foe.

"Yes; you certainly did fetch him a most fearful welt," he reflected. "Anyone with a less intelligent skull would have required what you will require within this next few minutes, Lindrum. I think you measured that blow remarkably well. And, as I say, it is a trifle distressing to see you so utterly unstrung, now. The years seem to have wrought a sad change in you." He dropped the poker back with a clatter in the grate. "Not surprising, I suppose," he muttered. "The years have changed me, too. Eighteen years in the quarry gang hardly tends to refine one's feelings or outlook. I think I have grown a little impervious, too. You may have noticed that."

He went back and stood behind Rackway.

"Why have you brought your guns out tonight?" he asked. "All of you; you've got guns in your pockets, and they're all pointing at me. All except Lindrum—and I can quite understand about him. You always were immaculately careful, Rackway. But why do it? Revolvers won't help you at all—and I told you last night that revolvers were offensive to me. Indeed, I even told Lindrum I would kill him first for no other reason than that he pulled a gun on me."

Rackway looked round at him, and his face was like a wooden image.

"Bunk!" he said angrily. "Look here, Grey. What damn-silly game do you think you're playing? This wholesale murder menace of yours is too absurd for words. Such things don't happen in these bright days."

"Your mistake," said Grey gently.

"You're acting like a silly fool—and overacting it at that. Do you think you're impressing us? Do you think you're frightening us?"

"Take a look at Lindrum," said Grey, and shook the ash off his cigar.

Rackway waved a hand. "There's Stephen Leeds," he said. "He can put three bullets into the ace of hearts, one on top of the other, at ten yards, without overstepping the red spot. There's Grayne—you've seen him score a line across a visiting-card held horizontally in your own mouth. There's Kann there, who can juggle three guns in the air and hit a ha'penny thrown ceiling high. And there's me. I'm not so good. I'm older now. But I can still hit a man's heart at five paces—and back myself at a thousand to one not to miss. And we've *all* got you covered."

"I dare say," said Grey. "But the whole statement is noncommittal. It a fact or a threat?"

Rackway cleared his throat.

"It's a threat," he said slowly, and went white round the mouth. "Damon Grey, you are not going to get out of this house alive. The first movement you make that might be construed into anything remotely resembling a gesture of aggression, and you will have four bullets in your chest at one and the same moment."

"I think not," said Grey. "You see, you have forgotten one little point. I am not entirely a free man. I am liberated on what used to be known as ticket-of-leave. Every now and then I have to report myself to a certain police inspector at Scotland Yard as long as I am in London. Quite a charming man. A really affable fellow. He had dinner with me tonight. He is waiting for me now in the street below. After I have settled this little matter we are going along to one of the cabaret shows for a spot of supper and a little—ah—light entertainment. I told him that if I wasn't outside with him again in ten minutes to make a few inquiries for me, which he certainly will do. Ever such a nice chap. I'm sure you'll like him. That is, of course, unless you have nothing but a quaintly incredible story to account for my absence."

He stepped over to the window and pulled the curtains aside.

"Look, there he is," he said pleasantly. "I wouldn't like you to think I was bluffing. Come over to the window and have a look at him. Seems rather impatient already—see, he's looking at his watch."

Rackway, Leeds, and Grayne went over and peered out at an overcoated figure below on the pavement. Kann stayed where he was with a smile on his face that was half contemptuous and half amused. He had lived half his life on bluff and he admired a man who could put up a super-bluff of his own devising when the need fell with stark and unexampled suddenness. He switched his head round at a tiny sound near the fireplace.

Lindrum, with eyes blazing with ferocious fright, had picked up the poker and was advancing towards the window, the back of Damon Grey's head turned full and unsuspectingly towards him.

Kann saw Lindrum's fingers gripping on the poker-handle so tightly that the blood was pressed back from them and they shone bone-white. A tiny dicker of expectancy slid across his face.

He himself hadn't the faintest doubt that Lindrum had, in merely touching that poker, voluntarily signed his name on his own death-warrant. He hadn't the faintest idea how it would happen, but he was definitely convinced that within the next second or two Lindrum would be a dead man. The two facts—Lindrum's contact with the poker and Lindrum's death—were simply an instance of cause and effect.

He fixed that assurance in his own mind purely on his own knowledge of the complex functioning of the criminal instinct. Damon Grey had not mentioned the incident of Lindrum's first connection with that poker for nothing; it was not merely to illustrate a point that he had re-established in Lindrum's brain the memory and action of that night in Walmsey House, Kann had very naturally made a study of his own profession, a profession that was mental as much as executive. And he was ready to stake his life on his conviction that Damon Grey had picked up that poker with a very definite object in view. Something had happened to that instrument, something had been done to it by Damon Grey between the time of his picking it up and putting it down. And that something had made it potent to kill.

Lindrum tiptoed across the floor with a ghastly caricature of caution in his step. He was keyed up and quivering, oblivious of everything else in that room save the unprotected skull of

Damon Grey two yards in front of him. The fingers of his left hand were sticking out like porcupine quills, and his insteps were bent like a ballet dancer's at every exaggerated step.

Lindrum himself didn't quite know how it happened.

His brain flashed the order to his arm to raise the poker. One more step and he would be within perfect hitting distance of that mocking skull.

But he neither raised the poker nor made that last step. The poker suddenly and without visible cause slid with a startling clatter to the floor. The noise of its fall was abrupt and emphatic in the silent room. The goup at the window whipped round.

Lindrurn stared like a drunken man at his right hand. There was silly, bibulous surprise in his eyes and his eyebrows were elevated in painful unbelief. His fingers had deliberately allowed that poker to slide out of their grasp. They had done it in flat contradiction to their ordered commands. So far as he was master of his own faculties the muscles and tendons of his hand were still gripping hard. He could swear he hadn't even eased his grip, let alone opened his hand.

Yet there the amazing thing was. Without any desire or volition of his, he had let that poker fall with a crash to the floor.

Kann leaned forward in his chair, watching Lindrum's face with almost mesmeric concentration. Rackway, too, was staring at him, but more in puzzled wonderment.

The surprise in Lindrum's eyes suddenly doubled. His right arm had started twitching, and he had abruptly arrived at the knowledge that all sense of feeling was oozing out of it.

Then the room went filmy in front of his eyes. The ruby lamps were but a dim sun glimmering redly through a fog, and the sound of motorcars passing in the square below droned away and died in a gradual silence that spread across his brain. All sound just seemed to fade gently away and go out. It was as though an utter deafness had come over him slowly and deliberately. And he was curiously cold. The air, the room, his body, everything around him and about him had suddenly gone unaccountably cold. There was a chilliness in his bones, in his very blood. John Lindrum swayed, turned halfway round, and fell over with a body-shaken smash on the floor.

For a few seconds there was a dead silence in the library, and then Grayne's voice broke the stillness with a whimpered "What—what in hell's happened?"

Stephen Leeds jumped forward hurriedly and turned the body over. He went down on one knee and opened Lindrum's collar and waistcost. He pressed his ear closely to the dead man's breast, but there was not even a flutter of the heart, nor even the faintest stirring of the pulse.

Rackway was trembling violently.

"Did you—did *you* do that?" he whispered, pointing almost in awe to the sprawling figure on the carpet. To Rackway it was inconceivable that Damon Grey could have had any hand in that tragedy. The thing had happened so suddenly, so inexplicably, and Grey was so far away from any possible chance of contact with Lindrurn.

Damon Grey shrugged and was prepared to take no further interest in the matter. He turned and had walked halfway towards the door when Rackway sprang at him and clung on to him by a shoulder—Rackway with a gun brandishing in his hand.

Grey turned, and the old ferociously wintry look was back in his eyes.

"Take your hand off me," he said, so quietly that only Rackway heard it. But Rackway's hand whipped off his shoulder as though he had suddenly discovered himself squeezing a cobra.

"Lindrum died because he threatened me with an automatic," went on the icy voice. "Put yours away."

Leeds looked up at him with accusing wrath from the floor.

"You—you murderer!" he rasped.

Grey nodded. "You can now probably appreciate my own feelings when—when they told me what you had done to my little woman," he said, "Don't get too self-righteous, Mr. Leeds—or you might be the next to go. You never quite know where you are when you're dealing with abani. Lindrum died of heart failure. So sorry to put you to the inconvenience of a coroner's inquest. The excitement of playing cards, I presume? Just one thing more—I shouldn't touch that poker yet for some time if I were you. It might bite you."

He opened the door and his hand lay long on the handle. "Nor this door-handle either," he said as he slammed the door behind him.

The four of them stood without moving, staring at the shut door, penned in without being able to move a finger to get themselves out. They gazed at the black, shining door-handle as though they half expected it to jump out at them and do a devil dance on the carpet. It was the focus-point for eight frightened, staring eyes.

For that door-handle had suddenly become to them a sign and a symbol. It was a silent, unwinking assurance of the utter inevitability of Damon Grey. There was death locked away in the porcelain soul of it.

And all it required was a touch, a mere press of the fingers—and life went out as swiftly as a lamp blown out in a gust of wind.

Kann was the first to speak. He knelt by the body and muttered: "It looks to me, Rackway, as though Grey has got us where we can't even squeal."

Rackway licked his lips.

"Is Lindrurn dead?" he asked, pushing the words out from between lips that were almost bloodless.

"Dead as a stone," the American answered.

They gathered round him as he knelt by the fallen man.

"Lindrurn held that poker in his right hand, didn't he?" he muttered to himself. He had taken out his handkerchief and bound it round his own hand. He opened Lindrum's fingers and examined them closely. But there was not a mark on them, not even a discoloration, either on the fingers or on the palms.

"Well, it beats me!" he said. "I'll tell the world it beats me. There isn't a mark on him. If it was poison, there isn't even a pinprick for it to have got through to his system."

"Better ring for a doctor," suggested Leeds.

"Yes—but we've got to get that door-handle opened first. And—and somehow I don't feel inclined to touch it. Grey was wearing rubber gloves. And rubber gloves are not exactly permanent fittings in libraries."

He crawled to the door-handle and inspected it. Rackway handed him a reading-glass, and he examined it under the lens, but there was as little trace of anything on the handle as there was on Lindrum's fingers.

Kann wiped his forehead.

"There's only one thing to do, and that's to keep our heads," he said. "It won't help us any if we start panicking round like a lot of school-kids in a thunderstorm. The only way we can get that door opened is to do it from the outside. Rackway, you'd best ring for your secretary. She will come in and open the door—and we must leave it open; wedge it open, if you like, until such time as whatever Grey has done to it has had time to wear off."

"Grey was right about that coroner," cut in Leeds savagely. "We must get some cards and bridge-markers out. Deal him out thirteen of suit. It only happens once in a thousand million times. Thirteen trumps all held in the one hand. You, Rackway—you dealt them. Lindrum picked up his cards, stared at them, and then something must have gone wrong with his heart. All we saw was that he suddenly staggered his hands up to his heart, and fell backwards over his chair. D'you get that? The shock—the sudden realisation of holding in his own hand the thousand million to one chance—was too much for him; caused a spasm or something in his heart muscles, and he went over. I'll rig out the markers so that it will appear that we had been playing for a couple of hours, and that we were all near about level, so far as winnings are concerned. Lindrum was a few pounds in, if anything—certainly nothing to do with his death."

Then Kann said:"Say, just a moment, you fellows." He was on his knees staring at the poker. There was something on the handle, some tiny suspicion of a film. He struck a match and held it to the flame. There was a little "pop," and the film began to burn with a bright blue flame, hissing ever so slightly in the silent room. It burned brightly for several seconds, and then it flickered and went out, leaving only a minutes wisp of smoke curling up from the handle.

"H'm!" said Kann, and tried the same experiment on the door-handle. But the door-handle did not react in the same way. There was no flames nothing at all to indicate that the door-handle had received similar attention to the poker.

"Bluffed!" said Rackway. "The cool devil."

"Yes," said Grayne uneasily. "But it makes it devilish awkward doesn't it? We won't know whether he—"

"Oh, shucks!" said Kann. "Some of you folk run around praying for trouble. Let tomorrow look after itself. Something has got to be done about this tonight. I vote we take the war to Damon Grey. All four of us pay a little visit to suite No. 4 at the Grand Imperial tonight!?"

Rackway looked a silent inquiry at the others and they nodded."This," said Rackway, pointing to the huddled figure on the floor—"this won't happen again. Twelve o'clock tonight—at the Grand Imperial? That definitely arranged?" And the other three, with sullen determined faces, nodded again.

V

Damon Grey walked out of the house into Grosvenor Square. The over-coated man who had been visible from Rackway's window walked down to him and accosted him.

"Good evening, Grey," he said quietly. "Can I have a word with you?"

Grey swung round, and his eyebrows darkened. "We've met before, haven't we?" he said.

"We have."

"H'm, yes. You're Ricks, aren't you—Mr. Dickie Ricks?

Ricks smiled. "Yes, that's me—spelt with an *i e*, if you remember," he said.

"Well, and what do you want with me?" asked Grey,

A less self-assured individual than Ricks would have bowed a polite "Good evening" to that voice and left it severely alone, would have been quite satisfied to have withdrawn from its neighbourhood with speed and decision. For there was nothing engaging in its timbre. It was wickedly hostile, ferociously malignant; the voice of a man who regarded every single one of the rest of mankind as an enemy, and an enemy whom he hated with every particle of feeling in him.

But Ricks, possessing as he did the sublime and rather proprietary self-confidence of youth, was colour-blind to signals when they were red. He linked his arm in Grey's and steered him across the square to one of the quiet hotels along Grosvenor Street.

"I want about five minutes of your time," he said. "Five minutes will be elegantly sufficient for both of us, I've no doubt."

He pushed through a door, and they went on into a quiet lounge.

"You'll have a drink, won't you?" he said.

"I never touch it." The words were like crackling icicles.

Ricks shrugged and offered a cigarette case.

"Nor those" snapped Grey. He lit a cigar and puffed at it frigidly.

Ricks tapped him on the shoulder.

"It's about that little matter we discussed last night," he said. "Those murders and things you said you were going to commit."

"Well?" snapped Grey.

"Just this—you are not going to do them," said the other blandly.

"Oh?"

"Quite."

Grey eyed him from under half-lowered lids, and there was a sudden little silence.

"You'd be rather amusing—if it wasn't that humour misses me, these days," he said. "Might I ask why you have arrived at this unique conclusion?"

"You may. It's because I've been making one or two inquiries about you, Mr. Damon Grey. And, between you and me, I've discovered one or two little things that rather—how shall we put it?—Tend to alter the case."

"Do they indeed!"

"They certainly do. So much so that you can wash all your silly threats out right here and now."

"Silly?"

"Yes, silly—idiotic."

"Dear me. I wonder whether Lindrum regards them in that light?"

"Why Lindrum?"

"Lindrum died tonight."

Ricks went white. "Lindrum—you—*what?*" he stammered.

"That's what I said. I killed him. They were all there, all the whole crowd of them—Kann, Rackway, Grayne, Leeds—and they all saw him die. And they don't know how it happened! You hear that, boy? They were all with me, all around me, watching me like rats watching a dog. But I got him! I picked him out from among the whole bunch—all of them with guns in their hands, guns they were itching to shoot, but daren't pull. And if you start antagonising me, you little fool, I'll pick you off just as easily as that."

"Well, you can call that a bet," came the heated retort. "You don't scare me, you lunatic." Ricks stood up and reached over for his gloves and walking-stick. He had lifted the gloves from the table, and his hand had gone on to within inches of the stick when Grey's voice pulled him up as abruptly as though he had collided with a house.

"Drop it!" The words almost leapt at him. They were alive, charged with imperative, crackling command.

Ricks, not quite comprehending, turned scared eyes down at the stick. A fly, a common, inquisitive house-fly, hovered for a painfully brief moment above the handle of the stick and then, with a sudden dart, settled on it.

Ricks blinked. The fly landed—and fell off again, all in the same second. It dropped on its back on the polished table-top and did not even kick. It was stone dead the moment its feet touched the stick.

"As easily as that!" said Grey in a voice that was almost toneless.

"Good God!" gasped Ricks, deathly white. He sat down again, a little shakily, and stared at the impassive face opposite.

"Do you understand now, you young idiot?" asked Grey.

"I—I—" Ricks swallowed hard. He thrust his hands into his pockets and continued to stare.

"Like that, eh?" he muttered.

Grey nodded. "Nothing elaborate, nothing theatrical," he said quietly."Just the simplest little action—and out you go. Opening a matchbox, pushing your chair back, taking your hat off, picking up your stick, Just the slightest, most natural little actions of life, sonny. And you are finished—as easily as that."

"Playing with me, eh?"

"No. Warning you. Keep away. You're young; too young. But perhaps you understand, just a little, now?"

Ricks drew in a long breath.

"Yes," he said softly. "I understand all right. A little more than you think."

"Indeed." The word was withering as the breath of the sirocco.

"Yes, indeed. You're a father, aren't you—?"

Grey suddenly stiffened.

"Well?" he rasped.

"Those inquiries I was making this morning—I—" Ricks stopped, fumbling for a thought, a phrase. Then he jerked out a sharp exclamation of sheer disgust. "Faugh!" he snapped. "Why should I? You're a damned murderer, anyhow. And a murderer isn't fit to be anyone's father. Find out for yourself. It's all in the records."

Grey's eyes burned as though live fires blazed behind them. He sat stiffly in his chair, a rigid figure cast in unforgiving bronze.

And then anti-climax stepped in. A situation that was rushing up headlong to a crisis petered out raspingly as footsteps sounded in the halfway leading into the lounge.

Grey sat back and reached over to the next table for an ash-tray. Ricks pulled out a handkerchief and wiped his damp forehead.

"Are you being attended to, sir?" The wine-waiter padded round a huge tub of palms and paused solicitously at their table.

Ricks opened out an evening paper with a flourish.

"Two coffees, please," he said, and buried his head between the printed sheets.

Damon Grey, lynx-eyed, watched him as the waiter disappeared. Then he broke the stick under his boot and thrust the pieces into the blazing fire.

Ricks ignored him, and when Grey returned he feigned a complete interest in his paper.

Grey paused above him, looking down at him with eyes that glittered like white-hot diamonds.

"Well, are you satisfied?" he demanded.

"Quite." Ricks didn't even raise his head.

"Have you anything more to say to me?"

"Not a word"

"Think it over, son. And, in the meantime, don't attempt anything silly. That little life of yours might finish off quite naturally in this lounge. Recklessness is the mother of heroes."

"I don't understand you," said Ricks coldly.

"The policeman you fetch to arrest me. He puts his unpleasant hand on my shoulder, and before we are out of this hotel he has an unaccountable attack of giddiness, and before he has had time to sit down in a chair he has a unique attack of death. The next one you call. He refrains from putting his hand on my shoulder. Instead he calls a taxi and draws a gun. He never gets out of that taxi, except to get into a hearse. And you—are you *quite* safe in fingering that match-stand?"

Ricks, who was about to strike a match, shied away from the thing as though it had suddenly put a thousand volts into him.

"As a matter of fact, it is quite safe," went on the calm voice. "I merely point out to you that you are playing with a brand of fire that is liable to burn you at any moment. In thirty seconds that match-stand might be too fiery to rest even one finger on."

Ricks looked at him. The bitter face was implacable. The old wintry look was back, more sullen, more unforgiving than ever. It was the face one sees occasionally out of the ranges of the Far West, solitary, wind-bittered, soured.

He swung round on his heel.

"Good night, Grey," he said.

"Wait."

Against his will, Ricks turned and paused.

Damon Grey, tense and strained, held up his hand.

"You mentioned something just now," he said. "Something concerning my parenthood."

"That was my good fortune—not yours!"

"What was it, Ricks? Have you news of my son?" Grey seemed almost to have pushed the words out.

"No, I haven't," said Ricks flatly. "I never knew you had one, and I don't particularly want to. If he is anything like his father, he had probably won his Blue by now for vivisection or something equally artistic. Whatever I discovered I prefer to keep to myself. If I could burn the books I would, believe me. The same avenues of information are open to you. It's quite easy—when you've found the clue. You go and find out, as I did."

Grey looked up with almost a hint of humanity in his eyes. They were softened with a look of yearning, of pleading appeal.

"I—am I asking so much?" he asked.

"Somerset House is free."

"Ricks, I took my breakfast yesterday morning in prison. I haven't burned much time."

"It was more important to you that you should kill a defenceless man."

"Not more important—more urgent," said Grey defensively.

"Well, tomorrow you just turn from the urgent to the important," replied Ricks acidly. "Perhaps after an hour's foraging with the registrar you will still think your destiny in life is to go round slaughtering those who have wronged you. And then again, you may not."

Grey's eyes flickered; the soft lights snapped out of them.

"Whatever the years have hidden from me, they won't rob me of my reckoning with Rackway and his gang," he said. "Urgent matters are still urgent. Stephen Leeds dies tomorrow night—whether Somerset House has yielded me its secrets or not."

"Two coffees, sir. Will you take black or white?" The waiter sailed in again with the coffee-tray.

"I will see to it, thank you. Put it down and run away." Ricks tossed him half a crown, waited till he had cleared out of earshot, and then turned irritably to Grey.

"Do you mean that?" he snapped.

"I certainly do. As sure as Stephen Leeds is alive tonight, he will be dead tomorrow."

"Well," said Ricks, ramming on his hat, "you watch your step."

He went out of the hotel almost at the run and raced back to Grosvenor Square.

Outside in the kerb a doctor's car was drawn up, the engine panting smoothly in the quiet of the night. In a few minutes it was joined by a second, a large white one with double doors at the back and big red crosses on the lamp-glasses. Two white-uniformed attendants got out of it and carried a stretcher in with them.

In the library a little group was gathered round the body of Lindrum, lying on the couch, and the doctor, dignified and serious, was listening to Stephen Leeds's account of the tragedy.

"H'm!" he said. "Very sad, very sad. But a case for the coroner, I'm afraid. I can't help myself. Much as I regret the unpleasantness and inconvenience, both to his relatives and to you, I'm afraid I have no other alternative than to report this to headquarters."

Rackway looked keenly at him.

"You are quite sure he is dead, doctor?" he asked. "It isn't some awful form of coma or paralytic seizure?"

"You haven't the slightest hope of ever seeing your friend alive again, Mr. Rackway. I'm awfully sorry to have to tell you so, but I cannot buoy you up with false hopes. This has been a terrible shock to you, no doubt, and I tender you my heartfelt sympathy, but Mr. Lindrum is dead. No pulse, no respiration, no reaction to either light or touch on the eyes ball, and—and everything else that points to death—unmistakable."

"And the cause, doctor?"

"A very obvious case of heart failure—too obvious really to need an inquest. But there it is—the law is the law and must be obeyed. If the coroner has any doubt he may even order a post-mortem. If so, I should like to be present and will willingly tell you the results." He glanced at the figure on the couch. "Odd," he muttered. "He doesn't look to be of the type that suffers from cardiac trouble. Colour good, eyes good, skin good, health good, general virility good. Rather interesting, happened, did you say? Card playing, were you?"

Rack way nodded. "Yes. Had been for nearly two hours. Nothing very exciting, of course. Rubber after rubber at bridge; stakes very modest—ha'penny a point, and there was very little in it."

"Often play together?"

"Oh, yes. Two or three times a week. We call it our solitary vice."

"Umph! Ha'penny a point doesn't sound as though it would precipitate a heart attack. Was Mr. Lindrum financially sound?"

"Oh, quite. He wouldn't worry about a thousand or two, anyhow."

"Well, something must have happened. You say he just stood up and fell over?"

"Yes. He stood up, swaying a little. Then he dropped his cards on the table, gasped, and fell over backwards with his hands pressed up to his heart."

"Very curious. And terribly sad. Where was he sitting, do you say—here?"

"Yes; those are his cards there. We hadn't even time to sort out our hands or start bidding. I dealt the hand, and I'd hardly served the last card and picked up my own hand when Mr. Lindrum crashed over."

The doctor had idly picked up Lindrum's cards while Rackway was speaking, and was making a neat little fan of them.

Suddenly a look of surprise and then of amazement overspread his features.

"Good Lord! This is extraordinary!" he ejaculated.

He spread out the cards on the table in a long line.

"Look!" he said. "Thirteen cards of a suit. Every heart in the pack! Amazing! The most extraordinary hand I have ever seen in my life!"

The others gathered round and made their own astonished comments. Stephen Leeds complimented the doctor on having so quickly divined the probable cause of Lindrum's heart attack.

"Very clever, doctor," he said, "and very quick, too. We might easily have packed those hands up without even so much as a glance at them."

Dickie Ricks tiptoed away from the door, for the bell had rung loudly, and the ambulance men were coming up the stairs with the stretcher.

He opened Lorna Rennie's room door and went in.

Lorna hurried forward to meet him as he entered.

"Dickie," she said nervously, "what has happened; what is all the excitement about?"

Ricks took her hands in his.

"Lorna," he said gravely, "you've got to get out of here—at once. There's no room for argument, and no time to lose. You've got to pack up all your things and clear out, tonight, now!"

"But, Dick, why?" asked Lorna.

"For three thousand five hundred and fifty reasons, only one of which concerns us at the moment," replied Ricks. "And that is that Lindrum is dead."

"Dickie! Not really?"

"They're just taking him downstairs now on a stretcher. And I won't have you mixed up in this vile business, not for all the Hildon Rackways that ever breathed."

"Dead?" Lorna was shocked beyond words.

"Yes, dead. Damon Grey killed him. He swears he will kill Stephen Leeds tomorrow. And I want to see you cleared out of here and away from all the horror of it before I go round to the police. You haven't a minute to lose. Pack your boxes and come away now."

"But, Dick, it's impossible. Where can I go?"

"I don't know, and it doesn't much matter. I'll think of something while you're packing. All I know is that you can't stay here. There be all the muck and beastliness of the police-courts—weeks of it—this affair is finished. And—" A tiny jangle pealed in the room.

Ricks looked up swiftly at the bell indicator.

"Who's that?" he demanded.

"Mr. Rackway," answered Lorna decisively. "He's ringing from the library." She picked up her notebook and pencil.

"But, Lorna—you aren't going to answer it?" Dickie looked surprised and incredulous in the same moment.

"Why not, Dick? He probably knows I'm here. The servants know I haven't been out of the house tonight."

"Yes, but—what earthly good can you do by going to see him now? If you show yourself you ruin the only chance you have left of keeping out of the police proceedings."

She patted his cheek.

"That the only reason, Dickie?"

"No. I don't like the idea of you being here with Rackway at all."

Lorna smiled.

"Green—eyed—monster!" she said, and moved towards the door.

"Lorna!" Dickie thrust himself between. "You aren't going to see that man tonight!" he said heatedly. "Neither are you going to leave this room except to go up and pack your things."

A swift change came over the girl. She coloured ever so slightly, and a cold glitter flashed into her eyes.

"Indeed?" she said with slow dignity. "And who says so?"

"I do!"

"Indeed again! And might I ask who granted you the royal charter, young sir?"

The bell rang again.

"Just stand aside, please. This room happens to be mine," she said coldly. "And so, by an odd chance, does Miss Lorna Rennie. Mine—and nobody else's! You just put on your hat and coat and go home, Master Ricks, *thank* you!" Lorna walked calmly past him.

VI

The doctor bade a sympathetic good evening to the little group in the library when the ambulance men had finished their task.

"I don't think there is anything more I can do tonight," he said "I will keep you in touch with anything further that may arise. I'll bid you good night, gentlemen; my time is rather fully occupied, you know. No, thanks, I won't have a whisky. Good night."

Rackway gave him his card and escorted him out to his car.

As soon as the doctor had gone, Kann called the others round him to a hurried conference.

"Now look a-here, you fellows," he said. "We are up against it—and badly. I reckon it's our first duty to admit that fairly. Damon Grey appears to have constituted himself a self-directing murder machine, with all the latest patents and safety devices attached. And he's gone the limit. Something has got to happen to Damon Grey! He has got us dangling halfway between hell and nowhere, and I guess it ain't over-comfortable for any of us. The arrangements so far are that we all meet at the Grand Imperial somewhere around midnight. Without going any further into details, I'd say our first job is to get our intentions cut and dried."

Leeds pulled out his watch and glanced at it.

"We still have more than an hour," he said. "The best thing we can do is to book rooms at the Grand Imperial and stay there the night. We can't very well excuse ourselves otherwise if we are caught roaming round Grey's rooms or the corridors leading to them."

"Mine's already booked," said Kann. "Got it over the phone. All you boys had better do the same. One of you can send an express messenger—just to dash a spice of variety; it's too late for telegrams."

Grayne proposed that a definite attempt be made either to put Damon Grey forever beyond the power of duplicating his first coup, or, failing that, to get possession of his supply of the mysterious drug. The suggestion was, in short, armed robbery at suite No. 4.

Kann nodded. "Nothing else for it," he said shortly. "Damon Grey has got to be put out of the way. He won't get a chance to murder *me*, and you can pile up your notes on that! I don't care a darn about his letters to Scotland Yard, either. He's just as liable to die from heart failure as Lindrurn."

Leeds fixed the final details. "Then we all meet as strangers in the Grand Imperial an hour from now. It will be either the card-room or the billiard-room, whichever offers the best opportunity. We can talk over the obsequies after we've got the lie of the land. Good night, you fellows. I want to book my room personally."

The party broke up, and after they had gone Hildon Rackway sat back in a chair, staring in front of him.

For him it meant the parting of the ways. He sensed the trump of doom in the tragedy of that evening. Grey had built himself into a position so impregnable that he was beyond the law. Old sins have long shadows, and Rackway had no tribunal to appeal to.

He was standing at the crossroads of doubt and despair. There were two alternatives ahead of him, both of them desperately undesirable. One of them was to stand by the gang and go through with it—an expedient that would see him standing in the dock on a score of charges the moment Grey's solicitors presumed his absence. The other was to cut and run.

And even flight was a barren sanctuary. He recognised the fact on sight. By running away he would brand himself guilty of every single thing Damon Grey had written about him.

But in flight there was just the painfully slight hope that he would get away to some small South American State where extradition warrants were anathema.

Rackway, for obvious reasons, was a man who kept most of his money in floating securities. In various parts of the house he had notes and bearer bonds to the value of many thousands of pounds. Elsewhere were jewels and proceeds of a dozen rich coups. With all those in his traps he felt he could let the rest go.

He could pull strings. Certain gentlemen connected with slipping affairs stood debtor to him for favours rendered. By paying the price, Rackway thought he stood a fifty-fifty chance of getting clear before the hand of the law fell with devastating weight upon him.

Sacrifices wouldn't matter. Life was sweeter than sacrifice—and then was Death mixed up in the counts against him.

But there was another price to be paid if he chose the way of flight—a price he was not prepared to pay. His steady eyes focused on a little photograph that stood in a tiny silver frame on his mantelshelf—a holiday snapshot of a girl with a laughing mouth and merry eyes, of a girl who wore daintiness as a queen wears a regal robe.

Rackway crossed over to it and studied it, leaning his elbows on the mantel.

There in that small picture was the sum total of all his desires, the culmination of his hopes. Lorna Rennie filled the great aching blank in his life, and filled it to ecstatic completeness. If it was odd that a man should fail to realise that he needed love until he found himself sailing through the tail end of the forties, it was odder still that his desires should centralise on one so young as Lorna Rennie. But old fires burn all the fiercer for long suppression. And Rackway's passion for his dainty secretary burned at furnace-heat.

He found himself sizing up the odds.

In all his knowledge he had never yet heard of the man who succeeded in getting clear after hampering himself with a woman. The list of fugitives from justice who took their woman along with them is exactly as long as the list of fugitives who found the woman too great a handicap. Man, on his own, when the prison gates open before his eyes, can become a most amazingly mobile animal. But with a girl in his caravan his speed drops to something under a half. She becomes the loadstone on which his plans are wrecked. The police no longer hunt the male. The female of the species is not only more deadly; she is as unchanging as the stars; and the police of the universe trail the man through the woman—and get him.

Rackway knew all that, sized it up, and admitted it.

And the dainty little face, with its clustering of curls and its softly browed eyes, peeped up at him with mockery and goading.

He looked at the picture hungrily, as he had looked at the original. It was a challenge to his soul, a gauntlet flung at his own common sense. And his vanity won! It always does when age is striving to make the conquest of youth.

His hand reached out to the bell-button and pressed it. Then he remembered. "Oh, of course!" he muttered. "I sent her off to the Majesty on that silly fool errand. Damn!"

And then Lorna knocked on the door and entered.

Rackway's surprise at seeing her there showed in a sudden line across his forehead. For a moment a wild fear went surging over him like a douche of cold water. But he pulled himself up on a tight rein. His nerves were going to the dickens, he told himself.

"Good evening, Miss Rennie," he said quietly. "You are back early, aren't you?"

Lorna smiled a trifle sheepishly.

"I—I didn't go," she said frankly. "I'm afraid I didn't take you seriously."

Rackway's eyes never left her. They seemed to be regarding her with a composure that was itself held under steel restraint.

"Miss Rennie, I never joke with you." Rackway said. "I am always serious. And sincere too. At least, I try to be. If I fail at times, it is only because I am humanly incapable of evincing a greater sincerity. But at all times I do my utmost. I wanted you to go to the Majesty Theatre tonight for a very special—and serious reason."

She met his gaze openly and said: "I think I know what that reason was, Mr. Rackway. You wanted me out of the house until after Damon Grey had come and gone."

Rackway bowed. "That desire was quite honourable."

"Oh, quite. I understand your motive perfectly."

"How did you know Damon Grey was coming here tonight?"

"I guessed it when I saw all your friends arriving. I was quite sure when you called me in and tried to send me out on such an extraordinary pretext."

"And you know what happened?"

Lorna nodded a very faint affirmative.

Rackway looked away. "I'm sorry you should have known; sorry you should have been dragged into this. My dear girl, there was no need for it. If you had only gone away as I wished you to, you would never have known anything about it. As it is, there is to be an inquest. Your evidence may be required. I'm awfully sorry. I tried to avoid it."

He knew that Lorna was looking at him keenly; he could almost feel her eyes boring at him. And he grew restive under her scrutiny.

"Mr. Lindrum died from heart failure," he said. And only he knew how horribly unconvincing the statement sounded.

"Heart failure, Mr. Rackway?"

"That is the medical diagnosis. The doctor has only just gone. And he is quite definite on the point. Heart failure caused by shock."

"What shock was that? Shock at seeing Damon Grey?"

"Oh, no. Damon Grey had come and gone by then. We were playing bridge, and I dealt him an extraordinary hand. Thirteen trumps. Er—unique. Simply wonderful, if you understand cards. Doesn't happen once in fifty years. Most unfortunate incident. Mr. Lindrum must have had a weak heart. Such a depressingly small thing to cause the death of a friends. Terrible!"

"Mr. Rackway, you weren't playing cards when you sent for me. There weren't even any cards on the table."

Rackway caught his breath. He realised how lame the whole thing sounded to a girl who had already taken down a letter to Inspector Harnden regarding the intentions of Damon Grey. But he had missed that point altogether.

"Er—no," he said, reddening. "As a matter of fact, we started playing bridge after Damon Grey left." He cursed himself for having told the doctor they had been playing for over two hours.

Lorna put her pencil and notebook on the table.

"Mr. Rackway," she said, "I'm afraid you haven't made out a very good case for yourself. Most men are poor liars; you are worse than most. You haven't the ability to tell a lie convincingly to a woman. I haven't asked you for information about it. Why tell me anything at all if you can't tell me the truth? If there's one thing I hate like poison it's lies."

Rackway pulled out a chair and looked profoundly uncomfortable.

"Won't you sit down?" he said. "I want to talk to you for a few moments. Put away that notebook; I'm not going to write letters, I want to talk to you about something ten thousand miles outside and beyond the realm of business."

Lorna sat down and put her hands in her lap. Rackway sat on the edge of the table, close up to her, one foot on the ground, his hands gripping the table edge.

"It concerns this affair tonight," he said gravely. "The results of it will react on me, rather seriously. I am at the crossroads, and the matter has become desperately urgent."

Lorna saw the sudden tenseness, the look of unbearable strain that had come over him. He was weighing his words and considering them as carefully as does a judge in summing up a life-and-death case.

"You know there is a great deal more under the surface of this than would appear at first sight," began Rackway.

"I know there is," said Lorna.

Rackway looked at her quickly.

"I know that Mr. Lindrurn was expecting to be killed tonight. He was murdered. And Damon Grey murdered him!"

Rackway gazed at her, and for the first time in his life he felt bitterly angry with himself forever having pandered to his criminal tendencies. While the lure of the hunt was upon him it was good enough. While he could match his skill, his brains, his coolness against the pack that was forever at his heels, the game was worthwhile. While he could lift priceless jewels out of the heart of the hum and glitter of great receptions, while he could beat even the relentless vigilance of the banking systems at their own game, while he could pit himself against the might and power of the police of a whole continent, the hunt was a living, pulsing thing in his veins; it gave him satisfactions and critical pleasures such as no other thing in the world could give.

That was, until his way of life crossed the road that Lorna Rennie trod.

And there he found his great cross-purposes. The pull of innate masculinity was all one way—the way that shunned the woman, the way that indulged his own quiet delights to the full.

But there was that other pull—the pull of the union eternal, the pull that is older than the hills, mightier than the mountains. And it was alive and dominant in Hildon Rackway.

It had missed him through the years that were gone. It had passed him by and left him untroubled with the doubts and fears and raptures that are most of its blessing and only a part of its curse.

But, then, he hadn't known Lorna in those days. And Lorna made a difference, a vast and insurmountable difference.

He flicked his thoughts up from the image of the girl and stared at himself eye to eye in the glass.

Full and square he looked into his own eyes, steel-grey and sombre. And they answered his question honestly and freely. "Leave the woman alone," they said. "She will hang you, as sure as your name is Hildon Rackway. Think sense! She is trouble, she is danger, she is all that links with heartbreak and despair. More, she is tragedy."

He dropped his eyes to her again.

Ah, but she was sweet. Her very loveliness was a tonic, a goad that pricked his manliness, a prize that challenged his courage.

Hildon Rackway turned to the girl and made his plunge. Knowingly, and without a single regret, he chose the path of disaster.

Lorna saw that definite change in his manner the moment he faced her. His sincerity had suddenly become vitally plain; it was a sentient, human thing. In some queer, indefinable way it seemed to ennoble him. It made him the man who was prepared to do all and risk all for the sake of his woman.

And in that same moment Lorna felt a wave of sympathy for him, a warm flood of emotion that, in a girl at all inclined to the sentimental, would have been as fatal as a draught of poison. She felt it and made no effort to shake it off.

"Miss Rennie," he said, "I most earnestly crave your indulgence for a few moments longer. If you object to anything I have to say, if I say anything that is in any way unacceptable to you, you have only to stand up and go out of the room. I shall understand perfectly."

Lorna looked at him without speaking. She saw the tremendous strain under which he was labouring. It showed in the drawn lines along his temples, in the rigidity of his mouth, in the hot lights that glittered in his eyes.

He waited for her; saw in two swift seconds that she was leaving the talking to him. He inclined his head over so slightly in acknowledgment.

"There have been times before in my life when I have had to face difficulties," he said, "but never have I had to face a crisis quite so serious as the one that confronts me now. It is all too involved, too hopelessly bound up in events that happened before you were born, for me to be able to give you any adequate understanding of the gravity of the situation. You would not understand it, and I would be more than a fool to tell.

"Suffice it to say that it concerns Damon Grey. You know that as well as I do. Tragedy and horror have been jumping about on a hairspring trigger ever since Damon Grey entered this house. I freely admit it. The return of Damon Grey to life and liberty is the most disastrous thing that ever happened to me. And because of things that happened in the years gone by I cannot come to grips with him. Unless I stoop to crimes as villainous as those he himself is committing, I am powerless. I cannot face him in open encounter, and the protection of the Law Courts is denied me."

He paused again, but Lorna preserved her defensive silence. Somehow she knew that Rackway was working up to nothing more nor less than a proposal of marriage. She read it in every sign he gave her. He was tremendously in earnest. And the girl does not breathe who would squash the chance of listening to a proposal.

Rackway saw the pink flush rising on her cheeks, saw that her hands had suddenly locked together in her lap, saw that she made not the slightest sign of wishing to leave him. And with a grip in his heart that was like the sudden pressure of a spring trap, he pursued his course.

"All I can tell you," he said, "is that Damon Grey has suffered because of me—suffered terribly. And—and I was in the wrong. Things happened a long time ago, so long ago that one would have thought the dust of the dead had settled upon their memory and obliterated them. But, as you see, Grey has come back. And he holds a knowledge that is death to me.

"I have but two alternatives ahead of me—flight or death! Do you understand that, little girl? Do you appreciate the deeper realities of such a statement as that? It is true. As true as I am sitting here in front of you tonight. From this night onward, from this very hour, the roads are opening to me. Flight one way—life, freedom, liberty, existence all that is worth living for and fighting for—and the other road leads to death.

"I am not joking with you, Miss Rennie. Believe me, I am terribly in earnest. Grey is, as you have seen, as relentless as he is fearless; He had tabled demands that simply cannot be complied with. We resisted him, and you have seen what happened. Lindrum paid the price. It was Grey's other alternative. My turn will come as surely as that clock ticks out the minutes on that mantelshelf."

Lorna's hands were gripping to a shiny whiteness round the knuckles, and she was looking at Rackway with horror awakening in her soul.

"But—but, Mr. Rackway," she protested, "surely there must be some way out? You—"

"Way out, little one? With Lindrum lying on a slab in the morgue? No. The only way for me is to take the road that leads to life and freedom. I am taking it tonight! Within the next few hours I stall be putting as many miles as is humanly possible between myself and Damon Grey."

"*Tonight?*"

Rackway leant forward, earnestly, pleadingly, his eyes yearning a hope that he begged would be fulfilled.

"Little girl, Miss Rennie, Lorna—will you come with me? Will you, *please?*"

Lorna sat back in her chair with a nervous little sigh. She was looking profoundly uncomfortable. The situation had suddenly got hopelessly beyond her. It was out of hand, running away with her.

The blaze of fiery passion that had suddenly flamed to life in Rackwey's eyes was so full of yearning that she averted her own gaze.

"I—I don't quite think I understand you," she said stiffly.

"Don't you? You do." said Rackway. "The girl isn't born who doesn't understand such things as I mean. If—"

"But, Mr. Rackway, please—you—really, I don't *want* to understand you. I—"

"You do! You do!" said Rackway, and his words came out in a tumbling rush. The pent-up feelings of long months of iron restraint burst out and overwhelmed him. "You know what I mean. You know that I love you with a passion that has become wellnigh intolerable. You know that from the first day you offered your services to me I have loved you with a love that has grown deeper every hour. You know there have been times when, with you sitting there in front of me, I have strangle down my emotions so ferociously that I have bruised my own soul: Lorna, my dearest, you surely—"

"But—please! Mr. Rack way, you—"

"Mr Rackway!" He looked at her almost wildly. "Not that—please, no more of that."

He held out his hands, as she attempted to interrupt him, looked at her pleadingly, and swept on in a breathless rush.

Lorna clung to her composure with a violent effort. A score of times she tried to break into Rackway's outburst. But he spoke with such impetuous yearning blazing out of his eyes that her tongue was muted by sheer inability to find words that would tell him the hopelessness of his quest and yet not hurt him. For no woman, be she queen or beggar-maid, can completely shut her heart to sentiment when a man offers her all that he has and is. It is the greatest gift he has to offer, and brutal rejection is only possible to a woman whose blood is colder than love that has died.

Lorna stopped him impulsively. "Mr. Rackway, you mustn't—you mustn't talk like this," she said hurriedly. "Really, I hardly know what to say to you. There doesn't seem to be anything I *can* say to you. I'm awfully sorry, terribly sorry."

"But, Lorna, you—"

"No. I can't listen, Mr. Rackway. I mustn't; I won't. It is a matter that should never have arisen. I am quite satisfied to be your secretary. More than satisfied. You have been kindness itself to me. Nobody could possibly have been kinder—or more thoughtful. I could not want for a better employer or a happier situation. But, please, no more than that!"

Lorna Rennie picked up her notebook and, without waiting for further permission, turned and walked out of the room.

Rackway stared after her long after the door had closed between himself and her. A dull cloud of hopelessness lay like a sombre pall across his brain. He felt deadened. Her refusal had come like a soul-destroying blow on top of the shocks that had already stunned him that day. He had never dreamed she would turn him down as coldly as that. In spite of his knowledge of the existence of Dickie Ricks, he had firmly believed that when the time came Lorna Rennie would not hesitate for long in making a decision in his favour.

His fingers were sliding slowly over the barrel of the revolver in his pocket. He saw ahead of him the only road—the lonely road—and its loneliness appalled him. And that which is denied is thrice coveted. For the first time in his life Hildon Rackway was frightened of himself. That road was too dreadfully empty for any human being to tread.

He pulled the gun out and looked at it thoughtfully. A click and a crack. That was all it needed. Just a little gentle pressure on the trigger and the temple, and the twin despairs of Lorna Rennie and Damon Grey would be banished forever. In a world that was peopled with darkness and despair life was not a gift to be thanked for, let alone treated sacredly.

And it was just then that a quick, vigorous hand fell upon the door and gave it a shove that jerked it wide open.

"Hallo! What are *you* doing here?" said a pleasant, cultured voice.

It was Stephen Leeds, the man to whom a pack of cards meant just fifty-two little slivers of will-o'-the-wisp magic.

Rackway felt his nerves flex in a tiny spasm when he saw him. Stephen Leeds, according to Damon Grey, was the next one marked down for death.

"I've just fixed up rooms at the Grand Imperial," said Leeds, coming into the room. "Everything O.K. there. Thought I'd just run in and let you know. The others have—Good Lord! A gun? What's up, Rackway?"

He reached forward and, with a dexterous twist of the wrist, flicked the glittering automatic out of Rackway's fingers. "Eh, what's up?" he demanded.

"Oh, just nothing," said Rackway, and, with a miraculous effort at composure, managed to make his voice sound unconcerned. "You're getting a trifle theatrical, aren't you? I was merely examining it in case of—trouble tonight, with Grey."

"Don't you tell *me*," retorted Leeds. "Not with eyes like yours! Why, good heavens,, man, you look as though you had been living on dope for months and supplies had suddenly been cut off."

Rackway drew in a long breath. "So they have, if you did but know," he muttered wearily. "Give me my gun. I'm not going to do anything silly. Not now. Sixty seconds make a difference sometimes. And I've just remembered Damon Grey. *He's* worth living for, anyway."

"Gosh," said Leeds, "you sound like a corpse. What's wrong? Anyone would think you had just proposed and, been turned down."

"Oh, go to hell!" said Rackway viciously.

Leeds was silent for several seconds. Then he said very quietly:"I see. Maybe it wasn't Grey that time? Never mind—I'm not asking. Just thought I'd run in and let you know everything is all ready at the Imperial. See you later."

At the door he paused and said gently: "And I should have a couple of brandies before going round there, if I were you. G' night."

"Bah!" said Rackway, under his breath. "If I were you, Stephen Leeds, I'd—I'd hit the outward bound before midnight strikes tonight."

VII

Somewhere in the gilded splendour of the vestibule of the Grand Imperial a melodious clock chimed a quarter to midnight. Only the softest echoes of it percolated through the great card-room at the back of the huge building.

The card-room at that hour was a temple of shadowed quietness, a myrtle-green sanctuary where majestic silence held court. Only a very few guests still played—quiet foursomes given over to the finer niceties of bridge or the wall-eyed intricacies of poker. But almost before the brass cylinders had ceased chiming the poker players counted out their chips with leisurely deliberation, settled up, and retired.

Before midnight chimed only two parties were left at the green baize tables, a little group of four, lackadaisically finishing off a rubber that had already become a foregone conclusion, and a silent couple who played casino without a word or a smile. Across in a corner a single lounger, perfectly dressed in American Tuxedo, read a current magazine, turning the pages without a rustle. The inexorable law of hush seemed to have communicated itself to even the inanimate objects, for a soda-water siphon ejected its contents into a glass with a surprising lack of "fizz," and even the cards themselves seemed capable of being shuffled without making a sound.

The casino players had brought their play to such a state of perfection that they jotted down their scores after each hand without reference to the cards.

One, a tall, well-built man, who looked as though he had been made for the clothes he wore, finished off a hand with a clever over-build, glanced at his companion and murmured: "Seven to me, I think?"

His companion, a slimmer, shorter man with raven black hair and a calm-featured face, nodded.

"Seven it is," he said. "Spades, big casino, and three aces."

"You had bad hands that time, all picture cards and small numbers."

"Yes, pretty filthy. I take five. One ace, little casino, and cards."

"Quite. That puts me out. Had enough?"

"Yes. I must have another dig at you some other time. Your memory is a little too precise tonight. I'm jaded, too. Had a tiring day."

"Dancing?"

The black-haired man laughed. "No—tennis. Trying to work up a service that will trot me through the summer tournaments. Good night, old man. See you tomorrow perhaps."

"Splendid," said Stephen Leeds with a chuckle. "To the manner born. You make a splendid foil, Kann."

"Don't we all?" smiled the American. "Nothing like a little practice before a good critic."

"There's that bridge-party breaking up. Now we'll have the room to ourselves. Grayne is over there in the corner just behind you, marvellously interested in the magazinical banalities of somebody's alleged reminiscences."

"Rackway not here yet?"

Leeds's brows clouded. "I've a nasty misgiving or two about him," he said, speaking in an undertone. "Went round to see him after I'd booked my rooms here and found him hugging a gun."

"No?"

"And looking as though his only wish at the moment was to aim at his own ear—and hit it."

"Nerves?"

"Seemed like it. I suggested that he looked as though he'd been jilted in his first love affair, and he flared up like a bad-tempered flapper."

"Shouldn't be surprised if you hadn't hit the nail." Kann was thoughtful for a moment, and then added: "He's gone completely potty on that stenog. My own impression is that he would cut and run if he could persuade her to pack up her grips and kick in with him."

"Right again," said Leeds. "You'd have thought so pretty definitely if you'd seen him this evening. Absolute cold feet, I thought."

"H'm! Not like Rackway!"

"No; but—" Leeds's unfinished sentence was expressive.

Grayne put his magazine down and stood up and yawned. The bridge players had departed, save one, who lingered behind finishing off the last of an excellent cigar. The card-room waiter entered silently with a large wooden tray and proceeded to collect the empty glassware lying about. The solitary remnant of the bridge-party smiled at a passing thought and laid out the cards for a game of patience.

"Silly ass," thought Grayne. "Why doesn't he go to bed?" He took a drink from a huge cut-glass jug of plentifully iced fruit-cup and strolled nonchalantly over to where Leeds and Kann sat in low-voiced conversation.

"Good evening, gentlemen," he said affably. "Do I intrude?"

"Not at all, stranger," said Kann, slipping into a strong American accent for the benefit of the midnight patience player. "Why?"

"Well, the night is not yet old. I wondered if you'd care for a three-bander. Play dummy?"

"We sure do, stranger. Staying in this hotel?"

"Yes. The third floor. I'm not a lounge sharp, I assure you."

Kann winked. "Couldn't we make up a four and play auction?" he suggested.

Grayne leant down and whispered in his ear.

"Damon Grey isn't in his rooms," he said.

"Not?"

"I've phoned three times and the call was not answered. The switchboard operator cut in to say he had doubled my ring several times and that suite No. 4 must be empty."

Leeds and Kann exchanged swift glances.

Grayne sat down beside them. "Anything fixed yet—where's Rackway? He's late, isn't he?" he said.

Kann leant towards him.

"I reckon we shall have to do without the assistance of Hildon Rackway," he said. "Leeds thinks he's quit. He's got the wind up badly over Lindrum." He rubbed his chin thoughtfully. "Somehow don't like the the idea of crediting Rackway with a yellow streak—we've known him too long to think that way. But there it is—he is the only one of us who hasn't turned up."

Leeds dealt out the cards to cover the low murmured hum of consation, and Kann outlined a plan for criticism.

"One of us had better make a casual tour round the lounges, co rooms, reading-rooms, and public sections. He's got to be located, had better do that, Leeds; you've got the air and the *flair*. You might find him in the billiard-room. Grey used to be pretty slick with a cue. And I reckon it's rather more than likely that he'd want to try his hand after eighteen years—billiards being an insidious game once you've got the hang of it. Grayne and I will go up on the landings and prospect around there. My room is on Grey's floor. I can see his bedroom door from my own room. It's at the end of a corridor running across at right angles to mine. No. 8A. You might look in there, Leeds, every now and then, while you are rummaging around."

"Well, and supposing I find Grey?" asked Leeds.

"Hang on to him like grim death till you see Grayne and me again. Keep him from getting up to his rooms."

"And what's doing while I'm holding him?"

"Grey gets a taste of his own medicine! By breakfast time tomorrow morning Mr. Damon Grey will know precisely how John Lindrum felt."

"Sounds sociable, but how?"

"You keep Grey away from his rooms. The rest will be up to us. This is how I reckon it out. Grey has got some place in his suite where he hides that damned dope of his. He has been up already and stowed it away there. And even if he hasn't, it stands to reason that he doesn't carry it *all* about with him. He's got a reserve stock somewhere—and where else would he keep it if not in his rooms? Well, Grayne and I will work it between us. Grayne stays outside on watch. I've got a whole hardware store of skeleton keys on me right now. If I can't get into Grey's rooms, and open every one of his locks inside five minutes—I'll eat 'em, makers' guarantees and all. Grayne will use my room as his own. D'you get that, Grayne? As soon as you get up there, hop into a dressing-gown, sling a brace of towels round your neck, and go ambling around looking for the bathrooms. Which same you will keep away from unless one of the hotel staff should be indiscreet enough to ask you what you're looking for. Then, of course, you will begin hunting for room No. 8A again, having lost your way. You will be humming a little snatch of song to yourself. And the moment you scent danger you will make towards suite No. 4 and break into a whistle. The tune will inform me that Sally is still queening it down the alley. Get all that?"

"Quite," said Leeds with a flicker of a smile.

"The rest is mine. I'll find that dope or bust. It's there, in his room, I'll swear. And, gee, when I get my hands on it I'll give him a taste of his own! I'll give him such a helping he will think he's drunk a bucketful, I'll flood his door-handles with it.

I'll wash his soap with it. I'll dip his toothbrush in it. I'll soak it into his pillow. I'll squirt it into his slippers. He will get a reminder of it from his shaving-brush and razors. I'll souse it into his collar buttons, I'll film his hairbrushes with it. The very pyjamas he sleeps in will be his own shroud."

He made a quick sign to Stephen Leeds.

"You get off on the job, old son," he said. "We'll give you a quarter of an hour to get back here. If you can't find him just look in here and let me know. If you are not back by half-past twelve, I'll know that you have found him and are holding him."

He glanced round at the man who still lingered at the bridge-table playing patience, smiling to himself when a good run opened up in the lay of his cards, frowning and puffing at his cigar when he ran into a doubtful proposition. He was too far away to have heard a word of the conversation, or even to have caught the subdued mutter of voices; but for some queer reason his presence there irritated Kann.

He looked what he apparently was, a silly old josser verging into the realm of second childhood and blissfully unaware of it. He was what Kann would call a stopper; a nasty reminder of the world at large.

"Silly old stiff," he muttered. "Why doesn't he go to bed?"

The silly old stiff, almost as though sensing and understanding the remark, turned and looked at them for a couple of moments, and then quietly resumed his game.

He was an oldish man, white-haired at the temples, with a pronounced cast in his eye. There was almost a babyish benignity in the utter affability of his features—a pleasant old johnny to whom all the world was still a very friendly recreation ground.

He had long white "sideboards" that came down two inches below his temples, and his complexion was a bright shrimp pink—the complexion of a man who was addicted to a very cold bath every morning of his life. That, and the benevolent beaming smile, and the cast in the eye—the whole *tout ensemble* playing patience—made up a picture that got on Kann's already irritated nerves.

Stephen Leeds moved quietly away and vanished through the swing doors. He went on diligently from room to room, through the spacious lounges and deserted bars, through the palm courts and reading-rooms, the roof gardens and billiard-rooms, but nobody even faintly resembling Damon Grey was in any of them. He made the whole circuit again, and then finally went back to the reception clerk and inquired again for him there.

No, Mr. Grey had not gone out. The reception clerk was quite sure on that point. He was certainly in the building somewhere. The front hall commissionaires were equally emphatic about it. Had Mr. Grey gone out they would have seen him. There was not the slightest doubt about it. Mr. Grey, being a first-floor guest holding a whole suite, received special attention, and it was unthinkable that they would have let him pass out of the hotel without acknowledgment. Such things did not happen at the Grand Imperial.

Leeds tried again through the billiard-rooms and drew blank again.

Having decided the question to his ultimate satisfaction, he went boldly up to suite No. 4 and knocked loudly on the door. There was not a sound from within. He knocked again, hard, with the stub of a patent pencil. He went to each of the doors in the suite and repeated his summons, trying each door after knocking, and finding them all locked.

He pulled out a notebook and scribbled a short note to Kann, sending it to him by a page.

Cannot find a trace of him. He is neither in the public sections nor in his rooms. Have tried all doors. They are locked. And I can get no answer to repeated knockings. Hall staff assure me he has not gone out through the front hall. Am of the opinion that he has either gone out through one of the staff entrances or else is in his rooms playing possum. Better come up and get on with it. I'll watch the stairs.

Kann read the note and frowned.

He passed the note over. Grayne read it, and put it in the ash-tray, and let a match flare under it till it curled up and turned black.

"Well?" said Kann.

"He's in his rooms," said Grayne with flat decision.

"You think so?"

"I'm sure."

"I think so too. Well, so much the worse for Damon Grey. Are you ready?"

Grayne nodded, and crushed the charred paper to dust with his thumb. Together they sauntered away through the card-room, passing the old gent as they went.

He turned a broad smile of disarming pleasure on them and murmured a polite "Good night, gentlemen." They got a closer look at him as they passed. That cast in his eye was certainly atrocious.

Kann returned his salute with a curt nod. And he whispered in Greyne'sear: "Gosh darn that old stiff. With a squint like that we're in for fifteen years' bad luck. It'll come solid, you see!"

The old gentleman appeared to dismiss them from his mind as soon as they had gone. He turned back to his patience game with a beatific smile.

They crossed the wide vestibule and traversed the lounge, keeping an eye lifting for Leeds. The lift attendant opened the gates to them, but waved him aside with a gesture of his hand.

They went up by the stairs and turned left down one of the wide corridors that opened out directly of the first-floor landing.

Grayne went into Kann's room at the bottom end, slipped off the coat, waistcoat, collar, and tie, and put on the American's purple dressing-gown

Kann halted in front of Damon Grey's sitting-room. He bent down and peered through the keyhole. All was in darkness within and there was not a sound to be heard. The great clock in the vestibule chimed again dimly from a distance. He glanced around. The whole landing was deserted. He pressed his ear close against the keyhole and listened with concentrated intensity for a sound from inside the room.

He pulled out a bunch of skeleton keys, thin delicate things that looked more like bits of twisted wire than keys. They were pliable and they glittered in the soft yellow light. He took a quick scrutiny of the make of the lock and selected a key, a short one with a double kink and a right-angle bend at the ward end. He slid it into the lock with the skilful and confident deftness of the expert. It seemed humanly impossible for a normal, thick-fingered man to manipulate metal against metal with such an utter absence of sound. The key did not even grate against the lock.

With a delicacy of touch and gentleness of pressure that was almost feminine, he began to turn the key. There came a tiny sound behind him, scarce perceptible in the silence. He spun round, on guard in a moment. A footfall sounded round the end of the corridor, a soft footfall preceded by a quiet preoccupied humming. He wiped his forehead and returned to his task. Grayne appeared round the end of the corridor, walked along, and passed him, still humming. There were thick Turkish towels round his neck and a bulging sponge-bag in his hand. He passed the American without a sign of recognition and disappeared round the end of the passage.

Kann turned the key. It grated ever so slightly, like a pin scratching on canvas. Then it stuck. With infinite care he withdrew it and inserted another. That, too, did not answer. It turned the lock halfway over and then jammed.

When Grayne passed Kann again as he was manipulating the key with a pair of steel pliers. Grayne padded past him without a glance in his direction. He was humming "Everything in the Garden's Lovely," but its inference was lost on the American, who, on his hands and knees, was swiftly busy at the lock again.

Kann slipped the key in the lock again and turned it slowly. One by one he heard the wards fall over, dropping open with barely perceptible clicks.

Then he lay flat on his face and pushed the door open inch by inch.

Still there was no sound from within. A wall of black silence seemed to well out from behind the door and envelop him. A service bell rang sharply down in the distant vestibule. It ceased abruptly, and the soundlessness that followed was pulsing and pregnant with expectancy. It was like a massed attack of silence that passed over and beyond him, and left him a quivering atom on the threshold of fate.

He began to crawl in. His heart was pumping against the walls of his chest, and he was breathing rapidly through distended nostrils as though badly out of breath. The nape of his neck seemed to be crawling up into his hair. Kann was keyed up to the last unbearable ounce; but he went forward. That was the biggest and greatest thing he did that night. Grayne admitted so afterwards. He went forward. With the palms of his hands all sticky with fear and the sickening anticipation of some jumble visitation from Grey crawling in with him inch by inch, he went forward.

He reached to his hip for his gun and fingered the safety cock. He gripped it in his right hand and felt for his electric torch with the other. For a few moments he lay, void of all motion, on the floor, listening, with every nerve fibre alive and pricking.

He rose to his knees and deliberately coughed. It was a loud, sudden noise in the nerve-rasping silence. He coughed again, gripping his gun tightly in his right hand. Still there was no sound or sign of life in suite No. 4. Kann took a new hold of himself.

He flashed the torch around slowly, without panic. The beam of light sought out the light switches. His hand shot out to them and snapped them on. A flood of white, searching light blazed out through the room, lighting it up with ruthless brilliance. With quick, incisive movements he searched the room. It was empty.

Grayne passed again outside, humming softly.

Communicating doors opened left and right from the sitting-room. Boldly he walked across to the left-hand one and pushed it open. That too, was empty. He switched on the lights and searched the place thoroughly. It was a bathroom, and not even a dog could have hidden there and escaped detection.

And yet there was something in that room that fixed and held his attention, something that told him instinctively he had got on the tail end of trail.

It was an attache-case, a very ordinary looking brown leather attaché-case, such as one uses to hold the few things necessary for a weekend out of town. There were neither marks nor initials on it and it was locked.

He fished out his keys, and in five seconds the bag fell open.

Kann stood back quickly, eyeing the contents. He didn't like the look of them at all. He knew that he had stumbled on the key to Damon Grey's secret poison—if only he knew how to get at it. He closed the door and took stock of the stuff, keeping his hands well clear of all contact with it.

There was a workmanlike little spirit-stove, with a super-heating arrangement attached; a bottle of raw spirit, several tiny little phials, some containing powders and liquids, some empty, a porcelain crucible, a pair of rubber surgical gloves, a mess of wet stuff that looked like a white branmash and gave off the sweet-sick smell of ether, and, right in the corner, away from the gloves, a little object wrapped in cotton-wool.

He wiped his forehead again, and realised that he had suddenly gone stone cold. "Phew!" he muttered. "Now for it."

He caught sight of himself in the glass and clicked his teeth irritably. "Richard Kann," he muttered fretfully, "I thought you'd got sand! You ought to go in for district visiting."

He glared at himself and seized the pair of gloves.

"And even these darned things might be doped inside out!" he growled as he pulled them on. "Well, if they are, Mister Grey, I'll give you credit for thinking ahead of me!"

He picked up the wool-packed object and opened it out. His eyes gleamed savagely when he saw the contents. It was a sprayer, a small glass bottle, such as hairdressers use for spraying the face after a shave. In the container was a liquid that was almost colourless. He stood it on a ledge and muttered: "Now for Damon! It's you or me this time."

With a gloat in his heart that might have come to the soul of a miser, he packed everything neatly away in the case again and put it back where he found it. He even locked the case again. Then he picked up the sinister little bottle with its rubber bulbs, shut off the electric light in the bathroom, and went out into the sitting-room.

There his work was swift and thorough.

Holding the sprayer out at arm's length and praying to his gods to help him handle the stuff aright, he pumped a thick coating of the deadly stuff over all the door-handles and electric light switches. A tray of glasses he treated in the same way, spraying the mixture all round the rims where the lips might touch. A silver cigarette-box, a cigar cabinet, a pack of cards, a pair of slippers, a nail file, the backs of chairs, everywhere where the fingers of Damon Grey were likely to touch he sprayed a trail of silent, inexplicable death.

The American looked at the amount of liquid left in the container. He had used nearly half of it. "Reckon that'll do for this room," he muttered, picking up a briar pipe as an afterthought and spraying the mouthpiece of it.

Then he went over to the bedroom door and listened. All was as silent in there as elsewhere. Gun in hand, he turned the handle and flung the door open wide. Grey was not there.

Kann switched on a flood of light, and for ten minutes without a break he toured the apartment with his instrument of death He sprayed a film of the deadly liquid on the silver hairbrushes, on the combs, and the razors. His collars and a thick wad of handkerchiefs, the bed-rail, the pillow, the evening papers laid out on the bedside table, the soap, the sleeping-suit box, anywhere and everywhere where the fingers of Damon Grey were likely to touch in the simple act of undressing and going to bed was sprayed with a thin veneer of the fatal liquid.

Then he pulled off the gloves, poisoned them, and tossed both the sprayer and the gloves carelessly under a tall chest of drawers.

He went out into the sitting-room, switching the lights out as he went. Grayne 's idle humming sounded outside; it turned the end of the corridor and changed suddenly to the hurried warning whistle. With ears that were stretched and quivering he heard the plaintive bars of "Sally in our Alley" piping urgently down the corridor.

And then a gust of wind from the wide-open window blew the door shut in his face.

Kann, with the perspiration breaking out all over his forehead, stood and stared at the poisoned door-handle.

He realised, all in a horrific moment, that he was trapped; penned in like a rabbit in a gin.

He heard Grayne approach and halt indecisively outside the door.

"That you, Grayne?" he whispered hoarsely.

"Yes. Get under cover!" The voice was a gaspy whisper but urgently imperative.

"Open the door!"

"I can't. Someone is looking at me."

"Who?"

"I don't know. Can't see him properly. Damon Grey, I think."

"Hell! Where is he?"

"Down at the end of the corridor. He's looking up here now. Got his eyes on me like rivets. Get away out of it—quickly. I can't keep this pose up much longer—I'm pretending to tie my bootlace."

"I *can't* get away out of it, you fool. The handle's doped on the inside."

"Well, hide under the bed—do anything. I can't open that door."

Kann whipped his deadly looking air-gun out and swore under his breath.

"Can't you go along and hit him over the head?" he demanded.

"No. Don't be a—"

"Why?"

"He isn't alone!"

"What?"

"There's somebody else with him."

"Who?"

"The manager!"

Kann began stiffing and blinding like a cornered rat.

The warning voice came again.

"I'm going to push off. I'll get somewhere where I can watch how things go. If anything happens I'll get Leeds up here. Quick! Hide! They're coming along!"

"Hide? Hide hell!" snarled Kann, and stood his ground behind the door. He left the lights full on, for even they were loaded with death, cocked his gun, and waited.

VIII

Stephen Leeds ran a clue to earth in the lower billiard-room of the Grand Imperial. It was when a page-boy sought him out and informed him that a gentleman very much resembling his description of Mr. Damon Grey was playing at one of the tables down there.

Leeds sauntered down the thick carpeted stairs and peeped in through the glass panels of the swing-door. There certainly was a man playing at the end table who resembled Grey slightly in both build and appearance. But it wasn't Grey. He recognised that at the first glance. The man was too young for one thing. He had the freshness and vigour of youth about him. And his hair was dark and plentiful; and his smile when he turned to grin cheerfully at his opponent was not the smile of Damon Grey. It was too merry, too ingenuous, too frank altogether. There was nothing bitter about it, nothing to suggest a soul that had been steeped in acid for half a lifetime, or a heart that had been pulped by the hammers of tragedy.

He wandered into the room, just to make sure. When he got nearer he saw that the face was boyish—alight with the vigour of the twenties.

"Not him," he muttered. "Handsome-looking youngster, though."

He nodded off-handedly to the players and glanced up at the scoreboard. Just below it was a booking block, the book in which intending players wrote their names to claim priority on any particular table or for any particular game.

Purely as a blind, he scribbled a name down. And the one immediately above his was D. Ricks.

"Ricks?" Leeds muttered. "Ricks? Now where on earth have I heard that name before?"

There were deep lines puckering down between his eyes. He stared at the name trying to recall a memory from the mere signature. But the style of the writing eluded him, and he turned and covertly scrutinised the young man at the table. He watched him intently as he made a stroke, a thin cannon up the table, that was made with a sure delicacy of touch. Ricks looked up as he completed the stroke and caught the card-sharper's eyes full on him, boring into him like gimlets.

But Ricks gave no sign of recognition. He just returned the greeting with a nod and a smile, and turned his attention to the game in hand.

Leeds was subtly puzzled. He felt positive in some queer, indefinable way that he had heard Rackway mention a Dickie Ricks. And yet for the life of him he couldn't think when or how.

He went out and walked slowly towards the card-room, turning the matter over critically in his mind.

He pushed the door open and glanced in.

The benign old gentleman with the chronic cast in his eye was still naively interested in his solitaire game.

He glanced up as Leeds entered.

"Ah, good evening," he said expansively. "Your friends seem to have deserted you. Perhaps I might offer you a game?"

Leeds laughed outright. The idea of that rather proper-looking old gentleman offering to stick him up at cards tickled him.

"I—I'm afraid I play rather well," he said frankly.

"Well, I'm not a bad hand myself," returned the old gentleman blandly.

"Really—I'd rather not play tonight, if you'll excuse me. I hate to decline your offer, but I'm afraid I must."

"Waiting for someone?"

"Well—yes; if you put it that way."

"Then why not give me a game till they come? Do you play casino?"

Stephen Leeds said "Do I!" And then he laughed shortly. "That, sir, was the first arithmetic lesson I ever learned," he said. "I was weaned on it."

The old gentleman beamed.

"Then, if you've nothing else to do," he said, "I'll give you a game."

Leeds looked around worriedly. He didn't in the least want to play the old boy. He floated at higher game. And besides, his job was to keep an eye skinned for Damon Grey.

The old gentleman looked up innocently.

"But perhaps I could help you find your friend? I live permanently at the hotel and know most of the guests. Is he staying here?"

"Oh, yes. Has a suite on the first floor."

"Then he's a floor mate of mine. What's his number?"

"Four."

"Yes, I know him. Came here yesterday. I took a liking to him right away. Morose, quiet-looking chap, looks as though he'd had the soul frozen out of him. Er—let me see now, Grey—Grey is the name?"

Leeds nodded non-committally. He fingered his chin thoughtfully. He was sorry now that he had mentioned the matter at all. The rest of the Silent Six would not have approved. It was against all their laws of scrupulous care in never leaving clues.

"He went out some little time ago, for a breath of fresh air before turning in. But you're bound to get him if you wait for him here—he said he would look in and have a Scotch and Polly with me before going up."

"H'm!" said Leeds. "Thank you."

"So you'll play, of course?" said the old gentleman with a smile. And the ferocious cast in his eye sat above that smile like a gargoyle grinning above a saint.

The old gentleman apparently took his invitation as something that carried its own acceptance. To Leeds's unfeigned surprise he pulled out a wad of five-pound notes and stacked them on the table in front of him.

Leeds looked quickly down at them.

That was a pretty deliberate challenge, he thought. The old boy seemed to have no small opinion of himself. Conduct like that was so totally at variance with his general appearance that Leeds was a little startled. The boot was generally on the other foot—men like Leeds had to force the game on men like the benevolent old gent.

Leeds pulled out a chair and sat down.

"Yes, I'll play you," he said gently. "What would you care to play for? A sovereign a point?"

"Certainly," said the old gentleman. "And—er—I wish you luck."

Leeds looked at him sharply, and the horribly squinting eyes stared back at him like a talisman of fate.

"Thank you. I don't need luck when I play cards," said Leeds dryly. But he said it so quietly that not even the good-humoured old gentleman himself heard it.

"Shall I deal?" asked the old gentleman.

"Certainly." Leeds didn't care a brassha'penny who dealt. He had ways and means of his own of accommodating the run of the cards to suit his own needs. And he was so immaculately slick at the gentle art of forcing the cards that he had played for long nights with professional card-sharpers and not even his partner knew he was faking the deal. He had lifted big wads of money off some of the cutest tricksters in hotel-land, men who knew they were being fleeced, men who knew every trick and of the game—and yet couldn't see how it was done. All they knew was that they lost money heavily, and that the slim, aristocratic man with the ice-cool countenance and rock-steady hands rose from the table with their money bulging his pockets.

The old gentleman shuffled and quietly cut his own deal.

Leeds did a mental grin. That was a new one on him. It was ineffable, something fresh from the grass; Sunday afternoon stuff with Aunitie. It was almost a shame to sting him. But there was one thing that Stephen Leeds did not see—and that was when the old gentleman bent his head down to look at his cards, he rested his eyes from their ghastly squint.

He looked at his hand. Four picture cards—utterly useless in play. Oddly enough, the next one was the same—and the next—and the next. Sixteen picture cards one after the other. Stephen Leeds, the most brilliant card manipulator in the metropolis, sat up and took a little notice. His lips pressed into a rigid line, and he slightly moistened his right middle finger. Sixteen picture cards, one after the other! That was going some: that was stretching coincidence out to the bursting point and some yards beyond it.

Meanwhile, the simple-souled old gentleman had taken in all four aces: big casino, little casino, three clear-boards, and a whole sheaf of spades. The old gentleman had won that game in the first four deals.

"Well, anyhow," grunted Leeds, "I can't get any more picture cards, can I? I've had all there are in the pack."

"That is quite true," assented the old gentleman coolly. "I always deal out all the picture cards first when I'm playing casino."

Leeds dropped his cards as though they had suddenly gone red-hot in his hand.

"*What?*" he gasped.

The old gentleman regarded him mildly.

"You seem surprised?" he said. "Why? It's a very safe plan, isn't it?"

Leeds was dumbfounded. The silly old josser was openly admitting that he had faked the deal, openly admitting that he had that amazing sequence of useless cards on his opponent. And, what is more, was admitting it as innocently and as blandly as though deliberate cheating was quite the accepted thing in card-playing circles.

"You—I—gosh!" Leeds gulped at last.

"Aren't you feeling well?" asked the old gentleman solicitously.

Leeds stared at him blankly. "Just—just a moment!" he managed to get out. "Did I understand you to say just now that you—that you deliberately planted that run of pictures on me?"

"Why, yes. Quite!"

"Phew!"

Leeds rose shakily from the table and as shakily sat down again.

The old boy was daft. Absolutely head first down into the uttermost depths of imbecility. Such a situation had never presented itself to him before in thirty odd years of gentlemanly card-twisting. He was beat.

He dabbed his forehead with his handkerchief.

"Then—you—you've been *cheating*?" he exploded.

"Why, yes, certainly—if you put it as bluntly as that."

"Well, what the hell's own game do you think you're playing?" Leeds became almost hysterical with a mixture of wrath, mystification, and downright amazement.

The old gentleman looked a trifle hurt.

"Why?" he asked gently. "You are a sharper too, aren't you?

Stephen Leeds blinked, blinked again, and then put his head back and laughed. He laughed aloud, riotously, unrestrainedly, only pausing now and then to stare at the unique old gent in front of him and then go off into another paroxysm, and then the wind went out of him like the slow collapsing of a dying pig. That absurd old party had called his bluff—called it as neatly and as unequivocally as any man's ever was since cards first put on a table. The astonishing coolness of it left him breathless. There was a wonderment sweeping over him that made him limp. He couldn't be angry, and he didn't know how to be exasperated. He was flat out. The ludicrous idiocy of it began to dawn on him.

"Holy Moses!" he muttered. "If that doesn't beat the band! And on *me*, too!"

He looked over at the old gentleman with warm appreciation. "Good lord—that certainly is one to you!" he said. "Have you been working this game long?"

"I—I don't think I quite understand you," replied the old gentleman, puckering his brows.

"I mean, I thought I knew most of the good men flying the Jolly Roger. There aren't ten in London worthy of the name. Race-course toughs mostly—they do it with a gun on their hip. It isn't card-sharping so much as highway robbery. I'd have thought I should have heard of you. Who are you?"

The old gentleman did not answer. He just continued to gaze placidly at the aristocratic figure facing him.

And all in a moment the blood began to drain out of Stephen Leeds's face. His jaw dropped and he went a sickly, unhealthy white round the mouth. He sat as rigid as a frozen rabbit, so stiffly, horribly flexed that one might have thought he had already been dead many hours and the rigor mortis had set in.

The old gentleman, without the slightest sign of either physical or mental perturbation, sat and gazed back at him.

In that flickering moment he had become such a despotic master of the situation that not a single word was needed to establish his kingship.

The old gentleman had not moved a muscle, had not made one single action either of accusation or aggression. Except one. And that was in his eyes.

And Stephen Leeds gazed at those eyes as though they had got him under a hypnotic spell.

For the ghastly squint had slowly gone out of them. The painful-looking astigmatism had disappeared as smoothly as though it had been rectified by hidden mechanism. The eyeballs attuned themselves to a normal focus, naturally and easily. And the eyes that gazed out of the shrimp-pink face were changed completely. There was life in them, fire, strength, virility. They were bitter, challenging, burning with hate, yet as wintry as the wind off the Poles. Steadily, without the flick of an eyelid, they bored their threat and menace into the soul of Stephen Leeds. All in that horror-filled moment he saw and understood.

Leeds's teeth began to click. It was a symptom of which he was entirely unconscious. He was oblivious of everything save the nerve-shattering presence of Damon Grey. Every shred of his keyed-up attention was fixed and centred mesmerically on him.

Damon Grey made just the slightest gesture of his hands towards him.

"A bad sign," he said gravely.

Stephen Leeds seemed to become suddenly aware of his chattering teeth. He shut his jaws with a slow effort.

"Well?" said Grey, with a deep frown. "I think our little gamble begins here?"

Leeds passed a hand uncertainly across his forehead, and he drew in a long, agitated breath.

"I—I wasn't expecting you—to see you—tonight," he said, struggling for something to say, something which would serve as a peg on which to hang his jolted faculties and hammer some sort of coherence into them.

Grey acknowledged the remark with a studiously polite inclination of the head.

"A little disconcerting?" he murmured. "I quite understand—and I'm sorry. But the fault is not entirely mine. It became necessary for me to advance my arrangements by twenty-four hours. What are known in diplomatic circles as unforeseen circumstances arose. And the step was rendered imperative. I regret it, of course, but it was a matter entirely outside my jurisdiction. Your erstwhile respected leader, Mr. Hilton Rackway, is endeavouring to clear out of the country. He is making every possible preparation to bolt while the door is still open. That, in a nutshell, is the situation. His flight leaves me no alternative. Unfortunately for Rackway, he has made a faulty assessment of the circumstances. The door is no longer open. Not to put too broad a point on it, it has been slammed in his face. The sailing dates of the steamers give me the key."

He regarded the other man dispassionately, almost in the casual way that a man might regard a friend of whom he has inquired an opinion on some trivial matter. "Ah, but I see," he said, "you don't quite grasp the point. Let me explain. The boat sailings offer Hildon Rackway his only avenue. They also point the direction to anyone on his trail. Glancing down *The Times* list today, what does one find? Under the heding 'Mails Today—Departures' one finds the name of the s.s. *Ruahontas* as sailing tomorrow evening. She is a good fast mail boat running out to the South American ports. She will be touching at half a dozen little republics where extradition warrants do not apply. The only other sailings are the cross-Channel steamers and the United States mid-week mail. He will choose the *Ruahontas*. He won't go to the Continent, because, in these volatile days, pursuit has evoluted to the aeroplane stage. Certainly also he will not go to New York—police officers in battalions might quite conceivably receive him on the landing stage. He will go by the *Ruahontas*, the only hope of permanent sanctuary. The boat train leaves for Southampton tomorrow morning at ten o'clock. Hildon Rackway will be on board that train. The *Ruahontas* will weigh out on the six o'clock tide. She will steam without Mr. Hildon Rackway."

Damon Grey gathered up his banknotes and restored them to his pocket.

"I remember, even in the old days," he commented dryly, "you could never resist the lure of a pile of notes and a pack of cards. But your memory must be getting a little—er—unreliable, Leeds—you yourself taught me that shuffle."

Leeds began to get something of a grip on himself. Grey was too persuasively gentle to be attempting anything brutal tonight. What his motive was he hadn't the faintest idea, but it seemed altogether beyond credence that he was contemplating one of his diabolical murders in that frame of mind. Leeds began to hedge in to safety.

"And you—you are going down to Southampton tomorrow, then?" he asked lamely.

Grey nodded.

"Yes," he said. "I shall go down on the boat train. I shall be rather interested to see Mr. Rackway's face when he recognises me. Yours was quite a study. So unconscious, so natural. The squint is rather a good disguise, I think?"

"It was—new to me," said Leeds in a painful whisper.

"Quite original. The general get-up is on the whole excellent. I shall have to alter it though tomorrow. These white sideboards are detachable: a little oiled pad rubbed over the face—and this absurd complexion is gone. Very helpful. With a skin like a Bognor prawn and lambs' tails down below the ears, one is so conspicuous. Should there be any hue and cry after your regrettable demise, my dear Leeds, the papers will be full of descriptions of 'the man with the squint,' 'the pink-faced man,' etc. Whereas, within three minutes of my getting to my room, I shall be just plain Damon Grey again. There will be no link, no connection at all. The whole idea, as I see it, is quite sound. Don't you think so?"

Leeds sat without blinking. The back of his throat had gone horribly dry. He saw, as though through a fog of fear, that Grey was deliberately baiting him. He could see it, stark and implacable, in his eyes. He moistened his lips and forced the panic out of his brain. The only thing he had to do was to keep his hands off anything Damon Grey had touched. So long as he kept his fingers rigidly out of contact he knew he was safe. And if he could only hold Grey off until a waiter or someone entered that room, he might manage to get away with it. Kann and Grayne ought to be down at any moment now. But at least one of the hotel servants, the night porter or someone, would be along in a minute to clear up the rooms. He thrust his hands deliberately into his coat pockets and looked across at Grey.

Grey smiled.

"And that brings me to another point," he said coldly. "Where are Kann and Grayne?"

Leeds was silent.

"Come, come—out with it," said Grey. "You were with them only ten minutes ago."

"I don't know where they are," answered Leeds sullenly. "Gone home, for all I know."

"That is a lie," said Grey evenly. "You know as well as I do where they are. Kann and Grayne are up in my rooms. And if I know anything of the internal organisation of the Silent Six, Kann is doing the job inside while Grayne keeps watch in the corridor." A flicker of contempt passed over Grey's face.

"I think I could even tell you what's happening up there," he added.

"After Lindrum's heart attack, you all had a bad touch of nerves," said Grey. "You went into urgent committee with yourselves, discussed the matter excitedly, angrily—with Kann the only one among you who kept both his nerve and his temper. Bah—you're too elementary for words. You concocted a little plan. A raid on my rooms. Your main idea—your only hope, too—was to get hold of my poison. You itched to pay me back in my own coin. By this time the scheme has probably worked. You were the downstairs guard, detailed off to prevent me going upstair until Kann and Grayne had had time to finish the job.

"Kann is in my rooms at this very moment. I'll lay you the odds—all Dartmoor to a pound of oakum—that he has found the poison. It's in a little leather attaché case in my bathroom. The locks wouldn't hold a tame canary. He's spraying liquid death broadcast in my suite. He's squirting it over every tiny inch of space he could possible imagine me touching tonight. I'd like to give you twenty to one that my pillow is damp with it now. And I wish him luck, Mr. Leeds. Luck and no regrets. For, let me tell you this: there isn't a gramme of poison anywhere in my rooms. The stuff that Kann is mucking about with up there wouldn't hurt a fly, wouldn't hurt a guinea-pig—not if you injected a pint of it into it, in gill measures, once every hour.

"It is a mixture of sugar and gin in which a little camphor has been precipitated. It gives off a slightly hospitally smell—quite enough to convince them upstairs that they are messing about with a half-pint of liquid annihilation. My poison is in my pocket, Stephen Leeds. I am going to kill you with it tonight."

Damon Grey spoke with a quiet decisiveness that was more wickedly inhuman than any prolonged tirade of passionate recrimination or vocal fireworks. To him, the man he had come to kill was less than a carcass of beef, a mere soulless automaton which had grievously offended him and was consequently about to be eliminated.

Leeds took stock of the threat but slowly. The full import of it dawned on him only after many seconds of chaotic thinking. And as slowly, his body stiffened. There was horror and helplessness running riot in his brain. It is not nice to catch a first glimpse of the Reaper and to eyes turned full on you, with his scythe outswung.

"You—you *what?*" he gasped and gazed rabidly at Damon Grey.

"You heard what I said," replied Grey, unmoved. "In the old days, Leeds, it used to be a cardinal rule in our operations that not a single move should be made until the organisation was complete. You see now the futility of trying to work effectively without efficient co-ordination.

"Those—those comedians upstairs are merely assisting me, keeping themselves out of the way until such time as I have fulfilled my obligations to you. My only complaint against them is that they are filling my rooms with the highly objectionable stink of camphor while they're doing it."

Grey switched off suddenly and watched Leeds closely for a few seconds. A red light was beginning to smoulder up in the card-sharper's eyes, the light of a man who has looked Death sheer in the face and outgrown his fear. Grey read the signs, and his voice went up a note. There was a deeper rumble in it, a note of warning, the single, deep-throated growl a bulldog gives before its jaws clamp home.

Leeds was no longer the terror-filled weakling, no longer appalled by the horror of the thing that was about to happen to him. There was a fighting spirit filling into him with every moment that sped. He was calling up his own reserves of courage and strength to employ shock tactics where brain had failed.

And Damon Grey beat him even at that. He did something that made the other man fall back in his chair cowed and beaten.

Without taking his eyes off him Damon Grey's hand went out to the ash-tray on the corner of the table. It was a massive thing of sheet brass, tooled and enamelled, with the arms and crest of the Grand Imperial embossed in the centre.

Grey's fingers closed over it slowly. Leeds's eyes followed the action in fascinated silence. The fingers flexed slowly, but with a deliberation that neither checked nor increased as the power went on. The heavy brass tray bent, crinkled and crumpled to a squeezed-out mass as the fingers closed. Leeds's eyes were staring, almost popping. The thing had been done with such a dreadful absence of haste or effort that the action stunned him.

The lean brown fingers opened and the receptacle, an attenuated ellipse of crushed metal, dropped back on the table with a little "plop."

"You see," said Grey gently. "I have had eighteen years in which to get like that: eighteen years during which nothing passed my lips except the scientific ideal of food quantity, quality, and weight. That eighteen years, moreover, was spent daily, hourly, at the quarry face. It hardened my soul, Leeds, hardened my heart ten thousand times harder than the granite hills I hacked and hewed. And, by God, it hardened my muscles, too! I could break your back."

Leeds relaxed in his chair, breathing quickly.

Grey collected the cards and began to shuffle them.

Leeds wiped his wet brow. "You—you murderous devil!" he gasped.

"Murder is a matter of degree, my dear Leeds," said Damon Grey. "You murdered the only soul in the world who could have made my return to freedom worth the price. You also killed me—but that does not signify. The fact that I continued to live is just a biological mistake, a problem in the higher studies of physics that does not enter. I am dead. I do not matter—not even to *me!*"

He shrugged. "That's all, Mr. Leeds. It's your turn."

He held out the cards. Leeds shied away from them as though they were crawling with bubonic. His fright was so real that his eyelids were bone-stiff and wide open above his eyes. His head was cocked forward on a neck that had suddenly gone wooden.

"You are reckoned something of an eloquent gentleman with these little things, I believe?" Grey poised the cards on the outstretched palm of his hand. "Please don't be frightened of them, Mr. Leeds—they won't bite you. As you see, I am touching them myself. I don't think there is any particular reason for you to go into apoplexy on their account. I haven't the slightest intention of committing suicide. Won't you take them?"

But Leeds still held frantically shy.

"As you will," said Grey. And the smile that crept into the corners of his mouth was villainously contemptuous. He leaned forward and folded his arms on the table, his hands out of sight.

"I was holding out a straw to you," he said.

"What—what do you mean?" stammered Leeds.

"Just this. You are probably the cleverest card crook in London. I heard about you even in Dartmoor. You were slick enough at it, God knows, when I last knew you. The nearest to you is a long way behind. You can do things with a pack of cards that almost can't be done, must have courage of a sort, or you could never rob a man under without turning a hair."

Grey seemed to be playing him up, dangling him on a string over a fire that was slowly but surely burning the very string on which he dangled.

"Well, what is it?" asked Leeds in a fiat voice.

"I wondered if you had the courage to try a cut of the cards with me, that is all. But I see you haven't. It—"

"But—I—what—" Leeds swallowed, "What is it you say?" he said.

"I offer you an even break on the cards.I put the cards on the table. You can shuffle them yourself if you like. We each cut.

The one who draws the highest card also draws the privilege of leaving this room alive. That is a fair offer. You have everything to gain and nothing to So far as the cards go the odds are 99 to 1 in your favour. There isn't trick, there isn't a pass, there isn't a sleight-of-hand movement in the wheels world of card manipulation that isn't known to you—there isn't a trick you can't perform."

Damon Grey tossed the pack neatly on to the table with a deft of his wrist. They slithered across the table in a tenuous line and Grey folded his hands back under his arms. He looked across at the other his eyebrows elevated, his whole face asking a question.

Stephen Leeds looked at him sourly.

"What's the game now?" he growled.

"Precisely what I say. It is quite immaterial to me whether you accept or refuse: if you refuse you will die just the same; if you accept you stand your chance with me of quitting this room with the breath still in your body and your heart still pumping."

"Just—just a minute," said Leeds with an effort. "Let me get the thing right. You give me the privilege of shuffling those cards?"

"Quite. All I ask is that you cut fair."

"I can give them any shuffle I like?"

"My dear Leeds," said Grey, with a short laugh, "I don't know enough about card manipulation to be able to tell whether you are stacking them up or not. All I tell you is that you'll play fair for once in your life—or die."

"The cards go face down on the table?"

"That is usual, I believe?"

"And then we each cut the pack?"

"Yes."

"Who has first shot?"

"Quite immaterial to me. You can, if you like.

"And if I cut out the highest card?"

"I shall make no further attempt to revenge myself on you. You will be quite at liberty to get up from this table and walk out of the room."

"That's not bluff?"

"Oh, no. You should know by now that bluff is a card I don't keep in my pack."

"Then why are you playing with me like this?"

"Simply to satisfy a little whim of my own. I've sworn to be revenged on the whole crowd of you. That is an oath I hope to keep eventually. But I thought it would give me a more aesthetic satisfaction if I got at you through your own particular failing. Yours is cards. Think of the overwhelming pleasure it would give me to be able to beat you at your own game. Not only do I rid myself of your utterly distasteful presence, but 1 have that secret satisfaction of knowing that I did it through a department of which you are a past-master. Lindrurn I killed because he was so superlatively sure of himself—and me. He was always the psychologist of our little crowd; he could always tell you what any particular person would do under any particular circumstance. An excellent precept that. Always attack where the enemy is strongest. Napoleonic, I believe? Grayne I shall get through his violin playing. The fiddle is an obsession with him. I shall kill him via that single ecstatic passion. Kann I shall get on his own nerve. I shall crack it first. The shock will kill him. Rackway—oh, well, Rackway is different. He has but one passion in life, these days. A mere slip of a girl. I shall take my revenge on Rackway through her. A simple matter. Simple and thorough and undeniably pleasing. Your pet foible is cards. I give you the chance. Will you give me the chance it offers?"

Leeds hesitated in painful indecision for a second or two and the perspiration began to bead out on his brow. Then he seized the cards with an animal yammer in his throat. Swiftly he shuffled them, his fingers slipping over the cards like a beautifully controlled machine. Leeds with a pack of cards in his hand was a piece of mechanical perfection. There were one or two tiny, barely audible clicks and then with a bold slam he tabled the shuffled pack.

Grey watched him with a titter of amusement in the corners of his eyes.

"Quite finished?" he asked pleasantly.

Leeds nodded, white to the ears.

"All right then—draw your card."

Leeds's hand shook visibly as he put it out to the pack. But no sooner had he tapped the pack with his fingertips than it became as steady as the table itself. He took about hall-way down for his cut and then whipped the card face upward. It was the ace of spades, the great big black ace that testified to his own expertly perfect manipulation.

He smiled a little when he drew it. But deep in his heart there was a ringing paean of triumph, for every other ace in that pack was held in the section of cards gripped in his right hand. He had neatly shuffled every ace into the top half of the pack, and that top half was his own cut. Damon Grey could neither beat nor equal that ace of spades.

Damon Grey stood up. The smile on his face was satanic.

Leeds gasped and then tried to spring at his throat. But his knees refused to support him, refused to let him stand on them at all. He had just seen Damon Grey's hands. They were cased in rubber gloves. And up his own arm a spasm shot: a spasm that went right on into his brain and turned the whole room black around him. Then even the blackness vanished and he toppled forward in his chair.

Grey carefully collected the cards, burnt them in the fire, and walked quietly out of the room. In the corridor he pulled off his white side whiskers, rubbed the oily pad over his face until every trace of make-up had vanished, and inspected the result in a little circular hand-mirror. He finished it off with a clean handkerchief, till the effect satisfied even his critical requirements. Then from under his dinner jacket he produced a flattened opera hat, flicked it open and put it on.

In the foyer, as he passed through, the lift attendant came out of his little cabin.

"Lift, sir?" asked the attendant.

"Yes, please."

"You're rather later tonight, sir."

"Yes. I've just been out for a little walk.

He went up with an infinite peace in his heart. He knew no pang of regret, he admitted to no single thought of sorrow. He told himself that his own affairs had thinned down to a point beyond any possibility of remorse.

There remained merely the matter of Richard Kann in suit No. 4

The lift stopped at the first floor and Damon Grey turned to the attendant.

"Might I see the manager for a moment?" he asked casually. "There is a little matter I would like put right in my rooms."

"Certainly, sir. I'll fetch him."

The lift went down again. Out of the corner of his eye Grey caught sight of a tall figure in a dressing-gown, with a swathe of towels round his neck, coming up the corridor towards him. He was humming unconcernedly and trailing a sponge-bag in his hand. He looked hard at Damon Grey, thrusting his head forward and staring at him under deep black brows.

He started badly and his humming changed to a flute-like whistle low and penetrating.

Grey turned away, ignoring him as though he neither knew nor wanted to know him.

The lift came up with the manager.

"Good evening," said Grey quietly. "Awfully sorry to trouble you so late at night, but I wanted to see you about a small adjustment I'd like made in my rooms. I'm being troubled a good deal with telephone calls, and I wondered if you could fix me up an instrument on a bedside table. At present my phone is in the sitting-room. I'll be staying here for several weeks, I expect, and if you could accommodate me in the matter it would be a great convenience."

"I don't think there will be any trouble about that, Mr. Grey," assumed the manager. "Let me come along with you and you can show me just where and how you would like the alteration made."

He smiled pleasantly, and they walked along together towards Grey's suite. Grey saw the man in the dressing-gown stooping down outside his sitting-room door. He was apparently adjusting a recalcitrant shoelace.

Grayne stood up as they approached, and with the utmost nonchalance addressed himself to Grey.

"Excuse me," he said. "Could you direct me to the bathrooms? I've been roaming about looking for them half the night, and they appear to me to be eluding me purposely."

"Haven't the faintest idea," said Grey, and he said it without moving an eyelid.

"Second on the left, third on the right," said the manager.

Grayne nodded his thanks, and strolled off down the corridor.

Grey turned the handle of his door and pushed it open. A blaze of electric light streamed out as he opened it.

"Odd," he muttered, loud enough for the manager to hear. "Very odd. I thought I switched the lights out before I went out. Still, come along in and I'll show you what I want."

He and the manager went in together. As soon as Kann, flat against the wall behind the door, saw the hotel chief enter he knew the game was up. Grey had bested him again. The murderous-looking air pistol, glittering wickedly in the glare of the light, slid slowly back to his hip pocket.

He stepped forward sheepishly.

"Say, you fellers," he said with a wry twist of his lips, "I'm most awfully sorry, and I apologise no end, but I kinder reckon I've made a mistake in my room number. I got in here, and it seems this ain't my set of rooms at all. I wonder—could you tell me where my own hang-out is? I'm a new arrival in this hotel, and haven't quite got the layout yet."

The manager jumped like a startled rabbit.

"You what?" he snapped. He scrutinised the American up and down. Hotel thieves were not unknown in his hotel. They seemed to regard the Grand Imperial as legitimate prey. He himself had been exasperated beyond measure by their cool audacity and devilish ingenuity. He hated the whole brood of them with every atom of feeling that was in him. And here was an obvious case, a chance to get one of the slim-fingered devils by the neck.

"Are you staying here?" he rapped.

"Yep. I got a room somewheres around here," said Kann.

"What number?"

"Lord knows. It's on my key, and my key is in the lock. This room was open and I just walked in. Before I could turn round and get out you two guys had come in. As I say, I'm most awful sorry, and I apologise for being in your privacy, but I just couldn't help it. If you'll allow me, I'll—"

"One moment." The manager stepped between him and the door.

Kann suddenly went white as a sheet of paper, and he felt the sweat breaking out over his skin. The manager, before he could put out a hand to prevent him, had closed the door. Kann's wide, horrified eyes saw his hand grip the door handle and deliberately push the door shut. Ten minutes earlier Kann had sprayed enough liquid over that door handle to have ensured its effects lasting all night.

Grey sniffed at the air.

"Peculiar smell in here," he said airily. "What is it? Camphor? Turpentine? Floor polish? Iodine—don't you notice it?"

Kann scarcely heard him. He was staring helplessly at the hotel manager, waiting, with a surge of horror sweeping over his soul, for the same awful symptoms to manifest themselves in him that he had seen in John Lindrurn when he took up the fatal poker.

He watched, in a state of fascinated trance, while the hotel manager locked the door with a master key. Damon Grey with his hands in his coat pockets, continued to sniff inquisitively at the air, pretending, with a monumental indifference, that the affair was beyond his orbit altogether. It wasn't that he was mystified or even puzzled; he was simply not interested.

Kann's eyes twitched as he saw the manager grip the handle again and try the door.

His gaze began to switch backwards and forwards from the manager to Damon Grey and back again. Grey walked over calmly to the table and picked up his silver cigarette-box. Kann's nerves began to dance. His thought-process went rocketing off in chaotic flights of incoherence. That cigarette-case was doped as viciously as was the door-handle. His frantic imagination conjured up an awful picture of first the manager and then Damon Grey himself toppling over the brink of inexplicable death—two dead bodies almost embracing each other. And he in the room with them—alone. The damnable business was getting beyond all bounds.

His own natural scruples fought a rapid fire action with his instincts of self-preservation. And in the twentieth of a second the humaner nature had won.

"For God's sake put that cigarette-case down!" he blurted.

The manager stared at him blankly, his eyes round with wonderment and his eyebrows elevated high in surprised interrogation.

Grey turned idly at the table, the case still in his hands.

"I—ah—beg your pardon?" he murmured.

Kann wiped his hand over his face and his eyes switched back to the manager. But the manager neither comprehended nor experienced disruption. He just faced round on the intruder and demanded explanations.

"Now, sir," he barked, "perhaps you will be good enough to explain something further about yourself."

Kann pulled himself up with a jerk. He couldn't explain anything without landing himself hopelessly in the mud. He couldn't even give the manager a hint as to why he had suddenly blurted his warning about the cigarette-case. There was nothing else for him to do but to bluff it out.

"Who are you?" demanded the manager.

Kann seized his cue with both hands and hung on to it like grim death.

"Say, suppose I first ask you who are you?" he suggested. "You come in here, find me in what I'll admit are somewhat unfortunate circumstances; you refuse to accept any apology or explanation, you turn the key in the lock and shut me in, and treat me as though I was a common criminal. All I ask is to be allowed to get out and around to my own room."

"I am the manager of this hotel."

Kann nodded his acceptance of proper authority. "Well, different," he admitted. "I'll allow you've got cause to ask unpleasant questions and to generate unpleasant thoughts. Who's your friend here?"

"That is Mr. Damon Grey, the occupier of this suite."

"Well, my name is Culmer J. Davies, of New York. You'll find it in your hotel register. And I repeat, I'm sorry I mistook my own room, but I can't remember numbers to save my life."

The manager stood silent for a moment regarding the American distastefully.

Grey strolled away from them humming, and poking about among his own belongings. His brown fingers touched half a dozen objects that had been extensively treated with the bottle-sprayer. And to Kann's increasing amazement he showed not the slightest sign of evincing any such symptom of paroxysm as Lindrurn had done before the poker slid from his fingers.

"Mr. Grey," said the manager, "are all the belongings intact? You haven't lost anything?"

"Nothing that I can see," answered Grey disinterestedly. "I should let him go if I were you. He seems pretty genuine. And I have no wish to embarrass a fellow-guest. I'm much more interested to find out what this peculiar stink is in here." He sniffed again. "It's camphor, I believe. And—and—'pon my word, I believe it's gin, too! Camphor and gin (sniff), camphor and gin. Now who in the world (sniff) has been messing about in here with (sniff) camphor and gin?"

Kann's brain began to crawl back to normal again. A gleam of intelligence shot in and sent him staggering. There was a note of ridicule running through Grey's voice, a red-hot note of mockery that was directed solely at him. He sensed it through a blank fog of incredulity. Grey was kidding him, laughing at him up his sleeve. He was looking at him with a gibe in his eyes. They were twinkling with a contempt that was bitter—degrading.

"Gin!" he scoffed. "And camphor! Phew! What a quaint mixture!" He sniffed again and opened the windows. And to Richard Kann it seemed that even his back view was laughing at him.

Grey turned his head sharply. There were sounds of hurrying feet down the corridor. They stopped outside the sitting-room door and someone knocked loudly. The manager looked at Grey, and Grey looked at Kann, definitely and keenly. A world of meaning, subtle, yet as naked as the day, went into that glance. It seemed to be saying:"Play games with me, will you? Well, you just listen to what's coming now!"

The manager called sharply. "Yes, who's there?"

"It's me, sir," said an agitated voice. "Me, the lift man, sir."

"Well, what do you want?"

The manager unlocked and opened the door. "What's the matter?"he asked irritably.

The lift attendant, white-faced and frightened, stood outside.

"It's—it's the card-room, sir," he stammered.

"The what? What's the matter with it?"

"There's a man in it, sir. A man—he's dead, sir. A dead body, sir—in the card-room." The words came out in a series of dry-throated jerks.

"Good God!" said the manager.

"The housekeeper found him, sir. All crumpled up over one of the card-tables. He was a guest, sir. Only staying here for one night."

"But—but what—"

"He—he seems to have had a popaleptic fit, sir. He crushed up one of them there brass ash-trays like it was a bit of paper, sir."

The American looked at Grey again. For a quick second they seemed to hold each other impaled on the steel in their eyes.

Then the manager jumped into action. He hurried out through the door, unmindful of Grey and his telephone, unmindful of the possible hotel thief he thought he had caught, unmindful even of Kann himself, who shot out of the room close behind him and rushed down to superintend the hushing up of this new horrid scandal.

Grey closed his door, locked it and bolted it on the inside.

IX

Rackway came to the desperate conclusion that his one hope lay in flight. That necessity stuck out at him, sheer and urgent, a landmark in his own life. Unless he made a race for safety, and won that race, he saw himself as nothing more than a line of black capitals on a tombstone, telling the story of yet another forward step in the progress of Damon Grey.

Quietly and methodically he set about making his arrangements.

He closely scanned the steamship sections of the newspapers. His first thought was for the Continent; a sudden, breakneck flight to that vast agglomeration of tiny new kingdoms and post-war republics that had cropped up like fungi in the night all along the western edge of Russia. A man might get away into that network of borders and frontiers and defy pursuit for years. And his good English money would be worth a millionaire's ransom among those ash-cans of empire. The police organisations in those light-opera kingdoms reckon hush money part of their wages; bribery is a normal perquisite, and extortion an honourable reason for delaying arrest indefinitely.

And then the memory of Grey's relentlessness came glimmering along his thoughts. Grey would follow him there. He would trail him and track him and keep him on the jump till life became a nightmare of cut and run, with nerves torn to ribbons and resources streaming away like water from a broken tin.

His eyes slipped down to the news of steamers that plied to ports afield.

The fast vessels seemed to be all weekend boats. The flying Cunarder wasn't leaving till Saturday—two days too late for him.

His creeping finger paused at the name of a speedy White Star boat. She was bound for New York. "Almost as bad as the Continent," he muttered. "I'd have to get right away over the Panama—a boat job again. He would be waiting for me in South America by the time I landed."

Ah! There was the boat for him. The *Ruahontas.* South America bound, leaving Southampton the following evening.

He wrote a hurried letter to the steamship company booking a first class cabin for the entire trip. And the cabin he wanted was a double one in the best part of the ship. He gave an assumed name and enclosed enough money in notes to cover the booking. He added that he would confirm the booking with a personal call in the morning, and would collect his ticket then.

Then he posted the letter at an all-night post-office and went along to a quiet little hotel near Waterloo terminus to spend the night. He had a painful dread of Damon Grey confronting him again in Grosvenor Square after the raid on his rooms by the rest of the Silent Six. And his stomach revolted at the thought of it.

He spent a wretched night. Sleep fled him. Every door that opened, every creak on the stairs, sent a trickle of terror along his spine. He saw the hand of Damon Grey on the handle of every door, sensed the pressure of Grey's foot on every board that creaked. He kept all the lights full on in his room, and wedged the back of a chair under the door handle.

At seven o'clock he rang for a strong coffee and turned out and dressed. After a breakfast that became more and more difficult to swallow with each mouthful, he hurried round to the steamship offices to confirm his cabin booking. Everything was in order there, and he phoned to a specialist friend to get him a South American passport made out before midday. That particular gentleman had assisted the Silent Six a score of times in a similar capacity.

He was a quiet man with an unemotional voice and a delicate penmanship; his passport forgeries were works of art.

"Who shall I make it out to?" he queried mildly.

"An old alias. You'll remember it, probably. R. D. Wentworth—and listen, make it out to that name—*and wife*! Her photograph is on the way to you now."

"Oh," said the specialist gentleman, gently surprised, as he hung up the receiver.

Rackway sent his luggage on to Waterloo and booked two first-class seats in the boat train special. Then he hurried back to the Grosvenor Square flat.

The maid answered the door.

"Anybody called while I've been away?" he asked.

"No, sir."

"Thank you. Is Miss Rennie up yet?"

"Yes, sir. She's in her room."

"Tell her I'd like to see her for a moment, will you, please?"

The maid withdrew and Rackway went through to the library.

Lorna came in in a few minutes, smiling a winsome good morning; but more than a little nervous behind that faint curtain of a smile. Another meeting with him within twelve hours was putting a girl at a pretty stiff fence. It was going to be difficult, to say the least—mere time itself can be such a gracious gift on occasion.

After the first swift glance she looked again. There was something tremendously changed in Rackway's appearance.

He, too, was doing his best to carry it off. There was a dead flat calm on his face. His eyes were expressionless, empty of life. Gone all the burning eagerness and pent-up fires of the night before. He just stood idly by the table, one hand in a coat pocket, the other holding a new-lit cigar limply between finger and thumb. There was a heaviness about the set of his figure that seemed to have altered him completely. It seemed hardly possible that the yearning lover of last night could be that same placid, unemotional human figure who regarded her then, dull-eyed, void of feeling.

And then the cigar twisted and flexed between his fingers. There was a dry little cracking sound, the cigar broke in the middle and frayed out like a torn rag. Hildon Rackway turned slowly away from her and stored out of the window.

"Er—Miss Rennie," he said, without turning round. "I'm afraid I have unexpected news for you."

Lorna looked at his back view oddly.

"Nothing—unpleasant, I hope?" she said with a wry little smile.

Rackway swallowed. "Er—no. I don't think it is unpleasant," he said. "Just a mere train journey and—and—I think I shall probably be closing the flat down for a little while."

Lorna reddened a little. "You aren't doing this on account of me, are you, Mr. Rackway?" she asked.

"No, no," said Rackway. "I assure you. Last night was a most regrettable affair—a ghastly mistake on my part. I beg you to forgive me. I regret it more than I can tell you. With your permission, Miss Rennie, we will not refer to the matter again."

Rackway, his shoulders sunk and his head averted, strove to appear interested in the quiet life of the square beyond the windows.

When he spoke again there was a note of forced nonchalance in his voice, an air of strained lightness that belied him.

"As a matter of fact," he said, "the whole business concerns my health, I've decided to take a little trip abroad. You already know I have reason—rather serious circumstances to cope with that were not of my seeking—and I think the simplest way out is to take the voyage which my doctor advised months ago."

"But—where are you going, sir?"

"This is strictly between ourselves, Miss Rennie; and if anyone should make inquiries of you, I must ask you to be as diplomatic as possible. Either give them an evasive answer or tell them deliberately that you don't know. Between ourselves, I'm making a run out to South America."

"But—sir! Am I to come with you?"

"Not unless you wish, Miss Rennie. As you know, I should be delighted to have you with me. You would travel strictly in your secretarial capacity; and I promise you that I will not thrust my company upon you any more than would be necessary to transact certain business which I must perforce take with me. I shall be using the wireless a good deal, and I shall have to engage a secretary, in any case. At least, I think so. If you would care to come I would be more than delighted—but, as I say, I won't press you either way. You must choose for yourself entirely."

Rackway's voice, halting and seemingly very unsure, trailed off into an unnatural silence. Lorna was mystified and just a little frightened. She felt she would have given anything for Rackway to have turned round and faced her just then.

But all she saw was the wooden stolidness of him as he stood there, immobile, in the flood light of the window. All she caught was the imperturbably quiet intonation of his voice, pitched in a low key that carried infinite respect and a great world of gentleness in its depths. With that sombre statue in front of her she could scarcely tell whether Rackway was in earnest or not. He seemed too detached from his own words to be fully appreciative of all they meant.

"But—but when are you going?" she asked impulsively—a sort of quick effort to bridge the disruptive little silence.

"Today. My arrangements are already made."

"Today?" Lorna gasped. "But, sir, you can't possibly go today, There are miles of business matters to be attended to—heaps of things that simply cannot be left—things that require your decisions A secretary couldn't possibly do them on her own initiative."

"That, unfortunately, cannot be helped. I am going today—this morning—now. The boat-train leaves in a couple of hours. I have booked two seats in it."

Lorna looked at him quickly.

"Two?" she queried.

"Yes. You will come with me as far as Southampton, at least. Bring notebooks with you. I shall have time to give you a great many instructions regarding the more urgent matters as we go down in the train. If you elect not to accompany me, you will bring those instructions back to town with you and proceed accordingly. Your salary will be provided for. I will address a letter to my bankers authorising them to credit you with the full amount of your salary monthly. That arrangement will continue. The rest of my affairs I leave in your charge entirely. You can dispose of them to the best of your ability. I depend on your own initiative in that matter. All I ask of you is to respect my confidence. If inquiries for me should be made direct to you, you will have no knowledge of my whereabouts. So far as you are concerned, I just went out of this house and disappeared. You understand?"

Lorna breathed out a stifled little "Yes."

He nodded off-handedly and turned towards her.

"Then perhaps you would like an hour to think it over?" he asked gently.

"How—how long do you expect to be away?" Lorna asked the question helplessly. She was in such a whirl of unrelated facts and incidents that she wasn't sure where she stood.

"I'm afraid I couldn't tell you," answered Rackway gravely. "Months, at least. Maybe years."

"Mr. Rackway! Surely you are not in earnest?"

Rackway smiled a tiny little smile that was terribly bitter. "I was never more in earnest in my life, little girl," he said quietly.

Lorna was nonplussed. Rackway, since Damon Grey's release from prison, had become such an amazingly changed being that she scarcely recognised him from the calm employer she had known. He seemed to have changed all in an hour—the hour that succeeded Damon Grey's first dramatic appearance in that room. He had become a creature of sudden inexplicable impulses, a man of panicky decisions and unuttered fears, so changed in his usual habits of life that she had lost all focus on him.

He smiled again, a trifle whimsically.

"Unless you wish to come in one morning and find me dead—from heart failure, of course—you must help me to get clear before my turn comes," he said.

"Goodness gracious me!" gasped Lorna. Rackway's face was so callously serious that she could not doubt the sincerity of his words. "Do you really mean that you are running away to avoid being murdered by Damon Grey?"

"To put it very briefly, yes. South America offers facilities that are not quite so—er—accessible elsewhere."

Rackway turned and peered out of the window again. The square was all bright and sunlit. Down in the gutter below him a couple of schoolboys played marbles together. Milk-carts were busy making their second round of calls; on the corner by Grosvenor Street a Punch and Judy show was getting more laughs from the grown-ups than from the half a dozen kiddies round it. The trees were all in the first young leaf, and there was an atmosphere of buoyancy, of joyous life, in the air.

But Rackway saw nothing of that. His mental vision was far away, right over the swimming miles of fragrant countryside and sunny woodland to the other end of the railroad, to the docks at the end of it, where the great *Ruahontas*, berthed at her pier, waited her sailing hour. He saw his own cabin there, saw her going into it, she all unused to the ways of the sea and the ships that sail upon it, saw him keeping her there under the pretext of taking down the last of his dictations, heard the "all ashore" bell clang through the ship, heard the gangways rumble over the side,felt the first mumbling beat of the great turbines pumping dimly through the soul of the liner.

He turned abruptly to her. "You will come with me—to Southampton?" he asked.

She nodded, her thoughts in a whirling tumult.

"Yes, I—I'll come with you," she said in a small whisper.

"Thank you." Rackway's voice cut back quick and short. He picked up his hat and stick. "I will call back in a car for you before midday. Good morning, Miss Rennie—thank you."

Lorna sat down again, and a queer little frown crinkled into her forehead.

"Lorna Rennie, my girl," she muttered between lips that were pursed up into lines of prim disapproval, "this is where you step gracefutty off the bus, phone for Dickie, and tell him all about it."

Ricks came round in a hurry. Lorna had him shown into her own room and, somewhat breathlessly, she gave him a rough outline of what had just happened.

"And I'm going to Southampton with him," she finished.

"What for?"

"To see him off on the boat."

"Are you?" said Ricks. "You—are—not!"

"Yes, I am, Dickie; now don't start being a silly jackass. It's purely a matter of business. There's arrears of work as long as my arm to be pulled up here, and I've got to go down on the train with him to get my instructions."

"If you are going down on that train, I am going with you," Ricks declared.

"Don't be so absurd. What earthly need is there for you to worry?"

"I don't like it, that's all. I don't like Rackway, and I don't like the rest of the crowd that comes here to talk alleged business with him. There's something fishy about the whole bunch of them."

Ricks was angry, out of temper, and in no frame of mind to bandy words with anyone. He was in the uncomfortable position of not being able to move for fear of dragging his sweetheart into the mire that must inevitably have followed on a showdown.

"Look here, Lorna," he said at last, "I don't want you to see that man Rackway any more. There's a bad patch in him somewhere. Put on your hat and go out for a long walk. Be missing when the boat-train leaves. I'll meet him and tell him you don't wish to accompany him."

"But I must, Dickie. I can't help myself. After all, he's my employer and he is entitled to some sort of return for his money. Goodness knows it's little enough I do for him as it is. An hour a day, sometimes—and he pays me treble wages."

"That's what makes it fishy," snorted Ricks. "The whole business of this place reeks of suspicion, and I hate you being mixed up in it."

"But, Dickie, you—"

"Look at what's happened here within the last forty-eight hours. A jail-bird comes back out of prison after God knows how many years spent in Dartmoor. There is a most terrible scene upstairs. Lindrum dies and no one on earth knows what he died of. Both the doctor whom Rackway called in and the police doctor at the mortuary last night certified heart failure.

That's preposterous, and I know it. Rackway knows it, too. Damon Grey *swore* he'd kill Lindrum. He told me so himself out in the gardens there. And that's not all. Stephen Leeds was killed last night!"

"Dickie!" Lorna's voice was a compound of shock and unbelief.

"It's true enough. Leeds is dead. And he died in exactly the same way that Lindrum died—apparent heart failure."

"But where did this happen?"

"At the Grand Imperial—Grey's own hotel. Stephen Leeds just crumpled up and died, and there isn't a sign or a mark to show what caused it. There wasn't a thing wrong with him—except that his heart stopped beating. That's two deaths in a single night."

"But, Dickie. It's all a ghastly mistake."

"It's no mistake," Ricks flared back. "I was at the Grand Imperial myself last night, and I know."

"You were?"

"Yes. I went there and booked a room for the night. Played billiards until after midnight just as an excuse for not turning in. Grayne was there, too. So was that American chap, Kann. They don't know me. But I knew them all right. Grayne and Kann were missing after midnight. The last I saw of Leeds alive was playing cards. I looked into the card-room and saw him there."

"Who was he playing with, Dick?"

"Some old chap with a fearful squint. That was all I could see. A squint and white side-whiskers. But if that old blighter wasn't Damon Grey, I'll cat my hat!"

Lorna looked at him, stunned.

"Dick, I can't believe it," she whispered.

"Maybe not. You will, though. That man Grey is a devil. He nearly got me in that Grosvenor Street hotel."

Lorna was too frightened to speak.

"That's why you won't go down in that train to Southampton," he went on doggedly. "That's why you'll never see Rackway again."

He strode towards the door.

"Dick, what are you going to do?" gasped Lorna.

"Do? I'm going for the police. What else can I do? I'm going to tell them the whole story." He groped under the chair for his hat.

"But, Dick, you mustn't—not yet. You're betraying my own confidence. Think of Mr. Rackway. You *must* give him time to get away first."

"Rackway! I don't care a blind bat for Rackway. All I care about is *you*! And you take my advice: put on your hat and go out. When Rackway calls for you, you'll be missing."

Ricks went out, slamming the door behind him. He banged his hat on his head and went down the stairs with an air of purposefulness in every stride.

And a few minutes after he had gone, while Lorna still sat on in a maze of doubt and indecision, Rackway's car drove up to the door and the hall bell rang.

Lorna was left dangling in mid-air. Rackway's step sounded on stair. She heard him go into the library.

He sent for her and asked her point blank if she was ready to start.

And almost before she knew it Lorna had breathed out an unhappy little "Yes."

After that the descent was rapidly simple. She was almost surprised to find herself saying:"I won't be—be two minutes, Mr. Rack way."

There was not a great crowd at Waterloo, and train accommodation was ample. Rackway had booked corner seats, and he flared up into a violent temper when he found his seats were allocated in a corridor carriage. The guard pointed out that there were no single compartments on the train—it was a boat-train special and was made up of corridor coaches throughout.

Lorna looked at him as he snapped and fumed. Nerves—nerves; he was eating them. She was shocked at the evidences of change that had so swiftly overtaken him. He, who was always so suave, so moderate and cool-headed, was as irascible as a gouty old misogynist over something that simply could not be helped.

The train had been under way nearly half an hour before Lorna had the temerity to mention the work in hand—sheaves of it in her portfolio.

He grunted that dictation was impossible on the vibrating train and that he would do it all on board.

He scrutinised his fellow-passengers under lowering brows, going over them feature by feature with covert intensity, and he positively jumped when anyone passed along the narrow corridor.

Lorna, sitting there immobile, seemed to exasperate him. Southampton and the *Ruahontas* were still a long way away. The safety he could only find when those great propellers began to swing was still a whole country away. And his irritability increased as the minutes sped.

Once, when the signals went against the train, and the brakes brought it grinding and jarring to a standstill, he sat back and bit his fingernails till they were all broken and bleeding.

"I—I'll go and see about some lunch," he blurted out at last, and jumped to his feet. Inaction, at that time of crisis, was having the same effect on him as the aftermath of drugs. His nerves twitched for an opiate that would remain inaccessible until the last mooring ropes had splashed into the water.

Lorna said: "Very well, sir; I'll wait for you," and put away her impedimenta in an attaché-case.

Rackway went for a walk up and down the corridor. He was even more nervous, more horribly apprehensive doing that than he was sitting down but he felt he had to do something or go mad.

And it was when he got to the top end of the long corridor the third time, and was turning round to come back, that a quiet voice said in his ear: "Good afternoon, Rackway. Not turning bird of passage already, are you?"

Rackway jerked back as though an electric shock had shot through him. At the same moment the train bumped solidly against the points and pitched him hard against the side. His hand went out in a wild grab the brass rail running along the inside of the window, and gripped on to it till the knuckle-tips shone white.

For a moment his brain ceased functioning. He couldn't think. He dared not. His eyes were wide open, but he could not see. He was only half conscious of being in a train at all. He wanted to turn tail and run like a hare.

"Not feeling well?" The solicitous voice came to him as though from a distance that was bounded not so much by space as by time.

He shrank farther back and tried to get a grip on himself. He found himself staring at the mesmeric features of Damon Grey, a face so delectably cool and untroubled that it might have belonged to some benevolent old clergyman. The grey-white brush of hair at the temples added to the look of gentle benignity that sat so oddly upon his resolute shoulders. He stood with his hands thrust deep into his trousers pockets, swaying slightly from the hips to the rocking of the train, and surveyed him with a look that came very near quizzical good-humour.

The change in Grey's attitude was a shock to Rackway. It was so obvious, in a horrible way. The steel-grey eyes were almost kind. They looked at him softly, almost, it seemed, with a hint of friendly affection in them. Rackway blinked and peered at him. It was almost like jazz music springing unheralded from the lips of a cathedral choir in the hush of a twilit dusk.

Grey put his arm under Rackway's.

"Come along down to the restaurant car," he said. "I can talk to you there. We can't talk here—you're too conspicuous. Your nerves must be in a fearful state, Hildon."

He steered him down through the swaying carriages.

Rackway stumbled at his side, helpless as a chloroformed patient being wheeled into an operating theatre. He was aware of firm fingers gripping masterfully on his forearm, and he took his volition from them. He was conscious of nothing save that cold, immense will that had, at the first moment of contact, engulfed and superseded his own.

Grey piloted him to a table, a small one for two, at the far end of the restaurant car away from the galley. He sat down and folded his arms on the table.

"Rackway," he said smoothly, "why this sudden journey?"

The hunted man said nothing. He shut his mouth like a trap and stared back at the hunter.

"Frightened?" A shade of disappointment crept into the voice.

Rackway hung on to his silence and interlocked his fingers tightly under the table. Whatever else might happen in that restaurant car, he was deadly determined that his hands should alight on nothing that might previously have been tampered with by Grey.

Damon Grey made a slight gesture of his hand.

"Rackway," he said softly, "you have nothing to fear from me."

Rackway looked up quickly, a sudden gleam of deeper suspicion in his eyes.

"What—what do you mean?" he growled.

"Exactly what I say. My dear man, I wouldn't kill you for all the wealth of the Indies."

A thundercloud settled on Rackway's brows.

"What game are you up to now?" he demanded.

Grey waved the question aside with gentle tolerance. "I assure you there is not the slightest need for you to run away," he said.

"I'm not running away!" Rackway snarled back at him fiercely. "Not from *you*, anyway. I want to get out of England. If I stayed in London I should kill you." Rackway's tones were savage, temper-ridden; his whole brain was breaking out into hot rebellion.

"Remarkable!"

"Is it?" retorted Rackway viciously. "The only reason I don't kill you now is that you are not worth the hell of a murder trial and the horror of the rope."

"Well, they would certainly follow," agreed Grey. "You probably know that Leeds has gone? I played cards with him last night."

"Go to the devil!" flared Rackway.

"That we are all bound that way, I haven't the slightest doubt," assented Grey.

Rackway stared sullenly out of the window.

Grey sighed to think that his friendly overtures should meet with such sour response.

He pushed over the wine list.

"We can't sit here ordering nothing. Won't you have a wine with me?" he asked.

Rackway's eyes went down to the purple leather card just under his nose. His locked fingers crushed into each other under the table, and there was a high red flush-spot on each cheek.

"I—I wouldn't touch that for—for a million pounds," he said thickly.

"You wouldn't? Very silly of you. And as I'm not likely to offer you a million pounds, very ungenerous also." Grey himself picked up the wine list and called the steward.

"A bottle of this," he ordered, indicating an item.

"That is a champagne, sir."

"Quite. Bring it."

Suddenly Grey leaned across the table, and Rackway shrank back as though he had been dealt a blow between the eyes.

"You are trembling for your own precious skin," hissed Grey, his eyes suddenly alight and aflame with passion. "And you needn't. It isn't you I'm after. I wouldn't hurt a hair of your head. I'm going to get you precisely as you got me. Go back. Go back to London and think it well out. Think what my life is today. Broken, robbed of all that makes life worth the labour of living, with all my dream castles tumbled about my ears, choking me in their own dust. Think it out. And think of all *you* had hoped to find in this world. Rackway, you are going to as I'm living now."

Rackway's jaw slowly sank. A ghastly suspicion had gone crawling across his brain, a thought so terrible and horrible that he tried to brush it away with his hands. His fingers unlocked, bone-white and dented with pressure. He touched them nervously across his forehead. They fell helplessly into his lap, and he gazed at Grey through unbelieving eye.

"What—what do you mean?" he gasped.

And Grey smiled. It was the wickedest, viciousest thing Rackway had ever seen in his life. It was bankrupt of humour, void of all intention of a smile; just a brutish grimace of stark animosity.

"I'll tell you what I mean," Grey said. "I mean that I'm going to give you a taste of what you're making me eat and drink and breathe every minute of my life. Do you think I can't see how things stand with you and that little secretary of yours? I saw—and understood—before I had been five minutes in your flat."

He broke off sharply. The old wintry look came hovering back over his face, and he asked:"Might I ask what Lorna Rennie is doing here on the train with you?"

"She—she is taking down a few instructions before I go," said Rackway mumblingly.

Grey sat back and glowered at him.

"May and December again, you old fool," he said. "Still, every man to his own madness. I'm not cavilling. So much the better; the barb goes deeper. Those others were easy—Lindrum and Leeds. Death was their biggest terror. They had a horror of it. My vengeance on them was complete and full when I killed them. You are different. Her death would hurt you so much more; and its memory would live with you forever. That is why I shall kill Lorna Rennie instead of you. You are going to live through all the miseries that are mine today. The ghosts of the past and the secret, bitter sorrows of the might-have-been shall be yours as they are mine today."

"Champagne, sir?" The steward bustled in with a great magnum.

"Yes, please; put it down there."

"Have a little?" he asked. Rackway shut his jaws tight and pressed back farther against the cushions.

Grey poured himself out a glass and sipped it.

"Here's to your soul when you first gaze on the dead face of Lorna Rennie," he said.

Rackway did not speak. He just sat and stared, glassy-eyed, at the man across the table. He felt a chill clamminess wrapping him about, as though every vestige of heat had drained out of the air.

Grey finished his champagne slowly. Rack way watched him, dazed. He saw him rise, toss a couple of notes on the table for the wine, and stroll off quietly towards his own carriage. He couldn't move; his muscles were fixed.

It was not until he had gone, gone with all the tyrannical aura of omnipotence that seemed to envelop him, that Rackway began to crawl back from his stupor. And the horror of his position welled up around him with all the inescapable torment of a nightmare.

Rackway, for all he was, for all he could never hope to be, rose up to a courage that was greater than he knew. The resolve went searing along bis brain. "That sweet child mustn't die—better by far the hangman's rope for me. Grey, you brute, when this train slides into Southampton Dock there will be a corpse on board, a corpse with a bullet in its heart. And they—they can have their way with me."

He felt back to his hip pocket, to the grim bulge of an automatic that rested there, charged with a death as swift and as sure as any evolved in the brain of Damon Grey.

Rackway lay back and began thinking things down to the finest points. There would have to be no bungling. Grey would have to be caught on the hop; for one second he would gaze into the single malignant eye of death—and after that would come the great oblivion. In that second he would taste the acids he had forced into other men's brains.

He would make ferociously sure, too; he would pump the whole cylinder into his brute body, if necessary, and if bullets failed to stop him, he would claw the windpipe out of him—anything so long as the shadow of honor was banished forever from the life of Lorna Rennie.

He sat back and poured himself out a full glass of champagne. Then another; and another. He signed to the steward. "Bring me a double brandy—no soda," he said, and drained off a fourth glass of champagne a draught.

"Nothing like a spot of Dutch courage," he muttered thickly.

The brandy was brought and he drank it neat. It brought a sudden swim of hot tears to his eyes, but in five minutes he noted its real effect. An absolute "still" settled over him, like the calm over a vast sweep of country before the storm breaks. It left him naked to his own intentions, a man with only one single resolve in his soul, and the definite ability to carry it into effect.

He held out his hand at arm's length straight in front of him. It did not quiver. He held a paper in it, and the paper did not even tremble. There was a tiny smile at the corners of his mouth. He knew those signs—the first symptoms of semi-alcoholism. That marvellous "still," that dependable calm, would probably last for ten minutes or a quarter hour.

He glanced at his watch. In ten minutes, he assured himself there would be a dead body in a compartment at the rear end of the train, probably two. He hoped there would be two. A bullet would be better than a knotted rope, whichever way you looked at it. It wasn't the rope so much or the standing on the drop, or the waiting for the bolt to fly—it wasn't that so much as the fearful business which would precede all that—the fearful business of the dock, and the ghoulish gentlemen in white wigs and black gowns who would argue and fight and fume over his case like's flock of vultures, whether he pleaded guilty or not.

He slid his gun under cover of the wine list and broke it open. Six gleaming little cartridge heads winked at him from the cylinder base. His snapped it shut and his hand, gripping the gun, stole into the side pocket of his coat. It made a bulge there, and he kept his hand on it, rose from the table, and walked steadily down through the corridors.

X

Lorna pulled out a book. She tried to fix her attention on it, jolting of the train continually blurred the print and her own unquiet thoughts kept trickling between her mind and the printed pages.

A shadow fell across the page. It grew darker.

She glanced up.

"Dickie," she breathed and jumped up. The book fell with a bump.

"Oh, Dick, I'm so glad you're here," she whispered. "There's going to be dreadful trouble. I have just seen Damon Grey on the train."

Ricks squeezed her arm.

"Don't worry," he said soothingly. "Stay up at this end of the train and you'll be out of harm's way. Sorry I couldn't find you before. Had a most unholy scramble for the train at Waterloo. Just managed to claw into a third as the train pushed off. Had a fierce morning trying to ram my sanity down the necks of a lot of uniforms. Not sure that I succeeded either."

Lorna's anxiety changed to sudden fright.

"Why, Dickie, what have you done now?" she asked quickly.

"Done?" he said bluntly. "I've spilled the beans. I've had Scotland Yard tuned in on me while I sang 'em the whole song, choruses and extra verses all complete."

"Dick! You haven't!"

"Haven't I? It took me two hours to convince them that I wasn't a pop-eyed lunatic. I got 'em in the end, though. Scored a couple of bulls with Leeds and Lindrurn and rang the changes on Grey's record. That drew 'em—unbelieving crowd of blighters."

"And what happened?"

"They wired Southampton. Detectives are meeting the train in. Damon Grey will be arrested the moment we draw in to the landing-stage."

Lorna's face went ashy white. That meant the entry of the Law with all its concomitants of publicity, embarrassments, and utter humiliations. It was inevitable, right from the first—but—

She shuddered.

"Simply couldn't help myself," defended Ricks. "Absolutely nothing else for it. Think it out for yourself and you'll see what I mean. The balloon was bound to go up, sooner or later. And we should have been in it! Right in it."

She sat down beside him, trembling a little.

"But, Dick, it's—it's horrible," she said.

"Bad luck, I know. But there 'tis; it's done now and can't be helped. If I 'd stalled off any longer we'd both have been in the dock with Grey." He stood up and peered up and down the corridor. "You stay on here," he warned. "I'm going down to see what's doing. I'll be back as soon as I can."

Before her restraining hand could get out to stop him, Ricks, full of the foolish, forthright courage of youth, completely unaware of the grand metamorphosis that had taken place in the heart of the hunted man, moved off to find Rackway or Grey—or both.

He went along cautiously through the swaying carriages, keeping step with that other drama that was roaring along side by side with the hurtling train.

The restaurant cars were fairly full, and he passed through them slowly. But neither Grey nor Rackway was in either of them. And it was not until he got to the far end of the train that he ran them to earth. It was in the little bay where the connecting doors open into the next carriage, a deserted little dead-end where no one ever intruded, for the connecting doors there were never opened, the carriages behind being merely baggage wagons.

They were already together, facing each other like two animals in the wild. Grey had his back to the side of the train, cool, steady, and amazingly controlled. Rackway was in front of him holding him penned in the bay with a drawn gun. His back was to Ricks, and he was crouching. Every line of him was tense, rabid, the very cock of his head was a loud yelled warning of tragedy rushing up to the break.

Ricks went forward, step by step, along the rocking corridor. It seemed that Rackway had just cornered his man. Grey had turned to find a Colt pointing in a rigid, nerveless line on his heart, and the eyes of a stone-cold fanatic glaring behind it.

No word was spoken; just for a couple of livid seconds the two men eyed each other, with death trembling between them on a hair-spring.

Then Grey's indifferent eyes flicked up to see Ricks's swaying figure looming a couple of yards behind Rackway's back.

"Pleased to see you, Ricks," he said distinctly. He seized marvellous chance the second it appeared. "You've arrived at an awkward moment again."

Rackway's head switched round, caught on the hop.

And Damon Grey leapt.

Hildon Rackway hadn't even time to be surprised. He saw Ricks for the hundredth part of a second as he turned his head, saw him lean forward and make a flying grab. In the same moment he heard the tiny scuff of Grey's feet on the floor as he sprang. He made a wild effort to level his gun again and fire. But he was overwhelmed, sandwiched between two assaulting bodies that collided with him simultaneously.

An arm as supple as a young conger eel slipped under his chin from behind and jerked his head backward. There was a sharp click as the fingers of Ricks's right hand connected on his wrist, and before he knew it his gun hand was wrenched downward and backward.

Grey's forward leap took him clear to the throat. A hand, brown and hard, clamped down over his mouth and fastened there solid. The gun went spinning from Rackway's fingers.

Then the train lurched heavily; Ricks sprang clear as the two men crashed to the floor.

Rackway fought like an animal, clawing and tearing with the wild ferocity of a mountain cat. The brandy fumes had got into his head. They were no longer a steadying influence, a drug to the nerves, they had progressed on and beyond that. They had become a goad, a red-hight incentive to fight and keep on fighting till every hope of victory had and every nerve and sinew was exhausted.

For two minutes they fought on the floor like maniacs.

Then Damon Grey twisted the other man completely over with an effort of sheer muscular strength that seemed impossible in one already touched with the fingers of age.

For a minute he held him there, flat on his face, helpless, immobile. Ricks picked up the gun and examined it. A Colt Six, loaded tight.

"Seem to have got here on time, too," he said, eyeing Grey.

The taciturn face nodded gravely.

"Looks as though he screwed all his courage up into one tiny little nickel bullet," he said.

Rackway, underneath, was foaming at the mouth. In between bursts of animal writhings he howled his frenzied hatred at Grey. Amid the profanity and general welter of words, Ricks heard sufficient to piece together the bald truths of the matter. At least, he got Rackway's end of it to the last letter.

Grey was unmoved. Motionless, he held his man down and waited for the storm to subside. He answered Rackway's slavering accusations with a sour wisp of a smile.

"Well, what are you going to do with him?" asked Ricks pointedly.

"Let him up, when he realises what a fool he is making of himself," replied Grey patiently.

"And what about me?" demanded Ricks.

"You? You don't count."

Ricks clicked his teeth. "You think not?" he said. "We shall be running into Southampton in a couple of minutes—maybe you'll readjust your opinion when you get there."

Grey looked up at him.

"Still too pig-headed to take a warning?" he asked.

"Much. One of the cardinal faults of youth, I understand."

Grey smiled frostily. "I like your nerve, my lad," he said.

"You admired it once before. You'll appreciate it still more when the train stops."

With a devastating contempt for the prone man, Grey rose to his feet. The train was slowing down, plunging into a veritable sea of red brick and grey slate that suddenly closed down about the metals.

Grey gave a quick glance out of the window. The old wicked glitter of ineradicable animosity was back on the face. A plumb-line intuition had given him the warning. To him it stuck out like a single porcupine quill—sheer out of the ominous phrase "when the train stops."

"I think I'll be getting along to my own compartment," he said.

"You won't!"

Grey's hand tightened imperceptibly on the window rail.

"Oh? And why not?" he asked gently.

Ricks twiddled the gun in his fingers.

"Because you'll stay right here and admire the scenery," he said. "*And* I'll trouble you to keep your distance."

"Frightened?"

"Not quite. But I'm not giving you a chance of unloading a cargo of heart failure on me. That's all. Keep your distance and wait for what's coming."

Rackway, sullen, wiping the floor dirt from his lips, was climbing slowly to his feet.

"Give me that gun, boy," he said thickly. "I'll square all this business up in two quick shots."

Grey's teeth showed in a wicked suspicion of a smile, "So you risked the champagne after all!" he tittered.

"Give me that gun."

"Sure," said Ricks, and tossed it over.

Grey turned his back on him and regarded the clutter of drab backyards sliding by. "Just below the left shoulder-blade—and a little to the left," he said.

Rackway made a horrible animal noise in his throat as he pulled the trigger—pulled it and kept on pulling it.

Ricks jingled the bullets in his trouser pocket.

"Rackway, you'd better sober up," he said. Here's the landing-stage just ahead—and there's trouble waiting on the platform. Go away. Go away and look after Miss Rennie, or you'll find yourself in a hell of a hole."

The train was bumping slowly over a maze of points and crossings. The first grind of the brakes grated noisily. Rackway, in that overwhelming second, realised what Ricks had done. Without a word, he dropped the revolver and almost ran back up the corridor.

Ricks picked up the gun and deliberately loaded it.

"Is that meant for me?" asked Grey.

Ricks nodded.

"You're threatening me?"

"You bet your sweet life. But not with this." He twiddled the gun again, and thrust it into his pocket.

"I should think not indeed," said Grey. "You'd have the shock of your life, youngster."

"Don't worry. The shock of yours is just coming to you."

Grey was looking at him out of half-closed eyes. "You've been to the police, haven't you?" he asked.

"I have. Plain clothes men waiting for you on the beach."

The tiniest suspicion of a shiver ran over Grey's face. It was gone in an instant. Except for a little higher quality of doggedness in his attitude, a keener look of sheer indomitableness in his eyes, the ultimatum left him unmoved.

He leaned against the carriage window watching the approaching forest of topmasts and spars that eternally hallmark Southampton's trade. He seemed to be considering the new bombshell in a speculative way. Lean fingers pulled thoughtfully at the stubborn chin. He even attained to an air of contemplative detachment. In some odd way it had the quality of making him valiant above ordinarily valiant standards.

It was the most amazing disguise he had yet produced.

He was silent for many seconds. Then, after a little while, he murmured: "I think you are very silly."

There was no more in his voice than that. Just the gently deprecating opinion his statement implied. But it was a sentence that was drawn from the very roots of his soul.

Damon Grey had boarded that train unarmed. His marvelous poison, his one dependable safeguard in any contingency, was in Load. Bluff was enough for Rackway. But the police would want something more than bluff to make them kick in. Ricks, of course, should have been eliminated when he first showed up.

His brain was working at lightning speed, sizzling along line after line of chance and deductive argument.

And every line, every possible twist of logic, came back unerringly to the dried-up little Hindu in the Berwick Market.

The platforms swam alongside the train. Brakes gripped harshly on the wheels and the train came down to a slow crawl and then, with a fuel grunt, to a standstill.

"Southampton!" said Ricks. "And you won't need your return ticket!"

"And that," said Grey, nodding off-handedly towards the barrier, "is the detective?"

"That's him right enough," assented Ricks. "Come on—shall we go out to him or shall I call him over?"

"Oh, we will go over by all means," said Grey. "It is not seemly that the mountain should go to Mahomet."

Doors were opening and slamming all down the length of the train. The arrival of a boat-train causes a minor eruption of activity on a landing, stage, and the *Ruahontas* was sailing with a fairly big crowd. Amid the bustle and confusion of shouting porters and luggage-hunting passengers, the two men stepped out.

Grey sauntered across to the barrier without even a backward glance at the man who had kicked his plans sky-high.

"Good afternoon, officer—you are looking for me?" he said.

The detective wheeled and scrutinised him swiftly.

"Name of Damon Grey?" he snapped.

"Yes. My card."

"I hold a warrant for your arrest on suspicion of having been connected with the murder of either John Lindrurn or Stephen Leeds, or both. I have a cab outside. You'll come along to the station with me. If you've anything to say I must warn you that it may be used as evidence against you. Understand?"

"Oh, quite. I have nothing to say. This is neither the place nor the time for it."

"Wise man." The detective turned to Ricks. "I shall require a statement from you, too, sir. Can you step along now?"

"Certainly," said Ricks. The detective nodded and piloted Grey out through the Customs to the waiting cab.

XI

Two detectives were hurrying down from London. They were travelling by fast car, and were bringing a third party with them—a witness who, most nights in the week, worked the lifts at the Grand Imperial.

Grey had been put straight into a cell, and since then had neither complained nor asked favours. He caused a little mild excitement and a whole lot of curiosity when he arrived, for a great many luridly descriptive rumours had reached the station with regard to Grey's activities in London. But the exact story was still very much in the air. A jailer was detailed to keep constant watch on him, while Ricks made out a formal but concise statement for the benefit of the chief inspector and the charge-sergeant.

Ricks outlined the case to the best of his ability, and as his tale lengthened so the scepticism of the inspector increased. Towards the end he was frankly incredulous.

"Candidly, Mr. Ricks," he said, "it sounds too good to be true."

"I merely tell you what I know to be the facts," said Ricks.

The inspector ran his fingers through his hair.

"But there isn't any such poison in the world," he protested. "According to the authorities here, there is no such drug known."

"The secret of it may not be generally known today, but from inquiries I have made in the London museum libraries, I find that such a poison was used in ancient Italy. Cesare Borgia used it for one or two of his more spectacular murders. He put it in the fingers of gloves intended as gifts to political back-numbers. How Grey came to get hold of it I can't say. All I know is that he *has* got it, and that he killed Leeds and Lindrurn with it."

"But how does he use it?"

"Can't say. But you get it just when you think you've missed it. I believe he carries it about with him in a glass bottle in his inside coat pocket. There is an air-spray apparatus inside it. The nozzle, a little thing probably no bigger than a pin's head, projects through the cloth of his coat, and by squeezing the bulb he can spray the stuff out at will. I tell you, inspector it isn't safe to touch anything where Damon Grey has been."

"Phew!" said the inspector, and made a lot of notes on a pad.

"Well," he said," I'm afraid we can't do much more here till the men arrive from Scotland Yard. I'm expecting them at any minute now. They will take full charge of the case. That is, of course, if they decide that there is a case to take charge of."

"You're still sceptical?" said Ricks.

"Well, it is a bit of an amazing tale, isn't it? Do you know who this Damon Grey happens to be?"

"Yes, a released convict."

"That's right. He has only been out of Dartmoor three days. If all you say is true, he hasn't wasted much time, has he?"

Drake, the plain-clothes man who had brought Grey up from the railway station, came in with his own written report.

"Want this?" he queried, "It's only formal; but you might want to glance through it."

The inspector took it and ran a half-interested eye over it.

"Hasn't been searched yet, has he? " he asked.

"I don't think so, inspector."

"Better get it done, then. Fetch him out and I'll take an inventory of all he's got. Feeling ill?"

That last interjection was jerked out suddenly, for Drake had swayed at the knees and gone as white as a sheet. Ricks jumped over to him and the inspector clambered off his high stool.

"What's the matter, Drake, old man?" he asked hurriedly.

The plain-clothes man put his hand up to his heart and clutched at it wildly. His eyes took on an awful glassy look, and he pitched across a table, knocking it over with a crash as he fell.

The inspector was into action in a moment. First-aid eddies were at hand in the charge-room, and he applied them with deft and speedy skill. The police doctor was on the scene within five minutes, and he pursed his lips as soon as he saw the figure stretched on the floor.

In a few moments he had made his examination, and when he stood up he looked keenly at the inspector.

"He's had a shock, hasn't he?" he asked. "What happened?"

"Nothing, so far as I know, sir. Serious, is it?" The inspector's voice was very sober.

"He's dead," said the doctor.

"Good God!

The appalling suddenness of it held him transfixed.

"But—but he was alive and well—talking—only a few minutes ago," he stammered.

"Heart failure," said the doctor gravely. "Odd, too. I never suspected Drake of that. Still, there you are—that's how things happen. Heart disease shows up suddenly in the man you least suspect. Married man, isn't he?"

The inspector nodded dumbly—unable to speak.

"Poor little woman." The doctor looked round at Ricks.

"What was he doing?" he asked.

"He just brought in a prisoner from the boat-train. A man arrested on a double-murder charge: man named Damon Grey. He has already killed two men—just like that!"

Ricks was shocked, angered.

"Just like what?" said the doctor, his eyebrows going up in puzzled surprise.

"Just like that. Poisoned them with a concoction of his own that leaves no trace except heart failure."

He turned savagely to the police inspector.

"Lindrum died like that," he flared up. "Pitched over all in a heap and was dead before anyone could get to him. Stephen Leeds went in just the same way. They found him collapsed over a card-table in Grey's own hotel. Perhaps you'll believe me now."

The inspector motioned him to silence with a gesture of his hand.

"If Grey did this it looks as though he's still got that poison on him," he said.

"Not a doubt of it. I wonder you didn't search him when he first came in."

"There's a telegraphic order against it from headquarters." He motioned to two awed and silent constables to carry the body of their dead colleague into a more private room. "And better send for Mrs. Drake," added the doctor.

"I'll search Grey myself," said the inspector grimly.

He called an order for Grey to be brought in. "I'd like you to be present, too, sir, if you don't mind," he said, turning to the doctor. "Looks as though there's more in this than meets the eye."

"Certainly I'll stay," said the doctor. "But I'm not subscribing to any poison theories. I know cardiac trouble when I see it. I'll hold another examination presently, but—Drake died from a faulty ticker."

Footsteps sounded outside in the cell corridor.

Grey came in, ushered by the gaoler.

The doctor studied him keenly. Certainly that wasn't the face of a murderer. The atmosphere of calmness, of quiet repose, that hung about him, deep as a woodland pool, was altogether too authentic. There was nothing melodramatic about him, not a spark of vindictiveness, or anything approaching malignity. He was just a very self-composed, exceptionally well-preserved man of gentlemanly appearance, and with a memorable cast of features. It was obvious that all this unpleasant business with the police was utterly distasteful to him. And those eyes, too— The doctor shut his thoughts off with a snap.

The inspector was speaking again, speaking with a cold-bloodedness that seemed positively brutal, if it wasn't for the fact that he was trying to catch Grey off his guard.

"Damon Grey," he said, "Mr. Drake is dead!"

"Is he?" said Grey gravely. "And who is Mr. Drake?"

"Mr. Drake is the detective who brought you here!"

Grey stepped back. For once that monumental poise was shaken. Unsuspecting as he was, the awfulness of it struck him with the same horrific force as it did the others. The thing had gone home to him. It was intimate to him, personal to him.

"Drake? Dead?" he muttered unsteadily. "How? When? What happened?"

The doctor's thoughts snapped on again. That man guilty? Absurd! The actor didn't live who could have bluffed that part. Grey was genuinely staggered by the news. Whatever else he had done he had had no part in the sudden end of Detective Drake.

"What happened?" repeated the inspector. "That's what I'm asking *you!*"

Grey looked at him with a puzzled frown.

"Asking me? Why?" Grey's perceptions were not working with their old facility. The news had dulled them.

"You know the charges against you?"

"Y-yes—certainly."

"Well, you can think, can't you?"

"But—but it's preposterous!" protested Grey. "You're charging me with the murder of Mr. Drake?"

"I'll tell you that after the inquest. We'll see what the coroner's dozen has to say about it. Meanwhile—I'm going to search you!"

The inspector watched him narrowly as he barked out his last sentence.

But for all the effect the intimation had on Grey, the inspector might just as well have asked him to sign his name in his autograph-album; He did not even look surprised.

"I'm afraid you won't find anything very exciting on me," he said.

The inspector surveyed the accused man sourly. There was not actual fear in his soul, but only a violent antipathy, plus a strong distaste to being murdered for doing no more than his duty.

"Got any firearms on you?" he jerked gruffly.

"Oh, no! I never use them. I know several people who do, though—Grey's eyes flickered across to Dickie Ricks—"personally, I consider them much too dangerous." He smiled. "And quite unnecessary," he added.

The inspector rubbed his nose.

"Well, turn out your own pockets," he ordered.

"Certainly," said Grey. "You'll find it a third rate collection, I fear."

He began, idly enough, turning out his possessions, laying each article carefully on the inspector's table. They made, as he said, quite an ordinary array.

A handkerchief, a fountain-pen, a patent pencil, a pair of nail-scissors in a small leather case, a handful of loose change, a little gold watch-charm, a return ticket to Waterloo, a wallet containing several hundred pounds in notes, a cigar-case, a box of matches, a gold watch on a silk fob, a nail-file, three small keys on a tiny ring, a letter from his solicitor, a gold cigar-cutter, a slip of paper with some notes of train times, a spare handkerchief neatly folded, a toothpick, and then, after a final fumble, a small leather card-case.

"Is that all?" demanded the inspector.

"Yes, that's all—at least, that's all that would interest you."

"That so?" The rejoinder was doubly hostile. For Grey hadn't so much as put a hand anywhere near that inside pocket.

"All that would interest me, eh? And what's in that inside pocket?"

"Which one—this?" Grey's hand dived into his left.

"No, confound you—that other one—that one you haven't put your hand in yet."

"Oh, this?" Grey opened his coat and fingered the top rim of his right-hand pocket.

"Yes, that. What have you got in there?"

"Nothing. Nothing, as I say, that would interest you."

"Turn it out!"

The long, tanned fingers slipped obediently in and came out again with something held in the palm.

The inspector drew in a long, slow breath.

"Ah-h! And what might that be?" he snarled.

Grey laid it almost reverently on the table with the rest.

The inspector craned his head forward and looked at it.

It was a small square case, about three inches square by half an inch deep, a beautiful thing. It was made of dull yellow metal, tooled out and chased with exquisite workmanship.

"Gold!" muttered the doctor under his breath.

"What is it?" snapped the inspector.

Grey repeated his last assertion. "Nothing that concerns you!" he growled. And there were crackling fires of menace in his voice, so pregnant with bottled-up hate that the inspector started back as though Grey had struck him.

"Well, what is it, anyway!" he demanded, eyeing the box and Grey alternately. "Open it!"

"You have hands of your own, surely? Pick it up. Open it yourself. It won't hurt you. Only—" a sudden blaze of light leapt to his eyes—"if you value your ability to keep on breathing—handle it gently!"

The inspector's hands were behind his back, and so far as he was concerned he intended to keep them there. There was a dead body outside in the ante-room to serve as an unholy reminder of Grey's possibilities.

The doctor, highly nervous, but undeniably interested, looked at the other three. He was still an unbeliever. He based his creed on his knowledge of the British Pharmacopoeia. And to the very best of his very wide knowledge there was no such element extant that could kill in the way the charge against Grey suggested. Doctors are scientists, and scientists demand the proofs of test and experiment before they relax one shred of their own proved opinions. His curiosity got the better of his own slight aversions.

"May I open it?" he queried.

"No; let him do it himself," cut in the inspector. "One coroner's inquest is quite enough for one day."

A ghost of a smile, frigid and contemptuous, flitted into Grey's eyes for a second, and as quickly vanished.

He put out his hand, picked up the little box, and pressed a spring. The thin box clicked open like the two halves of a locket. Reverently he laid it back again on the inspector's table.

The doctor gasped.

From the opened jewel two little pictures looked up, one from each half of the case. They were miniatures, painted in natural colours with miraculous skill. It was almost as though real human features, femininely lovely and laughingly delightful, had been caught alive and perpetuated in tiny miniature there in that little book of gold. The two pictures were of the same face, fair hair all a cluster, round ears that were shell pink and dainty, blue eyes as roguish as any that ever peeped out from under elfin eyebrows. And they laughed out of a bower of diamonds and rubies and emeralds. The whole interior of that little golden box was a nest of precious stones that winked and glittered in a myriad flash-points of coloured fire. The exquisite little paintings were nested in diamonds, dowered in rubies, a beautiful, wonderful resting-place for the memory of the tragic little soul who had long since sought her eternal rest in the peace and quiet of the grave.

All three of them looked up suddenly from the wondrous little thing. Grey was looking back at them. There was neither anger nor hate nor bitterness in his eyes. They were emotionless, sombre, almost, it seemed, the eyes of a man who had known so much compressed misery that they had burned out.

Without a word he picked up the precious thing again, closed it gently, and returned it to his pocket.

The doctor was studying Grey. He, of his higher sensitiveness, had read the story that Grey would never tell, though the rope coiled round his neck and he stared full-eyed into eternity. In all his experience he had never known another individual whose features could have so driven themselves into a dead neutrality as Grey's had done. And he vowed to himself again that that man—that marble-like man who sanctified his memories in a coffin of such utter loveliness that its cost must have drained a five-figure account bone dry—was no wanton killer of a helpless police officer carrying out his duty.

The inspector, looking and feeling more than a little sheepish, went over to Grey with a newfound courage. He felt he had let himself down badly over the searching of Grey. He owed it to himself, to his own personal and professional pride, to go through with the job according to police regulations. He knew that Grey still might have that deadly poison bottle secreted about his person somewhere, and that there was every change that he might put his hand into Grey's pockets and pull out a handful of sudden death.

But he went through with it. He turned out every pocket in Grey's clothing, and, except for a small key which had escaped Grey's own fingers in a waistcoat pocket, he drew a blank. His pockets were empty.

Grey was taken back to the cells to await the arrival of the detectives from Scotland Yard.

He bowed slightly to the doctor as he turned and left him, and then for an hour he sat on the hard bench in his cell reading the local afternoon paper which the jailer tossed to him before he slammed the door.

Outside in the charge-room, while the prisoner read quietly on, the inspector was making notes of the numbers of Grey's banknotes and entering them up in the property-book.

And then a motorcar, mud-spattered and panting, drew up at the door. Two men got out, nodded to the constable on duty, muttered the one word "Yard" to him as they passed, and hurried into the charge-room.

The inspector looked up to see a couple of keen, business-like looking men, on whose square shoulders sat the air of official authority. They looked competent, being, as they were, self-contained units of that mighty whole which regards the rest of mankind as something to be kept under continual observation.

"Afternoon. You the inspector?" asked one briefly, pushing all preliminaries off the earth.

"Yes. Rolleson my name. You're from the Yard?"

"Yes. Harper and Standy. I'm Standy—and in charge of the case. That is, if it *is* a case. Looks to me like a blow-fly, though. Evidence nowhere; cross-trails everywhere; nothing tangible anywhere. Whole thing seems to be up in the clouds. You had phone messages from headquarters about us?"

"Two." The inspector was just a little short in his answer. Drake's body was over there in the ante-room; and Drake was an old triend.

"Anything to report?"

The inspector fingered Damon Grey's cigar-case.

"Grey was arrested within two minutes of the boat-train pulling into the landing-stage," he said.

"You've still got him?"

"He's in the cells now."

"Good work. Who arrested him?"

"The late Detective Drake."

Standy shot a sudden darting look of interrogation at the inspector.

"The late? I don't quite get you," he said gruffly.

"Detective Drake is dead. He died less than a quarter of an hour after bringing Grey in." The inspector looked, with slightly flushed face, at the two men from the Yard.

Standy slowly pulled out a notebook, while a frown of incredulity spread slowly over his face.

"Drake dead!" he muttered in shocked surprise. "Dead? Good Lord! What happened, inspector?"

"I don't know. You know more about the case than I do."

"But how? How did Drake die?"

"How can I tell you? He just pitched over and died—there where you are standing now. I applied artificial respiration till the doctor came. But I knew he was dead even while I worked on him."

"The doctor has been then?"

"Yes; here within five minutes."

"And what does he say?"

"He swears it's heart failure—just plain heart failure."

"Nothing more than that?"

"No. But he is getting the coroner to call for a post-mortem."

Standy and Harper looked at each other, their eyes meeting for a full, bold searching of each other's thoughts.

"Well, what do you know about that?" muttered Standy.

Harper looked back at him grimly.

"I think we had better see this Damon Grey," he said.

Standy turned back to the inspector, and there was a set frown of determination on his face.

"Has Grey been searched yet?" he asked, eyeing the little heap of personal belongings by the inspector's elbow.

"Yes. This is his stuff here." The inspector pushed his fingers into the pile and spread them out.

Both Standy and Harper inspected them critically.

"You know you were ordered not to search him till we arrived?" Harper asked the question, and he asked it in the nettled tone that called for an explanation rather than an answer.

"Yes; I know," replied the inspector. "But what would you have done? What else could I do? He had already killed my plain clothes man. And one dead body was quite enough for me. The staff here isn't so numerous that I can afford to lose good men for the sake of obeying a foot of red tape. I stand by whatever I've done."

Standy nodded. "All right, inspector," he said. "I'm not lodging complaints. All I want to do is to get the hang of things. Doesn't look as though there's anything marvellously murderous here."

He picked over the various bits of personalia with the air of a sceptic, fingering them gently.

"This all there was on him?" asked Harper.

"Yes."

"Does he know Drake is dead?"

"Yes; I brought him in here to be searched and I challenged him right away."

"How did he take it?"

"It seemed to stagger him—took the wind completely out of his sails."

"Genuine surprise—was it?"

"Seemed to me so. But he's such a self-composed devil you scarcely know what to make of him. He might be the finest actor I've ever seen for all I know."

"What's he doing now?"

"Sitting down as calm as you like, reading the paper."

"Doesn't seem worried about his arrest?"

"Not a bit."

"Talk well, does he?"

"Yes. Good accent, roughened a bit."

Standy and Harper conferred together at some length. They seemed to be discussing certain details of the case with which the inspector was unacquainted and which they deemed it necessary to keep to themselves. Their talk was in whispers, very earnest and very rapid.

Once Standy turned his head and snapped out, "Ricks isn't anywhere handy, is he?"

"I don't think so," said the inspector. "He went out some little time ago. But he may be back."

Standy pondered for a moment.

"That young fellow knows what he's in for if Grey happens to be innocent, I suppose?" he asked after a little while. "If Grey gets away with this, young Ricks will be in it up to the neck. He'd have the whole crowd of us by the ears."

"I should say he would be a bit of a marvel if he got out of this lot."

Standy rubbed his chin.

"You don't seem to get me, inspector," he said uneasily. "The thing is this. We've taken the step; we've arrested the man, and we've simply got to justify our action. We've got to get the evidence against him, Upto now there isn't a single shred, not a line, not a bit of anything we can get our teeth into. That order to arrest Grey went through to you on the pretty sure conviction that something incriminating would be found on him. And you say there's nothing."

"Not a thing. There wasn't even a hope in the turn-ups of his trousers."

The two detectives talked together again, and then Standy took the inspector on one side.

"We had better be perfectly frank with you, inspector," he said. "This is exactly how the matter stands. To begin with, this young Ricks is all he sets himself out to be—a purely impartial informer with no axe to grind. His *bona fides* are above reproach. We have satisfied ourselves completely on that point.

"Medical evidence on the two dead men points to the heart failure theory, which has already been put up by your own doctor here in the case of Detective Drake. Grey's rooms at the Grand Imperial have been searched inside out, and there isn't a vestige of anything suspicious in any one of them. Expert searchers have explored every nook and cranny of the suite. The result was just plain nothing—not a sniff of anything incriminating in any shape or form. And now you've just searched him again and drawn an equal blank. Inspector, unless we can get our hands on to something tangible before very long, we are up against a brick wall—a very solid brick wall."

"Have inquests been held on the two dead men yet?" asked the inspector.

"They are being held this afternoon. They are probably finished by now. Post-mortems have been ordered, and we shall know the result as soon as we get back to town. That is the whole case against Grey. You'll admit it's very wild and inconceivable. It's all up in the air, and there doesn't seem to be anything more against him than Ricks's bare word, and the fact that two men are undoubtedly dead."

"Well—it all seems to be hanging on the results of those inquests," said the inspector.

"And on Drake's, too," said Standy grimly. "As much depends on that as anything."

"And what is the case in his favour?" Standy looked glum. "So far as I can see, headquarters are rather of the opinion that they've broken into a mare's nest," he said.

"Do you want to see Grey now?"

"Yes, bring him in," said Standy. "Leave it to us. We've got a line of action we want to try out. There's a man out in the car—a witness—when I give the word, go out and get him."

"Right," said the inspector. He called an order to the jailer.

There was a metallic clank of heavy keys in the corridor, a bump of a door, and Grey was brought in.

Standy and Harper fixed him with critical eyes as he entered. First impressions count for a lot with men who spend their lives studying the criminal physiognomy, and Harper and Standy had come to bank on their own abilities. Their keen, searching eyes bored into him feature by feature, and finished up with a shrewd stare that rested right on his eyes.

Grey scarcely seemed to notice them. Beyond a slight, casual glance at them as he came in, he appeared not to have seen them at all. The two men from the Yard were something just slightly less than vacuity.

Standy stepped over to him.

"You are Damon Grey?" he demanded.

"That is quite true."

"Last Monday you were released from Dartmoor prison?"

"That also is true."

Standy glanced back over his shoulder at the inspector.

"Has he been warned?" he asked.

"Yes. He knows what the charge is."

"Well, I'll warn you again, Damon Grey. Anything you say may be used in evidence against you. You needn't answer a single one of these questions unless you like, but if you don't you will have to answer them all elsewhere."

"And where, pray, is elsewhere?"

"In front of a magistrate."

"Interesting—but rather depressing. May I ask—why all this ritual?"

"You are charged with the wilful murder of John Lindrum on the night of Tuesday last and with the wilful murder of Stephen Leeds in the early hours of Wednesday morning last."

"Dear me! Sounds very dreadful."

Standy felt the cynical humour that lay behind the immaculate politeness of the words. And deep down in his soul he was aware of a tiny spark of animosity. He had come there to interview Damon Grey—not to be interviewed by him.

"Damon Grey, I challenge you to answer—and I require from you nothing more than a plain yes or no. Did you or did you not, on the night and morning of the eighth and ninth respectively, murder John and Stephen Leeds?"

"Oh, don't be so damned silly," said Grey peevishly.

"But I demand an answer. Did you or did you not?"

Grey looked at him with a half-smile of contempt at the corners of his mouth.

"What do you think I am," he queried, "a peripatetic murder burean?"

"Something on that line, apparently," said the detective blunty.

Grey thrust his hands into his pockets and gazed disdainfully out the window. Warm sunshine was pouring down, and the afternoon was drifting towards evening on pleasantly lazy wings. Everything seemed beautifully peaceful and still out there. It always does when one is cooped up and held captive behind the bars of circumstance.

"How came you to be acquainted with Lindrum and Leeds?"

"Merely professionally. They are both on the Stock Exchange. So was I before I went to prison."

"Nothing more than that?"

"No, I don't think so. I didn't get engaged to half a dozen of their daughters, if that's what you mean."

"When did you last see Leeds alive? "

"On Monday night."

"That's the night you came out of prison?"

"Yes."

"But you were round at Lindrum's on that night?".

"Yes. Leeds was there, too. They were both alive and talking when I left."

Standy scratched his head. This was a new phase to him, and very unsettling.

"Tell me. Where did this interview take place?" he demanded.

"At a flat in Grosvenor Square."

"Whose flat—Lindrum's?"

"No. Belongs to a man called Rackway."

Rackway? Rackway? The detective's memory did a quick back over the statements already lodged by Dickie Ricks. That was where Lindrum had died.

"Who is this man Rackway?" he asked.

"Oh, I don't know. Sort of mutual friend of the others. It's a little Stock Exchange clique. They work stock deals between them. I was in that set before I went to do a little job elsewhere."

"But—but, this man Rackway. Wasn't he at his flat when Lindrum died?"

"Couldn't say, I'm sure. You see, I wasn't there when Lindrum died. Lindrum was alive and kicking when I left the flat. But I believe I have already mentioned that, have I not? How many times do I have to say so before I take game and set?"

"Was Rackway there when you left?" The detective's voice crackled.

"Oh, yes, he was there. He showed me to the door."

Grey lobbed in his bombshell with all the calm disinterest of a man eating his breakfast egg.

Standy blinked, and blinked again. His surprise was writ in block capitals on his incredulous face. Grey seemed to have been leading him up the garden to introduce him to the plum-tree he hadn't got. He turned on Grey a look of startled wonderment.

"Then—then this man Rackway is a witness to your own innocence!" he said. "If Rackway was there with you when you went away, he can prove that Lindrum was still alive when you left the flat?"

"Something like that."

Grey seemed to be taking less and less interest with every spitfire question shot at him. He had the air of a man bored stiff. The blatherings and yappings of these inquisitive asses had even ceased to irritate. They only wearied him. He gazed out of the window with the pointed rudeness of a man doing his utmost to intimate that the conversation had begun to pall on him.

Standy was silent for a while. Both he and Harper had got their thinking-caps on, and the grey matter under them was working at high pressure. Grey had got them both flabbergasted. The more they thought about it the more diffuse the case became, and the more they thought about Grey the more enigmatic he appeared.

Rackway had become the cornerstone of the whole business. Indeed, it almost seemed that Rackway, and not Grey, was the man who ought to be under interrogation. More than ever Standy was becoming convinced that he had grabbed a ball of smoke or—as he expressed it—a blow-fly.

Standy wheeled suddenly as Grey was reading idly a framed set of Station Rules and Regulations.

"Damon Grey, what time did you go to bed on the night of Tuesday last?" he asked.

"Somewhere between half-past twelve and one o'clock, I should think."

Harper jabbed a pencil across a notebook and a flicker of reawakened interest went through him. His innermost thoughts were reflected in Standy's next utterance.

"Stephen Leeds died soon after midnight."

"Yes; you told me. Very sad. Very sad."

"Do you know anything about his death?"

"I didn't know he was dead till Mr. Drake so politely charged me with having murdered him."

"Where were you at midnight?"

"Out."

"What time did you get back to your hotel?"

"Soon after midnight."

"Did you see anybody there: anyone who could stand witness for you that you entered the hotel at that hour?"

"Oh, yes. Several people."

"Who?"

"The manager."

"Anyone else?"

"The liftman, as you know."

"The liftman. Right."

Standy made a quick sign to the inspector, who rose and casually strolled out of the charge-room.

Standy referred to Harper's notes.

"Grey," he said, "you have just committed yourself to a definite statement of fact. You declare that on the night of Wednesday last you did not return to the Grand Imperial until after midnight, and that when you got back one of the persons you saw was the hotel lift attendant?"

"That's quite right."

"Tell me. When did you see this same lift attendant?"

"As I came in through the foyer."

Standy's hand flicked behind his back, and the inspector came in accompanied by the lift attendant.

The liftman looked round wonderingly till his eyes rested on Damon Grey. Then a look of bovine surprise settled over his features.

Grey nodded to him with a quizzical smile.

"So they've got you, too, have they?" he murmured. "And many people have you killed?"

Standy, red in the face, pointed at Grey and turned to the liftman.

"Do you know that man?" he asked.

"Yes, sir. He's Mr. Damon Grey."

"How do you know him?"

"He holds suite No. 4 at my hotel."

"When did you last see him on Tuesday night—at what hour did he return to the Grand Imperial?"

"About twenty past twelve. He had just come in. He went up in the lift."

"Had the dead body of Stephen Leeds been discovered then?"

"No, sir. Not for some time afterwards. Me and the managers found it in the card-room after he had gone to bed."

"And Grey went straight upstairs? He didn't go into the card-room?"

"I've never known him go into the card-room, sir. I took him straight up in the lift with the manager."

"With the manager, eh?"

"Yes, sir. They went up together. Lucky they did."

"Why?"

"There were burglars in Mr. Grey's suite."

"There were what?" gasped the detective.

"Burglars, sir—in Mr. Grey's rooms."

Standy turned exasperatedly to Grey.

"Say, why didn't you tell me about this before?" he demanded, runing his fingers through his hair.

"I didn't think you were interested. Surely I can have a few burglars in my rooms without having to scream it from the housetops?"

"But—but this is ninety per cent of your case—you fool!"

"Is it? You seem to be frightfully interested in my case. Much more so than I am myself. And, anyhow, it's your funeral. Get on with it."

"What were burglars doing in your rooms?"

"Minding the baby, naturally."

Standy was rattled. His case was going all to pieces.

"Why the blue blazes don't you tell a straight story?" he snorted. "Eh? Do you think it clever to sit back and try to make a fool of me?"

"I've answered every single one of your questions, Standy. That, I take it, is all I have to do in the circumstances. It's your game. You began it—you hoisted me into it very much against my will. I can't do much more than give you the answers to all the silly fool questions you keep asking."

"You're only out to pull my leg."

"You shouldn't jump to conclusions. I strongly object to being badgered like this. At any other time I should be extremely resentful. In my present humour I merely find you tiresome."

"Will you please answer my questions? What were burglars doing in your rooms?"

"You see? Jumping at conclusions again. As a matter of fact, there weren't any burglars in my rooms on Tuesday night—nor, to the best of my knowledge, on any night."

Standy mopped his forehead.

"Really, you're the most trying devil I ever met," he said. "If you're innocent, why the devil can't you give me a bit of help in the matter? I'm only doing my duty. You don't think I enjoy getting a man on a murder charge, do you?"

"That's better. That's much better," said Grey softly.

Harper cut in on the liftman.

"You say there *were* burglars in Grey's suite?" he said.

The liftman looked uncomfortable.

"That was the rumour going round the staff quarters, sir," he said awkwardly. "You know how servants talk in big hotels, sir. But we may have been all wrong. All I know about it was that somebody was in Mr. Grey's rooms when he opened the door."

"Somebody who had no right to be in those rooms?"

"Yes, sir. At least, I understood so."

"What have you got to say about that, Grey?"

"The liftman is slightly inaccurate. Quite an excusable mistake, of course."

"Who were they?" Harper was getting on the right track at last.

"To begin with, there was only one. Some johnny or other who had got into the wrong room."

"Oh. A visitor in the hotel, was he?"

"Yes. Somebody who had got his number all mixed up and found himself in my rooms. Why are you so keen to know about it? I was under the impression that I was being charged with a couple of murders, not with acting as host to hotel thieves."

"I'll tell you why, Grey," said Harper. "According to our information yon have discovered the secret of a new and rather extraordinary poison. You are accused of killing two people by means of that poison. Your actual method of administering it is, so far, unknown to anyone. This morning your rooms were thoroughly searched. Three expert searchers from the Yard spent two hours exploring every inch and nook and cranny of your suite."

"Hoping to find the poison?"

"Yes."

"Any luck?"

"No."

"I should think not, indeed! I'm surprised that two sane men like you could bring yourselves to believe such a cock-and-bull story."

"It occurred to me that such a poison as that might be extremely valuable to others," said Harper quietly.

"Not a doubt of it. I'd rather like a tinful of it myself—be very handy for getting rid of troublous folk like you."

"If a person went into your rooms, an unauthorised person, looking for your poison, and found it, that would account for its not being there when our officers made their search?"

"As a bit of pure logic that earns a complete bun," smiled Grey.

"Have you anything further to say about it?"

"Oh, no. The whole thing lacks cohesion, sense, and probity."

"Any question to ask this witness?"

"No."

"You'll come back to London with us, under arrest."

"Now?"

"Yes, immediately. In the car."

Standy collected up all Grey's belongings and sealed them in a little canvas bag.

XII

Within ten minutes the car was slipping smoothly along out of Southampton into the long, rolling miles of the London road.

Harper and Standy sat back in the car glumly, talking together in short broken-off sentences. The case had gone all against them; if they failed to shake Grey's story, then there was nothing left but to polish up miles of apologies.

Their job when they got back to London was a swift round of inquiries. Up to now they felt they were on a treadmill—working hard but getting no farther forward. Grey seemed to have that exasperating knack of denying nothing and admitting even less. They hardly knew whether he was too clever, too uninterested, or too contemptuous to give them any help. He seemed to be leaving them to their own distasteful job of letting them prove themselves to be fools.

They watched him leaning forward in the car, taking an almost youthful interest in anything and everything along the white dusty road. A huge clattering corn elevator in a vast field delighted him; an aeroplane, droning along overhead, amazed him; a great cavalcade of chars-a-banc, noisy with the employees of some big industrial concern or other, brought a smile to the corners of his expressive lips.

The lift attendant sat mute and still, slightly fearful. Grey saw his embarrassment and handed him his newspaper. The man took it with an unhappy grin of relief and buried his face in it. The rest of the journey was passed in the silence of boredom.

Grey was lodged in one of the special cells at the Yard. Night had fallen—the third night since Damon Grey's release from prison, and already Grey was back under lock and key again, held fast in the great brooding temple of law and order that sits like a squatting ogre at the top end of the Embankment.

He sat down quietly in the shadowed gloom. There was nothing for him to do but wait. He had laid out a network of lines that he could not connect. That was the police job. And so he waited, in a cold sweep of contentment that was completely untroubled.

Out in the heart of the mammoth building Standy sat down to write out a closely detailed account of his investigations for the benefit of his chief, while Harper took the car and hurried round to get into touch with Rackway.

Rackway, white and worried, had just got back from Southampton. He had followed on by a later train when he discovered Lorna's absence. His nerves were on edge. It was just dawning on him what a mad, what an insane, thing he had come so near to doing down there in Southampton.

Then Grayne rang up. He seemed vastly relieved to find his leader in. He had been trying all day to get in touch with him, and repeated rings and calls had proved fruitless.

"That you, Rackway?" he asked in a tense voice. "I've just heard that there is a warrant out for Grey's arrest. Heard it this morning about midday."

"A warrant!" said Rackway. "He's already been arrested!"

"And they've really got him, have they?"

"He's in Scotland Yard by this time."

"Thank God for that!" The voice was fervent in the profound depths of his relief.

"Don't you be too sure, you fool. You don't think Grey is going to lie down and take everything that comes, do you?"

"What's the charge?"

"Murder. Two counts. Leeds and Lindrum. That young fool Ricks stepped in and lodged an information. Grey will kick like hell. We shall all be in Vine Street before the night's out."

"Don't you believe it. Grey's playing a deeper game than that. If he hadn't got something up his sleeve he would have pulled the whole story on us long ago. I've found out one thing, Rackway—that was all bluff about letters lying in his solicitor's offices. Bunk! Every word of it. He put the fear of God into us on a bluff."

"Well, we can't talk over the phone. Come round in the morning."

"Right. Good night."

Rackway rang off, and paced up and down the room.

A maid came and knocked at the door.

"Come in," said Rackway. It took him ten seconds to get the words out, and when he did he looked at himself foolishly in the glass, his voice was so unrecognisable. It was a thin squeak, dry and nerve-ridden.

The maid entered, closing the door quietly behind her as she came in.

"A Mr. Harper to see you, sir," she said. "He wouldn't leave his card."

"A Mr. who?" queried Rackway.

"Harper, sir. He says he's from Scotland Yard, and that he must see you on a very urgent matter."

The maid was quite at her ease. With a sudden death in the house it was not surprising to her that a police officer should call.

But Rackway went green round the lips. He felt his mental self swaying.

"Show—show him up," he said shakily, and turned away as the maidwithdrew.

His knees gave out and he collapsed in a great armchair.

He was still sitting there when Harper came in, his coat still on and his bowler hat under his arm.

"Good evening," he said. "You Mr. Hildon Rackway?"

Rackway clutched at a wild hope in that "Mr."

He nodded, and indicated a chair.

Harper remained standing.

"I've called to see you with reference to a man named Grey—Damon Grey. I understand you know him?"

"Oh, yes, quite well."

"I must inform you that he is under arrest."

"Good Lord—what for?"

"We are holding him on a double count for the murder of John Lindrum in this flat and for the murder of Stephen Leeds in the card room at the Grand Imperial Hotel."

"But—what a dreadful thing!" stammered Rackway. Hope was beating again in his heart. By the detective's very manner he saw that he had come on no mission to arrest him. He was too respectful, too lacking in the high-handed note of grim authority. It was all too plain that he was on inquiry bent.

"It is—if it's true, of course," agreed Harper. "But there are doubts. Nothing at all is proved yet; he is only arrested on suspicion. Now, I want you to listen to me for a moment—I won't detain you any longer than is necessary—but I must ask you to answer these questions frankly and fairly."

"Certainly," said Rackway.

"Damon Grey is now in custody at the Yard. I have interviewed him. And so far the evidence against him is of the slightest. We have failed to establish a case. On the contrary, he has made out a perfect answer to the charges. He has declared an alibi on each count. You are one."

"*Me?*"

"Yes, Mr. Rackway. He says that you were with him all the time he was in this flat with Lindrurn, and that Lindrurn was alive and well when he left. He says that you can prove his innocence, that you showed him to the door, Lindrurn being then in the best of health and spirits."

Rackway's head swam.

The insolence of it! The cheek of it! The cool, blatant daring of it! It took his breath away. He saw the full beauty, the flawless perfection of it in a single shocking second. By the threat he held over him, he was demanding his release on the perjury of Rackway. He, Rackway, had got to swear that his greatest enemy on earth was innocent.

And in that same awful second he knew he was helpless in the matter. He dare not do any other than comply with Grey's orders, even though it meant liberating the man who had sworn to kill Lorna Rennie. The trap seemed to have snapped down on him with ferocious suddenness and bewildering completeness.

Dimly, as though through a mental mist, he heard Harper talking.

"Is this story true, Mr. Rackway? Think back to that evening and try to remember what happened. Did Grey leave here before, or after Lindrum's death?"

"Oh—before—before—a—a long time before." Rackway forced the words out through lips that twitched.

"H'm! You're quite sure about that?"

"Oh, yes. Quite. I couldn't have been mistaken about it."

"How long before?"

"Oh—er—a couple of hours, at least, I should think."

"As long as that?"

"Yes. We—er—we had played several rubbers at bridge before Lindrurn died."

"Oh. You didn't start playing cards till after Damon Grey had left the house?"

"No. He had been gone some time. And then one of us—Leeds, I think it was—suggested a rubber to finish the evening. We often—play cards here—we four, that is. A little group of business friends, you understand. It must have been a couple of hours afterwards that—poor Lindrurn died."

"H'm! You were present at the inquest?"

"Yes. I was the principal witness. The verdict was death from heart failure."

"So I've heard. The post-mortem was held early in the morning, wasn't it?"

"Yes. It was hurried forward at your people's request, I believe."

"Government pathologist present?"

"It was on his evidence that the verdict was returned. He said there were unmistakable signs of heart trouble when he came to examine the organ."

The detective was silent for a while. The news, although by that time more than half expected, was depressing. Every mortal thing seemed to be going against him in the Grey case. Every avenue they sounded seemed to be pointing away from the man they had got.

"Tell me," he said, "was there any bad blood between Grey and Lindrum? Any private quarrel, or anything that might have led to—to trouble?"

"Good heavens, no! They were the best of friends," said Rackway, and he could have screamed at the devilry that had forced him to say that.

"Why did Grey come here?"

Rack way shrugged non-committally. "We were friends, you know, in the old days. Cronies on the Stock Exchange. I heard he had been released and, naturally, I asked him to come along. You know what I mean. I didn't know how things were with him and—naturally, we wanted to see what we could do for him. Why you should suspect him of murdering poor Lindrurn—well, you people know your own business best, but, frankly, I can't understand it."

Harper stood up.

"All right, Mr. Rackway," he said. "I'll be getting back to headquarters. Sorry to have troubled you so late at night."

"Not at all," said Rackway, and bowed him out.

When the front door closed between them Rackway collapsed shakily on a chair.

Harper was back in the Yard with all the speed he could get out of his car. He hurried in and found Standy just finishing off his folios of written evidence.

The two held a brief consultation at once, Harper outlining the trend of things as he had pieced them together at Rackway's flat. Standy, already glum and aware of the fact that he was eating a bad egg, looked glummer than ever.

"Um," he said, "pretty well what I expected. The whole thing is a false alarm, a fizzle. And the sooner we get out of it the better, I'm going through to see the chief in a moment and I'll advise him to that effect. Heard the result of the Leeds inquest?"

"No."

"Heart failure. Doctor says it was the most obvious case he has ever autopsied. He found a blood-clot big enough to have killed ten men."

"Blood-clot, eh?"

"Yes. Been climbing up the artery for years—and getting bigger, Stephen Leeds was bound to die as soon as that lot touched the heart."

"And Lindrum's case was pretty much the same."

Standy nodded. "I'll be getting along to see the chief. See you later."

He collected up his papers and went straight through to his chief, a big, ponderous-looking man, who looked up stonily and pushed out a chair as the detective entered.

"Been expecting you, Standy," he said; "keep it short."

Standy mopped his forehead and sat down with a grunt.

"It'll be short all right, chief," he growled. "We've found as quib. I've been doing nothing all day but prick bubbles. And finding nothing in 'em. That young feller Ricks is either a practical joker, an hysterical alarmist, or a lunatic. In any case, he's a public nuisance."

"Well, what happened?"

"Roughly, nothing. I've completed inquiries at both ends of the line, and found nothing—except that we've got hold of the wrong man. That is, if there is a man wanted at all—which I doubt."

The chief nodded, as unemotional as an ox.

"Grey was arrested at Southampton according to instructions," went on Standy. "He was searched. And nothing was found. Neither was there anything suspicious in his rooms at the Grand Imperial. Not a trace of this alleged poison anywhere. Both inquests have returned deaths from natural causes. Grey himself treats the matter more as—as a joke that has got beyond a joke, if you understand me. He started by being flippant. And then he froze up. You can take it from me, chief—Grey will be a hellishly awkward customer if we carry on baiting him."

"Tough type, is he?"

"Wire, whipcord, brains, and resentment. He's pulled an alibi on each case. He was out at Grosvenor Square hours before Lindrum died. Rackway himself admits it. He never even connected Lindrum's death with Grey. Seemed amazed when I told him Grey was in custody. In the other case, Grey was out all the evening. Didn't get back to his hotel till round about midnight. When he did he went straight up to his room. Liftman took him up. Recognised him down in Southampton the moment he confronted him. The manager, too, confirms it. It's a blow-fly."

The chief nodded again and fingered his chin.

"So, so," he muttered. "Quite as I expected. Inquiries made today at this end led me to expect something of this sort. We were a trifle premature in issuing a warrant for Grey. But you never can tell with these long sentence men. Grey was just the type who would harbour a grievance, nurse it, and let it canker on him till it ate him. And we always go for the safety line."

"Does that mean I'm to release him?"

"Yes, release him," said the chief. "Release him and send him through to me. I'll sound him and see how he takes it."

It was a very short interview Damon Grey had with the police chief. Very short and very frosty. He looked more reserved, more completely drawn into his shell than ever, when he was ushered into the presence of the great man. And there was a formidable glint in the grey, wintry eyes that seemed to mutter their warnings ahead of him.

"Ah—good evening, Mr. Grey," said the chief expansively. "I am more than delighted to have the pleasure of seeing you in person. I have a very pleasant duty to—"

"Quite!"

The word dropped all hot-and-cold from Grey's lips. It pinged into the room like a steel pellet dropping in a tin can.

"There was a—er—a slight mistake made in the matter of arresting you. We—er—"

"Quite!"

"Won't you—won't you sit down?"

"Thank you, no."

The chief twiddled his toes and tried again.

"I—er—I wish to tell you that you are no longer under arrest."

"Thank you."

"That is, you—er—you are quite free to go whenever you wish."

"That is awfully good of you."

"I might add that—"

"Please send my belongings to my hotel."

Grey, with his hat on, was halfway through the door, with quiet, measured steps and an air of finality about him that put an end to that conversation as completely as though a frozen wall a mile thick had suddenly slid down between them. It left the police chief staring at the place where Grey had been, with puckered brows and an uneasy feeling stirring about in his heart.

Grey went out, calmly and without haste.

Outside he raised his hat to the great drab building, and murmured: "No matter, Mr. Yard. I think, before we retire for the night, we will just have a few words with Mr. Grayne—Mr. Grayne, who has, according to *The Times* today, a little appointment at Airdrie House tonight."

He taxied back to his hotel and went straight up to his rooms. When he got in he peered round with an air of interested curiosity.

Evidences of the police search were visible in every corner of the suite. The hotel authorities had done much to cover up the traces and leave everything spick and span, but to Grey's analytical eyes the thoroughness of the ransacking stood out everywhere. Hearthstones had been lifted and relaid, windowsills raised and replaced, boxes, drawers, and luggage had been searched with the thoroughness of Customs officers going through the baggage of a known smuggler. Ventilator recesses had been turned out, pictures moved, and even the clock had been opened.

Grey went over to his dressing-table. His stick of shaving-soap had been cut in half; there were finger-marks on his collar and handkerchief boxes. The back of the mirror had been taken out and reset.

He almost smiled.

He picked up his bottle of hair-wash. It was a sprayer bottle with a rubber bulb at the end of a tube, just such a thing as a barber would use when spraying the face after a shave. He eyed the stuff quizzically for a moment, turning the bottle this way and that. About half of it was gone.

He wondered what the analyst would say when he found he had been exerting his uncanny powers on nothing more gruesome than a gill of a standard brand of brilliantine.

He went into the bathroom, pulled the stopper out of the bottle, and poured the stuff down the waste-hole of the bath. For ten minutes he washed and rinsed the bottle under the hot-water tap till he had got the thing glitteringly clean and free of every particle of oil.

Then he pulled on a pair of rubber gloves and peered down the waste-hole. There was a small brass grid over the hole, a neat little sieve allowed the water to escape, but prevented anything else from going down. Looped round one of the brass bars was a little piece of cotton stuff—such as might fray off a face-flannel.

"It is little things like that," muttered Grey, and raised a mental toast to the police searchers.

Damon Grey bent over the bath and painstakingly got the little thread between his finger and thumb. With infinite care he began to haul it up. A couple of yards of oiled silk came up, fragilely thin but strong as waxed thread. Then there was a tinkle under the brass grid, and, with a little gentle manoeuvring, the thing which dangled on the end of the thread appeared.

It was a plain glass phial about four inches long and very thin. Against the light of the electrics it showed more than half full of a thin, pale blue liquid that glimmered with an oily sheen.

He poured it carefully into the bottle sprayer, adjusted the whole thing neatly inside his coat pocket so that the nozzle projected a quarter of an inch through the pocket, tested it on a piece of blotting-paper, which he burned, and then went back to his sitting-room.

For a while he rummaged about in a drawer. He turned over a miscellaneous assortment of oddments till he found what he wanted—a little square of rosin such as violinists use to improve the grip of their bow on the gut strings.

The rosin was in a neat cardboard case, one end of which was open. From the open end about half an inch of rosin protruded, like the end of a shaving-stick in its silver wrapper.

Grey held the box in one carefully gloved hand and sprayed the exposed half with meticulous thoroughness, giving it layer after layer of the poison and watching it soak in. The rosin absorbed the stuff readily. The only discernible after-effect on its surface was a barely perceptible glazing, a slightly shinier glint on the deep, amber brown.

For ten minutes he treated the rosin, adding additional washes as soon as the last was dry. Then, satisfied with his preparations, he resealed the cardboard container, dressed, and went out.

Henry Grayne's home was a longish walk from the imposing doorways of the Grand Imperial. It lay off one of the beaten Kensington tracks, behind the Brompton Oratory.

He walked as far as the Marble Arch, then took a bus to the Oratory.

It was a dark night, with a smell of rain in the air. Wet clouds, big and black, were sailing in sullen battalions past the moon, and a warm, clogging wind pushed softly in his face.

He strode along, a tall, sombre figure in a long dress-coat and an opera hat, with a white silk muffler up under his chin.

Outside the house of Henry Grayne he paused and took a quick look up and down the road.

It was a typical thoroughfare of the back blocks of Kensington, wide, dark, and very quiet. It was half a mile from the busy bus routes, and the silence that hung over it was enhanced by the drab lime trees that stood drearily motionless at precise intervals along the edge of the pavements.

Gorlin Road is a respectable avenue in an ultra-respectable locality. The local council, sensing its innate goodness, had not seen fit to light it with the flaring arc lamps that blaze a trail of high lights along the main traffic roads of the metropolis. Corlin Road was lighted here and there with a single electric glimmer which only served to deepen the shadows among the trees.

At that hour the road was almost deserted. A couple of pedestrians, like Grey himself, dressed for the evening, and a stationary private motorcar comprised the whole of the traffic in the road.

Grey pushed in at the gate, treading quietly as a cat. Grayne's house was shrouded in darkness. Up at a bedroom a single Chinese of light gleamed, and that came from behind thick purple curtains imperfectly drawn.

Grey listened at the front windows, pressing his ear flat against the glass pane. For a little while all seemed as deathly quiet inside the house as outside. Then he heard the sound of a closing door somewhere in the back of the house. And the silence fell again.

He produced from a pocket in his dress-coat a long thin instrument, a cross between a strong steel table-knife and a very flat chisel. He slipped it up between the frames of the upper and lower windows, and after a second or two there came a very faint click. The operation was repeated at the other end. And Grey pushed up the bottom window.

He climbed in silently, and as silently closed the window behind him. He located the electric light switch and snapped it abruptly on and off again. In the brief, emphatic flash of light he got his bearings. Avoiding tables and chairs, he got round the room and cautiously opened the door. It appeared to lead into a big dining-room. He flashed a pocket torch. Dark oak panelling and darker furniture met his eyes.

The light snapped off. Ahead lay another door. And from behind it came the soft strains of a violin, exquisitely played. The piece was a fantasia, a bewildering succession of dainty little notes played at lightning speed, each note perfectly struck on the merits of perfect angering. Grayne was having a final practice before his big show at Airdrie House.

Henry Grayne was feeling supremely at peace with the world. The black horror that had hung over him like a thundercloud, immense, omnipotent, and dreadful, had slowly dissolved. Grey was under lock and key—and the police would not let up on him again. He felt safe in the safety of his own home for the first time since Grey came out of prison. The numbing fear of him was being slowly submerged and forgotten in the dreams pouring out of the soul of the old Cremona. It was a night of peace that Grayne had bought and paid for with raw, living nerves. And the aftermath was sweet—and worth the price. His thin fingers slid over the strings with the sure exquisite touch of the master.

Grey edged forward. His tall figure, well poised and strong-knitted under the aristocratic clothing of black and white, slid into the room, the shadow of an avenging Nemesis. Without taking his eyes off the swaying body, he closed the door as silently as he had opened it.

Grayne's little red rosin-box lay on the table beside him. Damon Grey could see it without turning his head. Also, in a half-opened drawer in the table, he caught the glint of a revolver butt.

Stepping with the catlike care of a panther, he moved over the thick carpet till he stood immediately behind the maker of music.

Grayne played on in a rapture, his soul out in the dim realms of beauty and lilting delight that Beethoven visioned and captured and held for all time in the magic of his melody.

"Henry Grayne, I want you!" The voice bit into the music like a lightning flash stabs into the night.

The Minuet in G broke off abruptly in a loud squeal as the bow sheered over the strings. Grayne spun round with a strangled gasp, as though he had been dealt a violent blow in the throat. For a moment he stared at Grey as though he beheld a ghost. His eyes were wide open, popping fright. An awful leaden pallor had swept over his face, the pallor of a man who has run into the shock of his life. He gazed at the motionless figure in mute, incredulous horror.

"How—how—" he stammered, then he licked his lips once, and fell over in a faint. He went over with a crash, knocking the music-stand flying, and sending the pages of music streaming over the floor.

Damon Grey looked down at him, asprawl on his face, one hand still clutching the violin, the other doubled up under him with the bow splintered to matchwood.

Grey, without haste or hurry, pulled off his white evening gloves, revealing a pair of rubber skin-tights underneath. He felt in his pocket for the poisoned square of rosin, pulled it out, and tipped the square of brown death out of its cardboard case on to the table. Grayne's own rosin was lifted out of its case, and in a moment he had effected the substitution pressing his own rosin into Grayne's case till it fitted perfectly. He closed the case and put it back in exactly the same spot on the table. The other piece he put into his own case and dropped it back into his pocket.

When Grayne came to he was lying on his back on a long leather settee, looking up into the dispassionate face of Damon Grey.

Grey was bending over him, dabbing his temples carefully with a handkerchief dipped in whisky. There was neither anger nor hostility in that cold face; it was just the face of a doctor or a vivisectionist bending over the stranger on whom he was going to conduct his next experiment.

"Feel better?" The question was utterly formal, divorced from all sympathetic interest.

Grayne had neither the strength nor the inclination to nod. His earth had suddenly spun backwards. And the jolt had produced nothing but an unbelieving bewilderment. The whole thing was inconceivable, a ghastly mistake on the part of his own brain. Something had gone wrong. That coldly immaculate devil couldn't possibly be Grey. Grey was in Scotland Yard, locked away inside four walls that would never again let upon him. It was Grey's ghost he was looking at. Grey was dead and had come to haunt him.

He covered his face with his hands. Mad; that's what he was. His brain had given way. And his dementia had taken this fearful form of imagining Grey in the flesh. The thought was awful. He could even smell the whisky on Grey's handkerchief.

Grey touched his hands. Stiff with horror Grayne looked up through his spread fingers. He could even *feel* Grey. The thought smashed across his mind that he must be stark, staring, raving—an imbecile.

"Do you feel better?"

Cold and precise Grey repeated his question. The violin player relaxed and waited for the next symptom.

The next symptom was nearly two minutes in coming. It came when Grayne, feeling his way nervously back along the road to sanity, sat up on the settee and turned round. Grey was gone.

Grayne sat on, afraid to move, afraid even to touch the settee on which he sat.

Grey was already in the outer room. He walked on with the quiet nonchalance of the man who knew his way and knew what he wanted to do. He switched on the light, went over to a big mirror on the mantelshelf, and pinked his cheeks with a bright rouge. From a waistcoat pocket he produced two false side-whiskers, very white and very fluffy, and with a little dab of solution he adjusted them to his satisfaction.

There was a telephone on a wall bracket by the door. He went over to it and gave a number.

"Is that you, Kann?" he asked. "Grey speaking—Damon Grey. Yes, that's right. No, I'm not at Scotland Yard. Sorry to disappoint you, but the door was left open. You will need more than luck to get my neck stretched. You agree? So do I. Now listen a moment. Scotland Yard *might* make a few inquiries about me tomorrow. Yes. Henry Grayne is liable to have a regrettable attack of heart failure at any moment. And the Yard might get peevish about it. If they do, you will inform them that I spent the entire evening with you. That is, from nine o'clock until nearly eleven. We chatted about Stock Exchange matters and modern conditions of the Continental currencies. From, nine till eleven. You understand? I never left your rooms. That's all. Thank you."

Grey rang off. In two minutes he was outside the window again and was walking calmly down Corlin Road.

XIII

Henry Grayne relaxed and did his best to steady his twitching nerves.

He swallowed a tumbler of brandy and tried to think down to a solid bedrock of fact and possibility. There were hectic spots dancing about in front of his eyes, and his wrists seemed to have gone unaccountably soft, as though they were physically unable to support the weight of his hands.

For over half an hour he sat motionless on the settee, not daring to get up or to touch anything in the room.

Somewhere in that room, he knew, the seed of sudden death had been sown. It had been planted there for him, and, from what he knew of Damon Grey, that death would leap at him suddenly, out of the very darkness or the light, precipitating him abruptly out of life into the shattering blackness of oblivion. And he was only just beginning to realise by how much life is indebted to the sense of touch. Fingers must always be touching something, every hour of every day.

It was when he had worn his nerves down to a frayed rag that Kann came in to the rescue—Richard Kann, the American, who alone among the members of the Silent Six seemed to have the power of mastering his own innate fear of Damon Grey.

The maid showed him in, and he entered, with his hands firmly in trousers pockets and a look on his face that tabled his unshakable intention of keeping them there. He waited calmly enough till the door had closed behind the girl. Then with a swift, shrewd look at Henry Grayne, he said! "Grey been here?"

Grayne nodded dumbly.

Kann looked at him half in pity, half contemptuously.

"Pull yourself together, man, for the love of Mike!" he snapped. "You're a long way short of an epitaph yet, ain't you? What are you scared about?"

Grayne indicated the room with a stiff little jerk of his head.

"I—I don't know what he's done. I don't know where he's put it," he said shakily.

"Well, you don't need to. That damned stuff wears off sooner or later, Go to bed. Let it sleep itself off."

"I—I can't. It might be on my bootlaces, for all I know. I—I fainted!"

"Well, sleep in your boots, you daft loon!"

Without another word the American took a box of matches from his pocket and went round the entire room, applying the flame test to everything in sight. The music, the music-stand, the violin, the broken bow, the table edges, the electric light switches, the violin case, the chairs, the tantalus, the handle of the soda siphon, everywhere and anywhere that his own ingenuity could suggest. Match after match he burned. As an afterthought he let the flame play over the rosin box. But Grey was still a jump ahead of him. The box was closed.

Grayne picked up his precious violin and nervously fingered it. He soaked down another stiff brandy and glared at the clock. Suddenly his temper flared out.

"To hell with Damon Grey!" he said fiercely. "I'll play tonight whether he kills me or not!"

He went over to his music cabinet and pulled out half a dozen new violin bows. "Music is the only thing worthwhile in this rotten world," he suddenly flared at Kann.

"Sure, boy; you're dead right there," assented the American pacifically.

With a fine appreciation of Grayne's harassed condition, Kann entered into his mood. He was meeting him more than halfway; he was helping him, humouring him, encouraging him.

But had Kann the slightest inkling of Damon Grey's real motive in ringing him up, he would have walked right out of that room, and never entered it again as long as he lived. Grey, with his uncanny intuition and his devilish knowledge of the psychology of his old associates, had sent Richard Kann into a trap that grew more cunningly perfect as the minutes sped. He had caught Kann on the hop. In a little while Grey would be back in his own hotel consolidating an alibi that no attorney on earth could shake.

And Grey knew, without the slightest shadow of a doubt, that as soon as the shock and astonishment of hearing Grey's voice on the phone had worn off Kann would jump into action. He would call a taxi immediately and hurry round to see Grayne, if only to ascertain what had happened there, and to see whether Grayne was still alive. And he also knew that Grayne, sooner or later, would go to his violin for comfort. The soul of the artist could not be denied that desperate help. He knew that he would crawl to music for his own salvation.

Kann watched his man keenly. Grayne had glanced nervously at the clock again. He had picked up the little red box, opened it, and was hurriedly rubbing the contents up and down a fresh bow which he had picked out of his case, his hands trembling with a new eagerness.

Kann sat down stolidly in a big armchair.

"Play me something from one of the operas, old son," he suggested. "'Il Trovatore.' You play that well."

Grayne looked round at him irritably, in some little surprise.

"Play?" he snapped. "Play here? Don't be a fool. Get me a cab. I'm playing at Airdrie House tonight."

"Eh?" Kann pulled out his watch. "Tonight?" he repeated. "You're daft; it's half-past ten."

"I know, I know. I'm playing at midnight. The Duke of Airdrie is giving one of his late receptions." Grayne's tone was short and irascible. "Oh, don't stand messing about there!" he snapped. "Get me a cab; get me a cab. Phone for it. Let me get out of this damned house, if only for an hour or two."

Kann stared at Grayne as the snapped-out orders shot at him. He half started to say something, thought better of it, and shut his mouth. It was no use arguing with a man in Grayne's condition.

Grayne looked critically at his bow. He gave it a little dab here and there with the rosin block where his trained eye saw unevenness. Then he passed his hand nervously over his forehead and looked round at the American.

"Please," he said. "I know I'm a bit difficult tonight. But I can't help it. I'm all on tenterhooks. Be a friend. Take no notice of me. Just help me a little. I need a bit of help just now."

"Grayne, you are in no state to play before a big crush like that."

"I am; I am. I'll play tonight as I've never played in my life. I must; I must. Dick, I've never yet broken an engagement, or failed to appear once I've given my word. Please get me a cab. I'll play for Airdrie as they've never heard a Cremona played. It shall sing to them, cry to them, thrill to them." He swept the bow with a flourish over the strings. "In the morning you shall read," he cried. "The papers will say it to you. You know their catchphrase. All society—*and* Henry Grayne."

Kann stood up. He was frowning but perfectly ready to stand by his friend in no matter what eccentricity he cared to plunge. He read the decision, the flat finality that stood out in Grayne's attitude. Grayne had given his word to play for his patron, and play for him he would, whether the effort played havoc with his nerves or not.

"All right, Grayne," he said. "I think you're a fool to attempt it tonight, but I guess I'll back you."

He went out of the room and gave a message to the maid to the effect that a cab was to be at the door as quickly as possible.

Grayne had risen to a newer and higher thrill of ardour. When Kann got back to him he was as full of keyed-up enthusiasm as any debutante preparing her Court toilet for the great and splendid occasion.

"Kann, you will come with me?" The words tumbled out of his mouth as he packed his violin into its case.

"Sure. You want a keeper tonight," said Kann bluntly.

Grayne took along a spare bow in a thin bow-case.

"Got everything?" asked Kann.

"Yes. Is the cab ready?"

"I guess so." Kann took a final glance round the room before he left.

The Duke of Airdrie's receptions were highlights even in the height of the dazzling London season. In that wonderful house near the Green Park the old Scottish nobleman entertained on a note that struck, and maintained, the highest pitch of magnificence. The Duke's receptions were eagerly anticipated, if only on account of their exclusive rarity. Airdrie House only opened its doors to their widest about twice in a brilliant season, but on those occasions, as the gossip writers alleged, coronets were plentiful as stars on a summer's night.

Guests had been arriving for over an hour when Grayne got there, his fingers gripping fiercely on Kann's arm.

A chatter of pleasure rustled round the great ballroom when Grayne's presence was announced.

"Henry Grayne? Splendid!" they said. "A delicately perfect thought indeed."

The rustle of conversation continued until Grayne entered, a single diamond blazing in his white shirt-front. With a scarce perceptible bow he took his stand on a raised dais at the far end of the room.

"Looks nervous tonight," said one."Very pale, isn't he?"

"Yes, rather unusual with Grayne. So at home with himself as a rule. The last time I saw him play was at a Royal Command, and he was like an ice-house."

"I believe the man is positively ill!"

"Oh, I shouldn't think so. Temperamental johnnies, these great artists, you know. Wild horses wouldn't make them play if they didn't feel up to it!"

And then Grayne began playing. As the opening notes of an exquisite melody edged into the silence he routed forever their doubts as to his fitness for playing. "Ah!" they murmured. "Svendsen! Svendsen's Romance! Perfection again."

And Henry Grayne that night played better than he knew. As the music worked up to its delirious rapture he abandoned himself to it thrails. He forgot the audience, forgot the brilliance, the bloom and the beauty that was all around him; forgot Airdrie, forgot himself—forgot everything save the wonder and mesmerism of the music he played. Flight by fight the music swayed higher and nearer to its marvellous climax. Grayne played to the soul that thrilled, alive and tremulous, in the melody. He played to a mighty hush that fell on the splendid assembly insidiously and as in exorably as darkness on a summer night. And when the end came—in that delicious petering out of a subtle movement that heralds the end of "Romance" Grayne was shocked at the thunder of applause that leapt at him out of the silence.

Grayne stepped backwards, the wild burst of acclamation roaring past his ears. The thrill of it numbed him. Half unconsciously he was rubbing the rosin block up and down his bow again, reinforcing the poison that was already crawling alive on the strings. He was aware, but only dimly of Kann's voice, hissing out a wild Americanism from the palms behind him!

"Another! Another! Play 'em another! Oh, boy! You've knocked 'em crazy!"

Airdrie himself walked up quietly to the dais and smiled a request for an encore.

"Wonderful! Perfect!" he said, his eyes alight with the pleasure of a host who, having offered his guests an inspiration, had seen that offering ecstatically received. "You will play us something more, won't you?"

Grayne heard him as though through the enveloping folds of a blanketing fog. He racked his brain to think of something more to play. But his memory had suddenly gone white and empty. In all his prodigious repertoire of great music he could not think of a single encore. Names and tunes and themes had gone blank. He couldn't even remember which piece it was that had evoked that spontaneous thunder of approval.

Then Kann barked at him again from behind. "Play 'em a contrast! Play 'em something different! Show 'em you're big. Go on, boy! Hit 'em while they're hot!"

The violinist backed still farther towards the palms.

"What? What? What can I play?" he asked dazedly. "I can't think. I've dried up!"

"Dried up hell!" came back the masterful voice. "Play 'em that Spanish dance—that Sarasate's thing with all the diddlum stuff in it." Kann hummed over the first few bars for him.

Almost in a dream he began to play it—one of Sarasate's Spanish dance pieces, with its tempestuous masses of intricate pizzicato work—swift passages where the bow is at rest and the notes are struck by the fingers of the right hand plucking at the strings.

He swept into the piece without a pause. He had to get on with it while the memory of its variations was still in his head. The first few bars struck into the clapping and table tapping, stilling it as though a magic silencer had descended upon the great ball-room. The music tripped daintily into the rhythm of the dance, a Spanish dance in which one only had to close one's eyes and listen to hear the thud of stamping heels and the click of the gay castanets.

At the end of the first whirling movement the melody broke abruptly into the pizzicato passages. His right hand plucked swiftly over the strings. Again he went back to the bow, and again his fingers jerked out a passage of pizzicato.

And then something went wrong with his right hand. He couldn't grasp the bow again. His fingers were growing cold, stiff. They were mutinous, failing to obey the orders his brain was frantically sending them. The music scratched to a sudden halt on a half-finished note as the bow slid jerkily to the floor. A blackness swam through his head. Five hundred guests, with surprise and alarm and wonderment written large on the wide-eyed faces, stared at the swaying figure. Airdrie sprang forward. But he was too late. Henry Grayne, in the midst of his mightiest triumph, crashed over among the flowers that ringed the dais.

XIV

Next morning Damon Grey crossed off another name in his mind.

"Kann goes next on the list, I suppose," he muttered, and thoughtfully puckered his brows. "But—but somehow I don't think I'll kill Kann. He's the only one who hasn't shown the white feather yet, and there's—other things. He's white. He's been catspawed, too. Been to prison and knows the hells I've been through. No—I'll give him the fright of his life—but I think he goes free."

Over his breakfast he was silent and reserved. He spoke to nobody. His mind was occupied with a mental stocktaking, and there was a hitch in the accounts somewhere. Something had gone wrong. The work had taken charge of the worker. It was all out of focus. Only two of the Six were left. Amnesty for one, for the other the gift of life.

And now was a time to slow down; a time to cool his blazing hate and... Somewhere in the world there was flesh and blood of his, the last priceless gift of his precious dead. Grey was just a little frightened, just a little cowed by the thought.

He finished his breakfast and went out.

The garrulous old woman of the dressmaking shop had given him sufficient information on which to open his own investigation.

His first visit was to the register office of his old district. It is an oddity of London that, while its face changes continually and persistently, its register offices stay fixed. Great emporiums, mammoth department stores, huge office blocks arise and are filled in a month; streets grow taller and grander and wider, but the poky little register offices of London Town stay poky and dingy forever. That same thought occurred to Grey when, on arriving at the register office, he found it just as decayed and decrepit as it was in that long ago when he first knew it.

"Good morning," he said to the clerk. "My name is Grey. Damon Grey. Eighteen years ago I lived in this neighbourhood. I came out of prison on Monday. I am seeking the whereabouts of my son. Can you assist me in any way, do you think?"

The clerk swallowed. "Beg pardon?" he said.

"Eighteen years ago I was sent to prison. Between then and now my wife died. I am informed that she gave birth to a baby a few hours before she died. A local gossip here gave me the news. She tells me it was a son and that the child was sent away to an orphanage—or a home of some sort. Can you give me any particulars?"

"I—er—struth! I'll have a look. sir. What name did you say?"

"Damon Grey. My wife's name was Iris Grey."

"I—I'll do my best, sir." There was something about Grey that precluded him doing anything else.

"I'm sure you will."

He was back in ten minutes.

"No trace, sir," he said. "I've searched the files for two years on either side of the date you mention. There is no birth at all during that period to anyone of the name of Grey. The child must have been registered in the district to which your wife went after she left here. Do you know where she went?"

"I believe, Lambeth. But I have no definite information."

"Then I should inquire there, sir, if I were you. Or, better still, go straight to Somerset House, and search the files. You'll find it there."

Grey leaned across the counter.

"The trouble is, young man. my wife was too ill to talk," he said; "she starved to death. And it is more than likely that she was unable to give her name or any details about herself at all."

"Oh! Um!" said the clerk.

"Today is Thursday. You will be closing early?"

"Yes, sir."

"Have you anything special to do this afternoon?"

"Well—yes—you see—"

"How much is it worth to you—the special business you have to do?"

"Well—it's hardly a case of money, sir. I want to—"

"Ten pounds?"

"Good Lord, yes—er—no. It isn't worth anything really. It's just that—"

"Here's fifty. You know all the ins and outs of this wretched file-searching ceremony. Take this card. On it are written all the particulars I know. Find me the definite evidence of my child's birth—and his whereabouts if still alive—and I will not ask to see your expense account. Good morning."

"Struth," said the clerk again as Grey vanished through the swing doors.

Grey took a taxi to the Lambeth office. He had laid out that line of inquiry with one very definite object in view. No matter what discoveries he himself might make in the actual locality, he knew that they would be either confirmed or disproved by that very competent young gentleman in the register office.

Over Westminster Bridge, through Vauxhall, and into Lambeth he went. His driver put him down outside the door.

Inside, Grey saw the registrar himself, an elderly man, with a kindly eye and a quiet, understanding voice. He lived in a difficult neighbourhood, where a spade is not so much a spade as an unbowdlerised shovel. Its people are golden-hearted but blunt—very blunt. And he had come to know them and their ways. His manner reflected it; the Government official called upon to deal broadly with very delicate matters—or, as he himself described the commodity in which he dealt, "love and life and death, with the—ah, frills off."

Grey outlined his case and detailed his requirements in a voice that he kept perpetually hard, but which only he knew how near it was to a nervous waver.

The registrar listened attentively, nodding his head as Grey ticked off his sentences. Then he frowned ever so slightly and said "Dear me—very extraordinary, very extraordinary."

For a long time he was absolutely silent. A slow flush was creeping over his face and a look, almost of incredulity, came dully into his eyes.

"Do you happen to remember the case?" asked Grey hopefully.

"I do. I certainly do. I remember it quite well. I mean, of course, about your wife and her child. It was a—er, how shall I put it?—A source of continual speculation between myself and my own dear wife, who, like yours, has since passed into the great beyond."

"Then you have the entries here?"

"Yes. I'm quite sure I have. Though if you had not told me your story, I'm sure I should never have connected the two cases. Really, your visit is so remarkable as to be—ah—dreadfully unsettling. Your wife came into Lambeth from quite a good neighbourhood, did she not?"

"From just off the Cromwell Road."

"Quite so, quite so. It is the same case. Extraordinary! You—you know that she was not—ah—known here in the name of Grey?"

"That is more than possible. She was starving, unable to speak, within a few hours of giving birth to a child."

"As you say. She was admitted to the infirmary here. My wife visited her twice during the short time she was alive. She was with her on the night she died."

Grey gripped the man's arm.

"Was her end easy?" he demanded, his eyes burning fiercely and his voice a deadly bottled-up whisper.

"I—I think so, Mr. Grey. My dear wife was there all night. Mrs. Grey died in her sleep—or rather she was—ah—unconscious when she died."

"Unconscious with pain?"

"There—there was a good deal of pain before she died. Yes—I'm afraid so."

Grey gritted his teeth. "So there was with—the others," he growled. Then he looked at the registrar.

"What happened to her child?" he asked.

"It was sent to an orphanage."

"Can you tell me the name?"

"Yes. Let me see now—it used to stand just round the corner off the Lambeth Road. The—er—the Brecknock Home for Waifs and Strays. It was pulled down years ago. The place where it stood is a great motor garage now. My wife visited the baby there for two years." He looked diffidently at the white-faced man in front of him. "We—ah—we had no children of our own; you understand, old friend?"

Grey nodded, and his forehead was damp.

"I—I'll talk to you about—that later," he said, and the breaks had crept into his voice. "Thank you—thank you, Mr. Man."

"But you need never worry about your little baby," said the registrar, a sympathetic smile lighting up his friendly eyes. "She was lucky, wonderfully lucky. She was adopted into one of the happiest families in London before she was five—long before the taint of the orphanage had had time to enter her little soul."

Grey looked at him blankly.

"*She?*" he said, in a puzzled voice. "*She?* What do you mean? My baby was a boy. I had a son!"

"Oh dear, no. Your child was a girl, Mr. Grey, a very dear, sweet little girl."

Damon Grey looked dumbfounded at the registrar.

"A—a girl?" he repeated unbelievingly. "A girl? Bosh! Utter and absolute bosh! My wife gave me a son! A woman told me so—a woman who lived within a stone's throw of my wife when she lived Kensington."

The registrar shrugged ever so slightly, and his voice held a mollifying note in it.

"That may be, Mr. Grey," he said; "but—ah—one can't get away from what one might call the—er—medical evidence, can one? Who was she, this woman who says she remembered?

"A local gossip. And that breed generally gets the facts right."

"Well, I'm afraid she hasn't in this case. Even local gossips can make mistakes—and yours certainly has. How could she know definitely? She was at Kensington, you say?"

"Yes."

"And your child was born in Lambeth. Half a city and a river separated her from the birthplace of your child. She only got her details third hand. And I assure you, Mr. Grey, she was quite wrong. Your child was a girl."

"But—but, man—"

The registrar held up his hand.

"Who should know, if not I?" he asked quietly. "I—who would have given ten years of my life to have been able to adopt that sweet child? I wanted her, Mr. Grey"—his voice became earnest almost to a point of bitterness—"I wanted her more than I wanted anything on earth. I longed for a baby of my own; I—I believe I would have committed a felony in order to have possessed that sweet child. Mr. Grey—Mr. Grey—*please!*"

Grey was lost in a swirling bewilderment. For the life of him he couldn't remember whether Mrs Herris had told him definitely that it was a son his wife had given him. He groped back blindly into the past, striving to remember whether the loquacious woman had mentioned the child by name, whether she had called it "him" or "her," whether she had definitely mentioned the word "son," or in what way she had succeeded in giving him the impression that his wife had given birth to a boy.

And all he could recall was that the woman had referred to the child as the kiddie, or your little baby, or it. It was he himself who had jumped to the conclusion of its being a boy. In some queer, indefinable way the word "kiddie" had suggested a boy to him. The notion had taken hold of him, had grown, added to itself, and became definite.

"Who—who did you say adopted her?" he asked after a long, dull-eyed silence.

"The doctor of the orphanage. A most charming, delightful man, a Dr. Morgan-Smith. He went from this neighbourhood some years ago to an extensive practice in the West End. You may have heard of him. He is still living, and is one of the most fashionable practitioners in Town. Your daughter was still with him when he left here. Whether she has left him since or not, of course, I cannot say. I lost track of them all after they—ah—crossed the bridges."

He, too, was silent for a while. He saw that his information had come as a bombshell to the man who was out searching for a son and heir.

Then he spoke again, gently and with infinite restraint.

"Your baby—I should have adopted her myself," he said, with a wisp of a smile—"only it is not right for a man to take a child into his house when—when the house is empty of a woman, is it? My wife died before the little girl was old enough to be released from the institution. A man can love much—but he can do so little."

Grey's eyes ranged drearily ahead to the opposite wall. He could not look the registrar in the face. There was pain and hopeless regret harnessed back to a mask-like expression of indifference on the lined face. And Grey had known too much pain of his own to see more.

"Morgan-Smith, you say the name was?" he jerked.

"Yes. You'll find him in Wimpole Street."

There was another little silence, tense, charged to the full with the memories and aftermath of the might-have-been. Then Grey said in a very unsteady way, "Could you—tell me where they—buried her? I—I think I'd like to—could you tell me?"

The registrar looked down at his fingernails.

"In Lambeth cemetery," he said. "My wife tended the grave until she, too, went back to the dust."

Grey looked out through the doors, out to the hot, dusty highway, with its clattering streams of noisy trams and rolling omnibuses. "Thank you, Mr. Man—I'll write to you!" he said awkwardly.

"Just a moment, Mr. Grey. I'll find you the entries in the files."

"No. No, thank you. Just make me out copies of the certificates, the birth and the death—and send them to me. I'm staying at the Grand Imperial. Register them, please."

"I will, with pleasure, Mr. Grey."

"Thank you, goodbye."

Grey did not look at him again. He stumbled out through the door, and the registrar saw him no more.

Shadows of evening were crawling out of the west when Grey found the grave. He only discovered it after a long consultation with the cemetery superintendent, who, in reference to the burial registers, located it from the interment date. It was overgrown with weeds and tall grass, almost obliterated. But Grey had come with his own gifts—a cabful of sweet summer flowers and a written card to say whose was the tired body that was resting there. And he left an instruction for a beautiful stone, carved and lettered, to be erected on that little oblong.

Later that night the competent young gentleman from the Kensington office called upon him. His information was terse, pithy, and very much to the point. It confirmed, word by word, all that Grey had discovered in Lambeth.

Iris Grey had died unknown, unnamed. She had been buried in a pauper's grave; the local guardians had borne the expense of her interment. The Silent Six had not even stirred themselves to save her that last bitter degradation. The child was a girl, born a week before her mother died. She had been adopted and registered provisionally in the name of her foster-father, Dr. Morgan-Smith.

"Thank you," said Grey stonily.

The clerk hesitated. He pulled out a handful of notes and silver.

"Your change, sir," he submitted.

"That's the way out." Grey pointed to the door and the look on his face was so icily polite that the clerk crammed the money back, muttered a hasty mouthful of thanks, and scuttled out of the hotel like a rabbit scenting a stoat.

Grey pulled out his little golden book and opened it.

"So they did that to you, little girl, did they?" he said. For many minutes he was lost in a dumb reverie: then snapped the case shut.

Friday dawned, calm and still over the echoing emptiness of the City streets. Grey opened his eyes to a day that was destined to be grim and portentous for him, a day that was to culminate in tragic accident and point the way of sacrifice.

He awoke as a knock came on his door. Grey had that rare faculty of slipping into complete wakefulness the moment he opened his eyes. With him there was no languid period of semi-consciousness; his brain picked up its action at the precise point where it ceased overnight.

Prison had done that for him. The harsh clang of the lock in his cell door had jolted his faculties into sudden motion so often that it had become part of his nature to be wide awake the moment the first light crept under his eyelids.

Grey glanced at his watch. "Eight-thirty," he muttered. "And a full day ahead." Half unconsciously he began reviewing his own immediate future. It was a knack he had acquired; to be master of himself in the morning, he argued, was to be master of himself all day.

His thoughts slipped along smoothly. There was Lorna Rennie and that interfering young fool, Dickie Ricks. He would get the job done and finished with—and then clear out of the country. Life wouldn't hold much for him after he had eaten his revenge out of the souls of those who had wronged him. Life would be a blank, a void, with only a memory left to canker in the heart. Ricks would have to go, of course. That was obvious from the moment he first went gabbling to Scotland Yard. He had deliberately pulled down the walls of doom on his own head. Well, more fool him. He had had a full and sufficient warning. But it was just like raw youth to go tampering with something that was miles above and beyond it. It had made a habit of meddling with dynamite and being astounded when the explosion came.

His thoughts sifted back to first considerations. Kann would be easy. He would put the fear of God into his soul; for one dreadful pulsating second he would show death to him in all its stark simplicity. And then call the dogs off. Kann was too good to kill. He was the type who would die with the bit in his teeth, fighting for his head when the shadows closed over him.

Rackway was different. Brave—right up to the death-point. Beyond that, yellow as a guinea. He knew that type, too. It was Rackway who had fired the shot the night Clifford Reese died. Rackway's bullet that had sent Grey to the frowning quarries of Dartmoor. There was death in the air when Grey stood in the dock with a murder charge lined up against him—and Rackway hadn't opened his mouth.

Well, Rackway should open his mouth this time all right. It would be difficult, revoltingly so. But Rackway should get his share though the heavens fell; he should get the taste of it so far down his throat that he would remember it to his dying day. He, too, should know the silent agony of carrying flowers to a cemetery.

It would have to be quick. Dreadfully quick. She would scarcely know that her life was going till it was gone. A string of pearls. So many lives and deaths had been strung on a string of pearls. The girl was not born who could resist them. Thank God for the postal service. He couldn't do it himself, not if fifty Hildon Rackways paid the price. A string of pearls. They were there on his dressing-table, all shimmering and quivering with the flash of the cold little fires that smouldered within them. A few slow pressures on that little rubber bulb, a few gentle hissings, soft as a baby drawing breath, and the beautiful jewel was a circlet of death.

The knocking came again, sharp and impatient.

"Yes, what is it?" he asked coldly. The chambermaid, bringing in tea and a sheaf of morning papers, paused at the door.

"A gentleman to see you, sir."

Grey frowned. "A visitor to see me?" he muttered.

"Yes. sir; he's in the vestibule," said the chambermaid.

"Who is he?"

"He wouldn't give me his name, sir, nor his card. He said you'd know bim."

Grey's forehead wrinkled into a broad furrow. He did a bit of quick thinking.

"About my own height—or a little shorter?"

"Yes, sir. About your own age, too, I should think, and rather good-looking."

"He speaks with an American accent, I think?

"Yes, sir, But not very noticeable."

"Quite. Thank you."

"Shall I send him up, sir?"

"No, not yet. Tell him to wait for half an hour. I must bath and dress. Then send him up. That will be just after nine o'clock, won't it?" he added distinctly.

"Yes, sir. Thank you."

The maid withdrew and Grey climbed out of bed. "Good for you, Richard Kann," he said. "Come to beard the lion in his den, eh? Good for you! That's the kind of thing I expected of you."

Grey was putting on his coat when Kann came in. Richard Kann, seemingly as nonchalant and unconcerned as ever, but with a glint of defiance behind his eyes that gave him the impression of holding a gun in each fist.

"Morning," he said shortly, looking straight at his man.

"Yes, that's about the right note," said Grey approvingly. "What do you want?"

"You!"

Grey brushed his hair with delectable care and surveyed the effect in the glass.

"So you want me, do you?" he said, and gave a little pat to the white fluff at his temples.

"Sure I want you!" said the dangerously quiet voice behind him.

Grey crossed his legs and lit a cigar.

"Tell me about it," he said, with a wave of his hand towards a chair. "Sit down and tell me about it."

Kann ignored the invitation.

"Last night you killed Henry Grayne," he said.

"Last night Henry Grayne was damfool enough to play the fiddle.

"He died in my arms."

"I rather guessed you'd be there."

"Not a nice sight."

"So I would presume. Grayne was of the type who would fight against death. Caused quite a stir, I was reading about it.

The morning papers are jammed full of it—look at them—there on that table."

"And I did a little investigating on my own," went on Kann.

"I trust the results were worthy of the labour?"

"They were. Not having ceased growing at ten, I found out a thing or two."

"You found that Henry Grayne carried his own death with him?"

"I discovered just that same. I found out all I wanted to. And this is where you get off!"

Grey rubbed his nose. "I'm awful sorry," he said. "Probably I'm a little dense, but really I don't quite follow you."

"You will!" Kann's voice was sourly deliberate. He sat with one leg over the arm of a chair and looked down at Grey imperturbably. "You doped that block of rosin," he rasped.

"That—is not news to me."

"You planted it on him."

"A simple matter, I assure you."

"You killed him with it."

"What of it?"

"Just this. I've got that block of rosin, Mr. Grey!"

Grey's eyes closed, ever so slightly.

"Have you indeed!" he murmured.

"I sure have. I spent a quick, panicky hour putting two and two together after Grayne died. Sure as eggs, they came to four. I worked it down to that rosin block by a process of elimination. You overlooked one little matter."

"Which is—?"

"That damnable poison of yours, on contact with gut, turns green!"

"Oh, yes?"

"Yeh! Grayne's violin strings were green as grass. I searched for that rosin block, *and* I found it."

"Awfully cute. You'd make a great detective, Kann."

"And I want to know what you are going to do about it?"

"Do? Do nothing. Why?"

"Because if you ain't—I *am*!"

Kann clicked the words out with steely incisiveness. It was an ultimatum, flat and definite, the defiant kick back of a man who had been driven beyond his limits.

Grey puffed his cigar and pondered the matter.

"You seem to be losing heart," he said quietly.

"You'll be losing yours if you don't haul in your sails," flared back Kann.

"Also—losing your sense of values," went on Grey smoothly. "You don't seem to recognise your own limitations."

"I've got none," said the American fiercely. "Listen, you big boob. I've just heard a mouthful about you that sickens me. I kinder want to get my hands round your throat and squeeze and keep on squeezing till you haven't a kick left in you. Rackway tells me you have just threatened to kill that little kid Rennie."

"I undoubtedly shall."

"You won't. Not if I have to go to Scotland Yard myself and make a clean breast of every damn thing I know."

"Your information wouldn't be worth a cent without that rosin block," said Grey imperturbably.

"But I've got it, you fool—I've already told you I've got it."

"With you?"

Kann checked up suddenly.

"No," he said. "It's back at my place."

Grey smiled.

The two of them stared at each other like a pair of animals spoiling for a fight.

"You've got it with you now; it's in one of your pockets," said Grey. "Let me see it."

"To hell with you!" said Kann, and reared up from the chair.

"Oh, you can have it," said Grey. There was a flicker of contempt in his eyes. "But I'll tell you what. Put that block on my hand. I'll hold it there, in my naked fingers for an hour, two hours. I'll hold it all day, if you like! The potency of that dope has worn off. That block of rosin is as harmless as a babe. You couldn't convict a fly on the evidence of the contents of that box. You couldn't even get it by analytic. Scotland Yard would be more likely to put *you* under restraint for being a dangerous lunatic. They'd laugh at you. Go away; you make me tired."

Kann stared at him without moving. He had suddenly gone dead white. There was a viciousness in his eyes that sprang, hot and trembling, from the wells of pure temper.

"Laugh at me, would you?" rasped Kann in a storm of fighting rage. "Laugh at me, eh? Well, you listen to this! See if *this* makes you tired!"

He made a wild grab at the telephone.

"Hallo, miss. Hurry! Give me Scotland Yard!" he yelled.

"My God! Kann! Drop it!" shouted Grey. He rushed across the room, his eyes wide open with horror, his fingers outstretched and clawing for the telephone.

But Kann, with a flaring red light in his eyes, pulled a gun and held him off. "Hey, miss! Hurry with that call!" he cried.

Grey pulled up like a shying horse, halted irresolute for a drastic moment, and then plunged forward again, regardless.

"Drop it!" he screamed. "Madman! It's—"

But he was too late. Kann, with a look of open amazement on his face, was slowly sinking to his knees. In those last few seconds that were left to him he saw the awful tragedy of the joke that life had played on him; he realised with what relentless thoroughness Grey had erected his barriers. He tried to drop the doped telephone receiver from his stiffening hand, but the fingers wouldn't open.

"Kann! Kann! I'm sorry! Oh, God, I'm sorry!" Aghast, Grey staggered back and buried his face in his hands.

"Sorry!" Fighting to the last, Kann's lips cracked into a helpless grin. "Not so—goddam—sorry—as I—am!" he gasped. Then he rolled over.

Grey, with his face white as wood-ashes, swayed limply against the table. Trembling, with every nerve and fibre in him in revolt at the awful, unnecessary tragedy of it, he stood and stared at the thing lying there on the floor. Then he collapsed into a chair, while the fog in his brain did a devil dance.

It had all happened in such a quivering, nightmarish moment that he could hardly bring himself to believe that Kann was no longer alive. There was a numbing brutishness in its very swiftness, in the madness in it unexpectedness.

He never knew how the rest of that morning passed. For hours he sat there, unable to move, unable to think. He seemed to see Destiny staring him in the eyes. Destiny with its face all twisted into a horrible grin unholy amusement. Destiny, with all its callous brutality and its grim inhumanity, could see the stricken humour of it—the murderer suddenly made murderer again against his will. Destiny was laughing aloud at him, digging him in the ribs and telling him he was no end of a comic devil.

Grey crawled to the windows and flung them open. He gazed down into the sunlit streets, into the wide white thoroughfares all filled with the hot, mellow air of the noonday, alive with the tuneless jangle of busy traffic. Circumstance had beaten him. His own methods, his own schemes, had turned on him and flung him headlong down into the abyss.

Someone knocked at his door and inquired if it was convenient to attend to the clearing-up of his rooms. The little voice of routine jarred him back to a sense of realities. Blind chance had flung him into a trap. Only a cool head could get him out of it. The knocking came again, louder and more imperious.

"No. Not yet. Come again in half an hour," called Grey.

The maid went away, and a newer and more relentless determination settled over the soul of Damon Grey.

There was a wild resentfulness upon him, a fierce railing against fate. And in his soul a greater ferocity than when he had first taken up arms against the Silent Six. In that hour Damon Grey reached down to the bitterest depths.

He dragged Kann's body to his sitting-room, laid it on the couch and covered it with a travelling rug. He locked the door of that room and informed the chambermaid that he would be busy in there all day and was not to be disturbed. He wanted to get away from that evil, terrible thing. Something would have to be done about it when he got back—but for the moment it would have to wait.

He pulled on his rubber gloves and sprayed the pearl necklace. Stone by stone the little pencil of deadly vapour covered the beautiful gems. He gave them three separate coatings, till the rope of pearls became a rope of death that would remain potent for days. Then he prepared a label, stamps, paper, and string and slipped the whole lot into his pocket. That package would lie in the G.P.O. all night, and he wanted to give the pearls another coating of poison before posting them later in the evening.

Then for some hours he was busy writing letters. A dozen of them. The longest and the heaviest was addressed to the registrar of Lambeth. He took them out and posted them.

The hall clock was just striking one as he slipped unobtrusively through the great swing doors and headed for Grosvenor Square. He walked all the way. Time meant nothing to him. The thoughts of the days and the years to come were blotted from his mind. He had become a walking automaton of ineradicable decision. Consequences mattered less than time. An hour, a day, a life, a death, they were as nothing: mere nouns, names bestowed on things that did not count in any earthly reckoning of his.

He rang the bell at Rackway's flat. A maid answered it, and told him that Rackway was out. Grey didn't know it, but that one single fact sealed his doom. All the scheming and planning in the world could not have saved him then.

He tried to burn time in the crucibles of patience. He went out and lunched. When he called back, Rackway was still out. He listened to glorious voices filling the great spaces of the Albert Hall, listened throughout a whole afternoon without a thrill or a rapture. His ear was not tuned to the voices at all—he was listening to the tick of precious seconds flitting by, and thinking of the horror under the travelling rug in his sitting-room. Rackway was still out when he rang again. He headed back to the parks, those spacious reaches of quiet green that stretch away from Park Lane in broad, shimmering acres, offering peace to the troubled and rest to the weary.

On a seat there he sat and waited. He was mentally certain that Rackway was still in London. Flight he had attempted before—and realised the futility of it. Grey pulled out the necklace and sprayed it again. Eight o'clock boomed from Big Ben. There were only a few peope about. He held the pearls close against his breast pocket in his gloved hand and sent the hissing death playing over them. With the utmost care he packed the parcel and stamped it.

Ten minutes later he stood beside a pillar-box. He dropped the package in. There was a little thud as it fell—and the wheel of Fate began turning on its last revolution.

Rackway was still out when he rang again. The maid asked him to come in and wait. Grey accepted, thankful for the knowledge inferred that Rackway was, at least, still in London and expected back.

It was ten o'clock before Rack way returned. Grey was shocked at the change that had come over him. Rackway was white, his hands twitched continuously, and about him was a lurk of leer-eyed fear that gave him a terrible hunted look. His face was worn and lined, there were dark moons under his eyes that told their own restless tale.

He started back when he saw Grey. Grey was sitting down, as coldly calm as a marble Buddha, and as unemotional. He looked at Rackway with eyes that were as level and serene as the horizon, and as indefinably distant. Rackway's eyes suddenly flashed to life. A sudden surge of animation swept through his stony features.

In that moment Grey was aware of a new element in the atmosphere. Something alive, vital, deadly, had jerked into motion. And for the life of him he couldn't make out what it was.

It was Rackway, in revolt at last. The fighting soul had jumped to life within him, and he faced Grey—a fighter, a man who had at last found the spirit, the grit, and the courage to fight for himself, and was going to, to the last valiant kick that was in him.

Grey shot to his feet. He saw what was coming. Destiny grinned at him, louder, more contemptuously than ever. Fate had again taken the affair out of his hands. He was confronted with a situation he could never have allowed for. There was not a word spoken. Rackway was at him like a tiger at a dog, sullen, purposeful, deadly. His fingers connected with the throat and stayed there, dug in and held their grip. They fought like animals. Grey, the fitter, stronger man, holding on to his strength against a man who had suddenly become whelmed in a fighting frenzy. Then Grey, with a heaving twist of his body, gave ground suddenly, and the two of them crashed over on the floor together.

Grey's coat had dragged up in the fall. And as they struggled there. Rackway's eyes saw the gleaming butt of the revolver in Grey's hip pocket. The rest was a matter of thirty seconds—thirty seconds of livid tragedy that paralleled the dreadful death of Richard Kann. And Rackway, too, knew how perfectly Grey had safeguarded himself when his fingers made that flying grab at the gun—that empty, useless gun with the deadly of poison all over the butt of it. Four times he clicked the trigger, with the muzzle thrust up into Grey's teeth. And when the sudden stiffening raced up his arm he seized it with the other hand and fired again—with the hammer hitting metallically on the empty cylinder-head; and Grey's helpless eyes staring up at him, numbed, bewildered, and half mesmerised with his own chaotic thoughts. Then Rackway, with glassy eyes and foam on his mouth, relaxed upon him, and Grey crawled out from underneath.

He swayed away across the room, flung his hands up to his head... went down on his knees. An agony went plunging through him like a white-hot arrow. Lorna Rennie—and the pearls in the post!

His shaking hands beat against his forehead. That damnable necklace. And he couldn't stop it! That package would proceed to her as surely and as inexorably as a river winds down to the sea. Absorbed in the giant organisation of the Post Office, it would be shuffled and dealt, carried and sorted and mixed, and when it finally emerged from the orderly chaos, an integral part of that organisation would carry it to her address and deliver it without a possibility of interception.

The sweat came out on his forehead in great glistening beads. With Rackway lying there dead, Lorna Rennie...

He put Rackway's body into the bed and pulled the bedclothes high over it, trusting to all the gods that are that it would not be discovered till the morning. Then he crept downstairs and went out into the night. All night long he walked the streets, a lone wanderer, afraid to sleep, waiting; only for the dawn—and the postman who would surely walk down that road.

Dawn came, with leaden skies and a grey chill light. It found Damon Grey weary and deadened, an immobile statue, waiting and watching by the trees in Grosvenor Square. For hours he had walked through the darkness, hoping and praying. Hope was all that was left to him. More hours passed, cold, cheerless, and fear-filled. People began to trickle into the thoroughfares, milk-carts began to rattle along the roads.

And then came the postman. Grey heard him before he saw him, the sharp double rat-tat that heralds ahead of him down every road in the kingdom. He knew it would be useless to ask him for that package. The postman never gives letters to strangers.

Grey walked calmly up the steps and knocked at the door two seconds ahead of the postman. The door opened and he asked to be allowed to see Miss Lorna Rennie. The maid took his message and put the sheaf of mail on the hall table. Grey's avid eyes saw the package of death lying there among the letters.

There was a quick footstep along the hall. In the pale light Grey failed to recognise the alert figure of Dickie Ricks, as he came hurrying out of an inside room.

"Ah—so it's you, is it? Thought I recognised that voice! And what the devil do *you* want here?" Ricks—as aggressive and defiant as ever.

"Oh, don't shout, man, for mercy's sake. Give me—give me that packet, please!"

Ricks sheered round at the tone of Grey's voice. It was weary, tired, lifeless, the voice of a beaten man, the voice of a man for whom circumstances have become too mighty to compete or struggle with further.

"Your number's up, Grey. The Yard are out for you. And they've got you right this time—you devil!"

"What—what matters? Give me that packet. For God's sake, Ricks."

Ricks had got behind him and had closed the door. There was a gun in his hand.

"What's the matter with it?" he demanded.

"I'll—I'll show you." Grey seized it. His nervous fingers tore at the wrapper, while his lips, in listless, disjointed phrases, forced out the story of what had almost happened.

Ricks looked at him hard.

"Damon Grey," he said, "Lorna and I are getting married today. I'am taking her away—out of it. We shall be gone for a long time—a very long time. Before we go I think there is something you ought to know—something she doesn't know herself. And, so long as I can prevent it, she never will know. You are looking for a son of yours, aren't you?"

"It was a—a daughter. I found out the truth of it—a little time ago."

"Quite so. Lorna Rennie is your daughter."

There was a tiny little silence. And then Grey laughed. It was the laugh of a man who was on the verge of a final breakdown. It was like liquid acid being poured on his own naked soul. The necklace was already in his twitching fingers.

"Her real name is Lorna Grey. I know it," went on Ricks, without pity, without remorse. "I'm marrying her in the name she has known all her life. Morgan-Smith adopted her when she was a baby. He gave her his own wife's maiden name—Lorna Rennie. You've played a magnificent game all told, haven't you? This "—he pointed to the torn package—"is just about the perfect finish. What are you going to do about it?"

Grey looked at him dully, with an extraordinary lack of interest. His eyes were fixed, glassy.

All he said was: "Is she here? My little girl?"

"No. She's staying at an hotel. That's why I'm here—collecting her things for her. I vowed she should never set foot in this foul place again."

"All right, boy! Get you along to her. Leave me—I wish you all—all—" he stumbled.

Ricks looked down at his hands. They were clutching the poisoned pearls, clutching them in a grip that was crushing them.

A shadow passed over his face, swift and fleeting. "Go away me," he stammered. "Get out of the house—before—the police get here. Keep the taint of this from—from my—your—little girl." He struggled with his chilling hands. "Understand—what's happening?" He got the words out with an effort.

Ricks nodded and stood back from him.

"I'll be gone in ten seconds," Grey gasped. "You might tell Standy that I did not kill Drake. Drake just died."

He toppled over. Ricks looked down at him. He caught his whisper: "In my coat pocket—a little golden—book—for your—my—girl. Take it—please."

Dickie Ricks took it.

THE END